# VANTAGE POINT

Joe–

Thank you for your service!

Paul Miller

**PAUL MILLER**

Edited by Pat Morris
Cover design by Garrett Lofgren
Interior design, layout and typesetting by Thomas D. Heller Soulo Communications
Cover photography by Paul Miller

ISBN 13: 978-0-9778209-9-3
Library of Congress Catalog Number: 2009935183

Printed in the United States of America

First Printing: September 2009

13 12 11 10 09 5 4 3 2 1

Mori Studio, Inc.
2112 Broadway St. N.E., Suite 200
Minneapolis, MN 55413
1-877-788-4341
www.moristudio.com

*For Angie.*

*Without you, there's no page 1.*

# ACKNOWLEDGMENTS

Upon completion of draft one, I contacted a number of editors and asked them to take a look at my first effort. Of the few that called me back, one immediately stood out. She offered to sample edit a few pages. I sent her thirty, and asked if she could tell me if the writing was terrible but with potential or terrible and without. She called me back a few days later with the joyous words, "I want to see more," and "have you considered changing…" So, to my editor, Pat Morris—thank you for offering all the terrific plot suggestions, publishing guidance, and wonderful mentorship. This couldn't have happened without you.

Thank you to my frontline readers, Bill, Christian, and Leona. I appreciate so much your time, and your honesty. To Buddy, and Bob for your expertise that transformed hollow words into honest illustration. And thanks to Joe for providing the launching point for the story.

And lastly, to Angie—every time I think you're as good as it gets, you show me I've only, again, underestimated you. From day one, your unwavering belief in me and this book has propelled the project forward. Your energy is present throughout the story. You are nothing short of unbelievable.

# PROLOGUE

**Fort Collins, CO**

## 12 Lebanese Exchange Students Missing

The FBI alerted state and local authorities across the country today to be on the lookout for twelve Lebanese exchange students who arrived in the U.S. last month but never registered for classes.

The men, who range in age from 18 to 21, were a part of a group of 16 students due to begin a mid-semester, three-month-long program in world cultures and global economics at Colorado State University in Fort Collins, Colorado, just north of Denver. The group flew from Beirut and arrived in the U.S. on September 30. Four of the students reported as expected to the university but the remaining 12 men disappeared after clearing customs at Philadelphia International Airport. Officials said the no-shows violated the terms of their visas and they would likely be deported if located.

FBI Special Agent Brian Colt told reporters there was no indication that the men were involved in any terrorist activity. But when pressed on the issue, agent Colt did say that it is the largest group of foreign nationals to go missing since 9/11.

"At this point, all they have done is not show up for class registration," Colt said. "There is no current threat associated with these men."

"Colorado State officials tried repeatedly to contact the students," university spokesperson Chet Davies said. When they could get no reply, the officials contacted Homeland Security, a part of the procedures developed after September 11th, to track foreign students. The men who executed the 1993 World Trade Center bombings were also registered foreign students.

Davies said the school does not plan to have any contact with the missing students in the future and that the four students who did register on time are doing fine under the circumstances.

"But it is really a difficult situation for the other four to suddenly have so much press and public scrutiny placed on them for just showing up as expected," he said.

Agent Colt said terror levels would not be raised but officials are extremely motivated to interview the missing students.

# CHAPTER 1

## FRIDAY

A pair of sickly rats chewed at the fresh knife wounds in the man's abdomen. The pain vaulted from excruciating to unspeakable when the irregular tears from the vermin moved from his skin to fleshy muscle. He prayed that by the time the rats got to whatever organs lay behind, he would already be dead.

The young man strained to free his hands from the bailing twine that bound them, but the struggle only added to the rivulets of blood dripping from his wrists. Rocking himself free was also impossible; a three-inch nylon strap was secured tautly around his waist to eye bolts anchored in the wall on either side of the chair. A matching strap restrained his neck, making breathing difficult and preventing him from getting a good look at his gnawing attackers just inches below.

He was in what he guessed was a small bedroom closet. The only sounds he remembered were distant footsteps and the occasional opening and closing of a nearby door. Hours, maybe even a day, earlier, light from under the door steadily grew, which he assumed to be the arrival of a new morning. But after falling out of consciousness several times, he wasn't sure how many sunrises had come and gone to create the current pale grey glow beneath the door.

It had been a good amount of time since he last saw his two captors. Four hours? Eight? He had pleaded from behind the tape as one of them tore away his shirt, and then slowly carved three horizontal cuts across his abdomen. The plea turned to screams as the other man pulled the snarling rats out of a small cage and tossed them onto his lap to feast.

Just days earlier, his plan seemed to be working so perfectly—he'd been hanging out on the Colorado State campus, discovering new friendships and effortlessly assimilating into American college life. His fresh start at the school was the result of three long years pretending to share the goals of a group of extreme Jihadists in his homeland of Saudi Arabia. He spent countless hours during that time supporting their secret mission to destroy the current Western powers and restore Islam to its global dominance.

But the secret he carried was that he never intended to help destroy the mighty United States, rather, he only sought passage through its borders. All of the planning he'd done, and the discipline he'd shown while falsely working for the fundamentalist group, had been playing out just as he visualized. And after just a first few days, America was even more wonderful than he'd expected.

But now, his dazzling dreams were replaced with total darkness where the only feeling he could muster was pain, mind-bending, searing pain unlike anything he could have imagined. Until the door opened and saw the large familiar figure staring down upon him. Suddenly he was overcome by an emotion that muted the pain—terror.

The two rats turned, sat up, and sniffed at the intruder. Unimpressed, they returned to their feast. One of the men hovering around the imposing figure, the man who'd earlier sliced his abdomen, stepped forward and used the same knife to cut away the neck strap, then yanked the tape from his mouth.

The man, who Rafiq knew only as "the general," waited for the underling to step back, then leaned forward and spoke, his voice firm and thick. "You have been a great disappointment, Rafiq. You were one of the chosen. One of thirteen to be exalted as you greet Allah in heaven. But instead, you are here being fed to common rats." The speaker stepped forward and grabbed one of the furry vermin in his hand. The immense shadow from his heavy shoulders enveloped Rafiq in a foreboding gloom. He watched the man stroke the ugly animal gently with his left hand, a seeming act of tenderness had he not been choking it to death with his right.

"Please. I have made a grave mistake. I realize that now," Rafiq rasped. "If, in your mercy, you can give me a second chance, I promise I will not fail you."

The man stared at him, then finally said, "Allah is filled with mercy and he would have us, too, live in such a way. So yes, I will show you mercy as he instructs us."

Rafiq looked up humbly at the man, eager to show his gratitude and resolve. But before he could make eye contact, his head was suddenly propelled back from a swift, iron-like punch. His head throbbed so completely he was oblivious to the words the man was speaking to him. Until he heard a familiar name.

"... Who shall it be, Rafiq? Your mother? One of your brothers? Or perhaps little Sabriyah? Who shall I spare?"

"Please. No," said Rafiq.

Another punch rifled down. "Choose. Or I kill them all."

The words didn't immediately register as Rafiq's head was again awash in screaming pain.

"Fine. They all die!" commanded the man.

"No. Not Sabriyah. She is just an innocent child—she should not pay for my stupidity."

The leader turned to the man on his left. "Make sure the rest of the family is watching when you kill her."

"But you said... Allah's mercy..." The attacker covered Rafiq's mouth with his large hand and snatched the knife from his subordinate.

"How dare you speak Allah's name to me," The man growled. "Mercy is given to those who repent their sins, not to a weak animal begging for his life."

He drove the angled blade deep into Rafiq's abdomen at the spot the rats had concentrated their gnawing. Rafiq wondered, as he drifted from life, if the huge man silhouetted by the bare bulb was Allah himself.

The remaining scavenger scurried up to the new stream of fresh blood.

# CHAPTER 2

Five men stood, waiting, behind white resin patio chairs that circled the round patio table in the middle of the otherwise empty living room. Four members of the team had been together for over a year. The fifth, a member of the group of students from Saudi Arabia, by way of Lebanon, joined them two weeks ago. He had been recruited with, and had trained alongside, Rafiq and had worried when his friend did not show up at the rendezvous at the Philadelphia Central Library. His worry turned to bewilderment when he learned that his fellow bomb technician had, instead, continued on to the cover destination, Colorado State University.

He remembered how excited Rafiq had been three long years ago when the recruiters told the group how the intelligentsia in the U.S. was ashamed of the way their government dictated behaviors to the rest of the world. And how, after the brief prohibition of new immigrants following the attacks of 9/11, the academics filled their universities with students from foreign lands, trying to prove they welcomed the world's citizens with open arms rather than a balled fist. The militant group had used invitations from universities to infiltrate the country with hundreds of willing young men prepared to die for their cause. But thirteen more with specialized training were needed for a very specific and time-sensitive purpose. He and Rafiq were determined to be among those students.

Now he waited silently with the others as their guest, General Aasim Abdul Attar, washed his former friend's blood from his hands.

"Share with me, again, the details of the boy's capture," General Attar ordered as he strode into the room.

The leader of the Denver team, an American-born Muslim whose father emigrated from Pakistan, answered. "Sarmad and I approached one evening as Rafiq neared his living quarters with two students from the college. As he was trained to do, he was on constant alert and saw us coming out of the shadows. He jumped between the other students and walked the final twenty yards arm-in-arm—the two students provided perfect shielding.

"The next day I trailed him as he walked out of the bookstore. This time we anticipated his training and Sarmad intercepted him before he could turn for the busy student union."

"During daylight? Did anyone witness the capture?" the general asked.

"There were other students in the area, but Sarmad was dressed in a CSU sweatshirt and jeans. He pretended to be showing Rafiq something on his phone as he held the boy and guided him to the car. There were no further complications after that, sir."

"The blade was right in my hand near his throat and not a single student gave me a second look. Fools," Sarmad said.

"They are intelligent enough to distrust their government. Those *fools* will be standing with us one day," the general said. The men nodded. "Did anyone else see you?"

"No, General; it was late. And we took precautions to be certain we were not followed leaving the campus," said the group leader.

"Good. Then let's move on to more important business. The final member of your team has been with you for two weeks." He glanced at the young new recruit. "I expect you have familiarized him with the target by now. Let us quickly go over your assignments once more before I must leave."

The team leader delineated the plan just as he had many previous times for the general. At the conclusion of the meeting, General Attar thanked the men for their important work and invigorated them with his vision of the new world order, invoking the promises of "centuries of peace" and "generations of children growing in Allah's warmth."

The men in the house remained standing in silent awe long after the general departed for the airport. Finally, the Denver team leader looked across the table to the newcomer, "Do you know who just left here?"

"Yes. He is General Attar, the leader of the offensive," responded the young man.

"He is much more than that. It is he who conceived the great offensive to destroy the most powerful nations in the world and, in turn, create a new global power structure with Allah as its one and only true God. But I speak of something even greater."

"I do not understand," said the newcomer, looking at the knowing expressions on the other men's faces.

"You were embraced by the next caliph. And not just in title or merely as the leader of a particular sect of Muslims as we have seen for so many centuries. The defeat of the U.S. will be the propellant to reunite a billion Muslims around the world! For the first time since Mohammed, we have the opportunity to work through our political and philosophical differences and bring the force of Allah to all the earth. General Attar is a direct descendant of Caliph Abu Bakr, the first successor to Mohammed. Not since the Great Prophet himself has Allah sent us a man with the combination of omniscience, spiritual strength, and holy bloodlines. He is the leader we have been praying for over so many centuries. Allah be praised! This is a momentous time in the history of Islam."

Other team members spoke up to underscore the leader's suggestion that on the shoulders of such a grand leader, Islam was on the precipice of historic glory. The voices were growing in excitement and strength as the rhetoric continued, but within minutes the leader brought the conversation back to a more task-based discussion.

When the business of the meeting was done, the leader led the men toward the dining room where several ornate rugs were laid out in rows. The men took turns washing their feet in the bowl outside the doorway before entering the room for prayers. Once inside, each man knelt on a rug angled in the direction dictated by a small compass sewn into it. The compass pointed to the holy city of Mecca.

---

The plane ride was routine. It was the "routine" that put General Attar in such a foul mood. It began well enough—the security personnel at the gate and the agents at the ticket counter went out of their way to ignore him. This had become the pattern. For the fifth consecutive flight, the person going through the metal detector directly ahead of him was asked to step to the side for additional random inspection. And, as always, the ticket agent at the gate was "delighted" to look for an exit row or first-class upgrade for him. Neither, however, was available for the current flight; it was filled beyond capacity.

It was when he got to the gate area that his irritation began to smolder. He could feel lingering glances poking at him like sharp needles. The general was clean-shaven and had changed out of the black shirt and slacks and was now dressed in a pale green button-down shirt with khaki pants. But the contours of his face and the color of his skin shouted Middle Eastern. Each time he looked up, eyes quickly diverted from him.

One pair of eyes belonged to a Caucasian woman well over 50, whose hair was part grey, part brown, but mostly a color unnatural to this world. She was dressed in a pilling sweater adorned with snowflakes and pine trees and radiating-red polyester pants. The general found her unwavering attention more annoying than the others because each time she looked away to avert eye contact with him, she let out a sigh of inconvenience.

Her conspicuous glances and others' were the same in Denver International as in airports all across the U.S., with the exception of LaGuardia and Newark. There, no one averted their stares; they wanted him to know they were looking at him.

As he boarded the large Boeing 747, the occasional passive glances, like those from the woman, turned into more direct eye contact; an escalation with which the man was also all too familiar. As he squeezed his small leather carry-on between an overstuffed garment bag and a wheeled suitcase, a man with a neatly trimmed goatee seated in the next row stared hard at him. General Attar showed no reaction. On any flight there were one or two men who thought they could thwart a potential terror attack with nothing more than an intimidating glare. The general knew these men were the least of his potential adversaries. Anyone so naïve as to think a glare a deterrent would himself be stopped by a similar benign act. In the general's experience, the truly courageous didn't need to display it.

He had learned this lesson eight years earlier, on a lightly traveled road twelve kilometers south of Halab, Syria, when ten men on a bus returning from a Sunni rebel meeting were stopped and told to disembark. The travelers immediately began bartering and pleading for their lives as the four men, who had staged a roadside breakdown, ordered the ten to form a line in front of the bus in preparation for their mass execution.

During the emotional bargaining, one of the ten , dressed in a light blue and white striped shirt, stood quietly at attention. Even in the thin sliver of moonlight, one could see him studying the situation, looking for the right opportunity to act. Seconds later, as one of the attackers stepped forward to slap the frightened man to his left, the stripe-shirted man pivoted on his left foot and slammed his right heel into the knee of the attacker, bending the leg to the side where it normally bent to the rear. As his victim fell, he snatched the AK-47 from the injured man's waist. He held the weapon firmly, waist-high, as the man literally fell out of the strap, collapsing in agony to the ground. Less than a second later he had full range of motion with which to move the weapon.

He put a round through the writhing man's skull then rotated toward the other three attackers standing in a row five meters away. He put the next bullet through the chest of the nearest man then continued down the line, putting a hole in the same spot of the next assailant. He was a moment away from finishing off the group when he was shot through the heart himself. That bullet was fired by the Arab man currently occupying the aisle seat of row 23 in the 747 descending into Minneapolis St. Paul International. Since that day, it was not the loud or physically intimidating men who worried the general; it was the quietly confident and perceptive ones to whom he paid close attention.

The Delta Airlines jet touched down without incident and after waiting on the tarmac for an additional 15 minutes to clear another plane, taxied to the gate. As the general retrieved his bag, the man with the goatee gave him a look that told him, "Damn right, you behaved yourself." General Attar glanced at the pen in the man's shirt pocket. In less than two seconds he could have that pen three inches into the man's neck, through his carotid artery. *Stupid American*, he thought. *Soon, you and the rest of your country will be nothing more than a footnote in history.*

General Attar kept his carry-on bag with him in the back seat of the taxi. The ride was a short one, just four miles down the Interstate 494 strip in the southern Minneapolis suburb of Bloomington. He checked in at the front desk of the Comfort Inn but instead of going to his assigned fourth-floor room, he went through the corridor to the adjoining Outback Steakhouse restaurant. He sat on one of the two open stools at the U-shaped bar and ordered an iced tea. Across from him, a younger man in a tweed jacket was reading *The Wall Street Journal*. The general looked blankly up at the wall behind the bar where a college football game was being broadcast on multiple TV screens. Several minutes later the bartender came by and asked General Attar if he would like a refill. The general looked down at his half-full glass and declined.

"So what do you think of the Gophers so far this year? Hard to tell what they've got with their cupcake non-conference schedule," said the bartender.

"Pardon me?"

"I saw you were watching the game up there. I was asking what you think about the Golden Gophers this year," the bartender explained.

"Gophers?"

"Can I get you anything else?" the bartender asked, surrendering. The general shook his head and dismissed him.

Minutes later, the man wearing the tweed jacket folded his newspaper, took a last sip of his drink and walked out. Shortly after, General Attar threw his bag over his shoulder and followed. He deposited his plastic hotel key card in the trash can outside the entrance before getting into the passenger seat of a waiting green Ford Taurus. The man in the tweed jacket put the car in gear and they were on their way to a house 30 minutes south of the Twin Cities outside the quiet town of Cedar River.

# CHAPTER 3

"C'mon, dude. What are we still doing here?"

"What?"

"It's 75 degrees in late October! We should be well into our second six-pack on the back nine somewhere, but instead, we're here in the middle of the damn woods working on your beloved deer stand—a structure, mind you, that has more man-hours into it than the Sears Tower," said Seth.

"Let's see; play golf with you and your physics-defying slice, or continue working with power tools, 20 feet off the ground? I'll stay here—it's safer," said Jason.

"Seriously, pal, you're a big-shot contractor and all, but putting a roof on this behemoth makes it look like a tree house. Are you going to create a secret handshake so only the cool kids are allowed in?" Seth asked.

Jason gave Seth a moody stare. "Too late for that. And how many times do I have to tell you, it's not a roof. It's a retractable weather barrier. And it'll only come out in emergencies."

A foot above the men's heads a tight stack of treated 1 x 12s were connected to the trunk of the tree. The lowest of the ten boards had two pairs of small finger holes drilled into it, two feet apart. Pulling the board unfolded the stack into a 6-foot slightly pitched "roof" that spanned the 8-foot-wide structure. The only work remaining was to create a decorative face plate to cover the stacked boards. Jason planned to rout vertical lines every two feet, then center drawer handles between them to create a facade that would look like a row of drawers across the tree.

"The rest of this is busywork. If we take only the power tools back to the truck, we can make it in one trip and have enough sunlight to get in a quick nine," Seth said.

"For Chrissake!" Jason said, "I should have asked Robyn to help me. She'd be downright tolerable compared to all the whining from your sorry ass."

"If you'd rather have Robyn here, fine. But don't call me a 'sorry ass.' It hurts my feelings—makes me feel like all those hours of Pilates have been wasted time."

"You wouldn't know a Pilates exercise if it walked up and strangled you."

"If some hottie in a leotard is doing the strangling, then bring it on."

"I'm telling Robyn you said that," Jason said.

"Again you bring up my wife. If I didn't know better, I'd say you have a thing for my hot mama."

"Let's hope whatever I've got for your wife ain't catching."

Jason and Robyn, Seth's wife, had begun their feud the very first time they met. Jason overheard her refer to him as "Captain Mullet" and it was *game on*; Jason never missed an opportunity to get under her skin and she repeatedly reminded him where he stood on the evolutionary scale. At one point during Seth and Robyn's engagement, she threatened to cancel the wedding if Seth didn't remove Jason as his best man. Seth stared her down, one of only a handful of times in their 15-year relationship, and she backed off.

"I believe the question about knocking off to play nine is still on the table," said Seth.

"If you want to be done for the day, that's cool; we can head out. But this is one of maybe three days out of the year that I don't feel like hitting the sticks."

Seth understood the defeated tone in his friend's voice. "No problem—let's just finish the roof and head home. I only wanted to play 'cause I figured you'd buy."

"Next week, I'll spring for 18. And let me say it again—retractable weather barrier!"

They finished the facade and attached it to the front of the stacked boards. Even close-up it looked like a set of drawer fronts. They tested the roofing system again before cleaning up.

The term "stand" implied a base upon which to hold something or someone. Jason's structure was more of an ornate deck than a stand. It was encased with a strong railing, complete with self-turned balusters. To the north, where most of the wildlife roamed, he had built a sunken rifleman's post. He answered the question of why the 4 x 8-foot post was eight inches lower than the rest of the structure by claiming it utilized the strength of the large limbs underneath for additional support. But the truth was he thought it added charm and visual interest to the stand. He knew when he constructed the pulley system to haul coolers, generators or other "supplies" up from the ground, that he was creating more of a retreat than a hunting platform. The fact was, he *needed* to build the extras, like the folding staircase and stacked cabinets, into the tree sanctuary more than he required their function. If pushed, he would have to admit the scents and unnatural look of the amenities did more to hinder successful hunting, than enhance it.

Seth climbed down to the ground to receive the supplies Jason lowered with the pulley.

"Who's taking care of your mom?" Seth asked.

"Kate agreed to stay with her for a couple of nights. Thank God for that—she was pretty much plan Z."

"I bet she didn't take much convincing," Seth replied.

"What's that supposed to mean? She's just a friend," Jason shot back.

"Of course she is. And I would never suggest otherwise." Seth took a toolbox and two cordless drills off the square wood base and noticed its detailing. "Dude! You stained and sealed the pulley platform? Are you going to start making me take my boots off before coming up? This isn't a deer stand; it's a monument!"

Jason's voice turned angry. "It's not a goddamn monument, asshole. It's just a frickin' deer stand. You got it? Deer stand—that's all!"

They made the half-mile trek back to Jason's truck in silence. Seth knew he'd screwed up. Jason had begun working on the stand exactly two years and one week ago, the day after he buried his wife and five-year-old daughter. What had started as a three-day project to keep his mind occupied and his hands busy turned into a fifteen-day mission to engineer the most efficient, elaborate, and productive deer stand in the history of hunting. The only people who saw Jason during that time were the cashier at the hardware store and his mother when he checked in once a day at the suddenly empty house they shared.

Halfway through the four-mile trip back to town, Seth broke the silence. "I didn't mean anything when I said 'monument.' I just meant that most deer stands are just a couple boards nailed to a tree. You, on the other hand, probably have plans for a projection screen and stadium seating," he said. "All I was trying to say is that your stand is rather…" He paused, unable to find the right word, "'sumptuous' for Cedar River." He saw a quick smile roll across Jason's face. "Uh, is 'sumptuous' a word?"

"Yes, sumptuous is a word," Jason replied. "But the stand isn't sumptuous. It might be a little extravagant or elaborate but it's not sumptuous. A hundred-dollar steak dinner is sumptuous. Beyoncé at the Grammys is sumptuous. My deer stand is not sumptuous."

"Would Beyoncé *in* your deer stand be sumptuous?"

"Are you kidding? In my dictionary, that would be the word's actual definition."

---

Kate Brooks looked down at the corner of her computer screen: 4:12 PM Less than twenty minutes until her much-anticipated weekend began. The three people in the St. Joseph College Admissions Department who had actual offices with doors that closed were gone by 2:30, the norm on Fridays. Though her responsibilities went well beyond administrative, she would not become, or be paid as, an official admissions director until one of the others left. So she dutifully sat at her workstation, urging the minutes to pass. A partition the color of a used sponge separated her from the other support person in the common area. Kate's station faced the door, because after six years in the department, she could answer virtually any question asked about the admissions process.

Glancing down again, she found only one minute had passed, which provoked an embarrassed smile and involuntary head shake. She felt like a 16-year-old all aflutter after the senior boy who'd been filling her personal fairy tales had just called her for the first time. She thought to herself, *You're 32, not 16.* "And he's not even going to be there!" She didn't realize she'd spoken aloud.

"What's that, Kitty Cat?" said the uber-perky voice from behind the partition. *Oh no*, Kate thought. *Now there's no way I'm getting out of here on time.*

Bonnie Schwartz sat on the opposite side of the dirty sponge. She was the other half of the support staff for the admissions department of the private liberal arts college. She'd received the office assistant job two years earlier behind the strong recommendation of her uncle, who also happened to be the tenured head of the English department. It had been a big step up from cashier at Millen's Bakery for the lifelong Cedar River resident.

When her mom, who was also her landlord, asked about the change, Bonnie stated rather coyly, "If you want to see a bull, you best be in a pasture." And now, at a fertile 24 years old, she sat in the middle of 1500 potential Mr. Bonnie Schwartzes.

"Did you say something?" asked Bonnie.

"No—just talking to myself," replied Kate.

The creaking of Bonnie's chair casters sent Kate's head falling back and a small sigh escaped her mouth.

"Anything I can help with?" asked Bonnie, leaning her dinner-roll body heavily onto the end of the partition. This position had tipped the movable wall from its base so many times during Bonnie's first six months that a custodian had to bolt it to the floor, rescuing it from the certain destruction two-hundred-plus pounds of eager assistance would have caused.

"Nope" replied Kate. "I just made a stupid mistake on this procurement order. And now I'll have to give them a call to adjust it."

"I thought for sure you were talking about someone being somewhere," Bonnie said. "Were you talking about the weekend?"

"Nope. Just trying to finish the order. Thanks," said Kate, focusing on her monitor.

"Well what *are* you doing this weekend?" Then an instant later, "Oh, that's right; you're hanging out with Jason's mom. That is so nice! Is she really old? Are you going to need some company? My Nonna hits the hay at like 7:30, I swear. So if you want me to come over, I could pick up a movie or something."

"I don't think I would feel comfortable with that. It's not my house and I really don't know Mrs. Kendall. You understand," Kate said in a soft, caressing voice.

"For sure. I totally need to get my mixes done anyway. Did I tell you I finished the Kelly Clarkson montage? Now I'm startin' the Mariah disc. Gawd, I can't believe how far behind I am."

"Sounds like you've got your hands full," said Kate.

Kate's cell phone rang; it was the default electronic ring. Hearing the Black Eyed Peas' "Let's Get It Started" each time Bonnie's cell phone went off was more than enough reason to resist uploading some clever ring tone.

"I better take this," said Kate, stepping through the open door into the hall.

"Hey Kate. It's Jason."

"Thank you," she said, gratitude filling her voice.

"Bonnie invasion?"

"You guessed it."

"Always glad to help," he said. "Listen. I finished my work a bit early, so how about I swing by and pick you up?"

"What time? I still have some work to wrap up here."

"Let's keep it the same time. I'll be at your place at 5:30?"

"That sounds great."

"Good. And Kate, thanks again. I know there are a million other things you'd rather be doing this weekend than hanging out with my mom. But with the Petersons next door away visiting their son in Des Moines, and Mrs. Jenkins not around, I'm basically out of options. Our former neighbor, Neil, would have been a possibility a couple months ago, but he's been coming around the house for the last few weeks; now he's the last person she'd allow to spend the night."

"Your mom is in a budding romance? Is that cool or a little weird?" she asked.

"It's more funny than anything else. I've known Neil forever and they'd be great for each other, so the weirdness quotient is pretty low. But they both act like nothing's going on, even though he only comes by when I'm not home, then leaves almost immediately whenever I show up," Jason said.

"Have you asked her about it?"

"No. I get nothing but a view of her back for at least an hour after he leaves," he said. "So anyway, you're really coming up huge for me this weekend."

"It's no problem—really. And stop thanking me. You're annoying."

"I get that a lot," he said and hung up.

Kate returned to the office to shut down her station for the weekend. As she waited for the various windows on her screen to save and close, she grabbed her jacket and bag, hoping to avoid walking out with Bonnie and facing another ten minutes of rehashed lunch conversation.

"Bonnie, something came up; I'm going to race out a few minutes early. Have a good weekend. Make sure you lock the door when you leave," Kate said through the cloth-lined partition.

"You're taking off? I thought you said on the phone that you had some work to wrap up," Bonnie said. She delivered the last sentence from her usual perch at the end of the partition.

Kate looked over, annoyed. "You could hear that through the panel and with me ten feet down the hall?"

"Well, I was packing up the muffins Jim brought in. So I wasn't totally behind the partition. You probably didn't realize how loud you were talking," Bonnie said.

Kate glanced past Bonnie to the coffee machine sitting on a faux wood stand between the first two office doors. Kate calculated that for her voice to get to Bonnie *accidentally*, it would have had to travel ten feet north down the hall, turned left through the office door, then south another eight feet, pushed through a large fake palm to Bonnie, who would have been facing the opposite direction.

"Well, anyway, I'm going to get going. See you Monday," Kate said, putting the strap of her bag over her shoulder.

"Okay, you too," said Bonnie, following Kate around the desk to the door. "I bet you're getting pretty geeked about spending a couple nights at Jason's house, even if he's not going to be there. God, he is fine! C'mon, have you seriously never been on a date together?"

"Never. Seriously," Kate called over her shoulder as she sped down the hall.

# CHAPTER 4

Jason made a couple of stops before heading to Vera's Diner for take-out. His mom, Hannah, was adamant about cooking a nice dinner for Kate in gratitude for her spending the weekend. And certainly the meal would have been as delicious as anything he could bring home from a restaurant. But Jason told her if she went to all that trouble Kate wouldn't feel needed. Hannah argued that it would let Kate know that she just had lupus, and that "I'm not crippled or have Alzheimer's or something." But in the end, because Kate was *Jason's* friend, he got his way. The truth was that Jason thought a home-cooked meal felt a little too "come meet my mom-ish." And as much as he enjoyed and cared about Kate as a friend, romance was not in their future.

The bell above the door chimed as Jason stepped into Vera's. The diner wasn't named after the owner; her name was Louise. It was named, instead, after the character from the 70s CBS sitcom *Alice*. Like the fictional Vera, Louise was a career waitress who was two parts super-server, one part dingbat. She could recite the style of eggs, choice of potato, and type of toast for each customer in her ten-table section, but then turn around and serve them hot water because she forgot to add the coffee before brewing.

One day in 1994 the manager on duty where she used to work watched Louise return $27.55 to a customer who had given her a twenty for a $12.45 tab. The manager, 20 years her junior, whose real title should have read, "Owner's Daughter," let Louise have it right there in front of the whole lunch crowd. The final remark in a string of rhetorical questions was, "Is that the only way you can get customers to sit in your section—pay them for it?"

Louise hadn't replied. She just walked back to the kitchen, grabbed her boyfriend, who was also the cook, and left. A month later, she opened Vera's two blocks down Main Street. The other restaurant closed soon after, while Vera's continued to serve the best food in town.

After waiting several seconds to let her customer's eyes adjust to the dark mahogany walls and floor of the former hotel bar, the teenaged hostess greeted him, "Evening, Jason. Meeting someone?"

"No, Penny—just need to grab something to go," Jason said, then moved toward the open end of the bar where Louise was rolling silverware into paper napkins.

"Excuse me. I'm looking for Weezie's, but I heard they're moving on up—to the East Side!" Jason called out.

"You must be thinking of Jefferson Cleaners. You'll need to ask for George," responded Louise, playing along with his *The Jefferson's* vs. *Alice* sitcom bit.

"That joke never gets old," said Jason proudly, putting his arm around her shoulder.

She responded by nearly hugging the wind out of him without leaving her stool. "If I live to be a hundred, it'll still be a kick in the pants to me."

"Well, that's good to hear, because I don't have a back-up line," Jason said. "What's the special tonight? I need some food to go."

Louise told Jason about the specials then hollered his order through the window to the kitchen where her boyfriend/cook, Sam, smiled and waved a spatula in the air.

"Has Mayor Pyan talked to you?" Louise asked, going around to the rear of the bar to pour Jason a glass of root beer he hadn't ordered.

Jason nodded his thanks for the home-brewed soda. "He talked to me a few weeks ago about adding another garage stall now that Audrey is turning sixteen. Why?"

"Well, he and Harry Clausen were in here having lunch a few days ago, talking about who should replace Harry on the council next year when he retires. I told them who I thought the best man for the job was and, of course, they agreed." She slapped her hand down on the bar and smiled. "And, by golly, if that gorgeous young man isn't sitting right here in front of me drinking a root beer right now!"

"Me? Run for city council?" Jason asked. "Let's see, jab a dull fork in my eye or get into politics? Hmmm. You have a fork I can borrow? Dull, if you got it."

"Don't crack wise with me or I'll stick that fork somewhere, and it won't be your eye."

"Yes, ma'am," said Jason, averting his eyes to his mug.

"Cedar River doesn't need a politician. We need someone who has a good head on his shoulders and isn't afraid to use it. That's why your father spent almost 20 years as our mayor or councilman. After his first election he didn't even put signs out. He didn't have to—people know when you're a good man; you don't have to go showing it to them," said Louise, the last sentence coming in a lightly scolding tone.

"Thank you, if there was a compliment in there somewhere. But Weezie, I'm not my father. He loved looking out for this town. He looked forward to the meetings and solving people's problem. I'm sorry, but that's just not me," said Jason.

Louise looked through the open rectangular kitchen window to check on his order. She didn't see Sam so she started in that direction. "We'll see," she said without turning back.

When she returned, she refused to allow Jason to leave with his food until he promised he would at least think about the idea.

---

Muhab Abdul Muhammad slid the .45 caliber pistol into its brown belt holster and clipped it on just inside his left arm. The case looked worn and tattered, depicting extensive use. The truth was he had used the gun for nothing more than target practice during the five years he owned it. But during a meeting in Egypt he noticed how battle-worn many of the other attendees' weapons were. So when he got home he used a file and a four-inch nail to give his sidearm and its leather case an "experienced" look, more in line with his abilities and position, if not his history.

A quick check of his watch told him he had plenty of time to make the 40-minute ride to the meeting site. He slipped on a blue sport coat, concealing the gun, and put his keys in his front right pants pocket and his cell phone in the right coat pocket. It was the small lessons spoken in passing that often had the most value. During his initial orientation into the group, someone mentioned keeping his keys and wallet on the opposite side of his weapon to minimize the amount of movement around it and the risk of exposure. This was one of hundreds of seemingly insignificant tidbits that became second nature to those raised in the Middle East region of the world, instincts he was never able to develop having grown up in Portland, Oregon.

Muhab made it to the rest stop off Interstate 35 five minutes early, then, according to established protocols, drove to the next exit and doubled back. After waiting a few minutes in his car, he watched two men in a navy blue Chevy Impala pull into a spot several stalls to his right. He got out of his car and walked to the painted concrete visitors' center. The door opened to a small room with floor-to-ceiling windows on three sides. In the center of the room was a kiosk containing large glass-enclosed maps of Minnesota and the United States. Centered on the only wall without windows were three vending machines. They were flanked on either side by doors labeled "Men" and "Women."

In the restroom, Muhab bent down to make sure the three stalls were unoccupied. He was checking his cell phone as the door opened.

"We're clear," said Muhab after the door closed. He hugged the younger man. "How are you, Khalid?"

"I am very well, thank you," said the handsome Middle Eastern man.

"And Omar?" asked Muhab.

"He is well also." Khalid removed his cell phone from his pocket.

Muhab waved it down. "We have a signal. I've already checked." If anyone approached the building, Omar would alert Khalid from the Impala by phone. Muhab leaned back against the row of sinks, his hands reaching wide to grasp the counter behind him. The movement had its desired effect; Khalid's eyes immediately flashed on the gun and he automatically straightened to a more formal posture.

"Let's get right to it; we may not have much time," continued Muhab. "As you know, we're still one man short of our full team. Happily, someone is traveling to Minnesota to join us as we speak. In fact, he is most likely already here. But Khalid, this man is no ordinary soldier. He is of a much higher rank than I," said Muhab.

"Will you no longer lead us?" asked Khalid.

"I will leave that to him. But I gladly relinquish that role if he asks," said Muhab. An uneasiness came over Khalid and questions filled his squinting eyes.

Muhab reassured him. "He is coming here because we are in need of specific expertise, not to replace anyone. The operative originally assigned to our group was unable to complete his duty. The man coming to assist us is more than just a peer or specialist, he is among the very elite in our struggle. If everything goes as planned over the coming days, this is the man who will rise to become our leader."

"Does our cause not already have a leader?" asked Khalid.

"I don't mean the leader of the Jihad. I mean the leader of Islam," replied Muhab with a knowing nod.

"A caliph?" whispered Khalid and looked in the mirror, struggling to imagine himself among such greatness.

Muhab nodded. "Yes. But let's not get ahead of ourselves. We have a battle to fight and a war to win before we speak of a new caliph. Besides, that is in Allah's hands."

"But it has been almost 400 years since the last caliph," said Khalid, his amazement continuing to swell.

"I know. Wonderful times are ahead for all Islam," said Muhab. "But let us first deal with the matters at hand."

Khalid nodded again, refocused and prepared to accomplish what was asked of him.

"He has certain requirements. That is why I called you." For the next several minutes, Muhab gave the young man specific instructions and left the room. Khalid was reciting the instructions back to the cell leader when his phone chirped. "Yes, Omar."

He nodded both into the phone and to Muhab. Khalid darted for a stall as Muhab pulled a paper towel from the dispenser just as the restroom door opened. A young bearded man smiled at Muhab who crumpled and tossed the paper towel in the receptacle, then stepped toward the exit. The man waited at the door and held it open for Muhab, who nodded as he walked through.

Khalid walked out of the restroom four minutes later.

---

Kate met Jason at the door of her stacked duplex with a small suitcase. The ride to his house took only a few minutes; he filled it with last-minute information.

"I know we talked about this when you first agreed to spend the weekend, but I wanted to just remind you how Mom's lupus works because the disease manifests itself differently on its victims. By limiting her exposure to the sun and minimizing stress, she lives a mostly normal life. But like most people suffering from lupus, she does get occasional flares and hers typically manifest themselves in seizures. It's been months since she's had one and I think she only had three in the last year. But when they come, they arrive at night, usually in her sleep, after her body shuts down.

"She has an alarm connected to her bed that will go off if there is more than five seconds of continuous movement—any less and it would go off anytime she rolled over. I've put the monitor in the guest room so you will definitely hear it. You just call 9-1-1 if it goes off and tell them she is having a seizure, then go into her room to make sure she can't hurt herself by hitting something or that sort of thing. I also stashed a list of emergency numbers under the phone in your room. It makes Mom feel helpless if she sees it.

"I'm not bringing my cell phone to the stand but Seth can come get me if anything serious comes up," Jason said. "But I'm sure nothing will," he added. Kate nodded in agreement.

"I know you're willing to stay through Sunday, but seriously, have Seth come and get me if you feel like you've had enough. The boredom will probably be overwhelming before then."

"Jason, I live with a cranky overweight cat in a rickety old duplex. I'm pretty sure a better offer will not be coming along before Monday. You take all the time you need and if the weekend isn't enough time, just let me know and I'll come back after work Monday," said Kate.

"Thanks. I don't think I'll be that long," he replied.

"I can't imagine what you're going through right now. But I think you've earned a couple days to yourself," she said and lifted her hand to his shoulder.

"Thanks, Oprah."

"Whatever," she said and pulled her hand back to her lap.

"Sorry," he apologized. "Gotta keep up my tough-guy façade, you know?"

"And good thing, too 'cause when I think Jason Kendall, I think bad-ass."

Jason shook his head, wishing he had a comparable comeback ready. They pulled up in front of the garage and walked across the stone path and through the back door. "Hey Mom, we're here," Jason called from the kitchen.

"Hello, hello," said Hannah Kendall from the living room at the other end of the hallway.

Jason set the dinners down on the counter and carried Kate's suitcase to the stairs at the far end of the hall. Jason noticed the extra make-up and fresh hairstyle as his mom approached from the opposite direction. "Look at you! Did Pastor Jenson move services to Friday? Nobody told *me*," he teased.

"Oh, hush," she said with a quick but substantial swat to his abdomen.

"Hello, Kate," said Hannah, moving on into the kitchen. "It is so kind of you to come. I hope Jason told you that I don't need to be waited on. Other than an occasional flare, I'm no different than any other dusty old woman."

"He told me that you are probably in better shape than I am," Kate said with a smile. "And it looks like he's right."

"I like you already, sweetie," said Hannah.

"Jason also told me you're a bit of a cribbage buff," Kate said.

"That's right. But as a warning, I don't care much for losing," said Hannah.

"That's one thing we have in common," Kate said. Hannah grinned, looking forward to the challenge.

"The dinner is on the counter. Two Friday specials—chicken ala king," Jason said, pointing to the brown bag rolled up at the top. "But you may need to warm them up a little." He shuffled toward the hall. "I'm going up to take a quick shower, then get out of your hair."

"You aren't going to eat with us?" Hannah asked, more annoyed than surprised. Kate wondered the same, hoping Jason would help the women get better acquainted.

"I don't like being outnumbered," he lied, taking Kate's suitcase with him up the stairs. A very long night still lay in front of him.

# CHAPTER 5

Khalid swiped the Visa card, flipped it over to verify it had been signed, then set it on the counter. While waiting for the machine to spit out a receipt, he bagged the skirt and denim jacket and handed the purchase to the customer. The woman signed the receipt and he gave her the bottom copy while wishing her and her preteen daughter a good evening.

"Who knows, maybe we'll be back later," she said and smiled at him in a way that was not entirely wholesome.

For more than a year, Khalid spent evenings and weekends ringing up purchases and straightening displays at the Rockwell Outfitter store in America's Megamall while attending classes at the University of Minnesota during the day. He originally applied for a job at the hip clothing store when he first arrived from Cairo, Egypt, but was told by a manager that he would need retail experience before he could be considered for the position. A few months later, after obtaining the necessary experience at the campus bookstore, he went back with another application but the same man told him they were not hiring. However, during the visit he witnessed a subtle interaction between two female employees that would bring him back that evening.

While dark eyes, angled cheekbones and curly black hair are common physical characteristics in Arab men, few possessed them in the startling magnificence of Khalid Bari. The striking features that set him apart in his homeland became only more distinctive in the ethnic diversity of the United States. It was not unusual for Khalid to catch a woman holding a gaze a second too long or, like the afternoon of his hire, witness a tap on the shoulder of one girl to another, nodding or pointing in his direction. It was the shoulder tap between the two female employees that gave Khalid the idea to return to the store that evening. Sure enough, the day manager's shift was over and a woman was now in charge of the floor.

Khalid arrived for "new employee orientation" at 9:00 AM the following Tuesday. He drove there from the hiring manager, Jan's, apartment.

After ringing up two more customers, Khalid returned to the floor. Muhab had given him a very important job and his shift at the clothing store was the perfect time and place to complete it. He was to acquire a gift for the leader of the nationwide offensive, who had come to complete the Minnesota team and was being introduced to the group tonight. The gift, he was told, was to be young, blonde, and "American."

An hour earlier, two young women, fitting the description perfectly, walked into the store. He played along with their dramatic act of "get noticed, giggle, and turn away." He walked toward them and was greeted by more silly laughter. He was about to launch into his well-honed routine that began with, "I bet I know what you're looking for," and ended with him receiving a phone number (usually with a smiley face written somewhere on the note). But before he reached them, he heard, "Khalid, I need your help over here, please." Jan had seen the game many times, too. And while she was well aware their relationship was not completely exclusive, her wolf was not hunting other sheep on her hill. Before he could complete her unnecessary task, the two blondes were gone.

He kept busy at the front of the store for another twenty minutes, refolding and neatening clothing to avoid again getting stuck behind a register. But the store was getting busier, and a line five customers deep formed at the cashier's desk with only Jan to assist them. She called Khalid to please help her at the adjacent register. He hesitated and she called again; this time the "please" conveyed the message, "I am your boss; do as I say." As Khalid turned to do as instructed, he heard the familiar giggles behind him. He spun back again—the target had been acquired and he was locked on.

---

Despite Hannah's mild protests, Kate cleared the dinner dishes and loaded them into the dishwasher.

"How about we fill our glasses before the tour," Hannah said, as Kate pressed the button to begin the wash cycle.

Hannah handed a wine glass to her guest, then led her across the hall into the family room. "Jason did all of this," said Hannah pointing to the detailed floor-to-ceiling mahogany entertainment and shelving unit. "Twice."

"It's beautiful. Why twice?" asked Kate.

"He built the first one when he was home on spring break his freshman year at Minnesota-Duluth," Hannah said. "His friends were all in Florida or someplace. Maybe it was Texas. What's that one island so many of the kids go to?"

"South Padre?" Kate asked.

"That's right, South Padre. Well, anyway, his friends were all off at spring break and Jason was stuck at home because he was playing hockey. Except, he *wasn't* playing hockey because his team was beaten in the playoffs the week before. So, after a couple days sitting in front of the TV, bored and feeling sorry for himself, Tom, his dad, gave him a list of things to do around the house. The first thing on the list was to put up some shelves in here. That night, Tom came home from work to a big stack of lumber in the middle of the room, and by the end of the week we had a beautiful entertainment center.

"That first one was smaller and didn't have these glass doors or anything," Hannah said as she rubbed the ornate detail. "But he tore it down and started on this one years later when Kelly was eight months pregnant with Grace. I swear he nested more than she did. Plus, I think he wanted to bring Grace from the hospital to a place that felt more like *their* home, not grandma's house. That may also be the reason he gutted the kitchen a month later."

"He doesn't do things halfway, does he?" commented Kate.

"No, he doesn't," Hannah said. "The baby's crying kept Kelly up all night and Jason's hammering kept her up all day—drove her crazy. But she knew plenty well by then that when Jason latches onto something he's not going to quit, so it's best to just stay out of the way."

"Is that what's happening this weekend?" asked Kate.

"I guess so. He's getting away to dive into his grief until..." Hannah paused, looking for the right words but not finding them, "until he overcomes it, I suppose. Last year the pressure built up over weeks in front of the anniversary, more, I think, than Jason realized. Then he left for a few days and when he came back it was like it was all behind him."

They moved down the hall. "Here we have the quilter's suite, formerly known as the living room," Hannah said. Three folded card tables and several padded folding chairs leaned against one of the sunny yellow walls. On another wall, stacks of patterns, utensils, and equipment sat in front of three-foot-high mounds of folded fabric. Three sewing machines and piles of finished and near-finished quilts sat against the right wall.

"Wow. It looks like we're standing in the middle of Cedar River's quilting headquarters. I bet you can keep an entire battalion of quilters busy in here," Kate marveled.

"We had fourteen women in here for five straight days last December. We sent 94 'Welcome Home' quilts to Habitat for Humanity that month," said Hannah.

"You touched a lot of lives, that's for sure," said Kate. Hannah smiled a thank you.

"Oh my! This one's beautiful," said Kate, looking at the quilt displayed in a large glass display cabinet.

"That's Grace's quilt," Hannah said. She pretended to fumble with the quilt as she composed herself. It was a difficult anniversary for her, too.

Hannah unfolded the blanket, revealing dozens of six-inch squares, each with shapes and scenes created from buttons of all shapes, sizes and designs, thousands in all.

"When Grace was born, Jason got tired of hearing how his daughter was 'cute as a button' so he sarcastically started calling her Button and, before you know it, he rarely called her anything else."

Hannah handed the blanket to Kate then gestured toward the decorative ceramic and glass button figurines displayed on the top shelf of the cabinet. "Kelly gave these to Grace on each of her birthdays. She knew how much Grace loved being her daddy's *little button.* She had a real knack for bringing the best of Jason into full bloom."

Kate refolded the quilt and handed it back to Hannah.

"I'm sorry, Kate. I don't mean to be an insensitive old bat," Hannah said. "The next time I go on about Kelly, just flick me in the ear or something."

Kate let out an embarrassed laugh. "Oh no, Mrs. Kendall, Jason and I are just friends."

"Oh, I know, dear," Hannah said, patting her on the hand.

Kate wasn't so sure she did.

---

It was 6:30 when Jason pulled off County Road 12 onto his eighty acres north of town. Three hikes later, all of the gear he'd packed for the weekend was in the deer stand. The last load consisted of a couple of twelve-packs of Killian's Red and two bottles of Maker's Mark whiskey. He'd hoped this amount of liquid mollification would last him through the weekend, unlike last year when he had to call Seth for more liquor by the morning of the third day of his four-day retreat. But this was the *second* anniversary of the hit-and-run death of his wife and daughter to a suspected drunk driver. Certainly, the pain would be more manageable this year.

## 8:00 PM

The avalanche of memories was unrelenting. One image begot another, and another; materializing like cards being dealt too swiftly to sort. He leaned forward, his elbows on his thighs, as his breathing grew more shallow. He tried to absorb each memory as it appeared—a trike on the driveway, a beach in Martinique, a hideous multi-colored Christmas sweater. But too quickly each memory escaped, replaced by yet another. Jason grabbed the beer at his feet and took a long drink, momentarily pausing the onslaught. But when he tossed the empty bottle with the others, the memories returned, again too briefly for him to consume.

Twenty minutes and another beer later, his breathing slowed and Jason was able to perform a mental triage of the memories. Those in the rear would just need to wait their turn or return later. He leaned back, closed his eyes, and enjoyed the mental slide show. He wept and smiled at the same time—both actions were involuntary.

*"I know her name."*

*"No, you don't."*

*"Yeah, I do."*

*"We agreed we wouldn't pick out a name until after we got to know her. She's only two minutes old."*

*"Grace."*

*"Grace?... Maybe... Where did you get that?"*

*"Her mom."*

*"I don't know what they put in* **your** *epidural, Jas' but I'm pretty confident my name's still Kelly."*

*"Grace. If she's a part of you, it can't be anything else"*

*"Hello, Grace."*

Jason wiped his eyes and took a long pull of whiskey.

---

Liz Pratt's head was screaming as she emerged from the blackout. As the fog dissipated, she realized she was sitting on a couch next to Maria, who was sobbing quietly. They were in a different room than when she'd drifted into unconsciousness. Her hands and feet, like Maria's, were bound with tape and their mouths were covered with the same. The large brooding roommate of the handsome man from the Rockwell Outfitter store, whose name she couldn't recall, sat near them in an oversized leather chair. He seemed to be unaware of their presence in the room as he watched an episode of *Gilligan's Island.*

While trying to shake the pain from her head, she thought of her parents and all the lectures and sermons they'd bored her with over the last few years—sit-downs about drugs, men, liquor, even panty choices. Certainly, the audacity of driving across the metro area to the apartment of a man she'd just met at the mall, like she'd done tonight, was covered at least once during the sessions. She would give anything to be out of this unfamiliar house in which she was now being held and back in front of her father, listening to a rambling thirty-minute "I told you so."

Earlier that day she and Maria had been at the mall, engaged in a contest to see who could complete the most Christmas shopping by

6:00. The bet would be decided by the most people shopped for, not the most items purchased. The winner would receive the usual prize—having her laundry washed and folded by the loser before the end of the weekend. But when they flirted with, then were asked out by, the gorgeous man at Rockwell Outfitters, whose charm equaled his physical features, the early Christmas shopping contest was replaced by splurging on new club outfits neither could afford.

Equipped with new figure-hugging clothes and their fake IDs, the girls planned to meet "Mr. Yummy" and his roommate for drinks at their apartment, then move on to a new dance club the men's friend just opened in Uptown, a narrow strip of shops and clubs where the young beautiful people of Minneapolis went to be seen. But they never made it through their first cocktail in the apartment, much less to the club. It was obvious that something had been slipped into their cosmopolitans.

Maria's sobs were growing louder behind the strips of tape. Liz gave her a soothing look to help calm her but it wasn't working. Liz then tried to speak from behind the restraint but the words came out like incoherent sounds from the world's worst ventriloquist. Maria returned the effort of mutual support with garbled sounds of her own.

All communication suddenly ended when the large, now-irritated, man lifted a silver handgun from his lap and waved it toward them, his eyes never veering from Gilligan swinging upside down from a tall palm tree.

---

## 10:00 PM

Using a penlight, Jason flipped through a photo album and remembered teasing Kelly about taking so many pictures of Grace as a baby, telling her that by the time their daughter was three, there wouldn't be any room left in the attic for his shoebox of old baseball cards. She shot him "the look" and he never got between a mom and her baby pictures again. Now, as he pored over the pictures, it struck him that she hadn't taken nearly enough.

*"Hey, Daddy, you're luckier than 'Lisabeth's dad. You wanna know why?"*

*"Let me guess. Because I'm so darned handsome?"*

*"No, silly."*

*"Okay, Button. Tell me why."*

*"'Cause you have three girls and 'Lisabeth's dad only gets to have two."*

*"Are you hiding two sisters from me?"*

*"No. Stop being silly. I mean you got me and Mommy and Grandma. He just has 'Lisabeth and Mrs. Thomas. He doesn't get to have a grandma with him."*

*"I'll tell you a really special secret if you promise not to tell Elisabeth."*

*"I won't."*

*"Are you sure? You can't tell anybody."*

*"I'm sure—really sure."*

*"Okay. Here's the secret: I don't just have three girls. I have the three* ***best*** *girls in the whole wide world. But you can't tell Elisabeth or anyone else. We don't want other dads to feel bad. Okay?"*

*"Okay. Besides, 'Lisabeth already told me her dad was the goodest. I just told her she was full of beans."*

## Midnight

Jason finished another beer, tossed the bottle into a brown EconoFoods grocery bag, and ripped open the second twelve pack. He hadn't anticipated drinking this much. He would definitely need more liquor before tomorrow night but, unfortunately, he couldn't call Seth for reinforcements this year. He'd deliberately left his cell phone at home—too many people wanted to check on him last year.

In the last hour, the recollections were far less frequent. Anger and resentment were filling the void. The images weren't dissipating only because he was at an emotional low, but because the number of memories he had of his precious family had decreased in the last year. Guilt seeped in with the already brewing fury and his two-year argument with God resumed. The accusations and questions were neither rhetorical nor forgiving.

"Where's the plan?" Jason shouted into the darkness. "We had a deal and I have been the good soldier. I've listened to you and your cronies tell me how things 'happen for a reason,' that you have a plan. Well, you show it to me. You show me this plan. Show me how things are going to get better, because I can't see it. All I see is more emptiness, more abandonment, more loneliness. It's not getting better; it's getting worse. Everyone else seems to have forgotten. I can't. I don't want to!"

Jason took another swig of whiskey and continued to rant. "Your 'plan' is the only thing I have left to hold onto. But it's been two years." He took another swig from the bottle. "Two years… and still nothing! I'm still empty." A fresh thought entered his head out of nowhere, bringing on more anger. "My whole life is still ahead of me?! That's all you got? Not good enough. Did you forget? You stole my life two years ago. Remember?"

He stood up for the first time in an hour and threw the half-full whiskey bottle deep into the darkness. Not anticipating the effect of the intoxicants, he lost his balance, slipped, and fell heavily onto a sturdy limb, which prevented a 20-foot plummet to the ground below.

Jason slunk back into his camping chair, embarrassed, as if the alcohol-induced near-fall diminished the righteousness of his argument. Quieter now and feeling defeated, he finished his argument. "I give up. You said I could get through this; that together, we wouldn't let them die in vain. Somehow we would honor Kelly and Grace."

Jason let out a long sigh that released the rest of his questions and the last of his hope. He leaned forward, his palms catching his forehead as a steady flow of tears started to puddle on the weathered wood planks beneath his feet. He looked back up to the stars and spoke in little more than a whisper. "I was wrong. It was all bullshit. You don't have a plan. Nothing's gonna come from their deaths. So just do me one favor; you owe me that.

"Put *me* in the next car."

# CHAPTER 6

For optimal security specific to the location, Muhab chose to wait until midnight to begin his meeting in Minnesota—far later than his Denver counterpart had. After prayers, the men replaced mats with two short rows of folding chairs and set a large dry erase board on a pedestal. Muhab waited as the men took their seats. Two groups formed naturally as this was the first time the two cells met as one. General Attar prayed in a separate room and waited there so he could be formally introduced by Muhab to make it clear to the group the significance of his arrival.

"Gentlemen, peace be with you," Muhab said. The men responded in kind.

"Tonight, our great journey brings us a wonderful gift. As many of you know, we have been awaiting another soldier to complete our team. Tonight, he joins us. But this man is not just any soldier. He has commanded many forces in the name of Allah." The volume in Muhab's voice built with excitement. "We are joined tonight by a legendary leader, the man by whom our destiny was conceived. What we undertake in the coming days, and the battle tens of millions of fellow Muslims take up after we are gone, was first conceived in the heart and mind of the man I am about to introduce.

"This is the man who leads our war to defeat the earth's infidels and return Islam to its just place in the world. But for his safety and your own, I cannot reveal his name and at no time should he be saluted or referred to in public by military rank."

Muhab turned around to the staircase landing. "Sir, we humbly await your address."

The men began to applaud. General Attar walked down the stairs and listened as the applause grew and random shouts of joy and thanks filled the room. He entered the room and allowed the cheering to crescendo, then wane on its own. He nodded at Muhab to thank him for the introduction and indicate to the other men Muhab's status within the group.

"Gentlemen, peace be with you and all glory to Allah."

"Peace be with you," responded the men.

"Centuries ago, there was a boy who had no father and, not long after, no mother. Grave dangers surrounded this boy and forced him into hiding. But this boy knew Allah and kept the faith. He did not back down. He did not turn from the truth," the general said, pacing purposefully back and forth in front of the men, shaking his fist as he spoke.

"The boy fought his way into manhood and others flocked to him. They rushed to him for his faith, for his righteousness, for his strength. They followed him because they could feel Allah's power inside him. The legion of faithful followers grew from hundreds to hundreds of thousands. I am, of course, speaking of the great prophet, Mohammed."

The men stood and cheered in agreement and praise.

"And only one hundred years after Islam was born, the number of true believers grew so large and strong under Allah's guidance and protection, they were able to overcome Persia to the east and Spain to the west. Not only were those countries much longer established in their own cultures, but they were two of the world's great military powers. It would be as if a country the size and strength of Egypt simultaneously defeated a fully armed Russia and United States today."

He paused and looked each of the seven men in the eye. "Think about what I just said to you. Egypt battles Russia and the United States at the same time and wins! That is what Allah has done for his people in the past and…" He looked down and passed back and forth in front of the men. When he looked up, each of the men was leaning forward in his chair. He had them.

"And that is what Allah has prepared us to do once again. We are the latest chosen ones. We are ready to rise up again!" He propelled his fist into the air and the men rose and mimicked his action, feeling his power.

He motioned them back to their chairs. "That is the amazing wonder of Allah. One day, his greatness will overpower the godlessness of the Russians and the Chinese. And we have prepared for such a day. But first, we must destroy the selfish arrogance of this godless America. Soon this nation of frivolous infidels who choose personal riches over life in the spirit will be in upheaval and political chaos." With a sweeping motion encompassing the men, he raised his voice to a shout. "An upheaval *you* will cause. *You* shall pave the way for our great victory! *You* will fire the shot that brings light to the world!"

Again the men rose in unison, shouting. They jumped up and down and hugged one another, praising Allah.

Gesturing for them to return to their seats, he continued. "But this giant, this superpower, like the foes at the time of our grandfathers, has a force greater than the world has ever seen before. We are attacking a massive army with fierce weapons and magnificent technology. So we will not fight against our enemy's strength; we will attack their weaknesses and, in doing so, we will neutralize their strengths. Let me show you the path to victory for Allah and Islam."

He turned to the white board and with a thick black marker, drew a rudimentary outline of the United States. Then he picked up a green marker and drew thirteen smaller circles within the outline; one was in the general area of the Twin Cities. He then drew five black squares, three along the coasts, two farther inland.

He turned back to the eager men. "First, we will use their own gluttony and greed to implode their economy. We will watch as their fear and godlessness paralyze them."

He turned back to the white board and slashed each green circle with a red X. His words became more hurried. "Then, as they point fingers and wallow in pathetic self-pity, we will strike the technology that has driven their laziness and opulence—the technology that they now rely on to *defend* them." General Attar drew large circles around each of the five squares.

"And with their defenses and communications destroyed, only fear and chaos will remain—victory for Allah will be swift and just! Where they fight with fear, we shall fight with courage!" he shouted, his fist now pumping above his head.

"Where they fight for possessions, we shall fight for righteousness!"

"Where they fight with no god, we shall fight with Allah!"

"Praise Allah!" he yelled, reaching a crescendo.

"Praise Allah!" returned the men, leaping to their feet.

"Praise Allah!" he yelled again.

"Praise Allah!" returned the men, in one voice.

They were on the edge of the cliff waiting, begging for a reason to jump.

General Attar took the .45 from his shoulder holster and fired it above his head.

They jumped up, cheering. The general waited a moment for the fervor to refocus on him. He fired again, creating a roaring frenzy. They had been committed to the cause before his arrival. But now they were committed to him as well, no matter the cost.

A third shot rang out, followed by a riotous roar from the willing martyrs.

Muhab flinched at the shots and the danger of being discovered. Sure, it was a small risk so far into the country in the middle of the night, but it was a risk all the same. He suggested to the general that the men continue their celebration in the hidden room under the home but General Attar disagreed. "The men need to feel like giants, not like worms," he said. Muhab rejoiced with the other men but silently prayed for Allah to keep them hidden from the world outside their walls.

---

Gunshot?

Jason turned left, in the direction of the sound. There was a light in the distance he hadn't noticed before. Jason replayed the sound in his head—could it be?

There it was again. Another gunshot! Like the first, it was muted and distant, but definitely coming from the area of the light. Jason stared ahead, perfectly still, watching for any movement, listening for any sound. He could hear his heart beating and for the first time tonight felt the breeze on his face from the west.

Then came the third distant pop matching the first two. But this one seemed different; not the shot, but after. Jason thought he heard faint cheers or shouting following the last shot, if that was what he heard. He leaned over to the bottom cabinet and pulled out a pair of binoculars. The magnified view was still a little blurry, but not because of the equipment. His eyes were focusing on the sight, which he now recognized as the single downward facing bulb of an outdoor garage light. He made out at least three cars in the driveway. He couldn't see a house but assumed the light-colored garage was a stand-alone outbuilding like the design of so many farmsteads that dotted the southern Minnesota countryside.

*Cheering?* Jason wondered. *Must be some St. Joe frat boys.* Jason wasn't so old that he didn't remember his college days, waiting until ten or eleven o'clock at night before leaving his apartment to hit the bars, house parties, and after-bar parties. He had been through a number of wild times that didn't end until a large breakfast in the morning soaked up some of the night's buzz. But guns?

If they were indeed gunshots, what should he do? He considered his next move; everything from alerting police to hiking to the garage for a closer look. But in his inebriated state and with no cell phone, he wasn't capable of much of anything, nor did he need additional complications tonight. His purpose for being in the stand tonight was to get *away* from people and ongoing daily strife. Eventually, he decided to turn his chair toward the garage light to monitor the area. He hung the binoculars around his neck and if he noticed any activity, he would react accordingly.

He didn't immediately hear or see anything, but the new concentration of focus was a welcome distraction from his self-inflicted misery. He took a sip of beer and thought back to the "good ol' days" of his college years.

---

After further praise and additional instruction, Khalid and the others left the rally, leaving just Muhab and the honored leader at the country house. Khalid drove to Omar's rented house in the southwest Minneapolis suburb of Richfield, eager to tell his friend about the amazing rally. In return, Omar told him that his night with the two blonde women had been basically quiet. Khalid squatted down in front of the women, who were sitting on the couch, and used his best "sensitive understanding man" voice to convince the two women that everything was okay. "No need to be scared... we're going to a terrific party... good times... have you home soon." His words had little effect on the women's fear so he gave up and, with Omar, led the two women outside. One of the women, the one not crying, drove her heel hard into Omar's foot, then turned and kicked him in the groin. But the kick was soft and hit Omar in the thigh as much as the more painful region. Still, it infuriated Omar; Khalid barely caught his raised arm before it could strike down on the woman.

"Omar, no! Remember your charge. Remember what Muhab said, 'beautiful and blonde.'" Omar was still fuming but had relaxed enough to allow Khalid to let go of his arm.

Forty-five minutes later, Khalid exited the freeway and began a series of turns leading back to the meeting site just north of Cedar River. He looked in the rear-view mirror at the silhouette of his friend Omar in the middle of the back seat, a beautiful but terrified woman at each shoulder. No one had spoken during the entire trip.

"Ladies, we are almost to our destination," Khalid said. "There is no need to be frightened. It is like I told you before. We are just going to a party to have some fun. No one wants to hurt you. They will be very glad to see two women as beautiful as you." Then to Omar, "Remove the tape from their mouths but not their hands. And do it gently."

Omar leaned to his left and peeled the layers of masking tape from the trembling woman seated next to him. The wide masking tape was preferable to duct tape because it pulled away much easier and did not leave tape residue or skin irritation. Omar turned to the blonde who'd kicked him and roughly ripped the tape off her mouth from the bottom up and pushed his hand into her nose, his knuckles knocking her head back.

"Omar!" Khalid yelled.

Omar continued to glare at the woman. No bitch kicks him in the balls. He hoped the man they brought her to entertain would treat her as brutally as he wished he could. He thought again about the pain her boot caused his groin earlier and lifted his arm across his chest, preparing to strike.

"Stop it! We're here," Khalid said.

Omar hadn't even felt the car brake. He looked out the windshield and saw a garage directly in front of them and an old farmhouse farther back and to the left. Khalid got out and opened the rear driver's door and pulled the crying blonde from the car. Omar reached over the other woman to unlatch the rear passenger door, then pushed her out and followed close behind. He held the woman's elbow in his right hand as he pushed the door shut with the other.

As the door closed, the woman spun to her right and delivered an elbow to Omar's right cheek, then tried to run. But he was too strong and easily kept his firm grip on her arm. He pulled her back, spinning her slightly, and landed a short left hand to her mouth. Her head snapped back as if attached to her body with only a wiry spring. Her knees buckled but his strong grasp kept her 110-pound frame from falling to the gravel. He was pleased; he'd thrown many punches in his time, and he was certain at least two of the bitch's teeth were loose if not out completely. He smiled at her and asked if she wanted to try again.

Khalid angrily chastised Omar for his temper and stupidity as they pushed the women up the sidewalk and into the house where Muhab and General Attar met them.

Muhab, seeing the two young women, turned to General Attar and said, "General, I told you we had a welcome gift for you. Khalid and Omar have brought them here for your pleasure. I hope you will allow yourself some enjoyment. Your days are filled with so much stress."

"What happened to this one?" General Attar said, grabbing the chin of the woman Omar had belted and examining the blood glazing over her swollen bottom lip.

Omar opened his mouth to respond but Khalid was faster. "I am sorry; she tried a number of times to flee and we needed to raise our level of force to make her fall in line. Please forgive us."

"I have been in the same circumstance myself in the past," General Attar said, not trying very hard to mask his anger. "But perhaps next time you will find a more subtle way of controlling the situation."

"Yes, Sir," replied Khalid, glancing at Omar with an "I-told-you-so" look.

"Clean this one up, and bring the other upstairs to me," commanded the general.

---

Jason was securing his sleeping bag to the stand when the car pulled up under the light in the west. He had given up his vigil after all the cars left together more than an hour ago. He only noticed the new car pulling into the property because he happened to be facing that direction while tying down the bag. He grabbed the binoculars from the chair, then saw a shadow figure get out of the driver's door and help another person out the rear door. The rear passenger door opened and a moment later a woman got out, followed by a man who towered over her. Jason was amazed the rear seat of the small car could hold such a huge man. The woman, standing maybe ten feet in front of the garage light, suddenly twisted into him then lurched away. Jason fell from his haunches when he heard the woman's scream and watched the man buckle her with a vicious fist to the face.

Jason sat for a moment in his fallen position, stunned by the sight of the sudden violence. He stood up to yell but all four people had disappeared around the far corner of the garage to the west. Once again he was confronted with a "next move" but this time he could not just stand back and mind his own business. He quickly decided that the safest response was also the smartest; call the police for help. He instinctively grabbed at his hip but his cell phone was resting quietly back home on top of his bedroom dresser.

"Shit! Now what?" he asked himself.

He looked up again in the direction of the light but found only blackness—the garage light had been shut off. He wasn't going to be able to make the quarter-mile hike over uneven and unfamiliar terrain in the dark. Plus, what would he do when he got there; especially in his deteriorated condition? Instead, he decided to return over the path he'd traversed dozens of times back to his truck.

"Hang in there—I'll be right back," Jason muttered toward the garage. Grabbing a flashlight, he descended the ladder as quickly as his spinning head would allow.

He reached the truck, but only after falling three times during the half-mile jog. His last fall slowed him significantly as his right foot had slipped on a jagged rock covered in dew, sending his foot flying back. His right knee took the brunt of the fall, slamming hard against the rigid stone. His pants were ripped and he knew his knee was bleeding pretty good as the cooling air licked the fresh wound with each new step.

When he finally reached the truck, he opened the door and lifted his foot to the cab floor. The full knee bend intensified the pain and in the truck's dome light, he could see just how deep the two-inch cut was. He grabbed a jean jacket from behind the seat and used the cotton lining to blot the wound. He climbed into the truck and straightened his throbbing right leg onto the passenger seat. Then he pulled the jacket arm inside out and wrapped it around the bleeding knee.

He leaned his head back and took a couple of deep breaths. The fresh night air, mixed with the alcohol, pent-up adrenaline and pain, bubbled angrily in his stomach. He leaned out the door just far enough to heave over the paint of the door well. Two more rounds of retching followed, briefly settling his stomach. Jason sat back and again laid his head back, willing his dizziness to stop. He thought about the empty bottles found at the scene where Kelly's car was sent over the guard rail and into the river two years ago. He guessed that driver was probably less drunk at the time than he was right now. He couldn't put the key in the ignition—not in this condition. Maybe he could flag down a passing car and get a lift into town.

Jason closed his eyes for just a moment to gather himself before going out to the road.

# CHAPTER 7

Jason woke with a start, his face warm from the sunshine pouring through the rear window. His neck ached as he lifted it off the top of the seat back. A moment later, his head began to pound, leading the on-rushing hangover.

"Dammit."

He straightened and reached to pull his door closed.

"Aahhh!" he screamed as his right leg bent at the knee, sending a shockwave of searing pain from the wounded knee to the rest of his body. He pushed the jacket sleeve from his knee, which pulled up congealed blood and reopened the cut. A new surge of blood filled the void as Jason turned the ignition and started for home.

A continuous loop of the woman's legs collapsing beneath her assailant's blow played in Jason's head during the ride home. He limped through the back door into the kitchen to find his mom preparing breakfast at the stove. Kate was sitting at the small table to the left, her hands warming around a coffee mug. She was wearing a faded yellow sweatshirt with the collar cut away and a pair of baby blue athletic shorts, probably the outfit she'd slept in.

Hannah saw it first. "Jason, what happened to your leg? I told you not too sleep way up in that thing,"

"It's nothing. I slipped and fell on the way back to the truck—it doesn't even hurt," said Jason, seeing Kate doing her own inspection of the knee.

"That's a lot of blood on your pants for a cut that doesn't hurt," Hannah said.

"Really, Mom, it's fine. I'm just going to run upstairs and clean it up," he said, and gave Kate a look that warned her from getting involved.

"You need to get it looked at. It's right on the knee, Jason. Otherwise, it's going to keep opening and never heal. Plus you'll have another big scar," Hannah said.

Kate chimed in. "Your mom's right. Do you want me to drive you over to the clinic? I can be ready in a couple minutes."

"Kate, believe me, Mom doesn't need back-up from you," he said.

"It's not about backing her up; it's about helping you," she said. "So do you want me to drive you or not?"

"No. I'll run by the clinic later to get it looked at. But right now, I'm gonna go get cleaned up."

"How much later?" Hannah demanded.

"Mom!"

Jason limped upstairs, keeping his right leg as straight as he could to minimize the bleeding. He got to his room and immediately grabbed his Blackberry to call Sheriff Pat Burnett's cell phone. But despite talking to him almost daily for the past month, he couldn't remember the number. *Technology is just making us more stupid*, Jason thought as he scrolled down through the phone's electronic phone book and selected Pat's number.

"Hey, Jason," Pat greeted him. "A little early, isn't it?"

"Why can't you just say 'Hello'?" responded Jason. "When somebody calls you, *they* expect to start the conversation. When you greet the caller with 'Hi, it's a little early,' it screws everything up."

"Do you want to hang up and call me back so I can answer according to the Jason Kendall rules of phone etiquette?" asked the sheriff.

"No, actually I have something important to talk to you about," said Jason. He told Sheriff Burnett about hearing what he believed were three gunshots from inside the house near his stand, about the number of cars that were at the house until 2:00 AM, and about the car that showed up an hour later carrying the woman who was hit by the man she was with.

"So these shots, were they fired, bang, bang, bang, or did you hear them at different times during the evening?" asked the sheriff.

"They were grouped but staggered," replied Jason, "maybe two or three seconds between them. And like I said, I thought I may have heard laughing or cheering after the third, so it may have just been a college party or something."

"One more question: why were you at your deer stand at that time of night? And why are you only calling now?" asked Pat. "I guess that's two questions."

"Grace and Kelly's accident happened two years ago yesterday, and I took some time to myself. I figured the stand was as good a place as any to get away from everything," Jason said. "I was planning on spending a couple of nights out there so I hit the juice pretty hard last night—ended up passing out in my truck before I could get help. I called you as soon as I got to a phone."

"All right. I'm not on duty today but I'll call Clint, tell him the story and have him go out to the house to take a look. I think I know the house you're talking about," said the sheriff.

"Can I ask you a favor?"

"Shoot."

"Can you keep my name out of it for now? Clint and I don't exactly get along, especially after I dropped him on the ice last year," Jason said. "I'm sure he's a professional and all, but I don't want my involvement to impact his interest level, you know?"

"That's right; I remember that. You laid him out good. What's he go? Six-two—two-ten, two-twenty?"

"It was a hockey fight—good balance and a lucky punch can take you a long way. Anyway, can you keep me out of it?" Jason asked again.

"Will do."

"Thanks, Pat. Let me know what you hear. And by the way, I'm thinking the basement should be painted and trimmed by Wednesday."

"Good news. I can get Mrs. Sheriff Burnett off my back," he said. "I'll follow up with you when I hear back from Clint."

Jason could hear the smack the sheriff got from his wife for his attempt at humor and the resulting, "Ow! I was just jok-" before the phone clicked off.

The Blackberry showed three messages. He checked to see who they were from and decided they could wait. He popped four Advils and took a quick shower. Afterward, he placed a gauze pad over the cut and wrapped it with athletic tape to hold it in place before getting dressed. He went downstairs and considered sneaking out the front door to avoid facing the two mothering hens who were undoubtedly awaiting him. He decided to behave like a man, instead, and found the women in the family room, each still with a cup of coffee, the smell of breakfast sausage strong in the air.

"Okay, I'm gonna head over to the clinic and get stitched up," he said to both women.

"I can make you some toast to take with you and there is some left-over scrambled eggs and sausage in the refrigerator," Hannah said.

"You saved scrambled eggs? Jeez—you don't pick my leftover Cheerios out of the garbage do you?" Jason asked and winked at Kate.

"Don't get smart," Hannah said.

Kate jumped in. "The eggs are seasoned and have onions, peppers, and a little cheese mixed in with them. Maybe some will find their way home with me."

"Okay, kiss-ass," Jason shot back. "I don't plan on going back to the stand tonight so you can take off whenever you want. Thanks again."

"Your mom and I already have our day planned." She glanced at Hannah then back to Jason. "So if she's still up for it, I might see you later."

Jason watched his mom's eyes brighten at the suggestion. "Okay, but don't go getting all crazy. I'll be inspecting the liquor cabinet when I get home," he said, then went through the kitchen and out the back door.

Kate caught him as he stepped onto the stoop. "Jason." She put a hand on his shoulder. "How are you doing? You know, with everything."

"I'm all right. I'll admit I was a little surprised how much it still hurts after this much time but I feel better this morning. Something else happened last night, too, that's got me pretty bothered. I'll tell you about it later," he said, and smiled at her before turning to leave. It was a good day to have someone care about you, he thought.

Jason returned the three calls while waiting for a doctor at the Cedar River Medical Clinic. His last call was to Neil Lockwood, who'd left a message asking Jason if he was still interested in getting together for their standing monthly lunch appointment. When Neil answered, Jason asked if they could move it up an hour to eleven o'clock; Neil agreed. Jason was already picturing the big juicy patty melt he planned to use to fill his empty stomach.

---

Liz Pratt drifted in, but mostly out, of consciousness during the night on the damp, rough concrete floor. Her hands were still bound by layers of blue masking tape but now rope was added as reinforcement. She sat up and leaned against the rear wall of the dark basement room, eyeing its only door. Although she was afraid, she was not in a panic. She'd been treated roughly and punched so hard in the mouth that she still couldn't bite down, but she still felt fortunate. She turned to Maria, lying unconscious and shaking in the corner. Things had been much worse for her.

A couple hours earlier the door opened and Maria was pushed through. Her hands were tied with rope, no more tape. She wore only a man's plain white t-shirt stained with blood and dirt, no pants or panties. Liz nudged over to her and tried to put her arms, with still-bound hands, around her friend, but Maria let out a frightened moan and pushed her away. Liz asked Maria how she could help, but the offer made her friend retreat further. So Liz moved back against the wall and watched Maria, her knees tucked inside the stretched shirt and her swollen, bleeding face curled into her chest. Her soft whimpering stopped when she fell asleep. The shaking didn't.

---

Jason walked into Vera's and waited for his eyes to adjust to the darkness, then scanned the room for Neil, but ran into Louise first.

"You already changed your mind about running for city council? I must've been even more persuasive and charming than usual." She paused a moment then, "Naw, ain't possible I could be more charming."

"No council; just lunch. I'm meeting Neil Lockwood. Has he come in yet?"

Louise sensed that her recruiting would be better served another day. "He's sitting on the other side of the TVs, along the wall."

"Looks like you've got a bad hoof there," said Neil as Jason approached the booth.

"Yeah, I took a bit of a header last night. Twelve stitches," Jason said.

"Ouch. Sounds like a perfect end to a really tough day."

Neil was a long-time neighbor of the Kendall family. He'd moved in next door the day of Jason's sixth birthday, so Jason's parents invited him to the small dinner they were having in their son's honor. Neil gave Jason a baseball autographed by Kent Hrbek, the Minnesota Twins first baseman who had hit 23 home runs the year before. That ball was number 21. Jason and Neil had a special bond ever since. After Jason lost his father, Neil took it upon himself to call and have dinner with Jason regularly, even though Jason lived and worked in St. Paul, forty miles to the north, at the time. Neil, who taught sociology at St. Joe's, had moved outside of town a few years ago but in recent months his car was parked in the Burnett driveway on a semi-regular basis. Jason wondered how or if his relationship with the man would change if, as Jason suspected, Neil and his mom were growing closer.

"I heard you spent another anniversary out at your deer stand. How are you holding up?" Neil asked.

"I'm fine. But it was a damn difficult night. I drank more than I normally do in a month. I suppose it was the only thing I had to do out there other than feel sorry for myself," Jason said.

"I don't think anyone is going to blame you if you partake of some drunken self-pity one night a year. Some men who have been through your kind of loss hope to get through one night a year *without* drinking," Neil said.

Jason gave an unsure nod. "Maybe. But it's damn embarrassing when I think about Kelly and Grace looking down on me. They deserve better."

"My field is sociology, not psychology, but I feel confident when I tell you this isn't the last time you'll get caught being human. Think about your expectations of Kelly if the roles were reversed."

The waitress came to take Jason's drink order; Neil was already working on a coffee. She left with an order for a club sandwich for Neil; a patty melt, a double helping of hash browns, and a large orange juice for Jason.

While they waited for the food, the two men talked more about Jason's struggle to deal with his loss and how to balance moving forward with keeping the spirit of his family alive in his life. As with most of their conversations, Jason did most of the talking while Neil was content to listen. Jason couldn't think of another person with whom he shared such a dynamic. The food arrived, along with Jason's second orange juice and first glass of water.

"Something else happened last night, too; that's how I banged up my knee," Jason said. He told Neil about the gunshots and about the girl he wasn't able to help.

"And you haven't seen this house before?" Neil asked.

"I'm sure I have. But I've never really noticed it. I don't spend a lot of time out there and when I do, it's typically in the summer when the trees are full," Jason said. "And maybe the light over the garage wasn't on other times, either, not that I have been out there at night more than a few times. I'm going to drive by there after lunch. It's probably a house I've seen a hundred times from the front."

The conversation gradually moved on to other topics, most of which were focused on Jason's emotional health and his short- and long-term future. Jason scraped together the last bit of hash browns into a final bite.

"Look at you. You aren't 170 pounds in a wet parka and boots and I need to unbutton my pants just looking at that many hash browns," Neil said.

"One seventy-five," Jason said. "Jim's got me on a new lifting routine at Irons."

His cell rang: Sheriff Burnett.

"Hello?"

"Why do you say 'hello' like it's a question? Didn't you think anyone was on the other end?" Pat said.

"Yeah, yeah." Jason quickly moved on. "Did you hear something?"

"Clint just called. He went out and talked to the occupant of the house this morning," Pat said. "But he came up empty."

"What?" Jason interrupted.

"The person's lived there for years and years but she just rents the place. She's a retired widow who apparently gets cheap rent from an out-of-town landlord while he waits for urban sprawl to make it down to Cedar River," Pat said. "What's more, she says she didn't hear anything last night and she was home all night and in bed at her usual time—9:30."

"What's her name? Do I know her?" Jason asked.

"I forget the name. I didn't recognize it—I know that."

"Nobody else lives there with her?" Jason asked.

"No, I guess not. She let Clint go in and have a look around downstairs and up. He walked around the yard as well; nothing out of the ordinary. He said the house even had that old-person smell."

Jason remained silent, digesting the information. The sheriff filled the void. "She did say that the landlord rents half of the garage to someone else. Some kids could have been in there partying—that's my idea, not hers," Pat said. "Did you actually see people go into the house?"

"No, I couldn't see the house; I just saw them kind of disappear around the side of the garage. Maybe they were just going into the garage. Remember, I was pretty messed up." Jason wasn't just talking about the alcohol. "Are you sure he got the right house?" Jason asked after a moment of dead air.

"I think so. Clint saw a light over the doors on the garage and some fresh tire tracks leading from the road to the gravel driveway. We'll track down the house's owner and run by there a number of times tonight and again next weekend—see if some school kids are taking their fun to the country. If they are, you bet we'll put a stop to it and find out if anyone was adding assault to the party agenda," Pat said, then followed the party angle. "Could you tell if they were young, like under-age kids?"

"No, it was too dark and too far away. But it felt like they were a little older than high school kids; I'm not sure why," Jason said. "Look, I'm in the middle of lunch. I should probably get going. Thanks for checking it out, Pat."

"That's the job. I hope it doesn't lead to anything more serious."

Jason lowered the phone from his ear but heard, "Oh, Jason?"

He lifted it back again. "Yeah?"

"I kept your name out of it—told Clint there was a message on my cell from a buddy who lives over in Dassel. Said he was driving by last night and saw a bunch of cars—and maybe a girl get smacked," Pat said.

"I appreciate that. Thanks, Pat." Jason turned off the phone and stared down at his empty plate.

"What happened?" Neil asked.

Jason filled him in on the parts of the call Neil missed.

The waitress cleared the plates and left the check. Neil tried to grab it but Jason was a split-second quicker.

"I think I'm going to run out there," Jason said.

"Where? The house next to your property?"

"Yeah, I just want to make sure they got the right place."

"Will you do me a favor and go home and check in with your mom first? Tell her you're doing okay? If you don't, you know she's going to call me and want me to recite our entire conversation, not to mention asking whether you got enough to eat," Neil said.

"You're right. I'll head home first," Jason said and winced from the pain in his knee as he eased up from the table. "And Neil, thank you for lunch… and everything."

Neil got up and patted Jason on the back and left the hand there for a beat. "Don't thank me; you're the one buying."

Jason decided it was good time to take a shot at finding out more about Neil's visits to the house. He went with the direct approach. "So, what's going on with you and Mom?"

Neil paused through a dry gulp. "At our age, you do what you can to keep up with good friends." Neil fumbled. "Why don't you go on ahead? I'm going to get a root beer to go."

Jason smiled as his mentor blushed and made a beeline for the far end of the bar.

# CHAPTER 8

General Attar was working on a laptop computer at the small rectangular folding table he was using as a desk in the dank eight-by-twelve-foot basement room currently serving as his office and sleeping quarters. He looked up and saw Muhab in the doorway.

"A police officer was here today," General Attar said. "He asked about gunfire and a woman being hurt."

"I know. Clara told me before I came down."

The general stood and turned away from Muhab, who waited silently for him to continue.

"You told me this site was safe. We waited until after midnight to begin the meeting because you assured me that we would not be noticed in any way," Attar said in a volume just above a whisper.

"General, according to my information, a car was passing by long after the meeting, just as young Omar restrained the woman. Clara was the lookout during the meeting and she told me not one car passed the house from eight o'clock through end of the meeting. And if the person driving by saw something, he heard something other than your gunshots—the timing was not right. The sheriff's department seemed satisfied after the visit. It was just bad luck. It could have happened anywhere."

General Attar erupted. "It should have been prevented! The old woman should have been watching for their return, and your man should not have hit the girl out in the open. He needs to be dealt with.

This situation needs to be dealt with, Muhab!"

"I understand. I have spoken to Omar; he is very sorry for his mistake and eager to redeem himself," said Muhab.

"I want to talk to him, personally. And his friend," the general said, turning to Muhab. "What about the police? How do we know they are not coming back?"

"We don't. But we have contingencies planned, just as you have taught," Muhab said, playing to his leader's need for praise.

"Tell them to me," the general ordered.

"Remember, they cannot see this bunker from outside or even from the other part of the basement—it's completely hidden. But if they do return, we will move you and the supplies to a secondary location. But I assure you, we are clear for a minimum of two or three days. I know how the local law enforcement works. Sheriffs are elected not by solving crime, but by giving the illusion that there is none. They'll just make a few extra passes over the next couple of nights as a precaution. And when they find nothing, they'll consider the matter closed. For that reason, we can't have any cars coming in or out of here for the next two days. It will not interrupt our schedule in any way."

Muhab sensed the general was not convinced. "We have planned many months for the Minneapolis attack—just as you have worked so hard nationally. We will not fail you."

"The planning is meaningless if we do not have the right men. The planning is meaningless if you do not execute." General Attar strode to Muhab. He stood so close the toe of his boot butted up against the tip of Muhab's shoe. "These are your men, Muhab. You are the man who recruited and trained them. They must understand that even when they sleep they are soldiers in Allah's army. What happened last night cannot happen a second time or your first command will be your last. Do you understand?"

Muhab nodded.

"We shall see," General Attar said.

The two men discussed additional mission-critical items, then agreed to minimal contact during the weekend. They decided Khalid, who had been asked to stay at the house overnight to guard the women, would remain in the house until Monday morning to serve in the same capacity. Before Muhab left, General Attar warned him about the price of failure, both to the operation and for him, personally.

---

Jason stepped through the back door to find Kate and his mom in the kitchen fixing lunch. Hannah was standing at the stove frying bacon; Kate was near the sink, tearing lettuce. He smiled a hello to Kate, who turned to greet him. Hannah, on the other hand, continued her watch over the bacon, ignoring his entrance.

"How'd it go at the doctor?" Kate asked.

"Coupla' stitches; good as new," Jason said, looking over the various food items being prepared for the meal.

"How many is a couple?" Hannah asked.

"Twelve," Jason said in a quiet guilty voice.

Kate cut in. "We're making BLTs. Your mom marinated the tomatoes in a Greek vinaigrette. How good does that sound?"

"So good I just might join you," Jason said, taking off his jacket and draping it over the back of a chair at the kitchen table.

"I thought you already had lunch," Hannah said, still not turning around, the irritation clear in her voice. "And I don't think we have enough bacon."

"That's fine. I'd probably explode if I tried to eat any more anyway."

"Oh, you might as well get yourself a plate," Hannah said.

Jason smiled and did as he was told. The three ate lunch together. Jason asked about ladies' night at the Kendall house. Hannah told him Kate was a formidable cribbage player, although she won four out of the seven games they played. Kate objected and added that the original plan was for a best two out of three series, which Kate won. She also won three out of five, hence playing the full seven games.

"And you think I'm competitive!" Jason said to his mom.

Before going upstairs to make herself scarce, Hannah placed the last quarter of her BLT on Jason's plate, which he happily finished. After lunch Jason filled Kate in on the previous night's events and how the sheriff's department found nothing in the morning.

"He asked if I thought the kids were minors. He's guessing it was some high school kids who found a place to party on a Friday night. He might be right; we did the same thing as kids. We'd search for some out-of-the way place in the country to share a twelve-pack. Unless girls came along; they brought those cheap wine coolers that tasted like Kool-Aid. Did you do that type of thing? Were you a feral youth?"

Kate nodded and shared a story about a not-so-pretty wine cooler adventure. They talked about how "beyond stupid and dangerous" booze cruising was back then. The conversation stopped uncomfortably as their thoughts swerved to Kelly and Grace.

Jason steered the conversation back. "It just doesn't feel right. I can't explain it, but it didn't feel like a typical teenager cruise." The talk of drunken driving was making his stomach slowly churn and he could feel his cheeks going flush.

Kate recognized the change in his appearance. "No matter what happened at that house, you've been through a terrible night and gotten what, an hour or two of sleep? Why don't you go up and lie down for a while. Maybe you'll get some clarity after your body has some time to recover a little."

"A nap isn't going to change what I saw," Jason shot back in frustration. But as he said the words, he understood her meaning. "But maybe I won't act like I saw Jack Ruby hiding on the grassy knoll, either," he said as an apology.

"How about I go home and overfeed my chubby housemate, then stop back in a couple hours to see how you're doing," she said. "I was planning on hanging out with your mom, anyway. Remember?"

"That'd be great. Thanks, Kate."

They stood and she gave Jason a quick but soothing hug.

Heavy shades darkened the bedroom and the world outside its walls was unusually quiet for a Saturday afternoon. But the peaceful environment wasn't enough to coax Jason into relaxation. His mind danced with images of the previous night, the events two years earlier, and happier times farther in the past. Even sporadic thoughts of Kate's hug and her warm, easy smile found their way onto his mental dance card. He wasn't sure how he felt about mixing current thoughts of Kate with those of his past life. He didn't get a chance to decide; his cell vibrated alive on his hip. The caller ID told him Neil was on the other line.

"Hi Jason. I haven't received a call from your mom. She must feel like you're in good shape."

"She was a little upset that I didn't call her directly from the clinic. But she's fine now; you know how she is."

"I sure do," the professor said. "But the reason I called is I was thinking more about the story you told me at lunch—about the farmhouse near your property. And I realized the woman who lives there is from my church so I went out to see her. I'm just leaving there now."

"You're kidding. Who is she?"

"Her name is Clara Riddle. You've probably seen her around town once in a while, but she's never been real active in the community."

"I don't recognize the name." Jason repeatedly mouthed the name, hoping a face would appear. When it didn't, he asked, "What'd she say?"

"She was very surprised to see a sheriff's deputy at her door—I can tell you that. She said she was afraid she was in some kind of trouble. I could see she was still shaken from it, so I asked her how she was doing. She said she didn't know whether she was more worried about the idea of a bunch of kids being in her yard or hearing that some man out in the woods was watching her house."

*Great. Is there no one I can't spread misery to?* Jason thought.

"But don't worry. I let her know you're a good friend of mine. I told her you called the sheriff because you found the late-night activity suspicious and were concerned for her safety."

"What else did she say?" Jason asked.

"Not much. Since she was so uncomfortable, I kept my visit short."

"Did you look around outside at all? Anything unusual about the garage?"

"I didn't really get a look at anything, Jas'. I was just trying to get a few more details for you," Neil said.

"Thanks for taking the time, Neil."

"You should wait a few days if you are still planning to go out there. She's still pretty spooked; probably not going to sleep much tonight the way it is," Neil said.

"Good idea. I'll keep my neuroses to myself."

"Be careful now, self-loathing is not a good campaign strategy for a future councilman."

"Not you, too?" Jason said in agony.

"Louise caught me before I left Vera's," Neil said. "Right now you need to work through your grief and take care of yourself." Jason was waiting for the "but" and Neil did not disappoint. "But when you're ready, you should consider it. The town needs good leaders."

"The minute I *can't* come up with a hundred guys more qualified, I'm in."

"The moment I come up with three that are, *I'll* call *you*," Neil said, then hung up.

---

Khalid rolled up the blanket that served as a substitute prayer mat. It wasn't a traditional prayer time, not that there was a wrong occasion for prayer, but the truth was he simply had little else to do. He had returned the chairs and dry-erase board to the hidden basement space, then, as ordered, spackled the three small holes in the first floor ceiling, all before the sun came up. The bullets went clear through the second floor and lodged in the ceiling of Clara's bedroom, missing her bed by less than a foot. Following the repairs, he spent a few hours catching up on sleep in the cramped supply room between the women's locked space and the general's quarters.

It wasn't until after the surprise visit by a sheriff's deputy that he was told by Muhab that he would be spending the rest of the weekend at the house. He took a quick tour of the top floors in search of something to occupy him mentally, but was unable to locate even a book in the sparse, almost barren, house. He returned to the basement confines and, other than making and delivering a small lunch to the women, kept himself occupied with prayer and made-up busywork in the storeroom.

He was removing latent marker strokes from the white board that could provide evidence of the offensive when he heard jostling movement in the room behind him, General Attar's room. Was it time for the reprimand he'd been warned about? Muhab had talked to him both last night and this morning and made it clear that because Khalid had recommended Omar for inclusion into the team, Omar's failings were his failings as well. Muhab also warned him that the general's penalty for Omar's lapse would likely involve "a good deal of pain." Khalid sensed when Muhab told him he would pray for the general's mercy in this matter, that "a good deal" meant "hellacious."

He heard a chair slide across the floor in the next room, then the leader's boots approaching in the hall. Khalid willed them to continue moving past his door. They did not. The dull black knob began to turn and fear welled up inside him. He prayed to Allah for courage but was interrupted before he could finish.

"Bring the girl to me; the one from last night," General Attar said. "Upstairs."

After giving thanks to Allah for the general's reprieve, Khalid walked down the narrow hall to the next room, lifted the padlock, and slapped the plate back. He opened the door and the woman with the split lip stared at him, her fear masked in defiance. He approached the other woman who was lying on the floor, facing away from him, her arms holding her knees tightly against her chest. He touched her softly on the shoulder.

"NO! NO! Please, I'll do anything! Please not again!"

# CHAPTER 9

Jason regained some sense of normalcy as the day went on. But he hurried out of the house after a conversation with Hannah that began with a discussion of how a girl as sweet and beautiful as Kate could be on the loose, and ended with how proud his father would have been to see Jason become a city councilman. His destination was the home of a local dentist for whom he was building a new den/sunroom addition.

Kate called while he was unloading his equipment. She was at his house and wondering why he wasn't. He apologized for not calling about leaving for the job site. Before hanging up, Kate mentioned she had told Robyn Jenkins she was free in the evening to go to the Cabbay party at the Jenkins' house.

"So you should be expecting a desperate call for companionship from Seth at some point," she said. Before he could ask if a Cabbay party was an opportunity to whoop it up with taxi drivers, Seth's number appeared on his call waiting. He hung up with Kate to take the call. Sure enough, Seth made the plea. Jason accepted his invitation to watch the University of Minnesota hockey game at The Scorecard but only on the condition that Seth promise not to mention anything about local politics. Though confused by the request, Seth agreed.

Jason let himself into the dentist's home, knowing the client and his family had taken advantage of the unseasonably warm weather with a last minute biking weekend in Lanesboro, a small tourist town near the Minnesota/Iowa border.

Jason was thankful for the vacated workspace. But it felt like it had been two weeks, rather than two days, since he had last been here. It felt good to be working again. He slipped the headphones of his MP3 player over his ears and selected the Steve Miller Band's "Greatest Hits" album. The music lightened his mood further and soon he was into a nice groove, installing and taping sheetrock to the frame of the room.

Despite the sky outside fading from a Carolina blue to a deep indigo, and listening to several full albums on his player, Jason lost all sense of time. When he finally checked the clock it was 7:45. He picked up his cell and scrolled through five new calls, all from Seth. He dialed his friend without listening to any of the three messages left and apologized for the second time that day for leaving someone hanging. He quickly cleaned up the workspace and was sitting on a bar stool, ordering a round of Newcastle, twenty minutes later.

"What the hell's a Cabbay party anyway?" Jason asked, then warmed Seth's cold shoulder by telling the woman behind the bar to put Seth's beers on his tab.

"I guess it's like Tupperware or those cooking-tool parties," Seth said. "A sales rep comes to the party, fills the women with wine and guilts them into buying her overpriced products. But in this case, instead of stackable bowls, it's women's clothing."

"Is it the company where if you sell a boatload of product, they give you a pink car?"

"First of all, no it's not 1982. And second, you're talking about Mary Kay, which is makeup, not apparel."

"Yeah, how could I have mixed those up? I feel so foolish," Jason said.

"Don't try to hide your lack of social awareness with sarcasm. It only makes you look more pathetic."

They ordered dinner during the second intermission of the game and the food arrived as the third period action started. The game had little intrigue; Minnesota was already up 5-1 over one of their in-state underlings.

"Pretty rough, last night?" Seth asked before taking a sip of beer.

"It was intense. It's like I'm fighting to get past the loss and working to keep the girls alive at the same time. I wish I could just skip over this week every year."

"I won't pretend to know what you're going through, but if there's anything you need—" Seth said.

Jason slapped his friend's back. "Thanks."

Seth nodded. "Did you use the weather barrier thingamajig overnight? The last thing you want is geese crapping missiles down on you when you're sleeping under the stars."

"I would have, but I ended up sleeping in the truck," Jason said.

Seth gave him a quizzical look. "Tree house too scary at night?"

"If I recall correctly, only one of us made it through the night in your tent that time when we were nine. I bet your Captain Kangaroo sheets felt pretty good that night."

"I've told you a hundred times, I had a leg cramp," Seth said. "And don't try to make this about me. Why'd you sleep in the truck?"

Jason repeated his deer stand story for the fourth time since sunrise. "Sheriff Burnett doesn't seem too concerned, but it's been bugging the hell out of me all day."

"Maybe that's good—keeps your mind off some of the other stuff you're dealing with. You know, kind of a mental or emotional transference."

"No, I don't know. Why don't you explain 'emotional transference' to me," Jason said as a dare.

"It's pretty complicated. I'm not sure you could follow along," Seth said.

Jason looked away, shaking his head.

"What? I know what transference is," Seth said, insulted.

Jason shook his head again, this time at Seth. "It's not that. I was thinking about last night. Something is gnawing at me about what happened at that house but I can't put my finger on it."

The conversation died out and they returned their attention to the game. The Gophers scored two quick goals, one on the power play, to lead 7-1.

"What's the 'no local politics talk' thing you mentioned on the phone?" Seth asked. "Did you run into some permit hassle or something?"

"I wish. No, my girl Weezie over at Vera's has decided that I should be the next distinguished Cedar River city councilman."

Seth shot a mock spit-take in response. "If you think it will help, you can re-use my campaign platform for South Elementary student council president."

"And what was that?"

"Chocolate Milk—Every Day!"

Jason couldn't hold back a laugh, "You won with that?"

"Damn right!"

"I don't remember getting chocolate milk every day," Jason said, more as an accusation than a statement.

"Turns out, milk selection was not under the auspices of the council president. What're you gonna do?" Seth said. The bartender cleared their plates and slid a fresh round of beers in front of them.

"So are you going to run?"

"No. Heck, I'd still be back in St. Paul if Kelly hadn't convinced me we needed to take care of my mom. You know I still plan to move back there at some point. I like being able to walk into a hardware store to pick up a roll of duct tape without needing to have a conversation with three different people and feel guilty about the other two I blew off. Even if I thought Cedar River was going to be my home long-term, I couldn't see myself knocking on people's doors to ask them to vote for me. It'd be like campaigning to be homecoming king; no thanks."

"I'm not telling you what to do, but now that I think about it, she makes some sense. You grew up here, but you've also lived in bigger cities, which brings a different perspective, and you're a business owner, so you have that angle. Plus, you lived in the same house as a council-man-slash-mayor all those years growing up. You should think about it. Keeping a small town in business isn't easy these days. Leadership matters."

"I thought you weren't going to bring it up."

"Bring what up?"

The hockey game was over; the final score was Minnesota 8, Bemidji State 2. At the request of a couple sitting a few stools down, the bartender switched the nearest TV to CNN. Jason and Seth passively watched the string of stories the way people stare at the flame when sitting around a campfire.

"How'd it go with Kate and your mom?" Seth asked.

"They've known each other, what, less than twenty-four hours? And already they're like old pals. Kate even took my mom's side against me at lunch."

"Gettin' in good with 'the mom,'" Seth said into his beer.

"Dude, let it go," Jason said. "Happy hour last Saturday, the party at Hammer's, book club. What do they all have in common?" He didn't wait for an answer. "I'll tell you: Kate and I are the only non-married, non-engaged people in the group. It's been that way for two years. Of course we're going to end up sitting together or talking to each other when the rest of you pair off. I like Kate a lot; she's great. But it's not a romantic thing."

"Whatever you say. I never should have brought it up," Seth said. "I'm just calling 'em like I see 'em."

CNN went live to a college protest in Colorado and flashed a photo of a man in the upper right-hand corner of the screen. Jason bolted forward, thought for a moment, then pulled out his cell to call Kate. No answer.

"Damn it!"

"What? Who are you calling?" Seth asked.

Jason turned to Seth and grabbed him by the shoulder. "How late is Robyn's clothes party supposed to go?"

"Robyn told me not to be home before eleven. And even then, I should call first, just in case."

"We're gonna crash it."

"The party? No way. Robyn'll kill me. I just told you; I'm banished until eleven."

Jason gave Seth a look that told him to be a man.

"No way, dude. Apparently the women just undress and try on the clothes right out in front of the other women. Seriously, you know Robyn; I'll be sleeping in the garage for a week! Then I'll probably get two more in the basement."

"In that case, I'm doing you a favor; let's go."

---

The second floor bedroom was quiet and dark. The general instructed Khalid, when he'd brought the woman to the adjacent bedroom, to stand watch over the road. The task was more stressful than he anticipated. Two cars had driven by the house in the last hour. The first was a pick-up truck. He wasn't sure whether or when to act. He was certain, though, that interrupting the general unnecessarily would create personal fallout for him. However, interrupting too late could compromise the entire mission. He held the turned doorknob as the pick-up whizzed past. No threat. He released the knob.

The next vehicle was more problematic. It approached from the same direction, but at a slower pace. Khalid took up his position at the door and watched the car approaching at half the speed of the pick-up and slowing. It was thirty yards east of the driveway when Khalid made out the bar on top of the car. Police! He froze for a moment; the fear starting in his chest and flooding out to his limbs. He regained his composure, opened the door and was about to knock on the general's when he heard the thrust of the car's engine as it sped west. Khalid darted to the window and watched the taillights until they became tiny red dots before disappearing into the night.

Movement in the next room interrupted a brief period of silence. Then he heard grunting and other base sounds. They seemed like the result of work rather than pleasure. He wondered where the line was between manipulating a woman into bed and forcing her there. Were his many conquests just further down the same scale as the general's?

Soon the grunts turned into a one-way conversation. The angry man's words got louder, and the unmistakable smack of a fist striking bone followed. It began a routine; a muffled question from the general, then the hard fist. The question/smack sequence played out another half dozen times. He heard the woman's whimpering but there were no screams. Those had stopped thirty minutes earlier.

Khalid felt the bile filling inside him. He ran through the hall to the adjoining bathroom where he heaved at the sounds of the beating. As he wiped his sleeve across his mouth, he thought of how the girls were giggling so innocently in the store yesterday. He looked out the window and told himself he was not like this man. He may not have loved, maybe not even cared about the women he'd taken, but he did not punish them for his pleasure, either. Nor did he want to.

"I'm not you," he said before arching over the stool again.

---

Jason and Seth parked their vehicles on the street a few houses down from the Jenkins' home. Like the driveway, the street in front of the house was lined with minivans and other family vehicles. On the way in, Seth debriefed Jason on their cover story for coming home early, which consisted of them simply grabbing a couple of beers from the fridge before going out to the garage to have Jason look at Seth's broken snow blower.

"I hope I can keep the story together," Jason mocked.

"It's a good story. What do you expect? I had six blocks to come up with it," Seth said and shoved Jason as he opened the front door to the split-level home.

Before they saw her, they heard Robyn's irritated voice from upstairs in the living room, "Who the…?"

The two men were waiting impishly on the landing for her consent to enter. They didn't get it. "Seth Jenkins, you damn fool, what do you think you're doing? It's barely after nine o'clock! I told you eleven!" They could tell she was just getting warmed up. "Women are half-naked, trying on clothes up here, and you two traipse in…" she didn't get to finish the thought as Jason rubbed his hands together and made a face filled with surprise and delight at her comment.

"Don't even think about it, Kendall. You two just turn around and go back to where you came from." Moving her gaze to her defenseless husband, "And dammit, Seth, you better call here before you come back!"

"Don't get mad at Seth. When he told me a bunch of babes were using your house as a dressing room, well…" Jason stammered. "It got me all hot and I needed a fix of Seth's secret *Playboy* stash out in the garage. We just stopped in here to grab a couple of beers first. It's been my experience if you don't have a beer in your hand during such an exercise, you just can't trust where that hand's going to end up."

Seth looked at Jason, his mouth hanging open, and suddenly dry.

Robyn turned flush as she felt the silence of the ten women to her left.

Jason let the silence hang for a moment, then said, "Calm down. I'm just kidding. Is Kate here? I need to ask her something."

Robyn gave Seth a look that told him what he could do in the garage tonight, then walked away. Seth shook his head at Jason, disbelieving what he'd just heard. Jason whispered to him, "You're gonna want to send those *Playboys* home with me for a while."

Seth clenched his teeth and shook his head again before walking out to the garage.

Kate came down the stairs, also shaking her head. "Why do you always have to push her buttons like that?" she scolded.

"If she'd stop acting like she's royalty, I'd stop reminding her she isn't."

Kate gave him a disapproving look.

"Listen," Jason said, changing the subject, "can you access the St. Joseph's student database from your workstation in admissions?"

"Yeah, why?"

"Can you sort by birthplace or national origin?"

"What is this about, Jason?"

"I figured out what didn't feel right about the people I saw at the house the other night, why it didn't seem like they were just high school kids out partying."

Kate waited for his answer.

"The men who left the house late last night and the two who came later with the girls were Middle Eastern."

"How do you know?" Kate said. Jason could see her doubt.

"CNN was on one of the TVs at the bar and they were doing a story about a missing Colorado State student. When they showed a picture of him, you could see he was obviously Middle Eastern—like the men I saw last night."

Jason saw that Kate followed how he made the connection, but the doubt on her face lingered.

"I'm not being racist and I don't have some wild terrorist conspiracy. I just keep thinking about that girl; what else did she suffer through because I didn't help her? I should have done something, Kate. I should have yelled or run to the house instead of my truck—something."

"How does that make the men you saw St. Joe students?" she asked.

"It doesn't. But Cedar River has basically no Arab population. I mean who'd emigrate to the U.S. to work at a glass factory? So if you remove the general population, the next logical conclusion is that they're college kids. I figure there can't be more than a handful of Middle Eastern students at St. Joe's. Like I said, Cedar River isn't exactly the vortex of diversity. If some of them live together in a dorm or a house off campus or something, they should be pretty easy to find."

"And then what?" Kate's concerns were holding fast.

"I don't know. I should be able to recognize the guy who hit the girl by his size alone. Then maybe we can get him prosecuted or at least teach him a lesson."

"It just doesn't seem like this is your fight, Jason. Why you?"

"What if that girl were you or your best friend? What if she were your daughter? Wouldn't you want someone to do something if they could? Wouldn't *you* do something?"

Kate looked away, not sure how to proceed.

"Do you think this is about Kelly and Grace?" asked Jason, thinking about Seth's mental transference diagnosis. "Maybe a shrink would tell me I'm transferring my grief and guilt about their deaths onto this girl. I don't see it, but so what if I am?! It doesn't mean those men shouldn't be punished or that the woman might not still be in danger."

Kate remained silent.

"So are you going to help me or not?" Jason asked.

Kate thought another moment before answering, then held up a finger. "One condition: you keep me in the loop and promise to stop if I think you've gone from a good place to a bad place with all this."

"That's two conditions, but you got a deal. How about we head to your office tomorrow morning?"

"That's not going to work. IT is doing an upgrade over the weekend; the system is down until Monday."

"Are you sure?"

"Why don't we drive over there right now so you can read the memo yourself?" Then, keeping up the sarcasm, "Oh wait—you can't. It's in my email, which is down for the weekend."

Jason considered firing back some sarcasm of his own but held back. "What time do you go in on Monday?"

"I'll be in by eight."

"I'll meet you there at seven-thirty."

# CHAPTER 10

## SUNDAY

Liz woke to a dull light permeating the thick grey plastic that covered the small storm window of the dank room. The sun was beginning its rise. The fresh light brought feelings of both hope and despair. Hope because they'd made it through another night; despair because their situation was unchanged. Maybe more correctly, Liz's situation was unchanged. Maria returned from another round away, further damaged. Liz only saw her face for a moment last night when the Rockwell Outfitter employee pushed her through the door, but it was gruesome. She'd looked like a cartoon super-villain; her face was swollen in some areas and sunken in others, blood smears, both wet and dry, accented the deformed contours.

Maria again lay away from her, but not in a tight ball as she had previously. Liz remembered how Maria pushed her away yesterday, but if they were going to get through this they would need to do it together.

Liz crawled across the room to her friend and brushed the matted and sticky hair from her face. The wounds were even worse in the light; it was as if they were fighting one another for space around her features. The ugly, foreign contours made her elegant face almost unrecognizable. Maria didn't react to Liz's touch so she continued to gently comb her friend's hair through her fingers. She was afraid to touch anywhere else, not wanting to cause more pain. She looked down upon her friend and admired how, through savage wounds, she was able to still look peaceful.

Liz resolved that she would show the same strength if she faced her own horrific encounter.

She bent down and softly kissed Maria on the forehead; it felt cool. She sat back up and held her friend's wrist, then staggered to the farthest corner of the room. Maria's peace hadn't come from strength. It had come through death.

# CHAPTER 11

## MONDAY

Jason was waiting outside the admissions office door with a large coffee when Kate arrived. She wanted to say something sarcastic about his eagerness but the best she could do at 7:20 AM was give him a what-are-you-doing-here-already glare. Jason, an anti-morning person himself, could only muster a "Morning," in return as he handed her the coffee.

Kate unlocked the door then led Jason through, making sure the door closed behind them to prevent any students from entering before the 8:30 office hours began. They waited in silence for the workstation to boot up. Two minutes later, the monitor presented the St. Joseph College logo, User ID and Password. Kate keyed in the information then called up the Student Data menu.

She turned to Jason who had pulled up a chair from the reception area. "Let me just say that anything I do from this point is illegal and not only could get me fired but thrown in jail."

"I know, Kate. And I've thought about what you said the other night; maybe this is more for me than for the girl who got hurt but, either way, I need to see this through," he said. "And I have no intention of playing some kind of bad-ass by making some kid pay for what happened to me and my family. I want you to know I'm going to follow this where it leads but only if something good can come from it."

"It sounds like you've got a good handle on things," she said, "so don't take this the wrong way, but if it leads to you turning someone into the sheriff, won't he want to know how you found him?"

"I'll be sure to keep you out of it," he assured her.

"Okay, but remember our deal; I want to be told ahead of time, just to make sure nothing gets back on me."

"Done. Now can we do this? I need to get to a job site."

"Wound a little tight for 7:30, don't ya think? You might want to consider staying away from the power tools today."

Jason gave her a list of countries that were considered a part of the Middle East and Indian regions of the world. She did a search of the students who were not U.S. citizens; there were only eighty-two. From that list, she highlighted the students whose country of origin fit the profile Jason created and clicked "Summary Report." The screen showed name, current address, when enrolled, major, class schedule and additional contact information.

Twenty-one students fit the criteria. Their summaries flashed on the screen. Jason had Kate delete the four women on the list, leaving seventeen potential targets.

"Now what? Kate asked. "Seventeen out of twenty-nine hundred isn't a lot. But you're only *one* person."

The screen held all of the summary information for one student and just over half of the one below it. "Can you scroll down through the names?" Jason asked.

Kate pressed the down-arrow key and held it. The lines of data moved up steadily through an additional two student summaries, then the speed of the scroll spiked.

"Whoa, whoa, whoa! Go back." Jason said.

"How far?" Kate asked and tapped at the up arrow.

"To about the third or fourth entry." She returned to the spot where the computer had jumped ahead. "Okay, right there. Now scroll down. Slower."

Kate gave him a glance, annoyed with the way he was giving orders. Jason was too focused to notice either her glance or his tone. She continued to tap the key until she reached the bottom of the list. They stared for several seconds at the last entry on the screen: Jusef Zayed.

Jason stood up; it looked like a dead end. He couldn't track seventeen people. Almost a minute went by while they each pondered the next step. Then Jason leaned down in front of the screen, reengaged. "Go back to the top, then scroll down again."

Kate did and seconds later they were again looking at the final listing. Jason grabbed a pen from a mug embossed with the expression, *Got Caffeine?* and wrote down the address, phone number, car information, and class schedule for Jusef Zayed.

"Okay now scroll back up."

Kate started tapping the up-arrow key.

"Stop." Jason copied down the same information for Shyam Amish, then folded the paper and stuffed it in his pocket.

"Why those two?"

"They're the only two names with driver's license numbers. The house near my deer stand is four miles north of town and I saw at least three cars there that night." He tapped his pocket. "One of them has to belong to one of these guys."

Kate gave him an approving nod, impressed with his powers of deduction.

"And what I didn't notice until I wrote down the information for the second guy—they actually share a place together. I'll bet you one of them likes to smack girls around or hangs with someone who does."

They heard a key struggle into the front-door lock, then watched it push open. The voice of Bonnie Schwartz preceded her appearance. "Is that you in here so early, Kate? I thought about you all weekend. Did you get to peek in Jason's drawers?" She laughed a little too loudly; obviously proud of the line she had likely rehearsed during the weekend.

She hung up her jacket on the coat tree just inside the door and continued her razzing, "Speaking of which, I bet he's a briefs man—those cute, colored kind, not the tighty-whiteys." She turned around and her face went so flush seeing Jason seated next to Kate, it looked like it might actually pop from the flood of blood to her cheeks.

"Hey Bon," Kate said, turning the monitor away from her embarrassed coworker. "Jason's just about ready to take off, then I'll come over and we can catch up, okay?" Bonnie nodded and quietly slinked behind the wall to her cubicle.

Kate tried not to look at Jason, afraid it would trigger uncontrolled laughter at Bonnie's expense. But when she could no longer resist, she was surprised to see that the social disaster hadn't even registered with him. Instead, Jason asked in a hushed voice, "Is there anywhere I can find a picture of these guys, see if I recognize 'em?"

Kate thought about it for a moment and whispered, "Each freshman class gets a class directory, in addition to the school phone book. It shows each freshman's school ID picture and the dorm they're assigned to. It's supposed to make them feel more a part of the student body. I'm sure there are some from the past few years floating around. Let me see what I can do."

"Thanks, Kate. I really do appreciate everything."

"No problem," she said. "Although, all of the favors seem to be going in one direction."

"I know. I'm not sure how I'm going to pay you back for everything," he responded.

"I'd start you a tab, but I doubt you have anything I want in return." She waved Jason away as he struggled to think of a return favor. "I'm just giving you a hard time. Get out of here."

After he left, Kate quickly closed the student information database and the computer screen hopped back to the standard main menu just as she saw an eager face pop around the partition. "Well?"

Kate rolled her eyes, then put on a smile and turned toward Bonnie.

---

Khalid arrived at work at nine o'clock, an hour before the store opened and a full half hour before he was scheduled to punch in. Jan refused to talk to him and stalked around the store with the look of a cougar ready to pounce. He'd flirted with customers before and always managed to soften up his manager/girlfriend rather quickly. But this time he'd compounded the problem by not returning any of her calls during the weekend. By Sunday she was suggesting very strongly in her string of messages that his disrespect may be a sign that they could no longer work together, and that *she* was not the person who would be leaving.

He completed several assigned tasks then got cornered by an annoying coworker whose single focus each day was sharing the ways the world was holding her down. Khalid gave the over-made-up, and over-teeth-whitened girl three excruciating minutes before checking his watch and walking away in the middle of her pointless Facebook friend-did-me-wrong sob story.

It was now 9:30; only thirty minutes until the cage at the door would be lifted and the store would be open to customers. He had hoped that Jan would engage him first, so he could use her anger as the impetus to resolve their dispute. But for his plan to work, the confrontation needed to happen before the store opened. She stalked to the back of the store, far away from the other employees working the pre-open shift. He caught up to her as she opened the door to the office and touched her softly on the small of her back then whirled around in front of her. "Jan, we need to talk. I know you are upset but I can explain."

She responded by trying to move through him into the office. She didn't try hard. Khalid shuffled sideways to cut off her path. "Please Jan; I was out of town with Omar. His cousin in Chicago called with tickets to the Fire game. It was spur-of-the-moment; we packed a backpack and left." He moved his hand to her shoulder. He could feel her tension melting a few degrees. "We left in such a hurry, I forgot my cell at home. I am very, very sorry," he said as he began to stroke her hair.

She tilted her head away, but not her body.

"I brought you a present," he said in playful whisper.

Jan responded in a voice that was two-thirds anger and one-third hopeful. "I have one question and one comment. What is a Fire game? And it better be a good gift."

"The Fire is the Major League Soccer team in Chicago." He grinned devilishly at her. "And, it is."

She put her hand out, palm up. "I'll be the judge of that. Let's see it."

"Not here, it is personal."

Her eyes went dark.

"It is in my backpack. We can take the morning delivery down to the storage area. I will give it to you there." He glanced back at the office entrance. "Trust me; you do not want anyone else to see it."

Jan retrieved the handcart and Khalid loaded two large boxes of men's sweaters, then topped them with a box of cologne and perfume.

He grabbed the backpack and slipped it over both shoulders, tipped back the handcart and started through the door. A hard poke between his right shoulder and pectoral muscle stopped him cold. "I better never see you talking to those two skanks ever again."

"I promise you, you will not."

They worked their way through the rear hall along the outer wall of the ninety-six-acre mall and took the elevator down to the store's basement storage area. Not all stores leased underground storage space. The single most important quality of a prospective employer for Khalid had been access to the basement area of the building. With some savvy calculation and a little good luck, Khalid found such an employer on the first try.

He had stayed away from the department stores, knowing they were so large they likely had storage within their main space. He focused on smaller stores that maximized the amount of square footage dedicated to retail space and, therefore, required a separate location for overstock inventory. Rockwell Outfitters' store seemed to extend as far back as any.

Khalid tipped up the cart while Jan opened the padlock then the chain-link door. The room was small and crowded. Cheap metal shelving ran from floor to ceiling along two adjacent walls and a three by six-foot table was squeezed in front of them. The storage units came in different sizes depending on what a store needed and how much they wanted to spend. But most of the units were not private; each was viewable to passersby through the reinforced chain-link fencing surrounding them.

Rockwell Outfitters was one of the exceptions; Khalid had seen to that. A month after he arrived he swiped four t-shirts by wearing them under his casual button-down shirt and pulled another half-way through the fencing. He had spent his entire shift the next day moving shelving and attaching blue tarp inside the walls and door of the room while his superior chewed out mall management for not having cameras in the basement and a general lack of quality security in the area.

Khalid carried the top two boxes onto their preassigned positions on the shelves and Jan followed with the third.

"No!" Khalid was on one knee rummaging through the backpack.

"Don't you tell me you just happened to lose my gift! There was never any present was there, Khalid? You piece of..."

"Look." Khalid pulled out a hat with a Chicago Fire logo from the pack. Jan wasn't impressed. "Omar and I have the same kind of backpack," he said. "I must have grabbed his by mistake. Your gift is much better than this silly hat."

He stood and snuggled up to Jan, pressing her against the end of the table. "When we were at the souvenir stand I saw something that I knew you must have."

"What?" she asked, still dubious.

"A little red thong that says 'Fire' on the front with little flames shooting out of it. First, I thought how good you would look in it. Then I thought how wonderful you would look *out* of it. That is when I knew you must have it." Jan showed him a smile that clearly conveyed something R-rated, then looked away, feigning innocence.

Khalid knew he was back on solid ground with her and, after the difficult weekend, he was ready for a release. He leaned his head to her ear and moved his hand up and down the front of her skirt. He spoke in a playful whisper. "Did you know my soccer coach always told me I was one of the best headers he had ever seen?"

A choked giggle escaped her lips. "We shouldn't do this. We need to open in fifteen minutes."

He kicked the door closed behind them, then lifted her skirt and roughly yanked her panties to her thighs. He literally felt her heat rising, "I will go extra fast."

She put both hands on his chest and held him back in protest. "Not too fast," she said then leaned back onto the table.

Twenty minutes later, still working to catch her breath, Jan grabbed her panties off the floor and stuffed them into Khalid's shirt pocket. "We better hurry up to the store before we get busted by mall management for opening late."

"You go on ahead; I need to wait for my little goalie to rest."

She looked down and saw he would need some time to "recover." Jan turned to the door and tried without success to brush the wrinkles out of her skirt. Before leaving, she twisted her head around and gave her lover a mischievous grin. "I don't know a lot about soccer but I thought goalies didn't get to score."

Khalid waited thirty seconds for his boss to be safely traveling up the elevator, then took a quick scan of the common area outside the room. All clear. He kneeled down where the two shelves joined together, opened his backpack and pulled out what looked like modeling clay.

The bottom row of shelves was filled with four filing boxes; the two on the left were marked "1992," the others, "1993." The boxes contained copies of receipts from the store's first two years in business before the store went paperless in January 1994. Khalid chose one of the 1992 boxes. It was less than half full because the mall hadn't opened until August of that year. He placed the six bricks of C4 explosive in the box, carefully covered them with the receipt slips, then returned the box to its original space.

He zipped up the backpack with the soccer logo hat in it and stuffed it behind a two-foot high stack of hooded sweatshirts. Jan's fragrance hung in the air. He thought about the fictional thong and how good it would look stretched over her soft round hips. He hoped Jan wouldn't press him about it, but if she did, he could put her off for a few days. After that, it wouldn't matter for either of them anyway.

He closed and locked the door behind him. On his way back through the common storage area he passed a mall security guard. Only someone on the lookout for it would have noticed the unnatural way they ignored each other.

# CHAPTER 12

Jason sat behind the wheel of his mom's tan Buick Century and kept a close watch on the small white house two doors down, on the other side of the street. His first-ever stakeout was not going well. He'd met Kate after work to get the photos of the two students from the freshman phone guide. Neither looked immediately familiar, but the two-year-old grainy images didn't eliminate them from being the men he saw Friday night.

He cut the black and white photos out of the directory at home before driving to their house, but he didn't realize until later that he'd cut off their names. He didn't know which one was Amish and which one was Zayed. That was mistake number one. Not a massive blunder, but if he saw or even confronted one of them, it would have been nice to know which one he was dealing with.

His next mistake was equally careless. He passed the time during the first half-hour of the stakeout looking over receipts and work orders when he noticed the Kendall Construction letterhead with the tag line "Done Right." It was the same color and font as the identical message painted on both sides of his truck, which sat several yards away from the suspects' house. "Note to self," he said into an imaginary recorder. "Have the idiot-chip removed from your brain at your earliest possible convenience."

Six minutes later he was back in the same spot, but this time he was sitting behind the wheel of the heavily potpourri-scented Buick.

The small two-story house of interest was part of a neighborhood just north of the campus that blended modest single-family homes with similarly styled houses converted to student rentals. The subject of Jason's attention was a standard three-bedroom home that, he guessed, was probably retrofitted into four or five bedrooms, as he'd done for a number of investment property owners in town. A driveway led up a gently sloped hill along the right side of the house to a detached garage in the rear. Several folded weekly shoppers littered the front stoop, telling Jason that the rear entrance, which was actually a side door, was the only regularly-used entrance. It was perched atop a four-step concrete slab guarded by a wrought iron railing between the house and driveway. From his angle just up the street, Jason had full view of the garage, driveway and main entry to the home.

The bench seat of the Buick was too stiff against Jason's back and too soft under him. It felt like the makers combined Momma Bear's and Papa Bear's chairs to make one seat that was equally uncomfortable for everyone. He bounced around the idea of taking his mom car shopping to upgrade her into something more comfortable, but since she never complained and probably didn't have a drive that lasted more than five minutes, he decided to mind his own business.

Sitting still was not Jason's normal style. Adding to his discomfort was the constant threat of being recognized, not by someone living in the house, but by a familiar face driving by. He didn't have a good excuse at the ready for being parked in the middle of a nondescript block in his mother's car, and trying to come up with one was driving him crazy. He cleared his mind by playing a mental round of golf at Willinger's Golf Club. He had used the same stroke-by-stroke technique on nights when racing thoughts about work or family kept him awake. He'd still never made it to the back nine before quickly relaxing and drifting to sleep.

An hour later, Jason was on the sixth hole of his second eighteen and had just finished hitting a perfect drive up the right side of the fairway when a rusty light-colored Grand Am slowed past him and turned into the driveway of the rental house. It angled slightly, and came to rest in front of the left garage door. The driver got out, lifted the garage door, then returned to the car and drove inside. Jason leaned forward in his seat. No doubt about it, the driver was the same person pictured in one of the photographs lying on the passenger seat. Jason was sitting so far forward his breath started to fog the driver-side window. He wiped away the condensation and heard car doors slam before two people emerged from the garage. A young woman waited for the driver to pull down the garage door, and then reached out her hand. The young man took it and they walked together up the stairs to the side door. Jason watched as the "girlfriend" waited on the top step while the "boyfriend" pushed open the door, then waited for the woman to enter ahead of him.

Jason did a quick mental inventory. The driver was one of the men from the database; the young woman was of Asian descent, although he didn't know if that mattered in any way, except she wasn't blonde like the women he saw at the house. They were definitely a couple—the way he opened the door for her was obviously a ritual. He wasn't sure of the make of the car the women and men arrived in Friday night, but it definitely wasn't a Grand Am. And most importantly, the man he just saw enter the house was small in size and didn't have the mannerisms of the man he'd seen punch the woman so hard her legs turned to marionette strings. He was not the guy Jason was looking for.

Jason watched the house for another hour and a half; the day's light was now completely extinguished. Only four vehicles had passed in that time and no one had come in or out of the house. Lights now lit up a number of rooms in the house. He guessed that most of the other tenants had already been home by the time he pulled up. He was getting a little bored and very hungry; he'd only had a bagel and small bag of chips at noon and it was now pushing 9:00. He called it quits for the night and pulled away from the curb. On the way home he decided he would get back to the house a little earlier tomorrow—before the other residents made it home. In addition, he would trade vehicles with Seth before tomorrow night to minimize suspicions. And he would bring dinner. He tapped the wheel and nodded—he was getting better at this.

Jason pulled into his driveway and pressed the button on the garage door opener. *The garage door*, he thought. "The kid got out to lift up the door and slide it back down—no locks," he whispered. He banged his fist on the steering wheel, then pressed the garage door button again, sending it back down, and backed out of the driveway.

# CHAPTER 13

Jason parked the car in the middle of the block around the corner from the house. He had last been outside in the early evening and the drop in temperature since then punched him square when he got out of the car.

"It's fall, dumbass. Start thinking!" he told himself. He looked down at his clothes, a forest green shirt, jeans, and boots. At least they were dark colored and the small Eddie Bauer logo on the shirt seemed forgettable enough. He remembered stealing apples one night with some buddies when he was in middle school and the only kid who got caught was Paul Gallivan. He had worn a hockey jersey with his last name on the back during the heist.

Anxiety percolated inside his belly as the front of the house came into view. His effort to appear "normal" only worked to make his stride unnatural and mechanical. Remembering he was here because he'd allowed a woman to get hit, and possibly much worse, steadied him. He briskly walked past the house and up the driveway on the other side of the house to the garage. He turned the knob on the service door—locked. Shit. He kept his eyes focused on the house as he shuffled over to the nearest overhead door. He groped for the handle behind him, found it, and lifted.

The door eased up. He took a deep breath and thought, *it's now or never* then raised the door up just above his waist, bent over and pivoted inside. He tried to find an inside handle as the door dropped from its own weight, but couldn't. It struck the concrete floor with a small bang, rattling the row of windows that traversed the door at eye level. Jason backed up a couple steps into the darkness and watched for house lights to come on and doors to fly open, but neither happened. When it was clear no one was coming for him, he turned around to look at the car behind him.

A sedan was resting quietly in front of him. Like the Grand Am in the stall next to it, it was an older American-made car that had been relatively inexpensive when new and now would be lucky to fetch one or two thousand dollars at sale. Initially, Jason could tell little else about the car in the murky darkness. He bent down and his eyes were within six inches of the metal nameplate before he could make out the word *Lumina*. He rose up and looked back through the line of windows to check that no one was approaching. Seeing no activity, he turned back around. *Is this the car from Friday?* he wondered.

It certainly looked like the car he saw the woman try to run from. But he was no auto expert; for all he knew there could be a half-dozen models similar to this one. The near absence of light in the garage prevented him from even matching colors. He quickly checked the house again—all clear. *What next?* He repeated the words over and over in his head. *What next?* How could he determine if this was the car from Friday night and, in turn, if the assailant lives on the property?

His eyes began to adjust to the darkness and the larger objects in the room began to take on shadowy contours as Jason moved around to the driver's door. He felt for the door handle, leaned back to check the stoop of the house again, then gently lifted the handle. The door released. Jason pulled it open, which triggered the dome light to illuminate the car's interior. The radiant light from the dome lamp made everything outside the garage go black. Jason didn't know what he was looking for but he knew he'd better find it quick; he could no longer see the house's door, but anyone coming from there could definitely see him.

The initial scan of the front seat brought no clues. No pictures, no hand-written directions or addresses, not even a Burger King wrapper. The car wasn't spotless and had a stale "guy" odor, but it was tidy. Jason leaned over to take a quick look of the back seat—same neat appearance, same lack of information. He sat down in the driver's seat. *What next?* He pulled open and pushed closed the ashtray—clean. He did the same for the glove box. Inside was a Minnesota driving map, vehicle registration, and insurance card. He pulled out the insurance card. Above "Insured" was typed, Shyam Amish. He put the card back in the glove box and closed it. When he did, he noticed the corner of a paper sticking out from beneath the front passenger seat. He bent down to grab it. The standard 8-½ x 11 sheet of paper appeared blank. Jason turned it over and saw a paragraph of sloppy block lettering, but before he got the chance to read what it said, the garage door flew open.

---

An open bulb blinked intermittently above the small worktable, a byproduct of the amateur electrical job installed in the hidden basement bunker. General Attar booted awake his laptop at the makeshift desk in the tiny room. He electronically leafed through the national and international news of the *New York Time*s, *Washington Post*, *The Wall Street Journal*, and *The Times* of London. Many newspapers released much of their morning editions to their web sites the night before to drive online readers to *their* sites first and, in turn, raise online advertising revenue. Three headlines drew his attention, but after scanning the articles, he found none of them affected the mission. After quick searches through several more news sites, he typed in: www.philcollinsrocks.com.

The screen flipped to a site that paid tribute to the music career of pop star Phil Collins. It listed his music with the group Genesis, his solo career, and the songs he wrote for other musicians. Viewers of the site were able to review Collins' memorable dates and events, filmography, awards, and future engagements. The site lacked some of the standard features of similar sites. No video of Collins performing was available, nor were Collins' CDs or videos for sale. But at the bottom of the short column of icons descending the left side of the home page was a button titled *PhilChat*. It was this icon for which the entire site was created. General Attar clicked on it.

The screen blinked to a chronological list of discussion topics initiated by various fans; the topic with the most recent user activity was at the top. As a chat room, this would have made any top ten list for the worst. During the existence of the two-year-old board, only six topics had been initiated and two of them were started for the sole purpose of criticizing the site and its viewers. "This site blows!" was the heading of one chat topic; another was titled "OMG! Does anybody here even understand Phil?" Those, like the other discussion topics, had fewer than five entries. Except one. "Let's make a live Phil chat happen" contained 372 unique posts.

The general clicked on that link and read the two entries posted earlier in the day, one from a poster with the moniker "Boxcars12" and one from "9lives." Although written as nebulous observations, both messages were local mission updates directed to the general from cell leaders in Houston and Atlanta. Plans were on track; no reply was required so he backed out of the site and shut down the computer. The time online had tensed his shoulders. He looked through the doorway to the locked door at the other end of the short concrete hall. One of the women inside the room was still fresh—as much as an American woman could be. He glanced at his watch: thirty minutes until prayers. He wouldn't have time to haul the bitch upstairs first.

---

Jason twisted out of the car and turned to the open garage door just in time to hear a man shout, "What in hell are you doing?" He was standing in the middle of the open doorway between two other men in their late teens or early twenties, the dome light giving form to their faces. Jason already knew three things about the boys/men. One, the person who yelled at him was not native to the U.S. A heavily accented, "What in hell are you doing" is not proper English for striking fear into an intruder. Second, their close proximity to each other and unwillingness to actually enter the garage was a dead giveaway of their trepidation about the situation. If the roles had been reversed, Jason's angry bark would have come from halfway around the car as he rushed the man, especially if he had two buddies backing him up. And third, the center man, was the other person whose picture lay on the passenger seat of his car parked just around the block.

Jason realized at that moment that if the police got involved, those pictures would be extremely damaging. The center man glanced to his left and said, "Ted, call 9-1-1."

"Yeah, sport, call 9-1-1," Jason shouted. "And tell them that the police chief's neighbor, Tim, is here. Tell them to ask the chief if the water heater I fixed for him yesterday is working okay."

Jason could see the confusion on their faces and so far, the friend hadn't made the call, so he pushed forward with the lie. "Yeah, pal, do that. And after you find that out, tell them that whoever owns this Lumina was shouting sick and deranged things at my eight-year-old niece today. Definitely tell them that."

The three men went from sporting mildly puffed-out chests to expressions that pleaded for mercy. Jason approached the fat man in the middle and stood eye-to-eye with him for a moment before the man leaned back a few inches. Jason leaned in and seized further control, "Do you really want my niece to lift her skirt and show you her ass, pal? Huh? Are you really going to do something that will make her scream, you sick prick! How about I make you and your boys here scream right now? How about we go for the ride you offered that little girl, and then we'll see who screams. I'll make it hurt real good!" Jason was almost over the man now.

"I-I do not know what you are saying. I do not see a girl today. I do not say those things to any person. I promise."

"What's your name, asshole?" snarled Jason.

"I am Shyam Amish."

"Did someone else have your car today?" Jason asked.

"No. Nobody." Amish answered.

"Why don't I believe you, asshole?"

"I do not know. I just go to class and come home. That is all," the man pleaded.

"He's been home since noon. I was here with him the whole time," said the man on the left. His phone was still in his right hand but harmlessly down at his side.

Jason glared over at him. "You open your mouth again, I'll drop you right here."

He glanced at the third man with the same glare then back to Amish in the center. "If my niece even sees this car again, I'll be back. And it won't be for a polite conversation like tonight. Understand?"

The boy who had been a man when he first opened the door managed an obedient nod.

"Good," Jason spat.

He pushed through the men, laying his shoulder hard into Amish's, and walked as slowly down the driveway as a man whose heart was drumming about 800 beats per minute, could.

He turned right out of the driveway and walked down the sidewalk, the opposite direction from his car. When he got to the end of the block he turned right again and glanced back down the sidewalk toward the house. No one was on his trail, so after another twenty feet of slow walk, Jason broke into the fastest hobbled sprint his injured knee would allow and kept the pace going around the block back to the Buick. It wouldn't be long before one of the students realized that if someone had really wanted to confront the person who assaulted his niece, he would have come pounding on the door, not pilfering through a car in a dark garage.

When he got home Jason was hyped and hungry. He fixed himself a ham and cheese sandwich, a small stack of chips, and a beer. As he sat alone in the quiet kitchen with his late dinner, the exhilaration of the night's encounter was tempered by the fact that Shyam Amish was not one of the men he saw Friday night. Amish must have weighed 250 pounds, maybe ten of which were muscle. None of the men he saw Friday had rolls of fat hanging over their belts. He thought about one of his dad's favorite phrases, *That's why they call it hunting. If it were easy, they'd call it catching*. Sometimes you do everything right during a hunt, but if a there is no buck, you still go home with nothing.

He wrapped the uneaten half of his sandwich and put it in the fridge. He knew he wouldn't eat the other half after the bread was soggy and it took on the flavors of the refrigerator's contents, but his mom would have been disappointed if she'd seen the sandwich remains discarded in the garbage.

His thoughts turned to the girl who was beaten and how he'd failed her again. And maybe he'd failed Kelly and Grace—the opportunity to do good in their honor was staring him in the face, and he wasn't able to snatch it. After a few minutes he turned off the light and went upstairs. This hunt was over and he'd come home empty-handed.

---

Khalid opened the door to the locked holding room in the basement. One woman was backed into the far corner. He saw a new fear in her that dominated her movement. Fresh cuts and bruising altered her appearance. Khalid wasn't surprised at the change; he'd received an urgent call from Muhab, who'd gotten an angry message from General Attar. Muhab told him that after the general's first encounter with the other woman in the basement, he realized there was trash in the room that needed to be removed. Khalid asked if the old woman could take care of it but Muhab clarified that he was talking about Attar's first conquest. So later that night, when there was less chance of being noticed, Khalid and Omar drove to Cedar River to dispose of the unwanted debris.

He gave the frightened woman a look of apology but it didn't have any effect. Then he spread out a blanket and lifted the lifeless body onto it. It reeked of a nasty combination of bodily excretions, blood, and general decay. Khalid focused on breathing through his mouth as he wrapped the blanket around her, which enabled him to keep the bile just inside his throat. For now.

He locked the door behind him, then carried the body out to the car where Omar was standing watch. Omar opened the trunk and Khalid laid the body inside. An arm fell out of the blanket as he pulled away. When he replaced it, the arm bent in a way it shouldn't have midway between the elbow and the wrist. He made it all the way to the dump site before hurling. The picture of the unnatural bend in the arm filled his mind the rest of his sleepless night.

# CHAPTER 14

## TUESDAY

Jason could see his breath as he unloaded paint and wood trim finishing supplies from his truck outside Sheriff Burnett's house. The cool temperatures from the night before had hung around and created a crisp morning.

The final job remaining in the sheriff's basement remodel was painting the walls and staining and attaching the wood trim. Originally, the sheriff was going to try to save a little money by doing the paint and trim work himself. But things had gotten a little busy at the department and Jason was a little short of work for his crew, so the two had negotiated a reduced price for the additional service.

"Morning, Jason." Sheriff Burnett came out the back steps in full uniform and jacket, sipping coffee from a spill-proof travel mug. "Can I move furniture in tomorrow?"

"Maybe tomorrow night. But I'd rather wait another day. It's best to let the second coat of paint completely dry before nailing on the trim. That way if it ever has to come off, the paint won't come off with it."

"How about *you* tell June she needs to wait until Thursday?"

"That's fine. She's going to confirm with me anything you tell her anyway."

"Isn't that the truth. I could tell her the house was on fire and she'd call the neighbor to get a second opinion. Do women think men go completely clueless after taking their vows or were they just pretending to respect us all along?"

Jason put up his hands as though someone was pointing a gun at him, realizing there were only wrong answers to that question.

"Well, I need to get into the office. Tonya's at training this week. When she's not behind the desk, the office is in chaos."

"Never good being a man short."

"Nope. Now the rest of us are saddled with extra work we don't like and aren't any good at. Nothing worse than a pissy deputy answering phones. Some of my guys will never understand we're in the customer service business. Protect and *serve.*"

Jason nodded like he'd just learned something new. He didn't want to feed the conversation. Pat Burnett was a guy who always had an extra fifteen minutes to shed some light on a topic that was quite comfortable resting in darkness. Whether it was the original shape of the STOP sign or which ingredients create the best omelet, the sheriff was ready to discuss it.

He started for his cruiser, then turned back.

"You know, Jason…"

*Here it comes,* Jason thought. He half sat on the tailgate of the truck; that way, he could get up at some point to signal he needed to get to work and thereby end the conversation.

"I wanted to let you know we did some extra drive-bys Saturday on that house on County 12. And we added it to the patrol Saturday and Sunday night, but the place was quiet as a church. We'll follow up again this weekend but I'd be surprised if we find anything."

"I came up empty, too." Jason regretted the words the moment they left his lips.

The sheriff studied him for a moment. The conversation was about to go in a direction Jason didn't want it to.

"What do you mean? How did you 'come up empty"?

Jason considered for a moment how to play it, but didn't want to wait too long and seem guilty of anything, especially after breaking into someone's garage last night.

"Well, you know that protest going on at that college in Colorado? Where the students are claiming the government is harassing and illegally holding that kid from Lebanon?"

He could see the sheriff wasn't following. He told the sheriff about seeing the report about the missing college student on CNN at the bar with Seth.

"When they showed the picture of the college student, I realized why I didn't think the people I saw Friday were in high school. The men I saw, including the one the girl was trying to get away from, looked like the guy on TV. They were Middle Eastern. You know as well as I do, Cedar River doesn't really have an Arab population, so I figured they might be St. Joe students. I..."

"Hold on here," the sheriff said. Jason could hear the change in tone. "You're telling me that *the next day* you decided the men you saw were from the Middle East? You're certain they weren't white or black, they weren't Mexican—they had to be Arab? In the dark, late at night, you're drunk, but you can tell the men's nationality?"

Jason needed to regain some control of the conversation. "That is what I'm trying to tell you; the picture on TV triggered the detail. Don't you have witnesses look through mug books to trigger their memory of who they saw committing a crime? It's the same thing."

"It's not the same thing, Mr. CSI Duluth. A witness looks through a mug book to identify an individual, not to narrow down his race."

"The comparison is a bad one, but I'm confident in what I saw. Middle Eastern people have certain common facial characteristics the same way people with distinct Scandinavian roots do."

"Sure they do but..." The sheriff shook his head at Jason's faulty logic. "I cut you off; go on with your story."

Jason looked at the back door of the house, hoping June Burnett would appear and provide a diversion—maybe pregnant with quintuplets or with flames shooting from her fingers. She didn't show, so Jason continued. "With the assumption the men I saw did attend St. Joe's, I got hold of some yearbooks and directories and jotted down the names and photos of students who looked Middle Eastern. And because they would need to drive out to the house on 12, I tracked that down too.

But it turns out the two students that had licenses weren't the men I saw Friday. Hence, dead end."

The sheriff took a moment to process Jason's account. "How do you know the two St. Joe kids weren't the men you saw Friday night?"

"Their pictures didn't fit the look of the men I saw from the deer stand." Technically, he was telling the truth.

"So would you be able to identify the men from Friday night, if you saw them again?"

"I don't know; a couple of them, maybe."

Sheriff Burnett took a long sip from his coffee mug, then licked the excess off his upper lip. "Let me tell you just some of the problems with the bullshit you just told me. First of all, labeling the men you saw as 'Middle Eastern' reeks of either racism or terrorism hysteria. I think you're too smart for either, so I'll dismiss it for now. If you were able to recall more about Friday night, don't you think we'd see that as relevant and want to know about it? And why would you be trying to investigate it on your own?"

Jason thought about the last question. He wasn't sure of the answer but he didn't like the initial suggestions that filled his head. The sheriff noticed the unsettled change in Jason's expression but moved on.

"But here is the most important part. Where did you come up with a list of the foreign students and who among them has a driver's license?"

Jason didn't respond, but the guilt on his face was obvious.

Burnett added a little fear to go with the guilt. Good wholesome fear was a tool he had used many times in his career to keep good people from making bad choices.

"I imagine someone could scour the DMV database and eventually come up with information similar to yours. Or..." the sheriff held it a beat for effect, "if you had a friend who worked in administration up at the college, you could get that same information a lot faster. The only problem with either of those two solutions is that it is completely illegal and the person who provided the information, if caught, would go to jail for a long time."

Jason had responses to the sheriff's comments but none of them were important enough to risk his big mouth getting him into more trouble.

"If you have any more information about Friday, you need to give it to me. Do you have anything else to add about that night?"

Jason understood the inclusion of the word "Friday" and was thankful he was not pushing the collection of student data angle. He stood up from his spot on the tailgate. "No, sir."

"Call me if you think of anything. Immediately. Don't go starting your own little made-for-TV investigation. I get that you're worried about the woman who got hit, but the best way to help is to let us professionals do our jobs."

"Will do."

The sheriff started again for the cruiser, then turned back. "When's the last time you were on a date?" he asked.

Jason laughed and picked up two five-gallon buckets filled with paint brushes, rollers and other supplies.

"I'm serious, Jason. No disrespect to Kelly, but have you dated since the accident?"

Jason looked at the sheriff, who was standing behind the open driver door, waiting for an answer. "No."

"You need some excitement in your life, a little adventure, before you end up in your mom's quilting clutch," he said. "I'll make you a deal; you go on an actual date and I won't ask how you found your two driver's license owners. Deal?"

"C'mon Pat."

"I want the name of the girl you ask out and the receipt from the restaurant." Burnett then added a little negative incentive. "Most businesses nowadays have software that monitors each user's keystrokes. It's typically used to stop employees from looking at porn and such. With a tool like that I should be able to find out who got you your data by the time I take my morning coffee break."

Jason guessed that the sheriff had no intention of following through with the threat but agreed anyway. "Fine, I'll go on a date."

"Good, I'll give you a week." He opened the door to the cruiser and added, "After that, I'm setting you up with one of my nieces. They might be a little more plump than you're used to, but you know what they say about beggars."

Jason started two employees rolling primer over bare drywall in preparation for the first coat of paint on the Burnetts' basement walls. He laid out drop cloths in the middle of the room then set up two sawhorses on which he would stain the oak trim. He was only midway through the second board when the phone on his belt chimed. He put the can of stain down but not the cloth filled with the walnut stain. He wore the phone on his left hip for times just like this. While his rubber-gloved right hand was already filthy with dark liquid, his left hand was still clean. The caller ID read, "St. Joseph Col." *Not an emergency* he thought and replaced the phone in its case on his belt. He rubbed stain on another four boards until the cloth became over-saturated. Jason disposed of it then called Kate back.

"Hey Kate. What's up?"

"I was wondering what happened last night."

He turned away from his employees before responding. "It didn't go exactly as planned, not that I had one. I sort of got busted breaking into a car by one of the two students and his friends."

"Jason!" Her voice boomed through the phone. He looked over his shoulder at the guys priming; they were both looking at him, smiling like two adolescent boys watching a buddy talk to a girl on the playground. He shook his head and rolled his eyes in disgust with the caller, but they weren't buying it.

He turned back around. "Calm down, the whole room can hear you. It wasn't that big of a deal. We talked like gentlemen about why I was there and then I left. It's fine."

"You told them why you were there?" she asked, surprised.

"I guess I should say I gave them a plausible reason for why I was there, which they accepted. Remember Kate, they're *under*graduates."

"I want to know what happened."

"Not now, I'm in the middle of a job; maybe after work. Which leads me to some other news." Jason measured his delivery before continuing. "I talked to Pat Burnett this morning. He told me they haven't seen any new activity at the house on County Road 12."

"Did you think they would?"

"I don't know, but that's not the point. After he told me about not finding anything, I kind of let it slip that I did a little investigating of my own."

"You what! Jason, we agreed..."

He cut her off. "I know. I screwed up, but it's fine. He just got in my face a little about leaving law enforcement to the professionals."

"Did you tell him you were here?"

"No, of course not. As long as I don't do any more snooping, he's cool. And last night was the end of it, so it's a non-issue."

"The students you found weren't the guys you were looking for?"

"No. Not even close," he said.

"Then what's the next step?"

"I don't have one. I feel bad about the girl who got hit. I think she was in some real trouble; her friend, too. But I've done everything I can think of. Hopefully, someone closer to the situation can give those guys what they have coming to them."

"So, that's it?"

"There is one loose end." He took a deep breath, then bulled ahead. "The sheriff thinks my life is kind of pitiful. He made me promise to go on a date in the next week, or else."

"Or else what?"

"That's between us guys." He tried to keep his voice even and cool for the next question. "So, will you help get the sheriff off my back and go out for dinner?" Then before giving her a chance to answer, he added, "You know, as a thank you for all of your help with my mom and everything."

"Only if it's *as a thank you*," she said. "You know, for your mom and everything."

Her sarcasm added to Jason's discomfort. "How about tonight? I can tell you more about what happened last night."

"Sounds good. How should I dress?"

"Semi-fancy. I need to show Sheriff Burnett the receipt. I don't think he'd approve of The Pizza Palace."

"Does semi-fancy mean you'll be wearing a jacket with those stupid elbow patches or does it mean you'll be in a work shirt, just not a dirty one?"

"Somewhere in between—and I don't have any jackets with elbow patches."

"So what do you wear with your pants that have the knee patches on them?"

"I better find a place with damn good food, 'cause it sounds like there's a good chance the company's gonna be really annoying."

"I'd say there's more than just *a chance*," Kate warned, then hung up.

Jason arrived home from work at 4:30. It had been another light day, which was starting to wear on him a bit. Late October was a little early for business to be slowing down. He sat at the kitchen table and was texting himself notes about the cost of the painting supplies when Hannah came in. She asked how he'd been feeling since the Friday anniversary. He told her that he felt a little better every day and that today was the first day he felt somewhat normal.

"Did something special happen today?" she asked.

"Not really. It was more last night," he said.

Jason grabbed a Diet Mountain Dew out of the refrigerator, then sat down at the table across from his mom and told her about what he saw Friday night and the events that followed. Hannah listened without interrupting and waited until he asked her opinion before offering a response. "You've been kind of a wreck for a few weeks now, Son. You did the same thing last year as the twenty-first approached. I understand it's a very painful and emotional time, probably will be every year. But going on stakeouts and breaking into garages? Don't you think that's a little out of character?"

"Probably. But maybe that's a good thing. I promised Kelly I would live a life worthy of her and Grace, yet two years later not a damn thing has changed." He twisted the cap off the bottle and took a swig of soda. "I feel like I should be doing something more, something greater. When I saw that woman get knocked around it was like Kelly was telling me, 'Put up or shut up.' But I didn't do it, Mom. I didn't do anything heroic. Instead, I ended up passed out in the truck."

He watched the soda's bubbles launch themselves from the bottom of his bottle. His mother didn't say anything. He looked up and saw her gentle eyes waiting for him to find his own way. "I don't know, Mom. It's like she put that house in front of me. I'm literally talking out loud to God, asking Him why He would take my girls from me, demanding to know His great plan, and all of a sudden I hear shots fired—and there's the house." He qualified his statement to separate the reality from the symbolic, "Obviously, it's been there for years and I've seen it before. But not that night." He waited for his mom to offer some consolation but again she remained silent. "So anyway, today is the first day I don't feel compelled to right the wrong. I guess life is getting back to normal and I'm done transferring."

"What do you mean, *transferring*? Hannah asked.

"Both Seth and Kate made it very clear that I was imposing my feelings about the accident on the activities at the neighboring farmhouse."

"Bull-cocky!" Hannah blurted out. "You didn't make up what happened, Jason. If Kelly or your emotions over losing your family inspired you to push a little harder than normal, okay. Then go with it. You've always known when to push and when to let go. We thought you were crazy when you decided, at five-ten and a hundred and fifty pounds, to walk onto the hockey team at Duluth. You ended up the captain and leading scorer of a conference championship team. But you also knew that your skills weren't good enough for the NHL and you stopped—even when the Capitals drafted you in the second round. The same goes for you and Kelly—how many times did she say 'No' when you first asked her out?"

"What did you expect her to say? She was dating my buddy at the time."

"Did you chase all your friends' girlfriends?"

"Just Kelly."

"Because you knew something was there." She waited a moment for the confidence of her words to burrow into her son. "If you have been locked on to this for the last week, it's not because you're emotional; it's because there is something there."

Jason nodded, more to himself than to her. "Hey Mom, do you know Clara Riddle? She's the woman who lives in the house."

"I recognize the name, but I haven't heard it in a long time. I think something happened to her husband a number of years ago if I remember right."

"So she's not a friend of a friend or anything?"

"No. I can't say as I can even put a face to the name. I'm sure I'd recognize her if I saw her," Hannah said.

Jason looked blankly out the window for a moment, then shook his head and looked at his mom. "I need to take a shower."

"Going out?"

"Yeah, dinner. I should have let you know earlier. Sorry."

"No problem. With Kate?"

"Actually, yes. You know, to thank her for coming o…"

"Yeah, yeah."

Jason got up from the table. Hannah stood up with him and hugged her son. "Stick with it. Find out what happened at that house."

"I think that ship has sailed, Mom. I don't have a next step," he said.

"What do I ask you every time you ask if I've seen your hat?" she asked.

"Do I remember where I saw it last," he recited dutifully.

"That's right."

---

Omar drove in silence from the Twin Cities to Cedar River. Out of the corner of his eye he'd watched his passenger scrawling notes and making calculations during the entire trip. He veered off I-35 onto the Cedar River exit.

"Turn right and get gas," General Attar said, without looking up from his notes.

"I filled the tank before I picked you up, Sir. We have plenty of gas," said Omar.

"Get the gasoline," the general said, still studying his notes. His voice was at the same volume as the first request and his cadence seemingly had not changed, yet the second order came through with great intimidation. Omar tried to straighten his already stiff posture and tripped the right-turn signal.

Omar swung into the last of the four pumps, keeping the car facing the ramp they had just exited. He pumped the gas while the general watched for any drivers coming down the exit embankment who appeared too curious about their surroundings or seemed to be searching for something. There were none.

Omar returned from paying for the two gallons of gas. He turned the ignition, then put his right hand on the gearshift, but before he could put the car into gear, General Attar reached out and snapped Omar's pinkie finger, leaving it dangling 180 degrees from the other three fingers. Omar tried to scream but the general's right hand was already covering his mouth. Even with the incredible pain, he was aware of his assailant's level of calm. General Attar hadn't even turned to face the man whose finger he so easily rendered useless.

Finally, the general spoke, his voice low and even. "Quiet."

Omar hadn't realized he was screaming into the general's hand, but somehow the threat in his superior's voice gave him the discipline to stop. General Attar continued to hold down the finger as he spoke. "When you struck the girl, you endangered a mission whose planning began more than five years ago. Your stupidity and lack of discipline could have jeopardized the entire operation. Thousands of men are prepared to die in the name of Allah and rid the world of the unholy United States of America." He finally looked over at his victim. "Normally, such a foolish mistake would have cost you not only the one finger, but also, the other nine. However, you are fortunate this day; we are too close now. Every person in this army has a job to do, even a pitiful menace like you." The general let go of the finger. "If you want to be a soldier in this war, if you want to receive riches before Allah in heaven, you must earn it. Are you ready to earn it?"

Omar nodded, sweat from his forehead stinging his eyes.

"Drive."

# CHAPTER 15

Jason was on time picking up Kate for dinner, but was about to make them late for their reservation.

"Where are we going?"

"I thought it would be better to get out of town. I read a great review in the Strib about a new Italian place up in Burnsville. I thought we'd give it a try."

A second-tier suburb south of Minneapolis, Burnsville was thirty minutes north. The restaurant was located on the edge of a dense retail area where I-35 split into 35W and 35E. The entrance to I-35 was directly west of town but Jason headed north instead.

"Did they move Burnsville?" Kate asked.

"We need to make a quick stop before dinner." Jason watched a car a quarter-mile ahead back onto the road and speed away from them. It was the same driveway he was seconds from entering.

"Is this a client of yours?" Kate asked as they pulled in front of a garage on a lightly grassed-over gravel drive.

Jason pointed to the northeast. "My deer stand is about a quarter-mile or so through the woods over there. The girl from Friday night got hit right about where we're sitting."

He could see the questions swirling in her head. He chimed in before she could start spitting them out. "Neil told me the woman who lives here was frightened by the fact that someone in the woods was watching her. I thought I'd apologize for any anxiety I caused. And though I naturally come off like a cuddly teddy bear, I figured a pretty lady at my side would make me appear even more harmless."

Kate sensed Jason's words were a bit rehearsed. "That's the only reason we're here? To make her feel safe?"

"What else would it be?"

They walked up the front stairs to a lifeless covered porch, which was, at a minimum, a doormat or a couple of rockers away from presenting a welcome to visitors. There was no doorbell so Jason knocked on the door and waited a few moments, but got no response. He knocked again, this time a little louder. They waited for a minute and in the middle of Kate suggesting that they may have caught her at a bad time, the dead bolt on the door slid open and a worn, grimacing woman appeared. Her greying hair hung unclean from her head, shadowing much of her drawn face.

Jason introduced himself and Kate to the woman whose scowl seemed to be her natural expression more than her opinion of them. He explained he was the person who called the sheriff last weekend and asked if they could come in and explain. After a brief visual examination of her obtruders, the woman backed up a couple steps to allow their entrance.

The door opened into the kitchen. Cabinetry wound around the corner to the right with a ceramic sink on the side wall. Against the opposite wall sat a seventies-era vomit-green refrigerator and stove. The countertops were void of any adornment or small appliance; drying dishes served as the only décor. At the far end of the cabinets stood a pantry, which looked like it led down to a basement to the left and out a side door to the right. The room was dated but clean and well-kept.

The three talked in a close huddle just inside the door. Jason spoke first. He told the woman that he owned the eighty acres directly east and north of her home, some of which he supposed the original owners of her house owned and farmed at one time. He explained that he camped on the land a few nights each summer and that's what he was doing Friday.

"Five minutes from home and I'm in my own nature preserve." He glanced at Kate, who appeared to be fine with the use of a white lie as an explanation for his being on the land Friday night.

The woman gave him a disapproving shake of the head. "Why would someone sleep on the hard ground when you have a soft bed at home? Young people always want what they don't have, even if it's a dirt bed."

Jason made his case for the allure of the outdoors but it was met with more disapproval. Rather than add to her torment with questions about what happened that night, he shifted the conversation to her home. "What a great place. I live in a turn-of-the-century house and I love it. This home has to be what, eighty years old?"

"I don't know," she said.

"You lived here long?"

"Since March of '88."

Jason rubbed his hands over a beveled cabinet door, making a small production of being impressed with its craftsmanship. "I'm a contractor and I can tell you, homes from this era are in better shape today than houses only ten years old. And more beautiful too. Bet you haven't needed much work done around here."

"None."

Jason walked left through the doorway leading to the dining room. The woman tried to cut him off but he easily slid by her. The room was neither large nor small. A cheap dining table and six matching chairs anchored the room. At either side of the curtained windows facing the road were original corner china cabinets.

"Look at these beautiful built-ins," he said, admiring the glass-fronted cabinets the same way he had in the kitchen.

"I was just about to sit down to dinner," the woman said as she arduously shuffled her way around the other side of the table, signaling the tour would end there.

"I'm sorry—hazard of the job." He felt her growing more uncomfortable but took a few moments to take in the full setting. The dining room led into the living room, which contained a standard older couch and matching chair. The suite was bordered by a nondescript coffee and end table, also matching. At the far wall stood a large, mostly empty, curio cabinet whose more updated style made it seem a bit out of place. Jason didn't want to add to the scowler's unease so he started back toward the kitchen. He was followed so closely by the woman that she almost ran into him when he stopped just short of the kitchen.

"Is this your son?" he asked, pointing to the single photograph on the small buffet that abutted the wall to the kitchen. The photo looked like a high school graduation picture, possibly from the late seventies or early eighties, judging from the style of the clothes. The photograph had a silver chain and medallion draped across it.

"Yes, that's my Robert."

"What does he do?"

"He was a soldier. He died in Afghanistan."

"I'm so sorry." Kate entered the conversation for the first time.

"Thank you. And thank you for coming by," she said, nudging them into the kitchen. Jason didn't want to leave; what he had seen so far only piqued his curiosity more. But the woman opened the front door and he followed Kate out before turning back to thank his host. "You know, in my business I have a hard time keeping my guys busy all the time. I noticed you have a cracked window over the sink. If you like, I can have one of my guys come out and fix it before winter. It could shift or expand and break when the temperature drops. I'd be happy to do it at no charge as an apology for frightening you the other night."

She took his card. "I wasn't scared. I can take care of myself fine."

"I'm sure you can, Miss," he paused. "I'm sorry. I didn't get your name."

"Clara, Clara Riddle."

"I can get the measurements and have that window in for you tomorrow, Ms. Riddle, if you like."

"I got your card. I'll let you know if it breaks."

"Believe me, you'll want to fix it *before* it breaks, especially with winter coming. I've got a tape measure right in the truck."

"The window's been cracked since I can remember. I'm sure it can make it through one more winter," she said, pushing the door almost closed.

"Yes, ma'am, sorry to be a bother. Good night."

They got into the truck and backed out of the drive.

"Lonely woman," Kate said.

*I wonder*, Jason thought.

---

General Attar waited a full minute, then used the handle attached to the rear left corner of the six-foot-tall curio cabinet to slide it along the wall, exposing the hidden entrance behind. He stepped up into the living room, then pushed the cabinet across the worn carpet, back into position. He walked to the window in the dining room and looked through the narrow opening in the drapes.

"They're gone," said Clara, who was watching through the small diamond-shaped window in the front door. "I got rid of them as best I could," she said, then walked over and handed him the business card.

General Attar stared down at the card as if hoping a clue would jump up at him. He tapped it in regular beats against his left hand. "If this man or anyone else knocks at your door, you do not open it. Talk to them through the glass."

"I just won't answer it next time," she said.

"No. We do not want anyone to get suspicious. The last thing we need is another visit from law enforcement."

Clara left the room and went upstairs. The general pulled out his phone and punched a number from memory. "Tell me about Jason Kendall."

---

The meal was terrific. Jason finished his large portion of carbonara; Kate's plate of chicken marsala was just two bites from clean. The waitress came by the table to offer dessert. Both declined but Kate asked for a cup of decaf coffee; Jason stuck with the beer he received with the dinner. The conversation meandered about, both pushing relationship topics to the very back of their dinner conversation catalog.

"I don't have a business to run and I'm definitely no construction expert, but what was with the hard sell on that lady's kitchen window tonight?" Kate asked. "If you're that desperate, you should come by my house. I've got months' worth of pro-bono work for you."

Jason thought about how much he should tell Kate. He had passed on too much information to the sheriff and that only got him a good ass-chewing. On the other hand, he could use a sounding board for his suspicions.

"There were a lot of things about that woman and her house that didn't add up. I wanted more time with her to figure out why."

"What's with the sudden Sherlock Holmes routine? I thought you'd given up trying to find the man who hurt that woman."

Jason shrugged. The Sherlock Holmes shot was preferable to the CSI reference the sheriff made earlier in the day but he didn't care for either comparison.

Kate went on. "I must be missing something. All I saw was a lonely old woman who might be a touch ornery and probably lives in the country because she wants to be left alone."

"My questions are as much about the house as Clara Riddle. But the two are definitely tied together. Let's start with Clara. She never even asked me what I saw going on outside her house the other night. Don't you think she would at least be interested, if not a little worried?"

Kate looked skeptical.

"And she said she was just sitting down to dinner, but dishes were already drying in the rack on the kitchen counter. She had just finished dinner," he said.

"Come on, Jason. So she told a little white lie to get us out of her house. Like you've never told someone you had another call coming in to get out of a phone conversation? Heck, you told her tonight you were on your property to go camping, which wasn't true." She shook her head. "I don't know, it feels a little thin."

"Maybe, but hear me out on the house."

She gave him an upward nod telling him to make his pitch.

"First of all, she says she's never had any work done on the house. There were three small patches in the dining room ceiling. And they were new—you could tell because the rest of the ceiling was yellowed with age. But the three spots were filled and recently touched up."

Kate straightened up to say something, but Jason held up his hand. "Let me finish." She leaned back in her chair and gave him the "I'm backing off" sign with the palms of her hands.

"Old houses like Ms. Riddle's have walls made from wood slats and mortar; usually a heavy wallpaper is slathered over them. Her house was the same way, except..." he waited a beat for effect, but Kate wasn't biting, "the wall at the other end of the living room. That wall was sheetrock like more modern houses. You can tell because it's smoother and paint adheres to it differently. Plus, it didn't have a window in it. Most older homes had a lot of windows to bring in as much sun as possible during the winter and let cool air flow through in the summer. Why would you knock out just that one wall? And why wouldn't you replace the window?" He gave her a "gotcha" look. "The last thing that is bugging me is the curio cabinet."

"Was there a chopped-off head in it?"

"Ha Ha." He waited as their waitress stopped to fill Kate's coffee before continuing. "I was going to say, before I was so rudely interrupted..." Kate rolled her eyes. "The curio was newer than the other furniture in the house."

"So she's not allowed to buy anything new? You're beyond reaching."

"It was empty and the built-ins in the dining room were empty. Hell, even the countertops in the kitchen had nothing on them. A curio is used to display things. She has nothing to display. And before you get all sarcastic, I'm pretty sure the carpet next to it was matted down like something heavy had been there. No way she's pushing that curio around."

"So what does all this tell you?" Kate asked with more curiosity than sarcasm.

"I don't know. But here's the last thing: she didn't have a hearing aid."

Kate shook her head. "Okay, now you've completely lost me."

"If I could hear things coming from that house from a quarter-mile away, she certainly could hear them, too."

"I'll admit the one thing I keep coming back to is that she never asked you what you saw or heard," Kate said. "It does make you wonder what she already knows."

"What are you doing tomorrow night?" Jason asked.

She waved him off. "One thank-you dinner is more than enough."

"Good, 'cause I was hoping you could stay with my mom again."

"Where are *you* going to be?"

"I'll be at Ms. Riddle's house."

---

The monster threw her back inside the dank basement dungeon. Liz Pratt fell hard to the concrete floor, opening a new wound on her right elbow. She didn't feel it. She wasn't feeling anything. She had just suffered through another brutal encounter with her captor but she defended herself tonight the same way she had the last two times: she left her body and did not return until he was gone.

Tonight was unusually violent. The beating was not to encourage or punish her sexual skills; instead, it seemed more like random acts of fury.

The man stood over her, seething with disgust. After each of the other attacks, he had tossed her back into the room, fastened the lock and left. But this time he was reluctant to go. Something had changed. She dared not look up; her eyes held steady on his worn brown boots, which were so close to her face that she could smell the combination of perspiration, dirt, and leather.

"American whores are the most terrible lovers in the world. I am happy to be finished with you."

He purposefully ground his heel down, crushing her hand as he walked out of the room. Hearing the door lock, she returned to her body. Her left eye throbbed. She reached up to blot the blood leaking from her temple. She gently rubbed the swollen bruises that lined the inside of her thighs. She looked down at the rows of purple and grey. "I am happy to be finished with you." The words rang in her head. The nightmare was finally over. She had made it through. She promised herself that she would continue to survive. No. Thrive. She was already a stronger woman than she was a week ago. And she would be even stronger when all this was over.

She looked over her body to inventory her wounds. She got to her elbow and saw it was bleeding. Part of her was glad. She had noticed she bled less each day over her four-day confinement. She attributed this to the single scant meal and one small cup of water per day. The part scrape/part cut was too large to immediately stop with just pressure. She elevated her arm above her heart and let it rest on the top of her head. The lofted arm also eased the throbbing in her mangled fingers.

Then a cold jolt shot through her body, blasting each bruise, cut, and broken bone along the way. Her eyes raced back and forth across the room in a panic. She scurried around the small space as she had so many times before, searching for anything that could help her escape. The current tour ended the same way as every other: no tools, no openings, no way out. She fell into a corner, covered her face and, for the first time since she was taken prisoner, began to cry. The words rang in her ears. "I am happy to be finished with you."

She hadn't made it through the storm. The monster was simply stating her destiny: she was the next to die.

She lifted her head back and let it fall against the wall behind her, the tears continuing to stream down her cheeks. Her gaze hung on the small grey storm window on the opposite wall. Faint moonlight was struggling to press through the layer of thick smoky plastic nailed to the frame. She touched her elbow; the blood was starting to congeal. She got up and walked to the window.

# CHAPTER 16

## WEDNESDAY

Two of the three crew members were already at the worksite when Jason arrived. Today's work was going to be easy. And fun. Most boys came out of the womb wanting to break things and Jason and his crew were no different. Demolition was on the docket—a fun diversion for most men who work construction.

Today was the second day of a new project. On the first day, the crew removed shelving, cabinets, and other items that the owner wanted to store for use in the three-stall garage upgrade Jason's company was going to build for him. The current design of the house and its attached garage did not allow for a simple third-stall addition, so they decided it would be less expensive to bring the old structure down and start fresh.

Jason walked the perimeter inside and out and set up a schedule for demolition. Without a plan, demolition can take a very long time and, more importantly, because things were coming down instead of going up, someone could easily get hurt. He was going over the plan with the crew foreman when his phone rang—Rice County Sheriff. "Shit," he muttered.

"Jason Kendall."

"Your story better be damn good. 'Cause if it ain't, you and I are going to finish this conversation down here in my office." If a normal phone conversation happened at a volume of three, Sheriff Burnett's voice was north of five.

"I'm not sure what you mean, Pat," Jason said.

"You know damn well what I'm talking about. What were you doing at Clara Riddle's house last night? And when you answer me you will address me as Sheriff or Sheriff Burnett!" His voice jumped another notch on the volume dial.

Hammering started in the garage. Jason walked down the driveway to his truck before answering. "Sheriff, I was doing what you told me." He could hear the sheriff inhale in preparation for a loud rebuttal but Jason didn't give him the opportunity. "I was on a date. My first date in ten years; I've got the receipt to prove it."

"Jason, are you going to tell me you weren't at the Riddle house?"

"I was there. But only to tell her how sorry I was for the trouble I caused. That's all."

"Why don't I believe that, Jason?" His voice dropped down to a four.

"I'm sorry if I did anything wrong but I should tell you I offered to fix a window for her so I may be going out there again at some point. If you like, I can call you first."

"Kissing my ass only reinforces my instinct that you are up to something. I don't know what is going on exactly, but this is my last warning. If I hear anything else about you, or that house, chasing students, anything, I'll nail you, Jason. I'll get you for trespassing, disorderly conduct, invasion of privacy, and that will be just the beginning."

Jason didn't have a response. "Are you reading me, Jason? I don't like amateurs playing lawmen and I won't tolerate it in my county. If this isn't getting through, think about the people around you. If you get into trouble, who's going to take care of your mom, not to mention the trouble your friend at the college will be in."

"I understand, Sheriff."

"Good, 'cause I am as serious as a heart attack on this."

"Understood."

"Now that we understand each other, where'd you go on the date?" Volume level three.

The demolition was going quickly so Jason took his crew to Vera's for lunch. They were waiting for the two men who were painting Sheriff Burnett's basement. Jason's eyes weren't allowed to adjust from the brilliant sunshine before he was summoned to Louise's executive stool at the end of the bar. She rumbled right through his unwillingness to discuss his nonexistent campaign and in five minutes had begun four lists on four separate pages in her spiral notebook:

Marketing

Donors

Volunteers

Talking points

He was standing at mock attention when he noticed Neil Lockwood sitting with another man in the back. Jason was allowed to excuse himself from the impromptu strategy session only after agreeing to stop back at Louise's stool before he left.

Neil saw Jason approach and stood to welcome him. "Jason. How's your knee? I don't see much of a limp."

"It's fine, just a little stiff. I've already done some light running on it. The stitches really itch, though."

Neil turned and gestured to his companion, "Jason Kendall, meet Albert Casillas. Albert is a colleague in the Political Science Department at St. Joe's." He turned to Albert. "Jason and his parents were my neighbors when I first moved to Cedar River."

After the two men shook hands, Neil waved to an open chair. "Won't you join us?"

Jason motioned to his crew. "Thanks, but I'm here with my guys. We're just waiting on a couple more."

"Until the others arrive then," Neil said, and pulled out a chair for Jason.

Jason sat down and was asking Neil's guest about his job at the college when Louise hurried by and rubbed Jason's back with one hand and stuffed a sheet of paper in his lap with the other.

"What's that all about?" asked Neil.

Jason held up the paper for the two men to see. "Subtle, huh? That's my campaign manager."

"I thought you didn't want to run for city council," Neil said.

"I don't. I'm not," Jason said.

"Why not?" asked Albert.

Jason held up the nearly blank sheet of paper for the other men. "I don't even have any talking points."

"Then use talking points already out there," Albert said. "The school district needs money to provide hot breakfasts to deserving students before school. Get behind something like that."

"But I'm not for it."

"You're not for children having a good breakfast? Studies are pretty clear that a good breakfast correlates with increased learning," said Casillas.

"I'm not sure we should be legislating breakfast," Jason replied.

"But if it gives children the best chance to be successful—" the professor countered.

"But doesn't that assume children aren't given that chance right now? Do you know that parents aren't already providing a good breakfast to their children?" asked Jason.

"Many parents do not," Albert said.

"Then send a note home from school illustrating the link between a healthy breakfast and learning. It could include a list of good breakfast foods or combinations of foods," Jason said.

Neil finally interjected. "There you go. You *do* have talking points."

Jason apologized to the professor. "Don't misunderstand me. I think it's very noble to want to help children, just as it is the elderly."

"So you agree the government *should* help," Albert said, leaning back in his chair.

"No. I think *I* should. Churches, other organizations should," Jason said. "Every time I hear 'The government needs to do this' or 'The government needs to provide more of that,' I hear 'It's not my job to be responsible for this' and 'Someone else should take care of that.'"

"So it would be your stance that it's not the government's job to help its citizens in need?" asked the professor, a touch of pretension creeping into his voice.

"No, that's not my position," Jason answered. "But in my opinion, every time you just give someone a fish you have one less person with the ability to fish for himself. Let me ask you a question," Jason continued.

"If a person is laid up and can't work for a while, would a good neighbor put him in contact with a Meals-on-Wheels type of program?"

"I would hope so. Would you do something different?" Albert asked, only partially taking the bait.

"I'd bring him dinner."

Jason saw the last two members of his crew walk through the door. "I should get back to my table." Offering his hand, he said to Casillas, "Professor, it was nice to meet you. Thanks for the back and forth; I hope it didn't take away from your lunch." Albert shrugged.

Jason turned to Neil and asked, "Can I talk to you for a minute?"

They got up and walked away from the table.

"How long have you known Clara Riddle?"

"I don't know, quite a while. I really knew her husband better than her," Neil said.

"Can you tell me anything about her?" Jason asked.

"What do you mean?"

"I went to see her last night."

"I thought we decided you should give her some space. She's been through enough."

"I know. I just wanted her to see that I'm nothing to be scared of. But when I was there, she seemed a little touchy, like she was hiding something. Did you get the same feeling when you went to see her on Saturday?" Neil shook his head hesitantly so Jason pried further. "Did she invite you in?"

"I didn't ask to go in."

"And she wasn't acting unusual in any way?"

"Other than being a bit agitated by the visit from the sheriff's deputy, no. What's this about?"

"I don't know. I just got a weird vibe from her."

"We all react to stress, not to mention strangers, differently. No, I didn't sense anything more." Neil turned back toward his lunch companion. "Enjoy your lunch, Jason—the meatloaf's wonderful."

"Okay, thanks." Jason turned to his party then pivoted back to Neil. "What about her son? What do you know about him?"

"Not much. Good kid, I think. Was killed a few years back."

Jason got to the table as the waitress was taking the first order. He ordered the meatloaf special, then walked outside to make a call. No one picked up, so Jason tried a second number. Seth answered on the first ring. "What are you doing? You know I'm not allowed to have my cell on at work."

"I didn't tell you to pick up," Jason said.

"Make it quick."

Jason could tell that he was nervous about getting caught talking on the cell, so he skipped any additional ribbing and asked Seth about his availability later in the day. They agreed to meet right after Seth's shift.

"What are we doing?" asked Seth

"Bird calling."

# CHAPTER 17

The door flew open and Khalid was pulled inside. The door slammed behind him as Jan threw her arms over his shoulders and locked her legs around his waist.

She was in a robe and her hair was still wet. "You're early," she said, then kissed him long and enthusiastically.

"Please do not misunderstand my enjoyment of your greeting, but you were upset with me on the phone earlier because I didn't invite you to my apartment. What changed?"

"I was upset because we've been together for how many months and I've still never seen where you live. I have great news and wanted to surprise you. I wasn't *mad*, just disappointed."

"I am here now. Let me hear your great news."

She kissed him hard again, then peeled herself off him. "I had a meeting with the vice president of the north region today and he told me I am one of three finalists for district manager! Can you believe it? I would oversee all the stores in Minnesota, Iowa, the Dakotas, and part of Wisconsin. This is huge!"

Khalid caught her when she leaped for him again and gave her a long hug. "That is wonderful news. I am so happy for you."

"I know. He told me it will be an uphill climb because I'm the youngest of the three being considered and have been with the company for the shortest period of time. But he said if I do well in the interviews, I have a great chance."

"Wow. That is so exciting," Khalid said. "They would be fools not to take you."

"That's not all," she said. "He told me to be thinking about who from the store would be ready to replace me if I got the job. I told him the person I'm thinking of should be moved up right now."

She rubbed her hands over Khalid's biceps. "I told him the company should promote you now before you finish school so they don't risk losing you later. And you won't believe this; he said there are a few stores short of quality management personnel. He's going to call you in the morning about a transfer."

Khalid didn't immediately respond. "What's wrong? Aren't you happy?" Jan asked. "You deserve it, Khalid. You've *earned* it. I'm not saying you need to stay with Rockwell Outfitters forever, but a real management title on your résumé and maybe a fifty-thousand-dollar salary by the time you graduate? That's not too shabby."

"It sounds truly wonderful, but the best part of my job is working with you. I am not sure what salary that is worth." he said. Her next kiss was longer and even more passionate.

Jan smiled at him, then backpedaled to the door of her bedroom adding, "Nothing is final, but I think we need to go somewhere and celebrate—just you and me." She untied her robe and let it fall to the floor, then curled her finger, signaling for Khalid to follow. "And I know just the place."

---

Seth pulled into his driveway moments after Jason eased his truck up to the curb in front of the house. The shift at Powell Glass ended at 4:00 but a managers' meeting pushed Seth's clock-out time to 4:20. He set the small cooler that held the remnants of his lunch on the back steps and headed over to Jason's F-250 and hopped in. They drove out to County Road 12 and parked at the inlet to Jason's land. Jason grabbed a small cooler out of the back and they were at the deer stand minutes later.

Seth pulled a Dr. Pepper out of the cooler for himself and handed a Diet Mountain Dew to Jason. The deer stand was a mess. Jason's sleeping bag was still in it's binds but with fresh holes puckering it, and bird dung and other darker stains spotting it. Pieces of spoiled sandwich and potato salad leftovers were scattered about. A brown grocery bag, which had been Jason's garbage receptacle, had holes chewed in the corner and the whiskey and beer bottles that had filled it were now spilling out.

"I bet some squirrel got a little more than he bargained for when all of these bottles came tumbling out." Seth said, standing the bottles up to prevent them from rolling off the edge of the stand.

"I hope he did," Jason said, wanting some vengeance against the critter. "I didn't think to bring any new bags with me, either."

Halfway through standing and organizing the bottles, Seth said, "Dude, look at all of these. No wonder you passed out in the truck; I'm surprised you made it *that* far." Seth said.

"My knee feels the same way."

"Oh, yeah. How is your knee?" Seth asked.

"It's been four days; thanks for all the concern," Jason said.

"Hey Bud, I'm sorry. But you know it's 'Take Oliver to soccer,' 'Help Annie with her piano,' 'We don't have any milk.' Pretty soon a week's gone by. What ever happened? Did the kids ever come back?" Seth asked.

"What kids?" asked Jason.

"I thought you and the sheriff figured that a bunch of kids were tipping back a few on the property over there." Seth pointed toward the Riddle property.

"Plenty of other shit has gone down since then." Jason caught Seth up on the week's events, from tracking the Middle Eastern students, to the trip to see Ms. Riddle. Seth took a long pull of his Dr. Pepper and considered the information. "Did Kate think the woman seemed suspicious?"

"I don't think she was looking for it. I bet she would if we talked to Ms. Riddle again," Jason said.

"Why was Kate with you, anyway?"

Jason sensed a little jealousy. "We were on our way to dinner."

"You and Kate went on a *date*?" Seth asked through a boyish smile.

"It was just a thank you for staying with my mom on Friday night," Jason said defensively.

"You went on a dinner date with Kate?" Seth asked again, his grin growing larger.

"Knock it off; it's not a big deal."

"Whatever, dude. Everyone's been waiting for over a year for this to happen. Hell, I was going to start a parlay board. You know, for five bucks people get to pick a time and place when you two hook up for the first time, closest gets the cash."

"Why? Because we're the two singles in the group of couples?" Jason fired back.

"No. Well, that's part of it, but it's not the main reason—it's like I told you before." He searched for the right words. "You should listen to the way she laughs at you. I mean, Dude, you can get in a good zinger once in a while, but you ain't *that* funny."

"Can we just change the subject?"

"Sure lover-man. Consider it changed." Seth sat down in a nylon camping chair and cursed the fact that it didn't have a cup holder. Jason sat down in the other chair; both were facing the Riddle property a quarter-mile away.

"So what do you think happened at that house on Friday? You haven't said it, but do you think it could be some kind of terrorist shit?" Seth asked.

Sheriff Burnett had mentioned terrorism to Jason yesterday but only to dismiss it. For the first time, someone had actually thrown out the idea as a real question.

"I don't know. It sounds ridiculous. Terrorists invading Cedar River! I can't go that far; there's no evidence. And why here? We're not exactly the crown jewel of the country, you know?"

"But you seem to be sure they're from Iraq or somewhere, though," Seth said.

"That's just it, I don't know their nationality. I don't know enough about that part of the world. I can tell an African American from an Arab, from a Latino. But I can't pick out a Somali from an Indian from an Iranian," Jason said. "Besides, being from the Middle East does not make somebody a terrorist." He took a swig of soda. "I'm trying to stay focused on the girl who was hit and dragged into that house." His voice filled with determination. “Someone was jacking around a helpless woman and maybe her friend. He is either in that house now or he was there Friday. And the old lady who lives there, Clara Riddle, knows about it.” He turned from the house and looked over at Seth. “I can just feel it.”

“So what’s the plan?” Seth asked.

“I was thinking I would hike through the woods over to the house and get a closer look.” Jason handed Seth a pair of binoculars. “If you see someone come out of the house or a car pull up or something, you do your cardinal call and I’ll ditch.”

“Okay, sounds good. But that’s not what I was talking about.”

Jason gave Seth a confused look.

“If one of the college kids who caught you in their garage had been the guy from Friday night, what were you planning to do? Or if you found something in that car, then what?” Seth pointed toward the house. “What if you hike over there and the woman you saw Friday is tied to a chair? Or what if she’s playing cards with the guys from Friday? Then what? I’m trying to figure out if you have a plan and why it’s your fight?”

Jason leaned back in the camping chair and took a swig of his soda. Both men sat quietly watching a line of Canadian geese in a V-formation flying overhead, honking wildly as they flew south to warmer climes. Then their eyes were caught by a white-tail doe and her two nearly grown fawns. The deer’s part gallop, part sprint always seemed as bizarre as it did magnificent.

“I guess I don’t have a plan, Seth,” Jason said, finally, “But I do have a purpose. I sat in this spot five nights ago and wondered if I was living a life that would make Kelly and Grace proud—if one of them were still alive instead of me, how the world might be a better place. And you know as well as I do, if Kelly had been in my spot Friday, she would have sprinted to that house and knocked the door down. It wouldn’t have mattered how much she’d had to drink or how big the guy was, she would not let those girls go alone into that house.”

“No, you’re right—she wouldn’t.”

“Kelly wouldn’t let go so neither can I,” Jason said. “Plus, that house just isn’t right; something stinks in Denmark.”

"Then get over there and find out what it is. But you better hurry. I've got to be at the middle school in forty-five minutes to pick up Chip. The last time I was late, Robyn shaved my ass with a dry razor."

Jason shook his head as he started down the ladder.

"Seriously! I couldn't sit down for a week."

Weak-jointed birch trees dominated the patch of land between the Riddle house and the stand. The result was underbrush filled with hidden twigs and branches in the tall prairie grasses, which slowed Jason's progress. Adding to the delay, the natural guideposts Jason had picked out to guide him looked much different from the ground and he was forced to feel his way as the woods grew more dense near the Riddle property. Finally, Jason saw the brick house, but the view he was angling for was wrong.

He bent low for the final twenty five yards and stopped a few feet from the tree line. From his crouched position he could see the entire east side of the house; the cracked kitchen window rested six feet off the ground in the left/middle of the first floor. The front of the house was also in view, but at an extremely sharp angle. The front porch supports along the front rail appeared stacked one on top of another. Jason had already seen the front of the house during his last visit; today he was more interested in getting a good look at the back of the house. He began to maneuver through the edge of the tree line in that direction.

Once behind the house, Jason huddled next to a large oak tree. He looked back in the direction of the deer stand but though most of the leaves had fallen, it was hidden by the thick copse of trees.

He turned back to the house and analyzed its architectural composition. The rear, like the front, had a porch, but this one was larger, extending the entire width of the house. The rails and posts of this porch had been turned on a lathe to add decorative interest. The stairs to the door rose beneath a gabled entrance with decorative carvings on its face. At the entrance stood a strong solid-wood door that once had a screen or storm door in front of it, possibly both, depending on the season. The door moldings were rather ornate for a traditional twenties-era farmhouse. A heavy copper light fixture hung at eye level, just to the right of the entrance. It was likely original to the house, its bronze color transformed over the years by a thin patina layer that left the metal framing a matted seaweed color. The entire façade was in a general state of disrepair, but it was obvious to Jason that the house once carried a subtle grandness to it. It was likely the home of a farming family who had built it *after* a number of successful years and strong return on their labors.

Looking now at the rear, Jason realized this was originally the front of the home and guessed that a road had probably passed to the north at one time and the house had faced fields to the west and north.

The garage, which faced County 12, was newer than the home; likely built in the sixties, maybe the seventies, long after the road to the north was abandoned and all other outbuildings had been torn down.

He moved west another fifteen feet and crouched behind a thick patch of prairie grass. In his current position he stood directly in front of the wall opposite the living room, the one that opened to the dining room to the south. The wall looked just like the façade on the rest of the house. Jason had expected to see newer brick that didn't quite match the rest of the house, the result of a major repair. Or even more likely, he anticipated some type of add-on room, perhaps a bedroom for an elderly family member, or a new mud or utility room—something that would justify the installation of the new sheetrock on the opposite side of the wall. Instead, he saw only a window.

It was a three-by five-foot double hung window, which matched the one equidistant from the door on the other side. He hadn't seen the window from the inside last night, just a flat wall behind the contemporary curio cabinet. Puzzled, Jason thought, *Outside: original window; inside: wall-to-wall sheetrock.*

Yellowing sheetrock covered the window. Or more correctly, sheetrock *filled* the window. It was cut to fit inside the window frame. Jason could see the imperfect breaks of the chalky material to make it fit inside the window. It was definitely an amateur job. A professional's first choice would be to replace the window completely. And at minimum, he would remove the window frame and insert a piece of sheetrock flush with the surrounding wall.

Why cover a window with sheetrock only to then cover the whole wall in the same material? And why sheetrock over just the one wall, not the entire room? Jason thought for a moment. Not only did it not meet code, but it didn't serve a purpose. Unless they were covering up something. "It doesn't make any sense," Jason said out loud. "What are you up to, Clara?"

---

Seth twisted off the cap to his bottle of Dr. Pepper before realizing he had finished it with the last swig. He opened the cooler and dug through the ice but found only two Diet Mountain Dews. *Real nice* he thought, then put his empty in the cooler and closed the lid. "One for me, and three for you; what a sweetheart." He looked back at the house, raised the binoculars from his chest, then retraced Jason's jagged path to the next property; still quiet. He checked his watch: twelve minutes until his thirteen-year-old would be waiting at the gym entrance. He cupped his mouth with his hands and whistled.

---

Jason moved right to get a look at the far side of the house before heading back to the stand, but two naturally felled ash trees lay directly across his path. The trees were lying four feet above the ground, their large exposed root balls providing height to one end, the canopy of branches doing the same at the other. Jason traversed the first log on his stomach and his foot squished down into a low muddy puddle covered by the thick grasses on the other side. He leaped toward the next tree and his other foot dropped hard into the same thick mud. After he rolled over the next log, Jason thought about how glad he was he had come straight from work. His boots held fast; the running shoes he would have changed into would still be stuck in the mud below, leaving him stocking-footed. The ground was higher on the other side of the second log and it stayed that way as he moved farther right behind a single eight-foot spruce a few yards behind the edge of the grass line north and west side of the house.

It wasn't a great angle from which to scan the house's west side, but because the property turned into an expansive grass lawn on the west side, it was the best he was going to get if he wanted to remain hidden. The good news was that the far side of the house was bathed in light from the descending sun. Jason scanned each level, giving special consideration to the windows. Everything seemed to be in keeping with the feel of the house, the full curtains covering each window gave it an aura of a fortress. But other than that, he saw nothing extraordinary. Yet something gnawed at him.

He flashed on his view of the living room from last night, and tried to think. But no clues or brilliant thoughts emerged—just the same gnawing feeling from last night that something wasn't right about the place. He checked his watch. S*hit! Already running late*. He looked toward the deer stand and thought, *why didn't he whistle?* He straightened from his crouch. He'd have to make up some time on the hike to the deer stand if he was going to get Seth back to town in time to pick up Chip. He took one last glance at the house and ran for the two fallen ashes. He suddenly braked twenty feet short of his destination.

---

A dozen cardinal calls and still no sign of Jason. Seth searched for and found a small patch of oak trees in the wooded area to the north. Oaks don't drop their foliage until spring, and he watched the bronze, gold and brown leaves flutter in the distance. The breeze causing them to dance was blowing from the west. He looked again at the garage and the distance between and realized his calls were being knocked down in the breeze; he needed a stronger signal.

He picked up the cooler with the Mountain Dews, pulled out the soda bottles, and dumped the ice over the side of the stand. The cooler which held the two Mountain Dews and empty Dr. Pepper was a small Igloo Playmate which used its lid as a handle for easy transport. The other cooler, which he figured Jason had brought Friday night, was much larger. Its handles were on the narrow sides, allowing for two arms or two people to lift its heavy loads.

Seth opened the lid of the larger cooler and lifted it so it hung just off the floor. Then he picked up the small Playmate and brought it down hard like a mallet against the large cooler hanging in his left hand. The loud crashing sound echoed against the trees. The force of the blow knocked the large cooler right out of his hand and almost over the edge of the stand. He scrambled over to it, and lifted it off the floor again, facing the open chest toward Jason. He slammed the Playmate mallet against it again. Another tremendous crash rang out. This time his grip on the large cooler held, and he quickly banged out two more alerts.

---

Jason turned back to the far corner of the house several feet short of the felled trees. *Was that –? I gotta go back*, he thought. He leaned forward and quietly stalked back toward the northwest corner of the house as if he were sneaking up on the area. He was two steps from a view of the west side of the house when a resounding crash came from his property on the east. He dove for the ground, his face landing in a bed of brittle leaves. "What the?… Seth?" he whispered. He remained flat for a moment waiting for his heart to stop pounding a hole into the ground.

He couldn't stay there in the open. The loud crack from the stand may have been heard inside the house. But he needed to see for himself if his eyes had deceived him, or if the image was real.

---

Liz Pratt sat in the corner of the musty room staring at the window that held her blood-drawn plea. She caressed her injured elbow, not because it hurt, but as a thank you for the beating it took to get the "HELP" signal onto the window. By the time she came up with the idea last night, her wound had mostly dried. She'd only finished the H before her "paint supply" dried up. She scraped the injured elbow hard across the rough concrete floor again to restart the blood flow. The stinging jolts worsened each time she stabbed at the open wound with her dirty fingers to get more "paint" but it was a price she was willing to pay.

And now she heard an unfamiliar sound—a distant bang coming from outside. It was unfamiliar not just in its volume but because it was obviously man-made. Then came another sound—different. This one was much closer but more difficult to discern. Small animals had run by her clouded opening to the outside world several times during her ordeal but this one was different. It was heavier. The dried leaves weren't scattered by the movement; they were crunched beneath it. She got up and walked quietly to the window when three more loud bursts boomed in the distance.

She leaped for the window, her forearm hitting the heavy plastic cover.

"The basement—I'm in the basement! Help me! You gotta help me!" She beat the window above her head continuously during her plea. Then she thought about her words and tried to eliminate the desperation in her request. "Please. I'm stuck in the basement! Can you help me? I'm stuck in here and can't get out!" Another of her dad's admonitions, "Never yell rape; always yell fire."

She didn't know who or what was outside the window. It didn't matter. She knew she was almost out of time.

---

Jason stood, finally. He just needed a quick glance around the corner to the west side of the house, then he could return to safety behind the tree line. Just then, three more beats from Seth disrupted the quiet. "Goddammit!" he said with no attempt to keep his voice down. No doubt, Clara and anyone else in the house could hear what he'd just heard. If they came out to inspect the scene for themselves, he was caught. Neither the woods nor its underbrush were dense enough to give Jason cover from someone searching for an intruder. His best hope was to beat them to the punch. He wheeled and took off for the stand. He hesitated momentarily, catching a series of muffled sounds coming from the west side of the house, the area he'd wanted to see a second time but never got the chance. As he hurdled into the tree line, he turned back and saw two things that bothered him. The basement windows on the east side looked different than those on the west.

And Clara Riddle was staring at him through the cracked kitchen window.

# CHAPTER 18

Through binoculars, Seth spotted Jason when he was halfway back to the stand where the treescape thinned. He was moving more quickly and in a straighter line than the hike to the house. Good thing, too, it was only five minutes until the end of football practice. He followed Jason's progress for another minute, then lowered himself down the ladder as Jason jogged up to the base of the stand. "It's about time. You forget I need to pick up Chip?"

Jason didn't answer, or even look at him. He just continued on to the truck.

---

Liz stopped pounding. Stopped yelling. Stopped hoping. She slumped down under the window. There had been a man outside. She'd heard his angry cry: "Goddamn it!" But he'd run away; maybe she drove him away.

She looked back at the window—the E and the L of her HELP were smeared beyond recognition from the pounding. The image went out of focus from welling tears. She rubbed her eyes hard with dirty knuckles until they began to sting. Tears weren't going to keep her alive. She kneeled down and ground her scabbed elbow across the concrete.

---

They made it to the truck in good time. Jason kept up a strong pace despite the burning sensation coming from his torn-up knee.

"I appreciate you rushing back, but I'm getting a little old for that kind of pace," Seth said, grabbing the side of the truck. "Especially in my work boots," he added after a deep breath.

Jason didn't comment.

"What is it?" Seth could see Jason was somewhere else. "Did you see something?"

"I don't know. I had to take off because of your stupid banging, before I could tell for sure."

"What did you want me to do? The wind wasn't allowing the cardinal call to get to the house, so I created a better signal. What do you think you saw?"

Jason pulled onto the road. "The basement windows on the far side of the house had grey Plexiglas nailed behind them. I didn't see them right away but as I got up to leave I thought I saw the word "HELP" painted on one of them. I was going back to look when you started your little orchestra, so I never got a chance."

"Holy shit! Are you going to tell Burnett?" Seth asked.

"I don't know. I only saw it for a split second. Plus, I'm not completely sure that's what I saw. The word was written backwards—even the letters were backwards," Jason said.

Seth wrote the word in the air with his finger. "Yeah, but from inside it would be written right to left."

"I got that—I'm just saying that with the letters going the wrong direction, I'm less certain if it actually said 'Help.' If it did, a couple of the letters were pretty malformed. So I'm not sure…" Jason shook his head. "I don't know."

"Do you want to pick up Chip and go back?"

"Can't. I gotta get home. Clara Riddle saw me running into the woods," Jason said.

"So? What can she do to you?"

"It's not what *she'll* do; it's what Sheriff Burnett will do. He knows about my little encounter with the college kids and was more than clear that I was to stay a helluva long way from Clara Riddle." Jason considered whether to tell Seth about what he thought he'd heard while at the house but he was still too unsure of it himself.

Chip Jenkins was the only kid still waiting for a ride and was not happy about it. He climbed in the back seat and slammed the door—hard. Jason and Seth each tried to engage the "disrespected" teen during the ride but their attempts only elicited a series of one-word responses. They were a few blocks from the Jenkins house when Jason used a new tactic. "Hey Bud, sorry we were late but we lost track of time planning the upcoming deer season. We both think you are ready to come along this year." The mopey teen straightened and leaned forward. Jason looked over at Seth who mouthed the words, "What the…?"

Jason came to a stop in front of the house and looked at Chip through the mirror. "You just need to okay it with your mom first." The newly energized teen hurried out the back door.

"Nice save," Seth whispered, then changed the subject. "So are you planning to go back out there tonight—make sure?"

"Absolutely. I need to know what I saw, maybe get a picture of it and get it to the sheriff. He'll be plenty pissed about me not letting go, but he'll also do the right thing and go take a look for himself."

"Give me a call if you want me to come along. I should be able to sneak away for a while."

"I'll work out a game plan and call you." Jason sat in the parked truck for a moment, staring ahead. The more he tried to envision the window, the less he was sure the markings formed a message. Maybe the others were right; maybe his grief over the wrenching events of two years ago was the true captain of the ship. He wondered if it had been steering him this entire time. A moment later he blinked back to action and peeled away from the curb.

Jason heard the phone ring just before he got to the door of his house. He burst through the kitchen to see his mom holding the cordless phone, reading the caller ID.

"Don't answer it!" Jason shouted.

Hannah looked at him, confused and a little bothered by his loud command. He grabbed the phone from her as it rang a second time and checked the called ID. He pressed the talk button, "What's up, Sheriff?"

---

"What did he say?"

"He said he would handle it right away."

"That was all he said?"

"He said that I wouldn't have to worry about this happening again. He sounded very angry."

"Good."

General Attar turned from Clara and called Muhab. "We need to move to a new safe house." He listened to the resulting question. "As soon as you can make it happen—safely!"

---

Sheriff Burnett pulled up to the Kendall house less than five minutes after ending the phone call. Jason met him at the front door and invited him into the living room. The sheriff shook his head at all the quilting material and equipment before turning his attention to Jason.

"So you say you've been home for the last hour?"

"That's right, Sheriff." Jason didn't dare address him as "Pat" after their last conversation.

"Why weren't you at work?"

"My men finished up the job at your house today so I came home to complete the paperwork; I can go down and get it for you." He paused and the sheriff shook off the idea. Jason went on. "My only other job is in demo phase right now and I let my employees do most of that on their own."

"Why did Clara Riddle claim to have seen you at her house a half hour ago? Her description was dead-on, Jason."

"I just saw her last night, Sheriff. Of course her description was dead-on," Jason fired back and wondered if he saw some doubt creep into the sheriff's face. It was his mom's idea to change his shirt and put on a baseball hat before the sheriff got to the house.

"I don't believe a goddamn word you're saying. I don't know what is going on with you and that house and I don't care. I am going to start patrolling that area myself and if I see you within five miles, you're going to jail."

"Sheriff, I own the land right next door. You can't bust me for being on my own property."

"You just watch me. I let the privacy thing with the St. Joe students slide 'cause you're going through a real tough emotional time. I can only imagine what it's like to lose your whole family, but this ends right now!" The sheriff was working himself into a real rage. "You're a good kid but something's going on with you, Jason. And whatever it is, you are not going to bother any more residents because of it. This is our last conversation about this. The next time I get a call about you, all bets are off. I'm hauling you in and we'll check out everything you've been up to. You got it?"

The threat pushed Jason's anger button. "Sheriff, I don't understand why you are hassling *me*? I'm not the one who made some woman my punching bag. Have you forgotten about that? Have you thought about how are you going to feel when some woman turns up in a pond somewhere and you're sitting at your desk making sure I don't step on my own property?"

"You best remember who you're talking to," Burnett threatened.

"What is going on in here?" Hannah interjected, striding into the room. Both men were silent for a moment, waiting for the other to explain.

"Have you been home for the last hour, Hannah?" asked Burnett, finally.

"All afternoon, Pat. Yes."

"How about your son here?"

"About an hour or so, I guess. He said he had some paperwork to do and went down to his office in the basement. I called him twice to light the grill half an hour ago and it's still not lit. We're having a special girl over for dinner tonight. You'd think he'd pay some attention."

Jason tried to hide the surprise about the special guest, but both Hannah and Sheriff Burnett caught the mixture of anger and alarm.

"When you're finished here, I still need that grill lit," Hannah said to Jason, then headed back to the kitchen.

Jason spoke first after she left. "I'm sorry, Sheriff, I didn't mean to get angry, but I don't understand what I've done wrong. I tried to find out who hurt that girl just like you would have if you were me. When I couldn't, I let it go. I told you that yesterday."

Burnett looked him over. "Bullshit." He walked out the door and turned back to Jason. "And your mom's a bad liar."

Jason walked toward the kitchen and saw three place settings neatly laid out in the dining room. "Thanks, Mom. I think he bought it," he said as he gave her a quick hug.

"You know I don't like lying," she said.

Jason nodded once and changed the subject. "Mom, please tell me you didn't invite Kate to dinner."

"I did. And you should be ashamed of yourself for not doing it first," she said, handing him a bag of frozen peas to open. "My condition doesn't require full-time observation. I get through each day just fine. If something does happen—and I can't remember the last seizure—it's going to occur well after my body shuts down for the night." She took the open bag from Jason and poured half the bag into a small saucepan. "I understand your concern if you are going to be out all night. *Are* you going to be out all night?"

Jason shook his head. "Probably not—but I thought she could stop by later just in case things go late."

Hannah shook her head as she flipped a pat of butter on the peas. "Then the real reason you want her here is because you want her here."

"Mom, you're not making sense."

"Yes, I am, and you know it. If you want to share the company of a wonderful woman like Kate, then you invite her for dinner. You don't ask her to come over, then leave, just so she can hang around to be here when you get back."

"It's not like that. I need to find out what happened at that house on Friday." He pointed a finger at her. "You're the one who told me to stay with this thing. Well, you were right—something's just not kosher and I need to double-check something before I pull Burnett back in. I wasn't sure how late I was going to be so I asked her to be here just in case."

"Oh, bull," she said as she pulled three massive bone-in chicken breasts from the refrigerator.

"I just took her out for dinner last night and now she's coming for dinner again tonight? Don't you think that's a bit much?"

"You can eat your dinner outside if you're scared," she said. "She's going to be here in ten minutes. I suggest you go get cleaned up."

"I thought you needed me to start the grill?"

"I bought the grill because it has a push-button start, remember?" She shook her head at the peas. "Sometimes, child..." she waved a wood spoon toward the hall entrance. "Now go on."

"I'm going, I'm going." And he went.

Kate was right on time. After some forced small talk, Jason went out to the patio to put the marinated chicken breasts on the grill. They were going to take at least 45 minutes to cook; there was no way he was going to make it back to the Riddle house before shadows covered the basement window. He pulled a chair up in front of the large Weber grill and thought about his expectations for tonight's trip back to the Riddle house. Seth was right-on with his question, "And then what?" "HELP" might be scrawled on the window, the sheriff was threatening him, and Clara Riddle was not only hiding something, she was now on the lookout for him. He needed to be better prepared for the eventualities that were to come—all of them.

He was staring blankly at the grill when Kate came through the back door with a beer and a glass of wine. She handed Jason the beer. "This is the second school night in a row I've been drinking," she said.

"I better not see it affect your grades," he said.

He pulled another chair in front of the grill, leaving the small bistro table all alone in the corner of the small concrete patio.

"You were looking pretty intense when I walked out. Care to share?" she asked.

He struggled to shake other thoughts from his mind, before gaining the moment. "No, just a lot goin' on."

"Anything I can do?"

He shook his head. "I'm sorry if you're getting too much Kendall time. I didn't know mom was inviting you for dinner."

"I'm enjoying it, but Sally isn't real tickled about it. She ran under the bed when I got home today and still wouldn't come out before I left."

"I'll talk to the cat—tell her it's my fault," he said.

"Unfortunately, I think we're beyond that. I've scheduled a counseling session for Tuesday. We have a lot to sort through."

Jason smiled. "It sounds like you two are doing the right thing."

Jason opened the grill and leaned back as pent up smoke billowed up and dispersed above his head. He turned the chicken breasts a quarter turn each, closed the lid and turned off the middle burner. Crisp, diamond-shaped grill marks set the tone for a great meal. He smiled, remembering his dad's words, "Take pride in your grilling. If a woman takes over your grill, your tools will be next."

"We celebrated a birthday at the office today." Kate said. "Normally someone brings in a little dessert but since the birthday girl is also going on maternity leave soon, my boss decided we should have lunch brought in for everybody. You'll never guess what I found out when I went to pick up the food."

Jason sat back down. "What?"

"It turns out I'm having dinner tonight at the estate of a high-brow future politician! How 'bout that?" She gave him a playful slap on the leg.

"Oh, for God's sake. Is Weezie greeting customers with, 'Welcome to Vera's, vote for Jason'?" he asked.

"I was a little early, so I told her about the great meal I had last night at Fresco. She asked me about it and obviously your name came up and off she went about her young, handsome councilman. I think she sees the U.S. Senate for you one day."

Jason took a pull of the beer and refused to respond.

"It sounds like you're pretty organized. I can't believe you haven't told me," she said.

"I didn't tell you because I'm not running," he said. "I swear if she tells one more person that I am, she's going to find her root beer laced with orange juice."

"Ooh, careful there, Slugger, aren't you in trouble with the law already? I'm pretty sure root beer tainting is a felony in this state."

"Just don't encourage her, okay?" he begged.

"I'm sorry. I got the impression you were on board. To listen to her talk, you'd think you had some real plans for the city."

"You know what my plan would be? Minimize the role of government. In a town this size, a council shouldn't have to meet more than once a quarter, every two months at the most. Put a plan together for the city and revisit it every few months to make sure things are moving in the right direction; if they aren't, make adjustments. My dad was a part of this city's government for years. He spent hour after hour dealing with people who would complain about ridiculous stuff like their property values going down because their neighbor's kids were leaving their trikes out in the driveway. People want all their annoyances settled and whims satisfied." He took another swig of beer to stave off a long rant. "If the topics were just changing traffic patterns, public safety, tax strategies, and so on, maybe. But listening to calls about lemonade stands requiring a permit—my head would explode inside a week."

"Do people seriously do that?" Kate asked.

"My dad once took twenty calls in one week from someone complaining that a neighbor had a Frisbee on the roof of his house and it was spoiling the 'feel' of the neighborhood. Finally, to make the phone stop ringing, my dad hauled his ladder over there and took down the Frisbee himself. And here's the best part: the people who lived in the house were on vacation at the time and the person who kept calling knew it."

"No way! Is that person still around? We should throw a bunch of Frisbees in his yard."

"Now you're the one wanting to break the law," he said. "Most people have common sense. The problem is, you never hear from those people. They take care of things on their own. It's that small vocal minority who are always asking for something," he said.

"The 80-20 rule. Twenty percent of the people causing eighty percent of the problem," Kate said.

"Sounds about right. The scary part is, it works. Look at the federal government. A far-right candidate runs against a far-left opponent because those are the candidates who represent the people shouting the loudest. The sensible people in the middle never have a horse in the race."

"Maybe we need someone to speak for the self-helpers… Jason," she said not so subtly.

"How long on the chicken?" Hannah asked through the screen door.

"Twenty minutes," he said and got up to flip the breasts.

"Ya know, Kate, you don't need to stick around after dinner. I'm not planning to be out that late." He looked up at the sky. "Plus, it's looking like it might rain."

"What are you planning to do?" she asked.

He didn't mention his visit to the Riddle house earlier in the day. "I'm hoping to close the loop on this thing from Friday."

"You be careful. Don't do anything stupid."

"I'll be on my best behavior. But like I said, it's not going to be all night, so no need to stay."

"Are you kidding? I brought fabric with me—your mom just gave me a short quilting lesson. I'm making Sally a cat quilt—figured I should start small," she said.

"Are you sure she won't think you're trying to buy back her love?" he asked.

"Just one more reason for the counseling," she said after a sip of wine.

Fifteen minutes later Jason opened the grill and pressed the meat with his finger. It bounced back nicely. Done. He never used a thermometer because it poked the meat and let the juices run out, plus his ego wouldn't allow it. Kate joined him at the grill and he instructed her on the "Jason Kendall rare-to-well-done touch methodology." He stepped back a half step to let her try. She poked at the thick part of the chicken breast and agreed with his assessment.

Their bodies were just a few inches apart. Jason noticed it first, and stole a glance at Kate. She felt it but kept her eyes on the grill. The moment held. He brought his hand to the small of her back and she curled to face him. Jason felt her warm breath and even warmer eyes on him, but he wasn't sure if he was ready for his first "first kiss" in ten years. Kate wrapped a hand around his head. She was absolutely ready.

The sound of a car rumbling to a halt in the driveway broke their embrace. Clint Baskett got out of the sheriff's department cruiser and strutted over.

"Jason Kendall, turn around and clasp your hands behind your back. You're under arrest."

# CHAPTER 19

Muhab pulled his Passat into the second row of parking spaces. The restaurant was rather busy for 8:30 at night. The parking spaces adjacent to the building were full. His car was parked in the middle of the next row—perfect.

He went inside and ordered a burger, fries and water to go. After receiving the meal, he walked back out to the parking lot and opened the passenger door of the car to the left of his Passat. The navy blue Chevy Impala pulled out and made its way to the interstate. Less than thirty minutes later it zipped by the old farmhouse north of Cedar River. Ten minutes and several rights and lefts later, it slowed back at that same farmhouse. Omar pulled into the gravel driveway. Muhab got out and hurried up the dark stairs and through the front door. The Impala backed out and sped back toward the Interstate.

Clara Riddle walked slowly down the stairs. A small .38 caliber pistol was hidden in the right pocket of the heavy denim dress that hung on her. General Attar had given her the gun after she saw the man she thought to be Jason Kendall scurrying into the woods behind the house a few hours earlier. He instructed her that if he came back and seemed a little too wise about the activities going on at the house, she should put a bullet in his chest.

"Hello, Clara. I understand you've had more visitors, recently." Muhab hadn't seen Clara since Friday night.

She recounted the visit from last night and how she spotted the same man in her yard earlier today.

"So other than apologizing for upsetting you, he only asked about the house?" Muhab was standing in the dining room with the lights still off, trying to put himself inside the mind of the intruder.

"He offered to fix my window. Some nonsense about it breaking all the way in the winter." She pointed through the kitchen to the cracked glass. "Been like that for five winters and never been a problem. I thought he was just a crook trying to scam money from an old woman 'til I saw him running into the woods this afternoon."

"What about the woman?" he said.

"What about her?"

"Yesterday. What did the woman have to say when they were here?"

"Nothing, really. I think she was embarrassed that they were here at all," she said. "Really pretty girl. She could do better than that swindler."

Muhab nodded and looked around the room again, visualizing what the man had seen. *What made him come back today?*

Muhab asked Clara to recall exactly what she had seen earlier in the day. She did, but he didn't hear anything new.

"What about the woman downstairs? Is she okay?" he asked.

"I suppose. I don't know. The other man told me not to feed her today, said it wasn't necessary."

He nodded slowly, considering the order. "Why don't you go ahead and give her something to eat—keep her satisfied, quiet."

"Okay. I was just doing like I's told." Her tone was defensive.

"I know. I am very thankful for your service over the years. Your reward is almost here."

She turned for the kitchen, the gun still uneasy in her pocket. She didn't want rewards; she wanted someone to pay for her son's death. She wanted someone to pay for the way her husband was denied his due compensation and respect after Vietnam. She wanted payment for his suicide and the weight with which it hung on her son. And she wanted vengeance against the U.S. military for attacking the harmless Taliban and snuffing out her only child in their loathsome barrage. "To hell with rewards," she mumbled.

---

Jason sat in the cell with a teenager whose pants hung as low as his sneer stretched tall. Jason thought about how much more effort it took for the punk to constantly pull up his pants than to just loop a belt around them once first thing in the morning. Or how easy it would have been to just buy pants that fit in the first place. He couldn't help but laugh when the kid started to stretch his facial muscles, which had obviously grown as tired of the forced sneer as Jason had.

The outer iron bar door clanged and Sheriff Burnett walked through the short hall to the row of cells, stopping at the third and final cell. "Hey, Ditch, your mom's outside again. Third time this month you've interrupted her dinner. She doesn't seem too happy."

"Is she really mad?" The kid didn't move from his perch in the far corner.

"Yep, she's damned pissed this time. What do you expect? You tried to swipe the TV from the waiting area of a car repair shop." Burnett paused and shook his head. "Ditch, you don't even have a car. You didn't think Myron might get a little suspicious?"

"That old man's got a lawsuit on his hands," Ditch said with the full sneer back again. He started limping toward the sheriff.

"I heard the TV got real heavy when the socket wrench hit you behind the knee," the sheriff said and opened the door. "You better include the TV's cost in the lawsuit because your mom says *she* ain't paying for one penny of it."

"Whatever," Ditch said. The sneer evaporated as he crossed through the cell door but the limp suddenly got much worse.

Burnett looked over at Jason, who stood up from the cot he'd been sitting on for the past two hours. "Sit down," he ordered. Jason complied. "That's the difference between me and Ditch's mom. If someone crosses me, he can sit in here until I'm finished with dinner. And when they really piss me off, I have dessert and read the paper, too."

"What is this all about, Sheriff? Clint wouldn't tell me anything. And I have to tell you, he's got some serious nightstick compensation issues."

"Shut up, Jason! If I ask a question, you answer it. Other than that, you keep your mouth shut," the sheriff said. "My lovely bride, June, made my favorite meal for dinner as a kind of thank you for finally getting the basement finished. Ham, green beans, and homemade au gratin potatoes. She even made me a raspberry-blackberry pie for dessert. The only problem was we didn't have any ice cream so I went to the store on my way home from work to pick some up. Turns out not everyone was having a terrific homemade meal for dinner. Your good buddy Seth Jenkins was also at the store picking up one of those rotisserie chickens and some fries from the deli. You want to guess where he said he was after his shift at the plant?"

"No idea," Jason said meekly.

"Wrong answer. It's getting to a point, Jason, where if your lips are moving, you're lying. But I have a long, good history with you *and* your family, so I'm going to give you a chance to turn that around. I'm going to make a call to Ms. Riddle and tell her we have her trespasser in custody. The believability of the explanation you are about to give me will go a long way to determining my recommendation as to how she should proceed with the prosecution of the offense."

Jason stayed quiet for a time before giving his explanation, "First of all, Seth was on *my* property only. He was nowhere near Clara Riddle's." The sheriff nodded. "When I visited Ms. Riddle last night, she didn't seem right. I can't put my finger on it, but she seemed uncomfortable in some way—like she was guarding something. You put that with the girl who was hit last weekend, the gunshots, and whatever else—I'm still afraid something bad is happening there."

"Why not call me or one of my deputies? I told you to stop your amateur investigation. I would have been happy to visit the home to follow-up my officer's visit Saturday morning. I could have judged her nerves for myself."

"You're right, Sheriff. It's just that after I screwed up the thing with the St. Joe students, I wanted to have something more concrete before approaching you. I know I'm missing something—something that could help you. I was hoping if I saw the scene again, something else from Friday might come back to me."

Sheriff Burnett looked down then up at Jason, shaking his head. "I gave you a chance Jason. Remember that." He walked through the door and slammed it behind him.

"Wait! Where are you going?"

"To get the truth… from Clara Riddle."

---

Working in the dark was standard operating procedure for Clara. She was no different than most people who lived in the same place for a number of years. Movement becomes second nature—cupboard height, the location of the power button on the TV, or the number of steps to the basement landing. She prepared the scant meal—a bologna sandwich, soda crackers, and a glass of water—under the cover of darkness.

Cup and plate in hand, she walked to the living room, leaned her back against the side of the curio and pushed. The curio began to slide and the light Muhab had left on in the entrance momentarily stunned her; she usually took the stairs in the dark. "Goddamn it." She was going to have to pull the curio back in front of the entrance to keep the light from the base of the stairs from leaking out to the main floor.

Clara stepped into the hidden staircase and down a couple steps, then turned back and set the cup and plate down on the landing. It was going to take all her strength to slide the curio shut. She grabbed the handle at the rear of the cabinet and slowly moved it across the carpet. She stopped twice to rest, but finally got the entire cut-out entrance covered. When she lifted the food tray, she saw the light switch high on the wall. With the light at the bottom of the staircase and having always worked in the dark, she'd forgotten about the second switch. "Goddamn it!"

With the curio covering the entrance, she didn't hear the knock at the front door as she started down the stairs.

# CHAPTER 20

"Food's here. Back up."

Liz was startled at first by the words spoken from behind the heavy wood door. Tonight the curt words from the old woman felt almost exhilarating. The food was unusually late. Liz was afraid it might not come at all, more proof that her death was imminent. She scurried to the other end of the room and waited for the door to open. It opened six inches, as far as the chain would allow. Liz was surprised to see light spilling in from the hall. *Food's late and the hall is lit? What is going on?* she thought. A paper plate was slid into the room. The sides bent as it was forced through the small opening, upsetting the plain bologna sandwich and six soda crackers it carried. A small Styrofoam cup of water was placed behind the plate. The door was closed and locked before Liz crawled over to begin her dinner. She reset the sandwich and piled the soda crackers in a neat stack next to it.

Four days earlier, during Maria's final encounter with the monster, Liz had received the same meal through the same small opening. That day she grabbed the cup and devoured the water so fast, small trails had run out both sides of her mouth. Then she put a whole soda cracker in her mouth, and choked, attempting to swallow it so quickly. She'd stopped eating and forced back tears. Liz had decided at that moment, *I may be in a cage but I will not act like an animal.* Tonight, she took a bite of the sandwich and forced herself to chew ten times before swallowing and following it with a respectful sip of water.

Before that first meal on Sunday, and each time since, she was warned to move to the opposite wall. She watched as the meager bologna and crackers were roughly thrust through the opening. The same meal arrived the following two days, at the same time; a couple hours before sunset. Tonight's meal showed up several hours late, but at least it had come. She looked at the window where she'd heard the person yesterday and told herself again, "Don't give up hope."

---

Sheriff Burnett knocked a third time with no answer. He wasn't completely surprised; there were no lights on in the house when he pulled up. He backed off the porch and walked around the house to the east, facing Jason's property. The curtain on the side door's window was a thin material that allowed only a veiled view inside. Burnett could see the entrance to the kitchen on the left and a basement straight ahead. He continued around to the back of the house but found only more quiet darkness before turning back. He stopped back at the side entrance then angled for the garage.

---

Clara was still breathing hard from having to pull the heavy cabinet open and closed again following her food delivery when she walked into the dark kitchen for a glass of water. After returning the glass, she spotted a figure moving in front of the garage. She pulled back the curtains slightly and saw the sheriff's cruiser parked in the driveway. Then she recognized the sheriff as he turned from the garage service door toward the house. She let the curtains fall and adjusted the position of the gun weighing down one side of her dress.

---

"I am considering making some alterations to your plan."

"Why?" It was a reflex. Muhab knew it was the wrong response before it got all the way out of his mouth.

General Attar rose and pointed his finger at Muhab, "Remember who you are speaking to! It is I who conceived this plan and rolled out the strategy for its success. I am the one sending the infidels of this opulent nation to their graves." He was standing in front of Muhab. "I am the man Allah has chosen to end six hundred years of despair for my people. You will not ask me 'Why.' You will do as I command."

Muhab was trying to summon up the courage to keep from cowering backward. It wasn't working.

"It is your inability to control your men or create a secure environment which has caused me to reconsider the plan and ready the necessary contingencies."

"What can I do?" Muhab asked after the general turned away.

"I am not convinced your group is ready—far too undisciplined. We will complete a full rehearsal on-site before the actual offensive."

"When?" Muhab caught himself. "When would you like to perform the rehearsal? We are just days from the attack. I will need to coordinate our resources."

General Attar showed him the schedule.

Muhab nodded. "If I may, sir—your plan is the definition of clairvoyance; I do not understand what you think could go wrong," Muhab said.

"The plan is only as precise as the men executing it. Our men are faithful but they are not elite in their abilities. Our best-trained soldiers have been reserved for phases two and three of the war, so we are left asking lesser men to perform simple but vital operations. And now a man who sent law enforcement here days ago was seen running from the property again today." He pounded his fist on the table. "This battle cannot be undermined by a stupid hunter plodding through the woods, nor can it be undone by a unit leader who has not planned for such a disturbance."

"It won't, General," Muhab said. "The situation is in complete control. This was a situation no one could have foreseen; it is being handled."

A soft knock interrupted them. It was Clara, again short of breath. "The sheriff is outside and he's coming this way."

---

Jason waited almost three more hours alone in the corner cell before the outer door clanged open and Sheriff Burnett walked in.

"What took you so long? Did you find anything?" Jason said anxiously.

"Nope. No ghosts, no goblins, not even a black cat," Burnett said. "Heck, I didn't even find Ms. Riddle."

"Where did she go? Did she move?"

"She was getting groceries while I was there. She's home now," Burnett said.

"Did you look around the yard while you were there? What about the garage? That's where I saw them Friday."

"It's not my first night on the job, Jason. I know how to follow my nose."

"What took you so long? It's pushing midnight."

"Like I said, I don't go out of my way for guys who dick me around," the sheriff said.

"So are you going to let me out of here? I need to go check on my mom," Jason said.

"You know what, Jason? You would do well to not speak again." The sheriff wagged his finger. "I already checked in with your mom, and someone is already with her, *as you know*. Now let me finish what I have to say. I didn't get to see Ms. Riddle because she was grocery shopping when I stopped there. But I left my card in the doors and she called me back a little later."

"What did she say?" Jason was holding the bars to the cell, begging for Burnett's response.

"Against my strong suggestions to the contrary, Ms. Riddle does not want to press criminal charges at this time."

"Why not?"

"You like it here that much? You want me to keep working on her?"

Jason kept his quizzical look on the sheriff. "So I'm free to go?"

"First, you need to tell me what you're holding back. You've never been a liar, Jason. Something has you spiraling down a bad path and you need to tell me what it is."

"When you were a cop on the beat, what did you do when you knew something wasn't right but you couldn't prove it?" Jason asked.

"I moved on to something I could prove. What is it that's not right, Jason?"

"Clara Riddle, the guys from Friday night, that house. I don't know."

"I've been at this a long time and I've got to tell you the thing that seems *not right*, Jason, is you. I won't charge you with anything tonight, but you've used up your three strikes. Next time, it's out of my hands. If you need some more time to get over your terrible anniversary or need to speak with a professional, then do it. But I can't allow you to keep breaking the law for some misguided emotional crusade."

Sheriff Burnett pulled open the door to the cell.

"How'd you do that? Don't you need a key?" Jason asked.

"It was never locked."

Jason saw Kate's car parked out front when he pulled into the driveway. He untied his boots under the light left on for him at the back door, and took them off after stepping inside. He thought about his dad telling him, after his freshman year of college, that he never waited up for Jason in high school because he knew when Jason stayed out past curfew. He just checked where Jason's shoes were. If they had been taken off outside, Jason was past curfew and trying to sneak to his room undetected. If they were inside the door, he was home on time and less cautious.

Jason's bedroom was the first door on the left on the second floor. But he went into the guest bedroom on the right. Kate was sleeping on her side atop the comforter with a thin floral quilt pulled up over her. She was still wearing her clothes from earlier. Jason sat down on the bed and put a hand on Kate's shoulder. Her eyes slowly opened and found Jason's. Surprise and delight wriggled through her sleepy voice. "You're home."

"Yep. You want to go home?"

"No," she said, less hazy.

"Good." He leaned down and Kate's arms wrapped naturally around him as if it were the thousandth time she'd done it.

The kiss was long and exciting, the way a first kiss is supposed to be. When it finally broke, they lay tightly against one another with their foreheads pressing together. Jason let the moment stand, fighting back the half-dozen corny or glib platitudes jumping around his head. After another kiss, Kate pushed herself farther into the middle of the bed and invited Jason to join her.

"This might sound a little juvenile, but I got kind of excited when I got home and your car was still here," he told her.

"I can top that. I put in two breath mints when I lay down—just in case." She started to giggle. "I woke up later because the side of my mouth was burning from the hot cinnamon."

They kissed more, then talked some and then kissed some more. An hour later Kate thought she heard a noise and told Jason to go to his room. He looked at her, confused.

"Your mom is just down the hall. I don't want her thinking I'm some kind of hussy. Now go!"

"Kate, I'm thirty-six years old. I don't need my mom's permission to be with a woman."

"Good for you. But you need mine," she said. "And I plan on being around a lot. So out of respect for your mom, I'm telling you to go."

Jason knew it wasn't an argument he was going to win. Plus, he found her wholesomeness kind of charming. He kissed her again until she finally pushed him away and he dutifully shuffled off to his room.

# CHAPTER 21

## THURSDAY

Jason was the first one awake in the house. He sat down at the kitchen table and dialed the number for Cy Corey, the only other full-time remodeling contractor in town. Cy answered on the first ring and Jason asked if he'd ever done work for Clara Riddle. The name wasn't familiar so Jason explained the location of the house.

"Nope, can't say I've done any work out that way that I can remember," he said.

"You're kind of an old duffer. How far back can you remember?" Jason asked.

"I'm young enough to kick your tail. I haven't done any work out around County 12 in the last twenty years; that long enough?"

"More than enough," Jason said.

"Farmers tackle most repairs and additions themselves. Most of 'em are more handy than you and I put together," he said.

"That's for sure. Thanks, Cy."

"When the hell are you moving back to St. Paul, anyhow? I'm getting a little tired of the competition—not that you provide much."

"I'll keep you posted," Jason said.

He clicked off the call and snapped the phone into its holster. The floor above the living room moaned; Kate was moving around in the guest bedroom. Jason walked to the cupboard and pulled out a package of coffee. He was halfway through reading the instructions when Kate walked in.

Jason held up the container. "I'm sorry. I don't know how to make coffee."

Kate walked over, took the canister from him, and kissed him softly. "Good morning." She was wearing a torn St. Joseph College pullover and jeans. She was not fully awake and her hair was tousled but not messy. To Jason, she couldn't look any better.

"So Jailbird, tell me what happened last night," she said.

"The sheriff ran into Seth, who told him we'd been at my deer stand. So I had to spend a good chunk of the night in jail until Sheriff Burnett could get hold of Clara Riddle to see if she wanted to press trespassing charges."

"You spent most of the night in jail because you lied to a sheriff. He called here right after Clint took you away. He told your mom he was disappointed in you and was going to waste some of your time the same way you wasted his. Then he called again about 9:00 to say he was going to make you sweat until midnight." Jason tried not to let her see how foolish he felt.

Kate picked up her bag. "Sorry to kiss and run but I need to get home and get ready for work."

"No problem. I need to get going myself."

She gave him another long kiss. "Call me later?" Jason nodded.

Jason's mind was on anything but work when he got to the dentist's house to continue work on the sunroom addition. He met with his crew while inspecting their work, then spoke with the client.

After a follow-up conversation with his crew chief, he left to meet with a new prospect. He stopped by a convenience store on the way to buy a liter bottle of Diet Dew. They were on special; two for three dollars, so he grabbed a second. It had been another restless night; he was beginning to need the caffeine to keep us his regular energy level.

Feelings of dread about not acting on what he saw in the farmhouse window clashed with the boyish excitement he felt about his budding relationship with Kate. Both emotions were still bouncing around his head as he pulled up to the prospect's house. He took a long drink of soda; the cold carbonated liquid scratched its way down to his stomach. He let it settle and took another long drink for the added energy kick. The second one went down more smoothly.

Jason knocked at the door and a short, slightly greying man greeted him with a warm smile. "Jason Kendall?" he asked. Jason nodded. "C'mon in. Let me show you what I'm looking at doing."

The two men walked down to the lower level of the split-level home. They stood on a bare cement floor, surrounded by walls of concrete block foundation rising halfway up and plastic-covered insulated wood framing running to the ceiling. Two by four stud frames surrounded two would-be bedrooms, a utility room, and a roughed-in bath. Storage boxes, half of which were labeled, "Christmas Decorations" nearly filled one room. A shelf above the washer/dryer and utility sink held assorted cleaning products. Other than that, the entire floor was empty.

Pastor Avery Strait had moved to Cedar River from a large suburban Wisconsin parish six years earlier as a last stop before retirement. He explained to Jason that he and his wife needed to finish the basement because they were adopting his brother's two pre-teen children. He didn't mention what triggered the arrangement, only that it was in the best interest of the children and agreed upon by all involved parties.

"Do you have any other children?" Jason asked.

"A son—Thomas; he lives in Montevideo. He and his wife have two small boys of their own."

"And you're willing to go through the teenage years all over again? You are a far better man than I," Jason said.

He gave Jason a broad, gentle smile. "You're probably right." Somehow the words came off as self-deprecating rather than insulting. "Do you give any kind of 'good cause' discount?" he asked, placing his hand gently on Jason's shoulder. It felt like he was sharing the spirit of God through his touch.

"My rates are always fair, but I think I can tighten my tool belt a little more on this job."

"That would be very kind. Thank you." Pastor Strait nodded as if he willed Jason's response. *This guy is good.* Jason thought, imagining money racing to the church coffers from the parishioners' pockets.

Jason inspected the site for any existing issues and they discussed timelines, strategies, and room uses. When the topic of design and aesthetics came up, Pastor Strait called upstairs for his wife, Helen, to join the conversation. The three of them discussed different design options. Helen introduced expensive ideas; Avery leaned toward a more simple approach. After getting measurements and discussing some technical details, they reached the familiar point in the conversation where the spouses were talking almost exclusively to each other.

Some first interviews took longer; others, like this morning, moved more quickly. But all couples' meetings ended the same way: spouses hammering out differences in vision. Initial impressions of the conversation told Jason this job would turn out like most of the other jobs he'd done for couples. He would soon be building Mrs. Strait's vision, not her husband's.

Jason stepped in and regained control of the conversation. "I'll let the two of you work out the details. In the meantime, I will get you a time and materials estimate for basic construction. We can incorporate the design elements later."

"Sounds good, Jason. I'll walk you out," Pastor Strait said. They got to the door and exchanged a few additional questions.

"How did you hear about us?" asked Jason.

"Neil Lockwood suggested we talk to you. He spoke so highly of your reputation, I asked him what we need to do to get you to visit us on Sundays." He patted Jason on the back again.

"I'm happy at Our Savior's, but thanks for the invitation," Jason said.

"Keep us in mind. I'm sure you know many in our congregation already."

"Funny you should say that. I might be doing some work for another of your parishioners soon."

"Who's that?" Strait asked.

"Clara Riddle."

The pastor's gaze moved to just above Jason's head, trying to place the name. "That name doesn't ring a bell. Are you sure she's a member of First Lutheran?"

"That's what I was told," Jason said.

"Maybe she just hasn't been to services for a while. I'll have to look her up," the pastor said.

Jason shrugged and handed the pastor his business card. "I'll get back to you in a couple days. If you or Mrs. Strait have any questions before, give me a call on the cell number."

Their handshake was interrupted. "What about knotty pine?" Mrs. Strait called from downstairs. Her husband gave Jason a look of pure dread.

Jason got in his truck and smiled through a drink of soda. Pastor Strait may have a whole congregation eating from the palm of his hand on Sundays, but when he came home, the power was in someone else's palm. Neil's neighbor in Minneapolis, Mr. Soucheray, had told him during the remodeling of Neil's parents' house, "A man only has the power in his home maybe four or five days out of the year. You gotta make the most of it." Jason smiled, "You're so right, Souch. You're so right."

Then his thoughts turned to Clara Riddle. *Why did you stop going to church?*, he asked himself. *And how does it fit?*

---

An overweight woman with a smear of frosting dried to her chin walked into the Rockwell Outfitters store, dropped two full bags of clothes on the cashier counter, tipped them over and let the contents spill out.

"I would like to return these," she said, offering Khalid a long receipt.

He looked at the woman then down at the clothes. He could clearly see that several of the clothes had been worn. "Is there anything wrong with them, ma'am?"

"Nope, just decided I didn't want them," she said.

Khalid folded the clothes and divided them into two piles: one with six items, the other with twice that. He placed the smaller stack of clothes between him and the customer. "These have been worn since they were purchased. I cannot take them back; they are yours to keep."

"What? I just tried them on, that's all. The tags are all right here," she said, needing both hands to hold up the mass of tags cut from the garments.

"None of the items have tags on them, ma'am. It is company policy to not accept any clothing in which the tags have been removed." He placed his hand on the taller pile of women's clothes. "We will take these back this one time, but we cannot accept anything that is dirty or worn," he said, moving his hand to the shorter pile.

"What am I suppose to do, take a shower before I try on clothes now?" she asked.

Khalid didn't respond, although he wanted to suggest a shower was probably in order.

"I am not leaving here without my money," she said.

"Perhaps you wish to speak with a manager," he suggested.

"*Perhaps* you can give me back my money for these clothes that didn't fit for shit!" she said, feigning outrage.

"I will get my manager and you can speak with her," he said, remaining detached from her drama.

"Let me have your name first. You're getting your ass fired for accusin' me of wearin' and dirtyin' this shit."

Jan walked behind the counter, passing behind Khalid and stopping at his right arm. Her hand lingered on his pants pocket as she stood beside him.

"Is there something I can help with?" she asked the woman.

"Are you a manager?"

"Yes, ma'am. What can I do for you?"

"Your boy here tried to insinuate that I wore all this before I brought it back. And that is just dead not right," the woman said, still full of fuss.

"Ma'am, as you can see, some of the garments are not fit to resell." She lifted the top shirt off the pile and laid it out on the counter and pointed to the red splotch at the breast line. "This has a food stain right here—maybe marinara or spaghetti sauce?"

"I didn't do that. It must have been there when I bought it," said the woman as she tried to scratch the hard stain away with her fingernail.

Khalid interrupted and asked Jan, "Would you like me to cover the floor?"

Jan nodded and he glanced at the woman again before heading for the back room. She made a sour face at him, forcing the frosting on her chin to crack.

Khalid accounted for his other coworkers' whereabouts before ducking into the break room. He grabbed the "natural" colored backpack with the phrase, "Keep'n It Green" stitched on it above a screen print of a mountain bike. Khalid shook his head at the irony of a person who works in one of the three largest shopping malls in the world promoting saving the environment. He wondered if it was more a commentary on American arrogance or American ignorance.

Khalid took a quick look back at the door, then opened the bag. Behind a pair of sunglasses and gloves with holes where the fingers should be was an oversized wallet attached to a long chain. Such a wallet was not allowed on the floor—it didn't fit the corporate image. He flipped it open. Looking up at him from behind a plastic cover was a picture of his coworker. The ID showed a young man with long black hair framing a dark Mediterranean face. Khalid pulled it from its plastic jacket and slid it into his pocket. He hung the backpack on its hook and returned to the floor.

Muhab would be pleased; it wasn't even noon and already Khalid had completed both tasks assigned him. First, as requested, he had exchanged shifts and was no longer working Saturday. Second, he now had a false ID with which he could rent the moving van for tonight's operation. When he got back on the floor, the upset woman at the counter was waving her arms around in forced disgust. The chunk of frosting dropped from her chin onto the counter.

---

The Pick Me Up was originally a butcher shop and deli located in downtown Cedar River. When a strip mall went up on the west side of town, with a large grocery chain store as its anchor, the owners saw their fresh-meat sales dwindle. However, their carry-out deli lunch business of made-to-order sandwiches and fresh soups remained strong. So, to augment the take-away business, they added earlier hours and a coffee and cappuccino bar. It brought in the additional sales they'd hoped for but, unfortunately, none of the coffee customers ordered sixteen-ounce rib eyes or smoked pork chops with their lattes.

A year later, the couple removed the refrigerated display cases and meat freezers and replaced them with a larger kitchen and more tables and changed the name from Main Street Meats to the Pick Me Up Coffee and Deli. Business professionals and professors from the college filled the eatery for lunch and students swarmed the comfortable surroundings at night. Later, they converted the apartment upstairs to additional seating and small meeting rooms.

Though not a coffee drinker, Jason was a semi-regular at the Pick Me Up because it provided him a quiet place to complete administrative tasks while avoiding the distractions of home. Plus it was the only place in town with reliable Wi-Fi Internet access.

Both of the rear corner tables, which provided the most quiet and privacy on the main floor, were occupied, so Jason set up his laptop and leather portfolio in a small upstairs meeting room. He spent the first hour working on the Strait basement project, then filed his notes and rough project estimate in an electronic folder.

He went downstairs to get a sandwich before starting his second project. The aromas got the best of him and he decided to add a cup of roasted roma tomato soup to the chicken Caesar wrap and carried the tray of food back upstairs. He opened his portfolio and started jotting down all the questions and points of interest regarding Clara Riddle and the events that occurred at her home. He had two full sheets of random notes and questions before he took his first bite of soup. A half-eaten sandwich later, he had nearly filled a third.

He pulled out a couple of fresh sheets from the yellow pad and labeled the first one "Timeline/Events," then restated, in chronological order, all of the "events" scribbled on the first three pages. He pulled another clean sheet from the pad and titled it, "House," then listed all of the items that had to do with the house. The next page was titled, "Facts," another one, "Questions," and the last, "Notable." The first item he wrote under this heading was "Middle Eastern Men—Terrorism?"

His cell rang. The caller ID read, "Seth."

"I thought you were going to call me about going back to that house last night?" Seth said.

"I thought you weren't supposed to use your cell at work," Jason replied.

"I'm on my lunch break. What's going on? What happened last night?"

"I spent the evening in the Rice County jail and got my ass chewed up good by the sheriff. Any guesses how that happened?" Jason asked.

There was a long pause before Seth offered his subdued answer. "Oh, shit. I told Sheriff Burnett I was at the deer stand, didn't I?"

"Bingo."

"I'm really sorry. Did he bust you? Are you in trouble?"

"Naw, Ms. Riddle didn't want to press charges, so I'm cool," Jason said. "But the problem is, I didn't get a chance to go back to the house to see if it was actually the word "HELP" that I saw on the window. On top of that, Burnett is more pissed than ever about my messing around. I'm at the Pick Me Up compiling everything from the last few days, hoping I can jog a memory, find a pattern, or whatever to take to him."

"Have you come up with anything?" Seth asked.

"As I look it over, it seems like a pretty compelling argument that something isn't right at the Riddle house. On the other hand, it could be seen as nothing more than a bunch of innuendo and speculation. Maybe I'll just hand it off to Burnett and hope for the best."

"What if he blows you off? If he's already pissed at you, he may not give it a fair look," Seth said. "If what you saw was a cry for help and someone in there is in real danger, it may be better to do something about it first and beg the sheriff for forgiveness rather than to wait and ask his permission."

"Burnett's a good man; he's not going to let someone suffer to punish me."

"I know. I'm just saying that your observations might be a little tainted in his mind," Seth said. He didn't receive an immediate response, so he backed up his point. "Do what you think is best, but just so you know, if you want go looking for a little more evidence, I am absolutely available tonight—for whatever."

Jason hung up and clicked the Internet Explorer icon on his laptop. When his Yahoo homepage appeared, he moved his cursor to the

Google search box near the top. He typed in the words, "Islamic terrorists" and pressed "Enter."

---

Four miles northwest of the Pick Me Up, another man was scanning the Internet. The laptop computer screen showed responses to a chat room topic. He clicked on the "New Post" icon under the discussion topic, "Let's Make a Live Phil Chat Happen!" then followed the prompts and keyed in the message.

> We are running into some interference. We need to move the live chat date forward to Saturday or Sunday. A#1 will perform a walkthrough on Saturday @ 12:00 PM central time. We will inform you immediately following the test of anything that may affect your particular location. Please be online, prepared to receive these updates as they arrive.
>
> Expect to go live Sunday @ 2:00 PM central time, but technical difficulties may warrant a launch immediately following the test on Saturday. Please coordinate your local resources to be ready for a live chat on both Saturday and Sunday. It may be difficult, but we have put a great deal of work into this. You are prepared for such adversity. Again, I cannot tell you strongly enough how critical you are to our long-term goals. You will be remembered forever for the great victory you achieve in the coming days.
>
> Please respond that you received this message and again after your resources are confirmed ready. If you are having difficulty, contact me through the appropriate channels.

General Attar reread his message several times and made slight alterations to the verbiage. Convinced it contained the "voice" of someone trying to launch an online celebrity interview, he clicked back out of the site, synched the information with his Blackberry and shut down the computer. Each of the thirteen regional cell leaders checked the site four times each day: 6 AM, noon, 6 PM, and midnight eastern time. He checked his watch and made a mental note to check the site again in two hours after the next regional ping.

The next order of business was to inspect the detonators. After that he would go over his revisions of Muhab's plan. The tactics and preplanning were sound, but the general wasn't convinced all members of the team were up to their assigned tasks. It was time to refigure who on the team would live. And who needed to die.

# CHAPTER 22

Jason's search on Islamic terrorists had segued into more instructive searches on "Islamic Fundamentalism" and "Muslim views toward women." He dumped the most informative sites into a "Favorites" folder for future reference. One article suggested a link between the Islamic portrayal of women in society to the practice of modern slavery. Jason went with the segue and keyed "human trafficking" into the Google box. Over three million hits came back. After perusing three sites, Jason considered that, although it was a possibility, the Riddle house didn't fit a typical trafficking site; those were typically located in densely populated, urban, or industrial areas. But he saved the articles into the folder anyway.

His cell rang again. This time it was Kate. The conversation started out a little tense. Jason got the sense, not from her words but from her tone, that she was disappointed that he hadn't called first and much earlier. He apologized and explained that he was in the middle of something that was taking much longer than he originally thought.

"So am I going to see you tonight?" she asked.

"I hope so—," he started.

"Good. Me too," she interrupted.

"But here's the thing—I might have something else I need to do."

"Oh. Okay." Her words were suddenly guarded.

"It's not that I don't want to see you—I do. I really do. But I'm working on something and it's sixty-forty that it's going to take up some or all of my night."

"What is it?"

"I'd rather not talk about it until it happens," Jason said.

"Okay, I guess. Call me when you know what your plans are," she said.

"You'll be the first to know—promise."

Jason clicked off the call and dialed Neil's office phone at the college. "Hey, Neil. I need a favor. Can you recommend someone in your Religious Studies department for me to talk to about the differences between Christians and Muslims?"

"That's an odd request," Neil said. "Do you have a new client who is Muslim?"

*Thank you for the out*, Jason thought. "Potentially. I don't know much about the culture and I have enough ways to lose business without adding 'sticking my foot in my mouth' to the list. I have a potential dream client over in Cannon Falls. He bought a fixer-upper, then figured out he's not so good at the fixing up."

"The best person to talk to is Dr. Iman Meshal in the Middle Eastern Studies Department. He's a great guy. I'm sure he'd be happy to walk you through Islamic traditions and their cultural conventions."

"St. Joe's has an entire department dedicated to studying the Middle East?"

"Not exactly. There is no degree available. It's under the International Studies umbrella. A student who majors in international business or religious history, etcetera, will need to take Mid-East Studies courses."

Neil gave Jason Dr. Meshal's office number, then transferred him directly to the professor's extension. The professor's lengthy voicemail message stated his teaching schedule, office hours, and email address. Jason checked his watch: 1:50. Office hours for the professor would begin in ten minutes; if Jason got lucky with parking, he could be there in fifteen.

Jason didn't need luck. He parked in the visitor's pay lot, which was never more than a quarter full. Most students living on campus had annual parking permits and those who commuted were not about to pay the exorbitant rates of the short-term lot. He was standing outside Dr. Meshal's office right at 2:00. He waited in the hall in front of the closed office door for twenty minutes and was about to leave when another man approached. "Are you looking for Dr. Meshal?" the man asked in a deep, heavily accented voice.

Jason nodded, "Yes I am."

"He is out with sickness. Is there anything I can do for you?"

"Dr. Lockwood gave me his name—said he was a good person to talk to about Muslim customs."

The man offered his hand. "I am Doctor Raznik, Department Chair. I may be of some assistance to you." He shook Jason's hand and ushered him into his office across the hall. Jason stumbled through some general questions about Muslim beliefs and how he could show proper respect when doing contract work in a Muslim's home. Dr. Raznik was both pleasant and informative but he wasn't providing the information Jason was really after.

"Are you finding a growing number of immigrants of the Muslim faith moving out past the suburbs and into more rural communities?" Jason asked.

"No. In fact, I am quite surprised to learn of your customer. Those of the Muslim faith live in communities where a mosque is near because continuous growth in faith is so important. I, for instance, live in Minneapolis and adjust my drive and class schedule around daily prayers."

"Maybe his job takes him farther south and Cannon Falls is as close as he can live to a mosque and make the schedule work," said Jason.

"Not a true Muslim. Faith before all else," the professor said sternly.

Jason shrugged a "beats me" look. He felt a little bad that Raznik was getting upset with an imaginary person. "What about the woman of the house? Again, I don't want to make any etiquette mistakes," Jason said.

"This is a little more tricky. In recent years interpretation of the roles and treatment of women according to the Koran began to change. However, most scholars still agree submission and..."

---

Kate was staring intently at her computer monitor when Jason approached the reception desk. "I'll be with you in a moment," she said without looking.

"Okay, but I'm melting." Kate looked up to see Jason holding an ice cream cone in each hand. "Blueberry cheesecake or mint chocolate chip? I've been working on both all the way from the student union and if I were you, I'd go with the cheesecake."

"What are you doing here?" she asked.

"I was in the area. You got time for a short break? I was hoping to go for a walk but raindrops started falling just as I got in the building."

"Maybe a short walk around the hall then," she said. She turned away from the entrance. "Bonnie, can you—?"

Her office mate jumped out from behind the partition. "Need me to cover the door?"

"That'd be great." Then she turned back to Jason, who was licking around the scoop of blueberry cheesecake ice cream. She pointed at him and said, "You! Get away from my ice cream."

They worked their way around the square administration building, then sat down on a bench near the front door and watched students racing through the now heavy rain outside.

"Tonight's not looking good," Jason said.

"When can you tell me what you're doing?" she asked. Jason couldn't tell if she was miffed about his secrecy.

"What I tell you needs to stay between us," he said. She nodded her agreement. "I know you still have questions about my suspicions of Clara Riddle but what I haven't told you is that when Seth and I went back there yesterday, I saw more unusual things. The worst of which was that it looked like the word, 'Help' may have been painted on one of the basement windows. I didn't see it well and need to go back and check again to be sure."

Kate put her hand to her mouth, then her eyes narrowed. "Why didn't you tell me? And now you're all hush-hush about what you're doing tonight—." She looked away and tossed her cone in the trash can near the bench.

"I didn't get a chance to tell you yesterday. I was in jail before dinner, remember? And I'm trying to tell you right now what my plans are for tonight if you'll give me a chance." He touched her arm and she turned her attention to him. "Remember how the men from Friday looked Arab? I spoke with someone today about Islam's view toward women. Many in the religion still see a woman as a possession to be used accordingly. If these men are fundamentalists, it could be really bad, Kate.

"I wasn't able to help the girl who got hit, and if that's where it ended, I'd be done with all this by now. But the house has been altered to hide something and now someone may be putting out a sign for help. One thing keeps leading to another with that place. Too many things."

"Did you tell Sheriff Burnett?"

"No."

"Why not?

"It's complicated. I probably should have and I still plan to. But when I do, it's not going to be with just suspicions; it's going to be with real evidence."

"Like what?"

"Like the person asking for help."

Jason jogged through the rain to his truck and dialed Seth's cell phone. "Are you still in for tonight?" Jason asked.

"You bet. What's the plan?"

"I haven't hammered out the details but the gist of it is this: we wait until after dark then when I get in place and can verify someone did, in fact, write a help message, you knock at the front door and give me time to make contact with the person asking for the help."

"What am I going to say?" Seth asked, suddenly nervous.

"Tell her you're a member of First Lutheran going around to members they haven't seen for a while, inviting them to Sunday's services," Jason said. "You'll just need to ask her a few questions to give me time to make contact with the person on the other side of the window. When I do, I'll buzz you on your phone; you'll need to set it to vibrate. That'll be the signal for you to wrap it up and head home."

"How are you going to get out of there?"

"I'm not. After I signal you, I'll call Sheriff Burnett and tell him what I found. It should be enough to get his attention, but if he is still suspicious or unwilling to hear me out, then I'll tell him exactly where I am and tell him I'm planning to break in. He's coming for Clara Riddle or he's coming for me. Either way, he's going to meet the person behind the window."

"It sounds like a good plan, but what about the hidden room and the guys from Friday night? Have you thought about them?" Seth asked.

"Are you asking if someone other than Clara Riddle is going to answer the door? The answer is, 'I don't know.' I think whatever is going on there involves more than an old widow—that's for sure."

"You have any idea who? Or how many?"

Jason could hear Seth's apprehension. "No. And I don't want to stereotype, but if I'm right about the men from Friday night being Middle Eastern… it kinda changes the game a little." Seth didn't immediately respond, so Jason said "I'm happy to swap roles. I figured I would go to the back of the house because I've been there before and I'm a better carrot for Burnett. But I am happy to be the one knocking on the door—I don't have a family at home to think about." *Anymore*, he thought.

"I just want to make sure we are in position to win, you know? Just like Coach Sayers told you way back," Seth said.

"I'm not following you."

"Remember when Sayers came to UMD after your freshman year? Remember what he said? He basically told you guys that you didn't have the talent of some of the other teams in the conference. But he didn't care. He said you were going to win right away for two reasons: you were going to think like your opponents, then were going to *out-think* your opponents. You did what he said and took second in the conference that year."

"He told us to think like our opponents then *outwork* them," Jason corrected. "He wanted us to do hours of study so we could anticipate what our opponents were going to do, then beat them to it."

"In that case, what I just said is *my* mantra, not Coach Sayers'. Think like your opponent, then *out-think* your opponent," Seth said. "And I think it's something we need to consider if we are going to make this work."

"I don't know much about this opponent—I don't have a lot of experience in this area. But I can tell you I haven't thought about much else for the last few days," Jason said.

"Piece of cake then," Seth said confidently.

"Piece of cake," Jason said, less certain.

# CHAPTER 23

General Attar got in a full one-hour workout in the cramped hall of the hidden substructure. Without weights or cardiovascular equipment he was forced to improvise from his normal regimen. Two years ago he'd read in an airline travel magazine about an elite athlete who significantly increased his power and explosion by following a routine created by a high-profile Hollywood trainer. General Attar had immediately flown to California and spent thirty grueling days working with the trainer, then left with a long-term plan for continued physical development. Already a naturally powerful man, the general built his 37-year-old body into an explosive, nimble fighting machine.

After his workout, he woke his computer out of hibernation. The same page was still on the screen, so he reread his message on www.philcollinsrocks.com. The importance of doing a live chat seemed overblown in the message, but not to the point that it would raise any flags with national security monitoring systems. He used the mouse to click the refresh button on the browser. A moment later his message flashed back again but this time thirteen new responses followed.

General Attar scrolled through all the responses. "Thirdgrader" wrote "We'll make it work. Further details to follow." Below that, "Seventh Heaven" wrote "I trust you are leading this endeavor for great success. We will make the necessary changes." The general read nine similar responses as he continued to scroll down through the chat-room messages. Two messages however, one from "Snake Eyes" and another from

"Niner's fan," expressed concern and questioned whether the changes were completely necessary.

He used the mouse to click through the protocols to input another message of his own: "Niner's and Snake Eyes, contact me off line." He sent the message then leaned back in the chair and folded his hands in front of him. Philadelphia and Houston were doubting him. He yearned to give them the message of what failure in their cities would mean to them personally. His eyes narrowed, and the screen went out of focus. The general didn't notice his tightly clasped fingers starting to turn blue.

---

Hannah was hard at work in the living room when Jason got home. He washed his hands in the kitchen sink before heading in to see her, but almost knocked her down in the hall on the way. It was rare that she got up from a quilt when Jason came home; it was his job to drop in *on her. Something's up*, Jason thought.

"We need to talk," Hannah said without any preface. *Uh oh, this is really serious*, Jason guessed.

They went into the TV room and sat down. Hannah picked lint off her pants for a time before speaking. "I am so thankful you and Kelly came to live with me when you did. And I know there were a lot of reasons after the girls' deaths when you would have rather been anywhere other than Cedar River or in this house." She looked up for the first time. "You put your own needs on hold for me and my disease."

She looked down again but couldn't find anymore lint. "What is it?" Jason asked.

"I don't know exactly how to say this," she said, looking up again, then rushed on. "I've decided it's time for me to be on my own."

"What about the lupus? I know it's been a while since your last flare but…"

"I called Dr. Hackbarth and he is looking into different technologies and care options for me when the flares hit. He says there are advances in both early detection of seizures and in the drug therapies for flare prevention and minimization."

"I'm glad to hear that, but still—kicking me out?"

"I'm not kicking you out. If anyone is leaving, it's me. Maybe I'll get one of those new townhomes going up on the west side of town, out by the hospital."

"Where is this coming from? Why now?"

"Plenty of reasons, I guess, but nothing specific."

Jason shook his head and crossed his arms, studying his mother. *Think like your opponent,* he thought to himself. "You know what I think? You saw a younger woman in the house for the first time since Kelly and you're trying to get out before I dump you for someone else."

"Aren't we a little self-absorbed?" she said. "I'll admit having Kate here has affected my thought process, but not the way you think. Being around her reminds me I've got a lot more life to live. Including relationships of my own. Your father has been gone for nine years now and I'm still only sixty-seven years old. What if the Lord keeps me around until I'm eighty-seven? That's a long time to be alone."

"Are we really talking about you and Neil?"

"No!" she scolded, then, "Yes, Neil and I have become closer recently but if any man is influencing this move, it's you. It's been a rough couple years for you, dear. It hasn't been easy, as your mother, for me to watch. But the ground beneath you has firmed up lately."

The comment caught Jason by surprise. He had assumed he was the caregiver in the relationship.

"You need to understand, sometimes a person just knows when the next phase of her life is beginning," she said.

"Sure, but it feels like this is coming out of left field," Jason said.

"It's not like I'm moving out tomorrow or anything; I still need to see what Dr. Hackbarth comes up with. But I've been thinking about this for a while. We've started to become sort of a crutch for each other and I don't think either one of us needs that anymore. Nor is it good for either one of us."

"You swear this isn't about Neil or Kate?"

"Like I said, it's a great many things, including Neil and Kate, but mainly it just feels like the right time."

Jason still wasn't sure about her motives, but he decided not to push until he had more time to consider the situation. "About Kate—." Jason rubbed his hand over his face but it didn't wipe away his discomfort. "It's not a big deal, but I should to tell you Kate and I are becoming more than just friends."

"Have you kissed her yet?" Hannah asked in a deadpan voice.

"Mom!"

"None of that French kissing, I hope. Girls don't want someone else's tongue in their mouth on the first kiss."

"MOM!"

"Oh, I'm just kidding. You're always so cute when you blush." Hannah got up and put her hand on Jason's shoulder. "I am really happy for you, dear. Kate is a terrific woman. And very cute."

---

Liz waited all day for the man outside the window to return. Hope, she realized, could be a wonderful thing, but it could also bring a load of anxiety with it. Since yesterday, when she saw the shadow and heard the man curse, each sound or small movement sent her heart racing with desperate anticipation of his return.

Overcast skies and rainfall made the room especially dark and damp. She guessed it was late afternoon. It was at this time yesterday when she'd heard the mystery man outside the window. "Stay focused, but stay calm," she told herself but her heartbeat refused to listen.

Suddenly there it was. She leapt to her feet and yelled, "Help me! Please help me!" She reached the window and leaped up to it, crashing her whole forearm against it. "Please, whoever you are, get me out of here!"

Then the shadow jumped away. Jumped? Liz followed her sinking heart to the floor. The shadow was different from yesterday. It didn't reach the top of the window. Probably just a fox or raccoon. And what about her plea? She'd rehearsed it a hundred times over the last several hours, trying to keep it conversational and nonthreatening. *Who's there? Hello? My name is Liz. Who is out there?*

The sun was setting and so was her hope for rescue. In the dark, her signal would be useless. She would again be separated from the world, alone in her room. Or, even worse, not alone. She couldn't shake the feeling that she had become an afterthought, even to the villain inside the house. "Don't you dare cry!" she told herself.

# CHAPTER 24

The plan was for Seth to pick up Jason a little before 8:00. They would drive to the Riddle house together and go over the plan one last time on the way. Jason was in the garage filling a backpack with tools and supplies he might need depending on the possible outcomes of the night's activities. He was considering different strategies in his head if the person behind the basement window wasn't alone, when Seth called.

"Hey, Pal. You're not going to believe this. I got called into work," Seth said.

Jason glanced at the clock over the workbench. "What are you talking about? Your shift ended three hours ago; what could they need you for now?"

"My boss called. Apparently, the four-to-midnight floor supe has a tummy-ache and has to go home," he said. "It's not the first time. His name is Rick but the other floor managers call him Always-Sick Dick."

"Can't you call someone else to cover?" Jason asked.

"I've tried. That's why I'm calling so late. There are four other guys who can do the job. Two of them already have too much OT covering for Always-Sick so they can't work it. The other two have other things going on. I can't get them to budge."

"C'mon, Seth. There's nothing you can do? What about just for a couple hours, then you can go back in and finish your shift?" Jason pleaded.

"I'm sorry, Bud," Seth said. "I think I know the answer to this, but do you think you can push it to tomorrow night?"

"I should have been there *last night*. If that girl is… no way can I wait another night. The more I learn about Islamic fundamentalists, if that's who these guys are, the more I regret not doing more when I first heard the gunshots on Friday."

"Why? What have you learned?" Seth asked.

"It's like here in the U.S. where Christians are basically kind, forgiving people. But there's the 'Christian Right' who distort the religion and use it to talk loud and pass judgment on everybody, usually in public. They give the rest of us a bad name," Jason said. "It's the same thing for Muslims, only a hundred times worse. The extremists have distorted their religion to the point where they believe they are called to wipe all non-Muslims off the face of the earth. Hell, they want to blow away tolerant and non-militant Muslims right with the rest of us 'infidels.'"

"And you think one of these groups is in Cedar River?" Seth asked.

"It seems far-fetched, and I sure as hell hope not. But if so, we need to understand what we're up against. You know, *think like your opponents*?"

"Then *out-think* your opponents," Seth finished. "I still like that."

Jason asked once more if Seth could find a way out of the shift but received the same answer.

"So you're going out there tonight for sure?" Seth asked.

"Yep."

"Jas– if it gets hairy, get the hell outta there. It'd be better to be in the back of a sheriff's car than the back of a hearse. You know what I mean?" Seth didn't wait for an answer. "I really need to get to work. They've called twice since we started talking; Always-Sick must be curled up in the fetal position."

"Yeah, I'll talk to ya later."

"Jason, call me as soon as you're clear from there. And don't worry about calling my cell; no upper management hangs around past six," Seth said, then hung up.

Jason looked up at the wall of tools and thought, *Looks like I'm on my own—didn't plan for that.*

---

Khalid sat in the driver's seat of small Ryder moving truck outside an apartment complex in the outer-ring Twin Cities suburb of Farmington. The worn bench seat was uncomfortable and smelled of grease and rancid food. He was sitting in the apartment building parking lot because he needed to kill a couple hours between the time he picked up the truck until the rendezvous time. People moved in and out of these buildings all the time, so a moving truck would not be conspicuous here. So far, there had been little activity in the lot since his arrival. Several cars had pulled in, but their occupants headed straight for the building without a glance in his direction.

Khalid passed the time by going over the operational details completed, and those still ahead, but his thoughts kept circling back to Jan. They were growing closer, and with good reason: she was a good person who represented what was right about America. She had a great relationship with her family, was wonderful to her employees, and brightened every room she entered with her brilliant smile. He knew it went against the rules of the mission to speak of their religion, but Muhab was very understanding. Surely he would be willing to allow Khalid the opportunity to enlighten Jan in the ways of Allah. After all, instructing any good person of the greatness of Islam is a virtuous thing.

If things went well tonight, he would discuss his plan for Jan's conversion with Muhab. But for now he needed to focus on the task at hand. He turned the key and pulled out of the parking lot. No one followed. Five minutes later he pulled the truck through the gates of a public storage facility along 35W, just south of County Road 50. He stopped at the second-to-last stall, where Omar and another young recruit, Nafi, were waiting in the Chevy Impala.

---

Working solo forced Jason to make some logistical and tactical changes to his plan. One was the start time; another was how to get in and out of the Riddle property. He drove past the worn entry to his 80-acre parcel, then turned on his high beams as the northerly road curved gently west. Less than a quarter-mile past the deer stand entrance was a raised berm in the roadside ditch. When Jason drove onto it, the heavy pick-up sank slightly in the wet soil created by the earlier downpour. He stepped on the gas, causing the tires to spin on the rain-slicked grass before eventually catching and lurching forward. Jason turned the wheel hard right and braked in a small clearing behind a mix of aspen and birch trees. He got out of the truck and inspected his path off the road. The tire tracks through the tall grass were obvious to anyone looking for them, especially Sheriff Burnett.

As a precaution he walked backward along one tire track and used his hand to sweep the grass back up to a more standing position. When finished, he walked up the driver-side tire path and repeated the procedure.

He stepped back and inspected his work. It wasn't perfect, but it would do. If the sheriff followed through on his threat to check up on Jason, there was no way he was going to be concerned about a little trampled grass a quarter-mile beyond the spot where he was expecting Jason's vehicle. If anything, his attention would be on the farmhouse that stood another quarter-mile around the bend. He turned and was relieved to see that his truck was basically hidden from view.

He opened the second-row door of the pick-up and unzipped the heavy backpack. He pulled out the larger of two flashlights, then pushed a twenty-four-inch piece of scrap pipe through the supplies to the bottom of the pack. He pushed the zippers on either side tight up against it, leaving six inches of pipe sticking out the top, then slung it over his back. He picked up the reflectors he'd bought at the hardware store earlier in the evening. He had asked for plain bike reflectors, which the attendant told him they didn't carry. But as usual, the hardware store had a better solution already waiting for Jason on the shelves.

If things went south tonight he would need to hightail it back to the truck through the dark woods. He couldn't afford to zigzag through the woods like he had the day before. He had come up with the idea of laying reflectors on the ground, which would mark his way with regular pulses from his flashlight. But the man at the hardware store had an even better idea: reflectors attached to three-foot stakes.

Jason hiked forty feet toward the Riddle house and slid the first reflector stake firmly into the wet ground. He marked the trail with reflectors at various intervals along the path, depending on the difficulty of the terrain. About two-thirds of the way to the adjoining property, Jason veered a bit too far north and had to pull up two of the stakes and replace them along a more westerly setting. When he got to the Riddle property, he was still carrying one reflector. He backed up ten feet and slid it under the tall grass. Two angled linden trees formed an arch that framed the entrance to his route back to the truck, eliminating the need for the final signal. More importantly, he didn't want anyone from inside the house to see it.

Jason made his way along the edge of the tree line to the single pine he'd used as cover yesterday, darting into the backyard once to get around the two fallen ash trees he'd scaled the day before. He knelt at his perch facing the north and west sides of the house and settled in for a thirty-minute wait. The new plan was to wait until 11:00 to approach the window. Without a partner to create a distraction, Jason hoped a later meeting time with the person behind the window would decrease the likelihood of being seen or heard by passersby on the outside or creating unwanted attention inside. His eyes moved in a regular arc over the two faces of the house—no light and no movement. He checked his watch again. Twenty minutes.

---

Muhab punched in the key-code at the front gate of the public storage facility, waited for it to slide back, then drove toward the third row of lockers. He was fuming by the time he pulled his car alongside the moving truck. He didn't know who he was more upset with, Khalid or Omar. Khalid appeared first, so he received the initial tirade.

"I told you a van! A van! Not a truck! People notice a truck. A moving truck in the middle of the night draws suspicion. I said 'van'!"

He watched Khalid cower slightly. This was the first time he'd shown anger to one of his subordinates. Khalid's reaction made him wonder if he should have done it earlier. It's never a bad thing to have your deputies fear disappointing you. He wondered what percentage of General Attar's outrage was anger and how much was show.

"Muhab, please understand. I called many renters. None of them had cargo vans available. This was the smallest vehicle I could get," Khalid said.

"This is the last time you fail me! Is that clear?" Muhab said. Part of his anger stemmed from his aversion to receiving more admonishment for his crew's failings from General Attar. Khalid nodded. Omar and another group member, Nafi, approached but kept their distance.

"Disregard driving an extra thirty miles before returning the truck. We will exchange the risk of having mileage tracked for getting the truck off the road. Get it back to the renter as quickly as you can," Muhab said.

Khalid again answered with a nod.

Muhab gave Khalid another long stare before turning to Omar and stepping directly in front of the larger man. "Why is your car here? I told Khalid that the three of you were to ride together. We don't need a convoy to Cedar River," he said, then added for intimidation, "Am I dealing with nothing but fools?"

Omar didn't cower as Khalid had. "No, sir. You are not dealing with fools. The general told me to drive separately in case there was an accident or something. Talk to him if you have a problem with it," Omar said.

Muhab seethed. Why was Attar contacting Omar directly? The last time they were together the general had practically torn off one of Omar's fingers. Muhab leaned in, "Get this truck loaded. We're on a schedule here."

Omar held fast for a moment, returning Muhab's glare with equal intensity, then turned toward the storage locker.

---

*Game time!* With the pipe in his left hand and the backpack in his right, Jason sprinted twenty yards to the first basement window on the house's west side—the "HELP" window. He leaned his back up against the foundation just to the right of the window, stretched out his left arm and rapped twice on the window. A few beats later he rapped again.

The knocks startled Liz out of a restless half-sleep, propelling her shoulder blades into the hard wall behind her. She rose and looked at the window, but saw only a rectangle of grey two shades lighter than the black that surrounded it. Then from the right came what looked like the moonlit shadow of a thick baseball bat or a two-by-four. It brought her two more knocks. It wasn't a bat or a board; it was an arm. She knocked back with the side of her fists and screamed. "Help! Please help me! You need to help me. Please!" *Damn it—calm down!*

---

General Attar was talking on his cell, waiting in the dining room for the moving van. The person at the other end of the call spoke Arabic through a phlegmy baritone voice. Between ornery dissertations he heard a noise. Was it the girl? He turned to the curio hiding the basement entrance and laid the phone against his chest.

---

"Okay. Okay. Quiet," Jason begged in a hushed voice. "Someone is going to hear you. Keep your voice down!"

The screams stopped and for a moment there was no sound. Then a quiet but anxious voice came from inside and beneath the window. "Can you still hear me?"

"Yes. I hear you fine," he said. He backed away from the wall and looked left and right along the house to see if the screaming had raised any suspicions, but no lights went on in any of the windows.

"What is your name?" he asked.

"Liz. Liz Pratt. I was brought here five nights ago with my friend. They have me locked in this room."

A shiver surged through his body—he had found her at last. "Hello, Liz. I'm going to try to get you out. What about your friend? Where is she?"

The woman's voice dropped. "She's dead. He killed her."

The words echoed through Jason's head. *He killed her.* What had he gotten himself into? The most serious violence he'd ever been a part of was a decent hockey fight against another team's thug. But that was a game with referees to break up any serious altercations; this was real—real people being murdered by real bad guys. *Maybe this is too much*, he thought; *it's time to call the sheriff.*

The woman inside the window must have sensed his trepidation. "Please, you've got to help me. They're going to kill me, too. It could be any minute now."

"Who? How do you know that?" Jason asked. The first question was a natural response looking for more information. But the second question was about fear. He needed one hell of a reason not to head back to the woods and call Sheriff Burnett.

"He told me he didn't have any use for me anymore. And tonight they didn't feed me," she said.

That wasn't enough. "I'm going to go call the sheriff. Help will be here in a few minutes."

"No. Wait. Don't go. Don't you see? I've been fed every day I've been here except today," Liz said.

Jason altered his body position to make a run for the trees.

"He's going to kill me. I could see it in his eyes. He went upstairs a few minutes ago. He never goes upstairs this late. I think he's up there getting a weapon." Her voice was getting louder again.

"Calm down. Someone's upstairs?" He backed away from the window and checked the windows again. All dark. If there was movement behind one of them, he couldn't see it.

"Yes. I heard him walk by and go up. Please. He could come back any second. You gotta get me out of here."

If someone *was* upstairs, he might be looking right at Jason, aiming a gun at him right now. Jason turned from the window and backed as hard as he could against the foundation wall, frozen. Make a run for it? They could shoot him out in the open; it would be an easy shot. What about calling the sheriff from where he was?

Jason was searching for a strategy to get away from the house alive when he was interrupted. "Are you still there?" the woman asked.

Jason listened to the combination of helplessness and panic in the woman's voice. It was the same desperate sounds he'd heard on the other end of an in-and-out cell phone call two years earlier. Kelly had the same terror in her voice: "Love you… much. He was on the bri… can't get to her… stop… crying… will always… you."

"Yeah Liz, I'm still here."

---

Attar continued to put up with the ramblings of the gruff caller as he waited for the moving van to arrive. At regular intervals he lowered the phone from his ear and listened for any more noises. But the only thing he heard was muffled rumblings worming out of the smothered cell speaker. Moments later, a flash of headlights appeared in the west though the thin opening in the dining room curtains. As they grew nearer, a second set of lights appeared directly behind the first, the second set riding closer to the ground. General Attar continued to watch through his concealed position until the vehicles slowed, then turned into the driveway. The general was through the front door to meet them before they were at a full stop.

# CHAPTER 25

Overlapping horizontal strips of two-inch blue masking tape covered the glass basement window. The first strip ran along the joint between the top of the glass window and its wood frame, the last one doing the same. At the sides of the window the ends of the long strips jutted out from the frame intentionally, creating vertical flaps on both sides.

Jason pulled the rubber mallet from his pack and tapped the center of the window. He heard the window shatter, but the firm seal between the tape and window prevented the glass from falling away. More importantly, the sound of the breaking glass was barely audible. He tapped the window twice more, breaking the pane more completely. Then he worked around the inside of the frame, striking the window hard enough to break the glass at the joint but gently enough not to rip or pull the tape.

When he finished, he grabbed the left end of the joined strips of tape with both hands and slowly pulled to the right across the window. The tape begrudgingly disengaged from the wood frame, then suddenly pulled away and a sheet of broken glass folded toward Jason as if hinged to the right window frame. After removing the tape completely, he gave the frame a quick inspection. Several small shards had dropped into the sill between the frame and Plexiglas and a solid row of similar shards were jutting from the narrow grooves on all sides. In the moonlight, it looked like a huge necklace of large diamonds filled the thin rut.

As Jason laid the sheet of glass to the side, a truck and trailing car braked on the road in front of the recessed house. Even though he was kneeling near the rear of the house, Jason instinctively flattened into the ground as the vehicles passed by. Lying face down, he heard them turn into the gravel driveway on the opposite side of the house. Liz heard them, too.

"What was that?" she asked. Jason didn't immediately answer. "Did they see you?" Liz's nerves were clearly at a breaking point.

Still, Jason gave no response. "Hello?" she asked. Frantic.

"Yeah. I'm right here," he said finally.

"What is it?" she asked.

"A car and a moving truck just pulled in. They're on the other side of the house. I can't see them."

They both heard the truck door open, then slam shut. Two car doors followed. Jason made a mental note; three new people?

"Hurry!" she said.

Jason considered his options. *Think like your opponent, then out-think your opponent.*

"Liz, I'm going to get you out of there, I promise. But I need to find out what they're doing first."

"No, don't you see? They're coming for me," she pleaded.

"I can't help you if I have a bullet through my temple. I need to make sure we can get out of here—all the way out." His confident tone belied his indecision.

He mentally flipped through his Internet searches from earlier in the day and cross-referenced them with the need for a moving truck. He came up with only one possibility: human trafficking.

"Liz, I need you to stay completely quiet. I'll be right back," he said, and didn't wait for an answer. He picked up the lead pipe and sprinted for the two fallen ash trees behind the house.

Safely nestled behind the large root ball of one of the fallen trees, Jason saw four men talking outside a Ryder rental truck. The men were not in a circle. Three of the men faced the fourth with their backs to the truck. The single man was pointing his finger at them as he spoke; he was definitely the person in charge. Jason could hear his voice but at this distance he was unable to decipher what was being said.

Moments later, two of the three underlings followed the leader toward the front of the house. The other man went around the truck, pulled out the ramp, walked up it, and threw up the rear overhead door. Jason saw a beam of light appear out the east side of the house, probably from the kitchen. A moment later the wire-thin opening around the sheetrock-covered window lit up. Jason held his breath for a minute, stuck helplessly out of the view of Liz's basement window. He waited. No yelling, no screaming. *Please God, let her be safe.*

He moved his focus back to the moving truck. The man had carried out several cardboard boxes but so far no people emerged. Then movement came from the front of the house. The two men who were dispatched to the house carried folding chairs to the truck; the leader wasn't with them. They picked up the boxes and turned back for the house.

"Think," Jason whispered to himself. He glanced toward the northwest corner of the house shielding Liz's window. Still quiet. Looking back to the moving truck, he saw the man was still inside the cargo hold. Jason rose from his tight crouch, preparing to race back to Liz, but was halted by more movement between the house and truck. It was the leader; he called to the man in the truck. Jason made another mental note: one man's name (not the leader) was Khalid.

Khalid bypassed the ramp and jumped off the rear of the truck and jogged over to the other man. The two men talked face-to-face with each other. The man on the right was older and thicker—thicker due to unusually dense muscle mass. He didn't slouch; if anything, he had unusually straight posture. But what made him look older was that, unlike the man he was speaking to, the years of gravity had pulled his features down. Jason did his best to study each man's profile. He might need to recall them for the sheriff in the coming hours. The men stopped talking when the other two returned, carrying a large dry-erase board from the house. When it was loaded, the two men carried a large box in each hand back to the house without additional direction. Khalid and the leader didn't move to help. Jason wondered if the younger man was second in command.

He turned his head in the direction of Liz's room but couldn't get to her. The leader and Khalid had ended their conversation but held their positions between the house and the truck. They went from looking directly at each other to varied glances around the yard, the way two men do to fill time to avoid idle chatter. The awkward fidgeting chained Jason to his position behind the fallen trees. Had it been just one person, Jason could have probably read his tendencies and timed his dash out of the man's line of sight. But with two, one's movements affected the other as they tried to avoid eye contact and appear spontaneous—keeping Jason nervously still.

Jason sat motionless as the other two men brought out two more small loads, one of which, Jason saw, was bedding. Jason again tried to think like his opponents but he couldn't put a white board together with bedding. And what were they bringing in? The four men met briefly at the spot where the leader stood, then three of them, including the leader and Khalid, went into the house; the other turned to close the rear overhead door of the truck. At last Jason was hidden from each man's sight. At that moment he sprinted for Liz's window.

He waited a moment, listening for activity behind the Plexiglas then whispered, "Liz, are you okay?"

"So far. But people keep walking by my door. Something's going on—where have you been?"

"Men were hanging around outside. I couldn't get back here without being seen," he said. "Hold on. I'll have you out in a minute."

He grabbed a short crowbar and a claw hammer out of his pack. The bar was fifteen-inch steel plate bent at a ninety-degree angle; three inches one direction, twelve the other. Both ends were tapered and flared with a notch to allow the bar to fit securely around offending nails. He jammed the short end of the bar between the thick Plexiglas and the wood frame on the left side of the window, then hammered it in the full three inches. He pressed the bar toward the Plexiglas, forcing it to bow into the room and extracting the middle nail.

He continued the procedure around the window as quickly as he could, praying the snug nails wouldn't squeak on their way out. He pried the two left-corner nails loose, then three more along the bottom of the window, then two more from the right side. Just two more nails at the top of the frame and Liz would be free.

Before he could thrust the pry bar under the top of the frame, the sound of metal slapping metal clanged at the other end of the room. Then he heard the sound of the room's door being yanked open. The partially secured Plexiglas pulled against the two remaining nails in response to the air being sucked out the doorway then snapped back against the frame. Jason wondered if the person opening the door heard the soft crack of plastic against wood.

The intruder didn't seem to notice the loosened window, but his menacing voice sent a chill up Jason's spine.

"Hey baby, you ready for a good time?"

# CHAPTER 26

Khalid followed General Attar up the stairs. The first door he saw made his dinner churn angrily inside his stomach. He could still hear the sounds that came from the room last weekend; flesh beating flesh and the agonizing cries of pain. He shook his head to drive out the terrified woman's terrible screams. General Attar glanced at the movement but didn't comment. The two men stopped in front the next door. The general turned to face him.

"Muhab has spoken very highly of you, Khalid. You have passed all tests given you," the general said. "I am presenting you with another opportunity tonight."

He pulled a semi-automatic pistol from the pocket of his leather jacket, slid a bullet into the firing chamber and offered it to Khalid, who did not immediately take it. The general pushed it to his stomach and Khalid took the weapon. It felt heavy and uneven in his hand.

"Own the weapon; you are in charge of its power," General Attar said and shook Khalid's wrist, forcing him to strengthen his grip around the gun. Khalid twisted his wrist in a circular motion, getting a better sense of the weapon's feel and balance. He had some training with similar weapons, but not since coming to the U.S. so many months ago.

General Attar put his hand on the doorknob. "The woman inside is prepared to go to Allah. It is her destiny. You are performing an act of great mercy and generosity."

Khalid followed the leader into the bedroom. He was surprised by the contrast to the rest of the house. Family photographs, some color, others black and white, adorned all four walls of the room. Additional photos sat atop an oak dresser and side tables. The comforter and other linen in the room displayed an American farm motif. The old woman was sitting in a side chair with a heavy blanket over her lap.

"Clara, we are leaving," General Attar said. "We cannot leave you here."

"Am I coming with you?" the tired woman asked.

"No. Your work is done."

Fear and surprise worked across her face.

"Allah has prepared you a special place," the general smiled. "You will finally be reunited with your son."

Clara nodded and a single tear meandered down her right cheek. She got up from the chair and lifted a picture off the dresser, then lay down on the bed. She looked at the general, unsure, then closed her eyes, her son's picture clutched tightly to her chest.

General Attar lifted a small pillow from the end of the bed and handed it to Khalid. "Put this in front of the muzzle to stifle the sound."

Khalid held the pillow a foot from the old woman's head and shoved the muzzle of the gun against it. A needlepoint image of a Siamese cat's head covered the pillow and the gun was pointed right between its eyes. The image bothered Khalid and he searched for a spot where the muzzle would both miss the cat and silence the gun. Unable to find one, he tried to move his line of sight from the pillow to the target. He let out a terrible yell as the gun fired.

The old woman must have wondered what was taking so long. She opened her eyes and looked directly into Khalid's as the gun fired.

---

"Wha, what do you want?" Liz said. She recognized the man. He was the roommate of the Rockwell Outfitter guy, the one who'd hit her so hard the other night.

"You see this?" the large Arab man held up his right hand. The last two fingers were taped together with white athletic tape. Additional tape ran from the fingers around his palm for additional support. "You did this, bitch."

He continued his slow approach. She had nowhere to go; she was already backed up against the wall under the window.

"I, I didn't do that to you. I swear."

"Oh, you did it. And you're going to pay every day until it's healed," he said. His voice oddly combined anger and laughter at the same time.

"If I did, it was an accident," she said raising her hands in front of her face, begging him to stop his advance. He was within a foot of her now. "Please. Please, I'll—" His fist was too fast; her head was crushed between it and the wall, and she fell in a clouded daze to the floor.

Liz was aware of the duct tape going over her mouth and around her hands but her relentless screaming and kicking was only happening inside her head.

---

Jason listened to the confrontation but couldn't see anything through the smoky plastic. The dull thud of skull against solid concrete sickened him. The blow had silenced Liz; the only sound he heard now was duct tape being ripped from the roll. He felt like a coward not acting, but what could he do? Did her assailant have a gun? Is that why she hadn't tried to run? Was it just one man, or more than one?

He strained to listen for more clues. Anything. He needed some kind of distraction to provide enough time to remove the final nails. Struggling through the small framed opening made a surprise entrance into the room out of the question. Should he take the risk? He needed to do something, but he was no good to Liz halfway through a tight window with bullet holes dotting his chest.

Then came a sound that gave Jason hope. It was the indecipherable sound of a person's muffled voice—Liz's voice.

But the man's voice quickly followed. "Look who's awake. Welcome back, bitch." Jason heard the powerful blow and the muzzled scream in response. The punch sounded different from the first, not bone on bone; maybe a punch to Liz's stomach or chest?

Liz's muffled expulsion of pain in response to the blow was the tipping point for Jason. Enough! The fear and self-doubt Jason had felt were gone, overwhelmed by rage and defiance. He simultaneously threw the claw end of the hammer under one nail and the pry bar under the other. He shifted his hands to the top of the tools and thrust both arms down and forward. The sheet of plastic shot forward then caught air and floated to the floor with a soft slap. Jason saw a brass latch at the bottom of the window frame. He turned it and slid through, feet first, pushing the frame up and giving him five inches of additional, shard-free clearance. His feet hit the ground just moments after the Plexiglas.

---

The old lady was still staring at him. She didn't want to die. Her eyes cried out for him to stop but he was already pulling the trigger. There was no doubt: he *murdered* the woman. White stuffing from the pillow floated softly over the woman. A larger clump fell on the bullet's entry point above her left eye and momentarily stopped the gurgling of blood before being washed away by the continued flow. He backed away from the bed but the woman's hard gaze stayed locked on him.

General Attar peeled the gun from Khalid's hand. "She is with her maker. Her work is finished. Ours continues, Khalid." He gestured toward the door. "Go check on the others. I will say a prayer for her soul."

Khalid slowly turned his gaze to the doorway, which seemed to be darting from side to side. After a moment, he took a first wavering step in its direction—away from the woman's stare.

---

Jason took a moment to get his bearings in the small storage room. It was empty except for the sheet of Plexiglas on the floor. The only light to the room was coming from a room outside the door, where he guessed the man had taken Liz. Jason shot through it but misjudged the unusually narrow make-shift hallway and slammed into the concrete wall on the far side. A hulking Middle Eastern man stood just a few feet from him. Jason recognized him as the man who had hit Liz Friday night.

*Was he the monster Liz mentioned?* Liz was on the floor behind him, duct tape wrapped around her hands and mouth. Jason's sudden appearance stunned the man momentarily and allowed Jason time to regain his balance.

"Who are you?" the man asked.

The out-of-place question caused Jason to pause momentarily.

The man followed his question with a big right hook. Too big. Jason arched back and to his left and the punch missed, hitting the concrete wall, instead. The man let out a loud cry as the skin over his first knuckle split open. Jason coiled at the knees, then checked the man into the wall before he could regain his balance from the errant punch. The man's face crashed hard against the wall. Jason was in too tight for a follow-up strike so he spun behind the man and shoved him down the hall away from Liz. It didn't do much good. The man was strong and showed good balance; he needed just two steps before he stopped Jason's momentum and turned.

But Jason was on top of him by then and a straight right connected hard to the man's nose. Jason saw his eyes glass over as he stumbled back. Jason threw a second punch, which also connected but with less force because the man's head wasn't as sturdy on his neck. The man ducked and retreated two steps to preempt a third punch. They were now more than three steps apart and Jason took a large step back increasing the distance to more than four. He tried to appear confident and waved the man forward.

"C'mon, big man. What're you waiting for?"

The man took a deep breath and growled as he leaned forward and charged at Jason. *Perfect.* Jason had taken a tactical step backward. Not only did it force his opponent to charge rather than punch, but it put him even with the door to Liz's room. As the man lunged for him, he threw the door closed with all his weight, hitting the man square and stopping his rush cold.

Jason pulled back the door, bent low and catapulted himself shoulder-first into the larger man. He hoped to send the man through the doorway, into the room, but he didn't have the angle and the man crashed against the doorframe instead. Jason heard the air hurtle out of the man's lungs and took advantage of the momentary shock to push the heavy man into the holding room, slam the door and slap the lock shut.

A moment later, the wood door erupted with a loud crack from a hard kick. Then another. Jason backed against the opposite wall in the narrow hallway and pressed his foot hard against the door near the knob. With his help, the door survived two more kicks, but it wasn't going to last much longer. He needed to get Liz out of there. They hadn't exactly been quiet; sooner than later someone else was going to come down to see what was going on. He looked over at Liz. She was standing now and, despite the tape, her eyes showed resolve. He saw the staircase behind her and decided to take a chance.

"There's an open window right behind you, dumbass," he shouted through the door. "Your mom raise you to be this stupid?"

Jason waited a few seconds with his foot on the door. When another kick didn't come, he grabbed Liz and ran for the staircase. As they hit the landing at the top of the stairs, they heard the man in Liz's room shriek in pain. Jason guessed that when he'd jumped up to grab the window frame to get out, he was greeted by the shards of broken glass across each hand.

---

General Attar waited to make sure Clara was dead, then checked the room for any evidence that could be traced back to him or the mission. As expected, he found nothing incriminating and started down the stairs where he saw Khalid holding the back door open, gazing into the darkness. "What are you doing? What is going on down here?"

Khalid pivoted back against the wall and turned his foggy glare up the stairs to the general.

---

Jason held Liz by the arm as they hopped out of the hidden stairwell into the living room next to the curio. He looked through the dining room, into the kitchen, and saw the front door was closed. Then he looked to the left where he saw the strangest sight.

The young man from outside, Khalid, was holding open the back door, bent over, coughing and spitting. He seemed unaware of their presence, and not in a strong position to defend himself, so Jason decided to take the risk. He took firm hold of Liz, then raced to the landing and right past the bent man, out the back door.

---

General Attar, who was standing halfway up the staircase, was shocked to see a man with the bitch from the basement run through the door. Khalid looked up, but didn't make a single move to stop them! *What happened to Omar?* He ran down the stairs and out the door, slapping Khalid as he raced by. "Come. They must not get away!"

Khalid, shaken from his sickness by the loud command, followed. General Attar, his .45 already in hand, saw two shadows disappear around the corner of the house on the right.

"This way," he said and sprinted after them, Khalid following right behind. He rounded the corner and saw his prisoner and her rescuer thirty feet ahead of him. Before he could raise the gun to ready a shot, they slipped behind the far wall of the garage.

---

Jason used his grip on Liz's arm to direct the wobbly woman across the yard. When they got to the far corner of the garage, Jason pulled her hard to the right along the wall, but she didn't immediately follow, causing the two to lose their combined balance and stumble clumsily forward. Jason's left foot slipped out from under him in the wet grass causing him to yank Liz further forward. He threw his right leg out wide for support as Liz's body fell into him, her bound hands unable to cushion the collision.

He was able to hold them upright, but the recovery put an odd torque on his leg; pain rushed through him as the stitches on his knee split. Worse yet, they had come to a complete stop. They regained their collective balance and Jason pushed them through the leaning lindens and saw two men to their left, gaining. The leader was raising his gun at them.

---

General Attar reached the garage and saw hurried movement up ahead in the trees. He lifted his gun, but was late again and couldn't risk the noise of the blast for a low-percentage shot. He lowered the gun and raced, with Khalid, along the garage in a dark corridor created by the line of trees and garage wall. The two they were chasing were now into the woods but the gap was narrowing. The general leaped into the woods at the point he saw the movement. "They must not get away!"

---

A minute earlier, Omar had thrown the frame open before his second attempt through the window. Scattered shards of glass scraped his chest as he wiggled his thick body through the tight opening. The resulting scrapes didn't cause nearly the pain of the deep cuts across each palm. He grabbed the pipe lying next to the backpack outside the window and raced around the front of the house when he heard General Attar yell from somewhere on the other side of the garage by the woods.

Nafi was getting out of the truck cab as he approached. "Holy shit! The others just chased two people into the woods. What do we do?" asked Nafi.

"Where did they go?" Omar yelled. Nafi pointed to the spot at the side of the garage where all four people had vanished into the woods.

"I am going to kill him," Omar hissed and pulled Nafi with him.

# CHAPTER 27

A few steps into the underbrush, Jason reached inside his jacket and pulled out a pen light. It illuminated a blue reflector ahead and to the right. He pulled Liz toward it and clicked off the light. Their pace was slow as they made their way through long tangled grass and over loose sticks and rocks. He could feel the men close behind. He willed Liz to move faster when he heard the man from the basement yell from further back. "General, we're right behind you."

They got to the reflector and Jason clicked the light on again. The small flashlight illuminated a strong, narrow beam. With a short wave of Jason's arm, it caught the reflector twenty yards ahead and slightly left. Liz angled that way without a push from Jason. They ran passed the second marker and he again clicked on the light. The next reflector was closer but veered thirty degrees to the right; they moved as one in that direction. Jason thought he had marked a nearly a straight trail from his truck to the house, but right now he was thankful for his poor sense of direction. The men behind him could not anticipate their course changes.

---

General Attar stopped thirty yards into the woods and listened. He had seen the two when he first entered and followed in that direction but he had yet to see additional movement. Khalid came alongside and pointed. "I think they are up to the right. Probably headed for the road."

The general held up his hand. "Quiet!"

He listened but only heard the plowing of the two men approaching them from behind. Omar and Nafi actually raced by them to the left without knowing it before General Attar called them back. The man and girl could be huddled somewhere in the dark cover of the wooded growth, but Khalid was right; the main problem was the road. If the man had a car waiting, they'd be gone.

"Khalid, you continue forward—keep your eyes moving. They may have stopped moving and are hiding somewhere," General Attar directed.

"But I do not have a weapon," Khalid said.

"If you find them, hold them and yell for one of us. Now go." Attar pushed him forward.

"You," he said, looking at Nafi. "Double back toward the house. If you get to the garage and do not see them, run into the house and tear out the phone. The might try to make it back to call for help."

"Omar, run for the road. If you see them, grab the man and call to me."

Before Omar turned to go, General Attar heard a noise. Omar heard it, too. It sounded like a large limb breaking several yards ahead of them and toward the road to the southeast.

"Go. When you get to the road follow it east, away from the house. I will continue on this course to the south east and keep them between us." He pushed Omar south toward the road and ran in the direction of the noise.

---

Jason knew it was going to be bad even before the snap. Most of the brush under their feet had made a soft mashing sound due to the earlier storm. But one thick branch was sitting up higher than most. It was denser than Jason thought and instead of giving easily under his weight, it bent, then snapped hard. The sudden bang from the splintered wood seemed like a clap of thunder in the relative quiet. Both he and Liz involuntarily ducked and slowed momentarily in response.

But the loud snap also served as an emotional slap to the face for Jason. His mind had been scampering around as quickly as his feet, but with the crack of wood, poise rushed in where panic had been. His focus was unchanged, but it was amplified by a calm confidence, like when he was on the ice at UMD and could relax and let the action flow naturally. Their pace through the woods stayed constant but instead of *thinking* about each move, they came to him instinctively.

Jason led them to the truck without the use of the final two reflectors. They ducked down in front of the driver's door and listened. He heard movement approaching on roughly the same course from which they came. But the sound was still many yards away—they had increased their advantage—*thank you hardware store*. He opened the door and pushed Liz through to the passenger seat. He turned the ignition and backed up a few yards to get even with the berm then turned the wheel hard right toward the road.

Before he could put the transmission into drive, there was a loud crash and the windshield became an intense white spider web. The glass in front of Liz caved in and small shards of glass fell into her lap. She tried to scream but the duct tape prevented its escape. Jason threw the truck into gear and pushed the pedal to the floor. The tires spun in the wet grass, preventing the tread from grabbing hold. Jason saw the man from the basement appear in the passenger window. He was swinging something at Liz. Jason grabbed her arm and yanked her toward him just as the lead pipe came smashing through the window, missing Liz by only inches. At that moment the tires grabbed hold of the wet dirt, lurching the truck forward. The right tires missed the berm and the trucked rocked violently before bouncing onto the road. Jason turned the wheel hard left, narrowly avoiding a tumble into the ditch on the other side of the road.

General Attar leaped out of the trees just in time to see the truck's right side slide across the far gravel shoulder and dip into the long grass beyond before catching and bursting forward down the road. He pulled his cell from his pocket and punched a number. A concerned voice came on the line. "What is it?"

"Your help is required."

Jason was off his seat and leaning to the left to see the road through a small patch of unfrosted windshield. He adjusted the rear-view mirror angle to match his awkward position—they were a half-mile down the road and still no vehicles appeared behind them. He glanced over at Liz. Her breathing was labored behind the tape and her chest and legs were littered with bits of broken glass, but she appeared relatively calm and focused. She felt his glance and turned to him. Blood from a half dozen fresh cuts from the smashed passenger window trickled down the right side of her bruised and swollen face. Yet all Jason saw in her eyes was determination and gratitude.

He pulled out his cell—for the first time in the last 30 minutes he felt he could safely call for help without being detected. He scrolled down to Sheriff Burnett's cell number. "Sheriff. I just left Clara Riddle's house. I have a woman with me."

The sheriff was instantly angry and started yelling. Jason didn't hear a thing he said; the sheriff would need to continue his bullying threats another time. He clicked off the call.

The phone rang seconds later.

"Sheriff, save your lectures and listen!" he shouted. "The woman sitting next to me is injured. She was a prisoner in Clara Riddle's house. I got her out but a group of men with guns chased us through the woods. This is serious shit, Sheriff. I am heading to your office now."

"Don't do that," Burnett said. "Take her to the hospital. I'll meet you there."

Jason parked the truck under the glowing EMERGENCY sign. He grabbed a utility knife from his truck bed tool chest and cut a line through the tape between Liz's thumbs. She lifted her hands immediately to her mouth, the back of her hands still stuck together by the tape as she clawed her mouth free and took in a long, deep breath. When the inhaling slowed she removed the tape from the back of her hands and looked at Jason. Tears slipped reluctantly from her eyes and comingled with the trickles of blood. The dam broke with the words "Thank you," and she threw her arms around Jason's neck and sobbed.

Jason held her frail, shaking body and let her cry into his shoulder as he kept watch on the roads leading to the hospital. Finally, after a few long minutes, she was able to pull away.

She wiped the tears from her cheeks then looked up at Jason. "I'm sorry. I don't even know your name," she said, triggering another small wave of tears.

"It's Jason."

She started to say "Thank you," but another wave of emotion washed it away.

# CHAPTER 28

Ten minutes later, Liz was being treated in an exam room and Sheriff Burnett was sitting across from Jason in the hospital lobby. The sheriff scribbled copious notes as Jason briefed him on what happened. The sheriff had already sent two squad cars to the Riddle property but realized, after Jason's story, two wouldn't be enough and called for three more.

"I better get out there. Stick around 'til I get back," the sheriff said.

"No problem."

Burnett gestured to the officer standing at the reception desk. "Deputy Guilmond and his partner will be here keeping an eye on you and the girl. Have one of them call me if you think of something else or need to get a hold of me for anything. I suggest you get that knee looked at, too." he said, pointing to the blood stain on Jason's right knee. Jason nodded and the sheriff strode for the door.

Rest was not an option for Jason. He tried for a minute to lie on the couch in the visitor's room but it was no use; only minutes ago he was navigating the most frighteningly thrilling ride of his life. He didn't know if it was thirst or anxiety, but he craved a Diet Mountain Dew.

The kitchen at Blessed Heart Hospital was used strictly for patient meal preparation; there was no cafeteria for the visitors and staff. He was directed down and hall and to the right to the vending area, which consisted of a wall of three vending machines and a small table that held a small microwave, napkin dispenser, and ceramic coffee cup filled with straws.

As he looked at his beverage choices, he realized the caffeine included in his first choice might send his already wired body straight through the drop ceiling. He kept coming back to the machine's water choices but on principle, he was against bottled water. *Why pay good money for something I can have for free?* But in this case, it would both quench his thirst and allow him a receptacle for refills. So he looked past his moral objection this one time and sacrificed a buck-fifty.

The twenty-ounce bottle was consumed and refilled twice before he returned to the waiting area. Too wired to sit down, he pulled out his phone and called Kate, who picked up on the first ring. After the initial greetings, Kate asked Jason where he was calling from.

"I'm at the hospital," he said, limping down the hall.

"What happened? Are you hurt?

"No, I'm fine. I said I'm *at* the hospital. I didn't say I'm *in* the hospital."

"Whatever. Why are you *at* the hospital?" she asked.

"It's a long story. A woman was being held prisoner at Clara Riddle's house—in the basement."

"Oh my God! Is she okay?"

"The doctor is looking at her now. It looks like they'd been beating her up pretty bad. And tonight she got sprayed with some glass when we were trying to get away."

"We were just there the other night! How… ? What about you, are you hurt?"

"I'm fine. Just a couple of bumps and bruises." He looked at the blood stain over his knee. "But Kate, the girl—I had to guide her through the woods to get away. And when I held her arm, it was like there was nothing left around the bone. I don't think she could have held out much longer."

"I'm coming down there."

"You don't need to do that." The hopefulness in his voice didn't match his words.

"I'll see you in a few minutes," she said.

Jason called Hannah next to let her know he was going to be very late. He told her some of what happened. Her response was the same as Kate's. "I'll be right there."

Kate got to the hospital first. She saw the blood stain on Jason's pants and immediately asked about his leg. Jason assured her it was fine and stood up to receive her desperate embrace. Having her next to him soothed Jason more than he would have thought. Her kiss drained even more of the electricity from his body.

"So, what happened? How's the woman doing? I told you to just call the sheriff."

"Would it be okay if we just sat for a while?"

Kate realized she was satisfying her own need to take care of Jason more than she was focusing on him. She eased him back down to the couch then lifted his arm and settled in underneath. She worked her hand through his hair and rested her head on his chest as Jason curled his arm around her.

They sat in silence for a minute as she slowly rubbed his chest in small circles. She broke the silence only once. "I'm so glad you're okay," she said. He squeezed her tight against him.

Minutes later Hannah rushed through the front door and saw Jason and Kate resting on the small sofa in the glass-walled visitor's room at the far end of the long hall. Her focus went straight to the dark stain over Jason's unnaturally straight leg. She continued on to the front desk and a minute later was standing alongside a nurse in front of her son. The nurse asked Jason to accompany her to an exam room to check out the wound. He declined. Hannah suggested strongly that he go with her. He looked at Kate, "I'll be right back."

Jason waited twenty minutes to see a doctor and another thirty before the old stitches were removed and new stitches were sewn in their place, along with eight additional to close the now larger cut. He inquired about Liz's condition but the doctor, and later the nurse, gave him the exact same response. "I am not allowed to comment on other patients—sorry."

Jason disobeyed the doctor and didn't wait for the local anesthetic to subside before leaving the exam room. Kate couldn't hold back laughter when she saw him hobbling down the hall; one pant leg was cut off above his injured, wrapped knee, the other still soaked halfway up his leg from his race through the wet woods. The real humor came from watching him brace himself against the wall, while awkwardly and unsurely trying to walk on a mostly numb limb.

"Thanks for the support," he said, holding back his own laugh.

"I'm sorry. You just look so pitiful," she said and eased under his arm to support him back to the visitor's room.

Hannah met them before they made it back. "Can I get you anything?"

"I had a bottle of water around here someplace," he said.

She looked around but didn't immediately find it. "I'll go get you some more," she said, and bounded out of the room.

"Have you heard anything about Liz?" Jason asked Kate.

"Is that her name? Liz?" He nodded. "No, they haven't told us anything."

"What about the sheriff? Has he been back?" Jason asked.

"No. The only people who have come through were a couple college kids. One had blood coming from his nose and eye. It looked like he'd been in a fight. Other than that, it's been quiet."

Hannah came back with two Styrofoam cups filled with water and set them on the end table next to Jason. "Let me know if you're still thirsty; I can get more."

Jason was about to crack wise about her eagerness but resisted. She had a right to be anxious, too. He took the next several minutes to replay his account of the evening's events to the women. An occasional question was asked, but mostly the women sat still and silent, shocked by the danger that had surrounded Jason.

By the time he finished, the local anesthetic had mostly worn off and he asked Kate to walk with him back to the vending machines. He wasn't interested in any refreshment as much as he was looking for a way to pass the time. He bought Kate a bottle of cranberry juice and she insisted he buy something for himself, too. They settled together on a bag of peanuts. He pulled out his cell phone on the walk back to the waiting area and turned it on. One new message. It was from Seth. He had called while Jason was waiting to get his knee re-stitched. The nurse had asked as a part of the standard patient interview if he had a cell phone with him. He said he did and she told him it needed to be off during his examination. "Hospital policy."

Jason asked Kate to go check on Hannah while he returned Seth's call. When Jason finished his quick recap of what happened at Clara Riddle's house, Seth started in.

"How is she now? The girl, I mean."

"I don't know. They've been with her for a long time. They won't tell me what's going on."

"So how big was the dude?"

"What dude?"

"The guy you locked in the room, the one who smashed your truck window."

"I don't know. Maybe six-three, two-thirty. No doubt he would crush me in a normal fight," Jason said. "It's weird. With a helpless woman standing there, you feel a lot more powerful. It's like you don't have any choice but to take him down."

"He ran into a door. I wouldn't call that 'taking him down.'"

"You're gonna start busting my balls now at one in the morning or whatever time it is?"

"No, just didn't want you to think you're some kind of big badass now," Seth said.

"Trust me. That's not gonna be a problem."

There was a pause in the conversation and Jason started to think they'd gotten cut off, then, "I'm sorry I wasn't there, Jas. I should have found a way out of work. I should have been there with you."

"No sweat, man. Next time."

"You can count on me—I swear."

"I know. I'll talk to you tomorrow."

Jason stopped by the front desk on his way back to the visitor's room and asked again about Liz's condition. After extended pleading, "She's sleeping now," was the only information the nurse would reveal.

Deputy Guilmond walked up to the desk next to Jason. "Sheriff Burnett is heading back here with Detective Mangemelli. They'd like to speak with you when they get here."

---

Muhab lay on the ground about to die of suffocation. He watched his commander looking down on him, his eyes afire with rage. He'd barely made it into the room before the general's hand had slammed into his Adam's apple, stopping the flow of air in and out. He fell back against the door, pulling at his throat, when a fist smashed hard under his ribs. He fell like a sack of feed onto the floor. He knew General Attar was screaming at him but the words reached him in cavernous echoes. Then suddenly his abdomen retracted and a burst of air rushed back into his lungs. He was grateful and amazed at the ease with which each breath came.

General Attar was still screaming. "… Do you hear me, Muhab?! The whole plan."

Muhab's eyes refocused. He saw the general's back rotate and his arm coil for another punch.

"Wait! General, wait!"

The enraged general held his ready position.

"I am very sorry for any problems I have caused," he said, "but the mission is still on schedule. We will execute it just as we planned. The United States will be in free-fall by this time next week. I assure you."

"Only because we have compensated for your incompetence! The isolated safe house was a terrible idea—I told you that," General Attar shouted. "You are not a tactician. You are but a… a theorist, a consultant. I will personally reconfigure the plan for Minneapolis and I will handle all tactical decisions from this moment forward. Is that clear?"

Muhab nodded, relieved.

"You must find out what the girl's rescuer knows. If he has seen me, he must be eliminated. The girl must be silenced as well. No one can be allowed to get in the way of our success."

"Won't that attract more attention? I am not sure that is a good idea so close to victory," Muhab said.

Attar kicked his heel into Muhab's ribs. "You are not a general!" Attar boomed. "You collect information. You get the information I need and *I* will decide how to use it."

He stepped over his curled-up subordinate and walked away.

# CHAPTER 29

Hannah, Kate, and Jason took turns pacing, checking their watches, and asking for—but not getting—updates on Liz Pratt's condition while they waited for the sheriff. Forty-five minutes passed before Sheriff Burnett and Detective Bill Mangemelli finally showed up at the hospital. The only characteristic the men shared was the badge. The sheriff stood slightly shorter than the five feet, ten inches at which he started his long career. Thirty of the sixty pounds he'd added since his rookie year hung over his belt in front, the other half sat under it in back. His greying hair was mostly uncombed and without the product that normally provided its slick, wet appearance. On top of that, he appeared generally disheveled, like he had slipped back into a uniform that had already been in the hamper.

Next to him stood Detective Mangemelli, who cleared six-five. His rich black hair framed his dark Italian complexion. He was younger than his boss by ten years but with perfect tanned skin and large, curious eyes, it looked closer to twenty. His suit was not expensive but was meticulously pressed and neat. The khaki trench coat neatly folded over his left arm finished the outfit smartly.

Hannah didn't wait for the men to come to a stop before she asked the question they all wanted answered. "Did you catch the men who chased Jason into the woods?"

"Not yet, Hannah. But it's just a matter of time," Sheriff Burnett said, not knowing how much Jason had told her.

"It's a big Ryder truck. I'm sure they can't get too far. Right, Pat?" she said.

Burnett gave Jason a disappointed look before answering, "That's right. Law enforcement in surrounding counties and the highway patrol are on the lookout. They won't get far."

"We were wondering if we could speak with you alone, Mr. Kendall," Detective Mangemelli asked. Jason nodded and rose off the couch.

"Ladies, this is a very delicate matter. It is imperative that you don't discuss anything Jason has told you. I don't want you to even discuss it with one another and alter what is fact versus speculation. At some point we made need to ask what you have already heard to make sure incorrect information is not being disseminated. We don't want anything to happen that might impact the apprehension or prosecution of the suspects. I'm sure you understand how important every detail is."

The women nodded, a little worried about the implications of their actions and a little impressed that they were insiders in such a critical situation.

Jason got up and followed the two men out of the room. The sheriff warned him that the interview might take a while and, with the time approaching 2 AM, suggested that Jason send the women home. Jason took his advice and after another strong command from Sheriff Burnett to keep any information regarding the night's events quiet, he walked the women out to their cars in front of the hospital. Kate offered to go home with Hannah, who declined, saying she wouldn't sleep anyway. Kate looked at Jason who nodded that his mom would be okay.

Her offer rebuked, Kate offered to wait at the hospital for Jason. It took a couple minutes of persuading her that nothing new was going to happen before morning and that he'd call her if it did, before Kate finally agreed to go home for the night. Even though he would have much rather had her near.

Burnett and Mangemelli were at the front desk talking to the doctor when Jason returned. Mangemelli intercepted him and escorted him to the hospital conference room while Burnett finished his conversation with the doctor. A cheap wildlife print hung behind a long faux wood table, which was surrounded by blue stackable chairs. Jason wondered if a designer intentionally tried to make it look as antiseptic as the exam and patient rooms.

Jason and Mangemelli had just sat down on opposite sides of the table when Sheriff Burnett entered and took the chair between them at the end of the table.

"What did the doctor say about Liz?" Jason asked the sheriff.

Burnett glanced at the detective, then back to Jason, pausing to measure what he was willing to release. "They're currently focused on dehydration and exhaustion. They're giving her fluids and letting her rest. Other than that, they just have to wait."

"She looked pretty beat up," Jason said. "Did they check for any internal injuries?"

"According to the doctor, they haven't found anything serious. Physically, after some time to heal, she should be fine. Emotionally? Who knows—may take longer to heal," Burnett said.

"That's it? Are you sure? I'm no doctor but she looked to be in bad shape."

Burnett cut him off. "Jason, let the doctors do their jobs. If anything comes up, they'll let us know."

Mangemelli straightened and pulled the folds from his sport coat. "Mr. Kendall, do you mind if we record this conversation? We don't want to miss anything that might help us catch the parties responsible."

Jason shrugged and the detective placed a small recorder on the table between them.

The sheriff spoke next. "Jason, can you walk us through tonight's events? Start at the time you got out of your truck and keep going until you pulled into the hospital. Don't leave anything out. What may seem insignificant to you may be a big help to us."

Jason recounted the night's events and the two men took considerable notes but didn't interrupt. When he was completely finished reciting his account, they began their questioning.

"And why were you there in the first place?" Mangemelli asked.

Jason looked at Burnett and then back to Mangemelli. "I needed evidence that something bad was going on there. I had nosed around a little after seeing Miss Pratt hurt last weekend but Sheriff Burnett told me to leave it to the professionals. My gut was telling me something still wasn't right, so I decided to get something more concrete for the sheriff to grab onto. I was there yesterday and, like I said, thought I saw the HELP message on the window. I figured if I could confirm someone was inside, that would give Sheriff Burnett cause to search the house for himself."

"But you didn't," Mangemelli said. "You didn't call him when you saw a message asking for help yesterday, and you didn't call him when you found the woman being held in the basement tonight. Why not?"

Jason looked down at the table for a moment before addressing the detective. "I was running the other direction when I noticed the message—I wasn't sure of exactly what I saw. I'd planned on going back to make sure but was stuck in jail last night. As for tonight, I called Sheriff Burnett the very minute we were out of danger. I got you involved as fast as I could."

"Forgive me, Mr. Kendall," Mangemelli said, "but it strikes me that you repeatedly refrained from calling law enforcement at times when you could have."

"Understand, I saw things going on at that house starting last week." Jason looked at the print of two ducks taking off out of a pond while he unscrambled his thoughts. "I'm sure the sheriff was being prudent in the way he approached the incident last Friday and the follow-up during the week. But I felt like his actions were more passive than active. Then last night, I was hoping he would see the HELP message for himself and act on it. When he didn't and didn't seem suspicious after later talking to Ms. Riddle, I figured I needed more evidence to convince him something was going on out there."

Sheriff Burnett slapped his hand on the table. "I can't act on what I don't know."

"You're right. I don't mean to make this about you, Sheriff." Jason responded, then turned back to detective Mangemelli. "My wife and daughter were killed two years ago this week. I first saw the men when I was falling-down drunk and an emotional basket case trying to deal with the loss. By the time I called you guys, there was no trace of the men and Ms. Riddle acted completely oblivious to what had happened. I knew I wasn't crazy—but maybe I needed to see the person with my own eyes to be completely sure."

"Or maybe you needed her as some type of bargaining chip?" suggested the detective.

Jason's confusion was obvious.

Mangemelli pressed on. "Maybe you and Ms. Riddle were involved together in some not-so-legal endeavors and when it didn't end well, you did your best to help the sheriff discover Ms. Pratt and put the target squarely on Ms. Riddle."

"That's crazy. I just met Ms. Riddle—what would we have been involved in?"

"You and Ms. Riddle were neighbors for almost three years but you never met? Then last week you hear and see violence coming from her house. Days later, she calls our office to tell us you were trespassing on her property, but then when we arrest you, she doesn't want to press charges. I'm having a hard time reconciling everything. It sounds to me like there is a lot more to your story than what you're telling us. It wouldn't be the first or even the second time you lied to this office, would it?"

Sheriff Burnett held up a hand. "Jason, would you care to have an attorney present?"

Jason could feel the sweat forming at his hairline as he disregarded the sheriff and stared at Mangemelli. "What do you think would be going on between me and Clara Riddle?"

"That's what we need to find out." Mangemelli said. "Let's back up for a minute. You told Sheriff Burnett you were alone and drunk in your deer stand Friday night. Is there anyone who can corroborate where you were or your state of sobriety?"

"Like you just said, I was alone. But the empty bottles are still in the stand if that helps. I'm no forensics expert, but maybe you can analyze the ground around my stand? It was doused with piss chock-full of Maker's Mark and Killian's Red."

"Why'd you wait until morning to tell me about the girl, Jason?" Sheriff Burnett asked.

"I told you. I passed out in my truck." Jason could hear the defensiveness in his words.

"And you couldn't call before then?"

"I didn't have my cell phone with me," Jason said.

"Is that a habit?" Mangemelli asked.

"No, but—" Jason stumbled.

Detective Mangemelli didn't give him time to recover. "Tell us about your relationship with Ms. Riddle."

"There is no relationship. I met her for the first time a couple nights ago."

"What about her son? What's your relationship with him?" asked Mangemelli.

"Never met him. I heard he was a soldier—that's all I know."

"Do you use drugs, Mr. Kendall?"

"What? No!"

"If I went to your house, would I find methamphetamine?"

"No, you wouldn't."

"What about guns?"

"What about 'em?"

"Do you own any?"

"Yes." Jason suddenly thought the shorter the answers, the better.

"Handguns? Do you own any handguns?" asked the detective.

"One, for target shooting. Why?" Jason replied, then stopped, looked at the sheriff and said, "Do I need to ask for an attorney?"

The sheriff looked squarely at Jason and said, "Clara Riddle was murdered tonight. We're going to need to see that gun."

# CHAPTER 30

## FRIDAY

The interview/interrogation continued for another two hours. Both officers asked the same questions over and over from slightly different angles, which Jason hoped he answered the same, truthful, way each time. When he got home, Jason found his mom asleep in an overstuffed chair in the living room with two squares of fabric in her lap. She was still holding a needle between her thumb and forefinger. He set the fabric and needle on the round end table next to her and laid a recently completed quilt over her before going upstairs. His mom had been right earlier in the day: it wasn't clear who was taking care of whom.

Jason went up to his room and considered the night he'd just endured. It was easily the most exhilarating and frightening ordeal he'd ever been through. It seemed like six days rather than six hours since he'd driven out to Clara Riddle's house and rescued Liz Pratt from her basement cell. Now, somehow, he was a lead murder suspect. How had things turned from overwhelmingly good to unbelievably bad so quickly?

It was almost lunchtime when Jason woke. He propped himself up and, having slept long past his 7:30 alarm, immediately reached for his Blackberry. *7 New Messages*—slept through those, too. He climbed out of bed and held down the 1 key on the phone, which signaled it to play the messages back in the order received. The first two were from his crew chiefs asking for a more detailed work plan for the day. Seth was the next to call—checking in again. Kate had called at 9:32. "Jason, it's Kate. Sheriff Burnett and a detective, a tall guy, just left here. They interviewed me in my boss's office for the last half hour. They told me that right now you're just a witness but I think they suspect you of being involved in what happened to Clara Riddle. I can't believe she's dead! Call me as soon as you can."

The next message was also from Kate; worried about why he hadn't called her back yet. The last two messages were from the crew chiefs, still waiting for direction. He called them back first, conferencing them together and putting a plan in place to finish out the week. He felt the throbbing in his knee and shoulder and decided to take a hot shower before returning any more calls.

After getting dressed, he went downstairs to grab a soda but found none in the refrigerator. He cussed his bad luck and slammed the door shut, then remembered the extra bottle he'd bought yesterday was still lying on the passenger seat of his truck. He slipped on a pair of tennis shoes and opened the back door to find Clint Baskett in his deputy uniform walking toward him, a nightstick in his hand.

Jason shut the door behind him and waited for Clint, who didn't acknowledge him until he was only inches away. "Mr. Kendall, you need to come with me. The sheriff has some more questions."

"*Mr. Kendall?* That's a long way from shoving my face into that alley and making me eat gravel when we were kids."

"If my folks had known you'd turn out to be a piece-of-shit murderer, I doubt I'd a gotten a beating for that one," Clint said. "So, you coming easy or you coming hard?" He tightened his grip on the nightstick.

"You look pretty comfortable with a little pole in your right hand, Clint. I don't dare mess with anyone who's obviously so practiced." He winked at Clint and lifted his arms in surrender.

Clint stepped to the side to allow Jason to lead the way down the path. "I bet the boys up in the Stillwater pen will enjoy that little wink. I always knew your little neighborhood-hero routine was a bunch of shit. It took some convincing, but now the sheriff knows it, too."

Jason whirled at Clint but the deputy was ready for it and jammed the nightstick in just below Jason's belt line. Jason fought the reflex to buckle forward. Instead, he remained ramrod straight and returned the deputy's stare. "You're the reason Clara Riddle's dead, Clint. If you had done your job, you would have found that girl last Saturday. You would have realized Riddle was hiding something. But I guess it's like they always say—never send a goon to do a man's job." He held his position, waiting for a reaction from Clint but only received a condescending stare.

Jason turned to start back for the car when his kidney was branded by Clint's nightstick. His back arched in response to the pain and Clint used the momentum to spin him hard to the ground. Handcuffs clicked tightly around one wrist as Clint spoke. "You shouldn't have resisted, pretty boy. It just makes you look more guilty."

Jason sat alone in the jail cell for the better part of an hour before being escorted to an interview room. Sheriff Burnett and Detective Mangemelli came in twenty minutes later wearing the same clothes from last night. The sheriff still looked disheveled and now the detective was beginning to follow suit.

Sheriff Burnett spoke first. "Deputy Baskett said you tried to assault him."

"So how does he explain the nightstick impression across my *back*?"

"So you didn't assault him?"

"No."

Burnett nodded in a way that signaled agreement. A good sign?

Detective Mangemelli cleared his throat and put the recorder from last night in the center of the table. "Thank you for coming in, Mr. Kendall. We have some additional questions from our conversation last night. Again I must ask if you would like to have an attorney present."

Jason shook his head. "I'm good."

"Okay, fine. So could you begin by again going over the events of last night for us as you remember them."

He assumed they were looking for any inconsistencies, so he recounted the same story, doing his best to include everything he had the night before but nothing more. Neither man gave any reaction during his narrative nor immediately after.

"Did you have anything to do with the death of Clara Riddle?" Mangemelli asked.

"No. Absolutely not."

"Were you in any way involved in the capture or imprisonment of Elizabeth Pratt?" he asked.

"No. I was not." Jason wondered if something had happened that solidified his position at the top of the suspect list. "I think it's time I included a lawyer in this conversation."

Sheriff Burnett spoke next. Jason sensed he was usurping the detective's strategy. "Here's where we're at, Jason. Either you are unbelievably smart and orchestrated a terribly heinous crime, or you're not very bright and your bumbling moves enabled or in fact, caused, the crimes to happen."

"So either I'm a brilliant criminal or an innocent but hazardous buffoon. I'm not very fond of either choice."

"I'm guessing the latter," the sheriff said, "but at this point we can't rule out the former, so here is how we are going to proceed: Detective Mangemelli is going to follow the evidence as if you're our lead suspect. I am going to follow the evidence as if you're not. So, you become both our key witness and best lead."

"Those titles are a little more complimentary," Jason said. "But isn't your best witness Liz Pratt?"

The two officers looked at each other and Mangemelli gave his boss a slight nod before Burnett explained. "Ms. Pratt isn't talking."

"Why not? Is she afraid they'll get to her again?" Jason asked.

"It's not us," Burnett clarified. "She won't talk, period. Her family is here, but she hasn't uttered a single word to them, the doctor, us, nobody. The doctor said it's not that unusual after what she's been through."

"Did he say how long she'd be like that?"

"Did *she* say. Jean Anderson is on the day shift. She said she's seen it a couple times over the years. It could be hours or it could be days. We're just going to have to wait," Burnett said. "So we're going to tell you some things that, if you're guilty, you know already, and if you're not, may help us with our investigation." Jason nodded. He was glad to be on the same side as Sheriff Burnett for a change.

"You mentioned the moving truck and the men carrying things in and out. What about Friday? Did you see the men leave with anything, even grocery bags, backpacks, briefcases, that sort of thing?" Burnett asked.

"No. I don't remember anything like that."

"Where was Ms. Riddle when you were at the house last night?"

"I never saw her, but I was in the basement for maybe a minute and the main floor for literally less than ten seconds."

"Did you notice any strange smells in the air?" asked the sheriff.

"Like what?"

"A chemical smell—like in a beauty salon."

"Boy, not that I remember, but that doesn't mean there wasn't any," Jason said.

"You'd remember it," Burnett said. "And you said you never knew her son?"

"No. I saw a picture of him the night I visited Ms. Riddle; she said he was a soldier who died in Afghanistan. That's all."

Jason answered a few more questions from the sheriff, then several more pointed questions from the detective. When he finished, Mangemelli nodded to Burnett, who spoke next. "I don't want to sound dramatic or ominous, but we need you to stay in town until we tell you otherwise." Jason agreed. "And I'm asking you as a friend to keep this conversation confidential. It won't be easy. A town this size is going to be submerged in talk of Clara Riddle's murder. And if you're innocent, you'll risk letting Liz Pratt's captors go unpunished."

"I'll do whatever you need," Jason said.

They led him out of the room and he continued all the way outside to check messages while he waited for a deputy to drive him home. His mom, Kate, and Seth had called again to check in. He called his mom first to let her know he was okay and to tell her not to talk to anyone about last night.

"I think we need to call someone, Jason—get some legal help," Hannah said.

"I've considered that, but I'm not quite ready to take that step."

"It's not just about being innocent, dear. We need to know how to prove it if we need to."

"I know. But I don't want to look like I have something to hide, either. How are you doing?"

"I'm just fine—it's you we need to worry about."

Nothing was going to be settled on the phone, so Jason told his mom he would be home soon and they could talk more then. He called Kate at her office next. She immediately hung up and called him from her cell phone a safe distance down the hall. Jason listened as she recounted her interview from the morning. Jason could hear her nerves actually fraying as she worked her way through the questioning. After she finished her story, she asked about him and whether they had spoken to him.

"They talked to me again. I think they are just hoping a lead drops out if they keep shaking the trees. It's their job," Jason said.

"Do they think you murdered Ms. Riddle? Be honest with me."

"I have a feeling a certain deputy pounded it into their heads last night and, unfortunately, it's going to take some time and convincing to get it all the way out, that's all," he said. "What worries me is that if I'm still a suspect, then they don't have any other strong leads. Maybe if I can rack my brain and come up with something to help the investigation—a memory, a detail I've forgotten, something distinguishing about one of the men, anything."

"Would it help to look at it from a different angle? I'd be happy to listen—be a second set of eyes for you."

"That might be a good idea," he said. Any time with Kate was a good idea.

"Why don't you come over tonight and you can bounce some thoughts off me? I'm going crazy just speculating on everything."

"Sounds good, but how about we get some dinner and just hang for a while first," he suggested.

"I'd like that." They made plans for when and where, then hung up.

The deputy came out and held up his keys. "Ready?"

"Thanks, but I'll walk. I've got a stop to make."

---

In a large metal garage with the rental truck parked safely behind them, General Attar and Muhab stared at the general's hand-written flowchart. A small wood-burning stove in the corner tried, but failed, to warm the cool autumn air in the uninsulated structure. Neither man spoke for several minutes as General Attar studied timing adjustments and strategy tweaks for the mission and their potential impacts on later actions. Muhab, whose expertise was cultural and sociological engineering, could only wait while the tactician completed his calculations.

"The risk of moving the timetable forward is significant, " General Attar said. "But I believe it is equally dangerous to wait—with a full complement of operatives in each city, waiting for the clock to tick, being discovered becomes a real possibility. If what happened here last night should occur in any of the other twelve cities, it could bring the entire mission down with it." He looked at Muhab. "You have not received any more information from your source with local law enforcement?"

"Not yet, but I expect an update soon," Muhab said, then gesturing to the chart, asked,"What is the solution?"

General Attar stared at the chart for another minute, then suddenly straightened, fresh energy radiating from him. He tapped the paper, picked it up, crumpled it, and threw it in the stove. "We turn a negative into a positive. We move up our schedule *and* increase our success rate. Ready your men!"

---

The door stayed open. That was the rule. Without the ability to speak, Liz made it clear that the hospital room door was not to be closed—not even during doctor's visits. A uniformed deputy was stationed at the door where inside, an older woman, probably her mother, was tending to the Liz; holding her hand at her bedside. Liz was the first to notice Jason standing uncomfortably out in the hallway. She reached out a heavily-wrapped hand and her inviting smile pulled him through the door. The deputy, seeing Liz's greeting, allowed Jason to enter.

The strong aroma from two enormous floral arrangements mixed with the harsh scent of someone clearly over-perfumed walloped Jason as he crossed through the threshold. He blinked involuntarily as he approached the bed. A man, who looked to be Liz's father, got up from his chair in the corner and stood behind the woman, bedside. They both looked over Jason with guarded suspicion.

Liz looked one hundred percent better. She was sitting up in her bed and the sunlight through the window seemed to concentrate its powers directly onto her smiling face. Her color was better and, while still naturally thin, the IV fluids of the past twelve hours had removed the hollowness in her face and plumped her skin. Even without makeup and marbled with cuts and bruises, she was a beautiful young woman.

"How are you feeling?"

Liz nodded and pressed her lips together.

"This is probably going to come out wrong," he said, "but you look much better."

Her smile grew. It did come out bad, but she understood what he meant and seemed to revel in his lack of social grace.

"I'm sorry I didn't bring any flowers or anything. I'm not good about that kind of thing. Do you think anyone would mind if I just added my name to one of the arrangements already in here?" Liz's smile broadened. *Not fumbling too bad*, he thought.

"I talked to the sheriff's office and they're really on top of things. They're going to catch the men who did this to you real soon."

She looked down and brushed at her gown.

"Well, I just wanted to come by and see how you were doing. It looks like you're in great hands here—."

She grabbed his hand a little tighter, denying his retreat.

"How do you know Liz?" asked the woman sitting beside her.

"We met last night." The woman understood and gave him a grateful nod as a single tear rolled down her cheek.

"You raised a strong young woman. You should be very proud," he said to the woman and returned Liz's firm grip.

"We are." She caressed her daughter's hair and smiled at her in a way that showed the tremendous level of respect and pride she had. "Very proud."

"I should go," he said to Liz. She nodded reluctantly.

He still felt responsible through his inaction for her being in a hospital bed in the first place. He wanted desperately to leave her with something inspirational or meaningful that would stay with her during the upcoming days and weeks of physical and emotional recovery, but could only find words that sounded pretentious and trite.

"I'm sorry. I'm sorry for everything you went through," he said, choking on the final words.

He turned to leave and was at the door when he heard it.

"Jason." Liz's voice was weak and jagged. A collective gasp from the room followed.

He turned back and saw her mother starting to sob. But Liz was smiling. "Thank you."

He nodded and swallowed hard. "You're welcome."

# CHAPTER 31

Jason felt weighted down as he slowly walked the eight blocks home from the hospital, not to mention his knee hurt like hell. His thoughts jumped from Mangemelli's arrogance to images of Kelly pushing Grace in her stroller down the same section of Fifth Street to thoughts of purpose and whether it's determined by God or the person searching for it. His pace slowed further over the last block, as he thought about all the ways the past seven days would impact Liz Pratt's future.

Jason found Hannah in the living room/quilting headquarters with two other women. She was cutting fabric while the others added decorative touches by hand to nearly completed quilts. One of the women asked if Jason knew about the shooting in the country and a quick roundtable of outrage, horror and speculation followed. Jason noticed his mom hadn't given away any inside information and closed the discussion by telling Hannah he wouldn't be home for dinner.

"Where are you going?" asked a woman whose shiny scalp showed through her thinning white hair.

Jason nodded, curiously. "I was thinking about having dinner at Vera's tonight, if that's okay."

"Is that an offer?" the woman asked. "What time do you want to pick me up?" The three women laughed as if she'd just scored one for the team.

"You know, I would much prefer *your* company but I'm already meeting someone else."

"Is it a girl?" the woman asked. All three women stopped what they were doing and looked up at him.

"In fact, it is. And that's the last question I'll be taking this afternoon, thank you."

Hannah waited a moment to see if her friend would continue the ribbing but she didn't. "I'm having dinner at Vera's tonight, too."

Jason looked at her to see if she was just continuing the fun but saw she wasn't. "What's the occasion?"

Her answer was a bit cryptic. "Neil called this morning to tell me about the shooting out in the country. He could tell I was a little bothered by it, so he offered to talk more over dinner."

"Good. Maybe I'll see you there, then." *Taking their relationship public?* Jason wondered.

"Jason, before you run off, can you help me bring in some more coffee and scones for the ladies?"

The third woman, who was the oldest but retained the largest percentage of original hair color, spoke up. "Hannah, don't you dare. You already fixed us a big lunch—I'm going to be leaving soon anyhow."

The other woman seconded the notion. "She's right, Hannah. Stop spoiling us and sit back down."

"Nonsense," Hannah said, and pushed Jason out of the room before they could argue further.

In the kitchen, Hannah cleaned the coffee pot while Jason filled the water to the instructed level. "Thank you for not telling your friends I was at Clara Riddle's house last night," Jason said. "What about Neil? Did you tell him?"

"He asked if you knew about the shooting and I said you did but that was all I said." She spooned fresh coffee into the filter and started the coffeemaker. "I think Neil could tell I wasn't telling him everything. That's why he offered up the dinner idea."

"I'd rather you hold off saying anything to him until I get my name completely off the suspect list. Plus, we don't want to do anything that might impact the sheriff's investigation. I'm sure everything that happened last night is going to get around town sooner or later, but I would much rather it be later if possible."

"I understand, dear. Neil will, too."

Jason offered to help his mom deliver the coffee but she shooed him away. He went down to his basement office and found himself full of energy with no way to expend it. He called both crew chiefs, asking if they needed any help, hoping one of them would need him to buckle on a tool belt and throw a hammer until quitting time. No such luck; things were right on schedule. He thought about other work-related activities requiring his attention and remembered the Strait estimate saved on his laptop. He printed it out and drove over to First Lutheran Church.

Avery Strait was in the middle of a telephone conversation when Jason arrived, but waved him in, then gestured to the chairs facing his desk. Jason hated sitting with clients when they were on the phone. The harder he tried to focus on something else, the more he tuned into the conversation. In this case, an angry father was upset that his daughter was witness to some kissing between two other kids during a youth-group hayride. Jason spent the first few minutes of the call pretending to review the proposal. Then, when the conversation moved to debating whether the youth pastor should lose her job, he closed the folder and scanned the walls filled with plaques, artwork, and other assorted memorabilia. Finally, the pastor ended the conversation, rose from his chair, and extended his long right arm across the desk.

"Hello, Jason. I must apologize. In my business, you never know when a two-minute call is going to go two hours."

Jason shook his hand. "You were on that call for two hours?"

"More like twenty minutes. But between you and me, sometimes it feels like *twenty days*, you know?" he said, then pointed to the folder in Jason's hand. "Is that the estimate for the basement? It doesn't look like there's much in there. I hope that's because the numbers are so small." The pastor laughed, but not convincingly.

Jason handed him the folder and walked the pastor through the itemized costs. In the first few minutes, the pastor had worked fifteen percent off the labor. Jason wasn't a bad negotiator, but he was an unworthy adversary to Avery Strait and he soon realized the longer he sat in the pastor's office, the more profit he was going to lose. He got up to leave the office before he ended up paying for the building materials himself. The pastor got up with him and walked him down the hall.

"Did you hear about the shooting?" the pastor asked.

"Yeah. It's unbelievable."

"I don't understand how she let those people make drugs in her home. And then they kill her? Terrible!"

"They were making drugs?"

"The man I was speaking with on the phone said the sheriff told reporters there was a big methamphetamine lab in the basement," the pastor explained.

"It was a drug house? That doesn't make sense," Jason muttered to himself.

"What was that?" asked Pastor Strait.

"I said it all seems so senseless," Jason lied.

"Oh, I don't believe that. People talk about senseless violence. There is no such thing. All violence is intentional. There are too many terms these days that make despicable acts seem understandable. A person may regret his choice later, but at the time, it made plenty of sense. I can't tell you what it is, but there's a reason those men took that poor woman's life." He shook his head. "Can you believe it? The first time I'd ever heard of Clara Riddle was when you mentioned her yesterday. And the very next day she is murdered in her own home. Unbelievable."

"So was she a member of First Lutheran?" Jason asked.

"No. I checked into that when I got here yesterday. I wanted to see if we could bring her back to a more active role. But she deactivated her membership a number of years ago, well before I arrived."

"Deactivate? Does that mean she quit?" Jason asked.

"It doesn't mean she quit God, if that's what you're asking. Usually someone chooses to deactivate when he or she marries someone from another faith, like a Lutheran marrying a Catholic. The person deactivates when he or she adopts the new church's covenants."

"Do you know why, or where she was going?"

"No. But I'll bet someone asked her at the time—to make sure there was nothing we could do to keep her. At least, that's what I'd do. But no, we don't keep records of that sort of thing," he said. "Who knows? If we had done a better job of hanging on to her, things could have turned out differently."

Jason had his doubts.

# CHAPTER 32

At 5:30, the line of hungry would-be diners filled the waiting area and was already spilling onto the sidewalk outside Vera's. Jason and Kate managed their way though the mass of people to the bar, but no stools were open and a thick crowd had swelled behind them. Louise shimmied through to the host desk near the front entry and told the teenaged hostess, Latangela, to quote a two-hour wait to people still arriving.

Jason and Kate were standing just behind her and watched the young girl, clearly overwhelmed, start to tear up. Louise put a tender arm around her shoulder, "Honey, when a table is open, we call the next name on the list—same as every night. If people are backed up around the block, they know better than we do, it's going to be awhile before they're able to sit down. You're doing just great, Sugar. I'm just so thankful you're the girl I have working the desk with me tonight." The girl nodded and wiped an eye.

Jason leaned down over Louise's shoulder and spoke in a hushed voice, "Hey, Weezie, I'll run for *mayor* if you give me the next table."

She turned around and swatted him on the arm. Her voice boomed. "You'll get a table when your name is called, just like everybody else."

"Okay. So are you gonna call my name next?" He gave her his most over-the-top charming smile and included a wink as a bonus.

She turned to the podium to see where Jason's name was on the list. She wheeled back around and swatted him on the arm again, this time even harder. "Your name isn't even on the sheet."

"I know. We just got here," he said.

Louise glanced over at Kate, then back to Jason. "You two together?"

"Don't make anything of it. Please?" he pleaded.

"I'm not making nothin' outta nothin.' I'm just surprised she's willing to be seen out with you and that scruffy mug of yours. You forget how to shave?" Louise looked at Kate and they shared a laugh at his expense.

He felt the two-day growth on his chin and decided to change the subject. "What's with all the people tonight? You got some half-price deals going on?" He twisted away from her third slug to his arm.

"No. This is all about that horrible murder. Look around," Louise waved into the dining room. "After what happened at that house last night, people want to spend time with those they love. They want to hold their family close. Heck, I'm going to be out of chicken fingers and macaroni and cheese in the next half hour. I got a busboy running to the grocery store right now to buy up all of their boxed mac-n-cheese. Bad stuff like this isn't supposed to happen in Cedar River, ya know? It scares everybody—it's not supposed to happen here."

Jason and Kate nodded.

"Your mom is here. You could join them if you want to; I don't know if they've ordered yet. They got in near the front of the rush."

Jason looked at Kate with a look that said, "I'd rather not."

"Let's at least go say hello," Kate said.

Louise gave them a push to clear up some space. "Yeah, handsome, go hug your mom; they're in the back. I'll put your name on the list, just in case."

Kate and Jason didn't get far before being stopped. First, they ran into Kate's boss, who was having dinner with her husband. She gave Kate an "aw, shucks" look—she had left the office at noon claiming a bad stomachache. Then they stopped by the table of one of Jason's recent clients. Jason tried to ask about the new entertainment center he'd installed as a part of a larger rec-room job, but all the couple wanted to talk about was Clara Riddle's murder.

They were still only halfway to Jason's mom when Seth called from across the room. He and Robyn were sitting at a large round table with three of their four children. When they got to the table, Jason harassed the kids for a couple minutes, which got both them and Robyn worked up, but in different ways. He could see things were ready to get out of hand, so he sat down in the open seat next to Seth.

Seth moved a children's placemat, wet with spilled chocolate milk, from in front of Jason's chair. "We were going to wait for Chip to get done with practice, but he called and wanted to have dinner at a buddy's house, instead. Robyn didn't want him to go. She's pretty upset about the shooting, but I convinced her it'd be worse if he was sitting here acting all pissy."

"Speaking of Chip, is he coming hunting with us this year?" Jason asked, glancing at Robyn. She was talking with Kate and didn't hear him.

"Are you kidding? Robyn dropped a serious hammer on that idea. He wasn't happy."

"How much did you tell Robyn about last night? Burnett was very clear that I wasn't supposed to share anything with anyone," Jason said, lowering his voice.

"Nothing, really." Seth gave the women a nervous glance. "I told her Ms. Riddle's house was near your land and that you could see it from your deer stand. She was curious if you knew her or ever saw anything unusual. I told her you never really noticed the house until just recently."

"Thanks, pal—I appreciate it. Give me a heads-up if or when you do tell her and make sure it doesn't go any farther," he said, then sarcastically added, "not that your wife would ever spread any gossip or anything."

Seth peeked at the women again. Robyn was wiping jelly off the hands of their four-year-old. "I'll keep it to myself, don't worry." Then, changing the subject, "Isn't it weird how someone could live in this small town for so many years, but no one really knew her—Ms. Riddle?"

"Yeah, I guess if you really want a private life you can have it—even in Cedar River."

"What's with the notebook?" he asked, pointing to the portfolio under Jason's arm.

"Consider this under the category of things I shouldn't be talking to anyone about," Jason said, glancing around the room. "Burnett's got a hair up his ass that I'm involved in the murder. I don't think he really believes it, but he doesn't seem to have any other leads to go on. So, Kate and I are going to deconstruct all the things that have happened over the week to see if I can come up with anything that could help him look in another direction and find the real murderers. Kate offered to be a second set of eyes so I'm going to bounce some thoughts off her."

Seth sat up. "I want in on that." Jason was searching for a reason to let him down when Seth looked over at the women. "Honey, Jason needs me to help him with something later. It's pretty important."

"Tonight?" Robyn was making a statement more than asking a question. Then she looked quizzically at Jason to see if he was behind the idea.

"How about if I wait until after Annie and Jake's bedtime?" Seth pressed on.

Robyn waited a moment before answering, then looked over at Jason. "Fine," she said, clearly perturbed.

"I'll see you at eight," Seth told Jason, who looked up at Kate. She appeared less than enthused.

---

Hannah and Neil were well into their meals before Kate and Jason finally got to their table. They were squeezed between two large round tables, each with parents struggling to control three young children.

Hannah showed mock astonishment at seeing Jason and Kate. "What a surprise, seeing the two of you here!" She gestured between Kate and Neil, "Kate, this is Neil Lockwood, our former neighbor. Neil, this is Jason's friend, Kate Brooks. She's the woman I told you stayed with me the night Jason was away."

Neil rose and shook Kate's hand. "Very nice to meet you, Kate. Have you been drafted into Hannah's quilting brigade?"

"I think I'm still a ways away from earning my way into that group," Kate said.

"Don't be silly. You're welcome anytime," Hannah said.

Jason chimed in. "Yeah, but isn't there a surcharge if you don't have your AARP card?" The comment earned him "the look" from his mother for the second time that day. He returned his own look that said, "What did I say?"

"Would you like to join us?" Neil asked, then spread his arms out wide, gesturing to the tables on either side of them. "The crossfire of crayons and soda crackers has died down greatly in the last fifteen minutes. But I can't promise a corn dog won't land in your lap at some point."

"Yes, please sit down," Hannah urged.

Kate deferred to Jason. "Maybe for a couple minutes. We were going to head up to the bar for a drink," he said, providing them an out. Neil noticed the portfolio before Jason could slide it under his chair.

"What do you have there?" he asked, pointing to the leather-bound pad.

Jason hesitated, then said, "The kitchen in Kate's duplex has almost no storage space, so we're going to try to pencil out a pantry, maybe disguise it as an armoire to go between the kitchen and dining room."

"You're in good hands, Kate," Neil said. "Jason transformed some wasted storage space under the stairs at my parents' house in Minneapolis and turned it into wonderful display shelves. The house is almost sixty years old and you'd think the shelves were original to the space. And he upgraded the stair banister—same thing." He put his thumb and fore-finger together in a gesture of excellence.

"Sounds beautiful," Kate said.

"It really is. In fact, I think you'd love it. You want to rent it? It's available!" Neil said.

"You still haven't found any renters?" Jason asked. "What's the holdup?"

"The real estate agents I've talked to say they're having a hard time filling vacancies lately. All they keep telling me is that it runs in cycles. But they continue to assure me it's just a matter of time," he said.

"You better get lucky soon. If it's still empty when the snow starts to fall, you might as well put out a sign saying, 'Burglarize me!'"

"Thankfully, Mr. Soucheray will make sure that doesn't happen," Neil said.

Jason remembered how the recently-retired neighbor spent as much time at Neil's house as Jason did during the renovation a couple years earlier. "You still owe him about five grand in labor. He did more work on your house than I did," Jason said.

"Well, I'll know where to find him," Neil said.

"In his garage," the two men said together, acknowledging one of the world's foremost putterers.

Hannah changed the subject to the food to include Kate in the conversation but, inevitably, like each of the other tables in the restaurant, the discussion turned to the murder of Clara Riddle.

"Neil was just saying before you arrived that they found a meth lab in the basement," Hannah said. "They think maybe old Ms. Riddle got in the middle of a drug war. Can you believe that? A drug war in Cedar River? How do you recognize something like that?"

Neil asked Jason, "Do you think what you saw Friday had anything to do with this? It's hard to believe that a bunch of kids just happened to be partying outside a house with a working meth lab."

"I don't know. It sure sounds like they could be linked. I've talked to the sheriff and now he knows everything I know. Hopefully it will help somehow," Jason said. "But I guess we won't know for sure until the sheriff finishes his investigation."

"I'm just so afraid that this is going to change everything," Hannah said.

"How so?" asked Kate.

"Like innocence lost. If we see some teenagers out acting like kids on a Friday night, are we going to think it's something else—something worse? Remember how things changed in St. Cloud after that poor boy was abducted while he was playing with his friends years ago? People started locking their doors during the day and not letting their children walk down the street to play. It really bothers me the way a couple of bad people can change an entire community forever."

The four of them talked for a while longer and Hannah pleaded with them to vow to keep things "normal" and to spread the campaign to others. Louise was scurrying past and noticed Hannah and Neil's finished plates.

"Sorry, folks. Just when we get caught up, everything gets backed up again," she said.

"No problem. But you can tell the waitress the two of us are ready for our check," Hannah said.

Louise scanned the restaurant, then turned back to Hannah with an unsure nod. "I'll get her here as quick as I can…"

"Don't worry about it. This one's on me," Jason said. Neil tried to object but Jason wasn't having any of it, so Hannah and Neil thanked him and excused themselves.

Louise looked around at the battleground of soda crackers, french fries and chicken finger parts. "I'll send someone over to get the table squeaky clean and bring you a couple glasses of chardonnay."

"I'll have a beer," Jason said. Louise lifted an eyebrow. He'd be getting a chardonnay.

"I've been a little pushy about the city council idea," Louise said. "But after today, can't you see why it's so important? A town needs good people leading it. What did Churchill say during the Great War? 'The bad guys win when the good guys stand around and do nothing?'"

"Something like that," Jason said.

"I never saw you as a kid who'd just stand around and do nothin'. You tellin' me I was wrong?" Jason didn't answer. "I didn't think so. Now do me a favor and order the walleye—nobody eats fish when they're feeling bad. Except for a mean old shark, I suppose."

She let out a loud, Marlboro Light-filled laugh and left to order the wine.

# CHAPTER 33

After the waitress took their plates, Jason and Kate talked about where to go next. Kate's duplex didn't seem like the right venue for a night together that now included Seth, so they discussed more public places to meet, finally settling on the Pick Me Up. As they made their way out through the crowded restaurant, Jason suggested they stop by the hospital first to look in on Liz.

Except for a new deputy, Liz was alone in the room. Kate stopped Jason before they went in and told him the door to the room was not her line to cross, that the room should remain a harbor for only those with a personal connection to the traumatized girl. Jason argued that he would feel more comfortable if she were with him, but Kate insisted. So Jason carried the piece of Louise's famous banana cream pie into the room alone.

---

A jazz trio was playing on a small stage inside Pick Me Up when Kate and Jason arrived. The place was packed with St. Joe students; some of them focused on homework, but most of them just hanging out.

"What self-respecting college kid would be caught dead in a coffee shop studying on a Friday night?" Jason asked Kate.

"Yeah, how dare someone not want to drink flat beer from a plastic cup in a dank, crowded basement? What's gotten into kids today?"

"Are you bad-mouthing house parties? What is wrong with you? I suppose you don't think apple pie has a place in America anymore, either—is that true?"

"Shut up, dork. Do you want to wait around for a table or what?"

"Oddly enough, I'm suddenly in the mood for a warm, flat beer," he said.

A few minutes later, they claimed the last open red-leather booth at The Scorecard. They ordered a round of beers and Jason called Seth to tell him their location. The beers arrived and Jason was in the middle of telling Kate about his two interviews with Mangemelli and Burnett when Seth walked up with his own beer.

"What are you doing here already? You told me eight o'clock," Jason said.

"Robyn and the kids were all watching a movie. When I got off the phone with you, Robyn waved me off and gave me the 'just go' look. So here I am."

"You're going to be in trouble for actually leaving," Jason said.

"I'll just do what I always do—blame you."

Jason shrugged. "Let's get to it."

"I'm going to use the ladies' room first," Kate said, sliding out of the booth.

Seth took her spot across from Jason and pushed Kate's beer next to Jason's, bumping his head on the vintage red globe light. "You two seem pretty comfortable together. How's it going?"

"We're taking it slow. But it's weird. Ever since you so discreetly suggested that she wanted to be more than just friends, I've looked at her differently," Jason said. "It's hard to explain, but one day she's just a friend, the next day she's a possibility."

"No disrespect to Kelly, but it's about time you pulled your head out of your ass. Kate wasn't the other 'single' in the group because guys aren't calling—they are. But her sights have been set on you for a while," Seth said. "At least, according to Robyn."

Kate returned and sat down next to Jason at the suddenly quiet table.

"What?" Kate asked.

"I was just telling Jason that the lines on the bottom of my feet look eerily like the face of Jerry Seinfeld," Seth said. Kate made a sour face. "Now you know why we stopped talking about it."

"Thank you for that," she said. "I think this is a good time to turn our focus to removing Jason from the suspect list. We can get back to your feet later… or not." Seth lifted his beer in agreement.

"The last I heard, they think it's connected to a drug war or something," Seth said. "Wouldn't that take him out of consideration right there?"

"Not necessarily," Jason said. "Detective Mangemelli asked if he would find any drugs at my home. I'm trying not to be paranoid, but if someone wanted me to appear involved, and I'm not saying they would, they could stash something in any one of a thousand places at my house and I wouldn't find it. Hell, it would take me a week just to look through the garage top to bottom."

"Between your reputation and your constant contact with people for your job, it should be pretty easy for you to prove you're not involved in a drug ring," Kate said.

"Don't misunderstand me. I feel the same way," Jason said. "I'm just saying that I'm not completely in the clear yet. So anything I can do to help Sheriff Burnett's investigation gets me closer to being crossed off the list." He looked over at Seth, "And like I told Kate, I just want to do whatever I can to catch the bastards who beat and raped Liz and murdered her friend."

"Did he tell you anything more than what he said to the reporters this afternoon?" Seth asked.

Jason shook his head. "Less. He never even mentioned the meth lab."

"Do we know exactly what he said at the press conference?" asked Kate.

Seth answered. "I caught most of it. According to the sheriff, a group of men set up a lab in a secret room in the basement of the house to cook meth. He's guessing something happened that made them decide to suddenly move the operation and kill Ms. Riddle."

"Unbelievable! It sounds like a news report coming from Minneapolis, not here," Kate said.

"I know," Seth said. "Robyn and I keep talking about how living on the north side—our kids' bus stop, the park, the ball fields—they're all within a few miles of that house."

"Hopefully, it's a one-time thing," Kate said. "Word around campus is that they think the suspects are from out of town."

"I don't buy it," Jason said.

"You think they live in Cedar River?" Seth asked.

"That's not what I'm talking about," Jason said. "I'm having a hard time with the whole premise." Kate and Seth gave him a look that told him to continue. "The sheriff's department walked into a house Thursday night with a hidden meth lab, a missing moving truck, and the resident of the house murdered. If that's the crime scene, it makes perfect sense—a group of meth runners need to bolt and kill Ms. Riddle because they're afraid she might talk or they had a disagreement along the way or whatever. It makes *perfect* sense."

"But?" Kate said.

"But that's not what I walked into," Jason said. "I heard gunshots from a late-night gathering and saw one of them hurt Liz Pratt. Then I saw a secret staircase to a sealed-off section of the basement. They held and raped two women for days; one of whom they murdered. Then before they took off, they killed Clara Riddle. That's a lot of violence for some podunk drug burners."

"I disagree. I still think the sheriff's theory works," Seth said. "Just because they are cooking the meth in the country doesn't make them hicks."

"How do you explain the fact they're Middle Eastern or the need for a concealed staircase in the middle of the country? And they were carrying empty boxes *into the house* last night. What was that about?" Jason asked. "And here's the big red flag for me: when Sheriff Burnett was playing 'good' cop, he asked me if I smelled chemicals when I was in the house last night. I didn't understand the purpose of the question at the time, but later, after getting more information, it became pretty obvious he was talking about the meth production."

"Yep, I asked Chip about it. They learned about it in their DARE classes. That's why they usually cook it in the country and not in larger cities; the odors from the chemicals are hellacious and if they don't ventilate the room really well, they could die from inhaling the gases or by blowing up the room. If they set up in town, all the neighbors would easily smell what's going on."

"Right, and I don't remember smelling anything, but I was only in there for a minute." Jason turned to Kate. "That's one of the reasons I suggested we stop to see Liz Pratt at the hospital; she's been in that house since Friday. I asked her if she smelled chemicals like in a beauty salon while she was there, and she hadn't."

"Maybe they stopped making it by then. That may have been what the meeting you saw last Friday was about," Kate said.

"Maybe," responded Jason, sounding unconvinced.

The waitress brought another round of beers and they discussed additional facts, but the evidence kept leading to the sheriff's conclusion for Kate and Seth, more reluctantly for Jason. They went through the activities of Jason's week but, despite a variety of ideas and questions, nothing surfaced that would assist the sheriff's investigation. The group was beginning to feel like it was spinning its wheels and Kate could see it was taking its toll on Jason, whose hand alternated between gently rubbing his leg and tapping the table.

"When you combine all these activities with the line of questioning from the sheriff, you're not able to come up with anything new?" asked Kate.

"Nope. They asked a lot of vague questions; what was my relationship with Clara Riddle? Do I do drugs? Did I know Clara's son?"

Seth cut him off. "Why'd they ask about her son?"

"I don't know. They were probably wondering if he was involved in some way. They must not have known he was killed in Afghanistan when they talked to me."

"He died in Afghanistan and his mom is working with a bunch of Arabs? That doesn't make sense," Seth said.

"I agree. I don't remember any send-offs, or memorials for that matter, in the last couple of years. Wouldn't there have been a big parade or something when he left?" She put her arm on the forearm of Jason's tapping hand. "Maybe we finally have something to take to Sheriff Burnett—he definitely missed her son." The men looked at her quizzically, so she explained. "Jason, remember when you asked who was in the picture when we were in her dining room the other night? Ms. Riddle said, 'That's my Robert.' It was the only thing she said during the visit that wasn't guarded."

"Maybe he didn't die; maybe they have him hostage somewhere and were holding it over her head," Seth said.

"So they can cook meth in Cedar River?" Kate asked doubtfully.

"Okay, it's a stretch," Seth said. "Did the sheriff ask anything else about the son?"

"Not that I remember," Jason said. "Now I wish I would have asked Clara more about him."

"What about the necklace?" Kate asked. The men gave her another puzzled look. She turned to Jason and shook her head. "You go to a woman's house and you notice that the dishes are done, but you don't remember a necklace hanging from her son's picture in the dining room? You are such a man."

Seth cut in and lifted his glass. "That's my boy!"

Jason clinked Seth's glass. "I remember the picture on the buffet with the little doily thing under it; it was about the only piece of décor in the house. But I don't remember the necklace."

Kate shook her head again. "It was a silver pendant with a moon and a little star."

"Was it a crescent moon? And was the star inside it?" asked Jason, twisting his body to her.

Kate nodded. "So you did see it."

"No. I still don't remember it. But I know the symbol; I learned about it online yesterday. It's a symbol of Islam; you know, the way the cross represents Christianity and the Star of David symbolizes Judaism."

"What do you think it means?" Seth asked.

"There's more," Jason said. "Pastor Strait at First Lutheran said Clara deactivated her membership a number of years ago. Something members do when they change religions." He explained that it usually happens after someone marries and converts to another religion.

Kate thought out loud. "Robert's Muslim, but he's fighting in Afghanistan?" They sat in silence for a moment, considering the impact of the possibility, then Kate said, "We should have stayed at The Pick Me Up. We could have Googled Robert and seen what came up."

Jason held up his Blackberry, "But here we've got Google *and* beer." He called up Google on his phone and typed in *"Robert Riddle" Cedar River MN.*

The first result was the jackpot. It contained all of the elements of Jason's search. He read aloud from the archived article from the *St. Paul Pioneer Press* titled "Casualties Still Arriving."

"Thirty-three-year-old Charles Riddle died of a self-inflicted gunshot wound on March 13, 1977… his widow, Clara, continues to live inside a nightmare… son Robert, 9 years old at the time of the suicide… 'His days as a boy just seemed to end that day. No more baseball, no more days at the lake. He hasn't had a friend over to the house in three years' said the widow through a solid flow of tears… The flagpole stands empty, as it has since the day he received word no payments would be issued from the Department of Defense for the chronic illnesses resulting from his third tour of duty in Vietnam… 10 days before he committed suicide… 'I can live with being poor, I am even coming to grips with the loss of my husband, but not seeing my son smile since his daddy's death, that is more than any mother should have to endure. Just one smile; even for a moment… 'No, no trouble in school, other than some issues with lack of participation. His teachers understand.'"

"No way was he fighting on the side of the U.S. in Afghanistan," Seth said. "Any other hits? Something more current?"

Jason scrolled through two pages of search results. "Not that I can find. There are plenty of hits for Robert Riddle but nothing related to Cedar River or Afghanistan."

"If Clara was about the same age as her husband, that would've put her in her mid-sixties," Kate said. "Seeing her the other night, I would have guessed more around late seventies, even early eighties. The last thirty years must have really taken its toll."

"She was murdered last night but she died a long time ago," Jason interjected. "How else can you explain standing by while men are raping and killing women in your own home?"

Seth took a sip of beer and shook his head. "If this country has a main enemy right now, it's Al-Qaeda and Muslim terrorists. And Clara Riddle was inviting them into her house to make drugs for our kids and do God-knows-what to innocent women. I don't care what the government did to you, it can never be enough to help our enemies hurt other innocent people."

"You can't understand the pain she went through," Kate said. "And with no resolution, her anger or sadness probably built on itself over the years. If my kid's life was taken because of something that could have been prevented, I'd be looking for vengeance, too. And Seth, we don't know she stood by and let the bad things happen. Maybe she was trying the help the girls and that's why they killed her."

"Maybe I'm at broken-record stage," Jason said, "but the combination of Islamic fundamentalists and drug-running just doesn't jibe for me."

Silence hung over the group again before Seth slid out of the booth. "I think better alone. I'll be in the can if you need me."

Jason laid his hand on Kate's thigh. "Not exactly the most romantic start to a relationship, huh?"

"I'm sure your plans to whisk me off to Paris on your private jet are still in the works. And a little FYI, I've cleared my busy social schedule for next weekend."

"So a pick-up ride to Milwaukee won't cut it?"

"Maybe a bed and breakfast up on the North Shore," she countered.

"I'd be willing to throw a free brewery tour into the Milwaukee trip," he said.

"You sure know how to make a girl melt."

They kissed each other with the yearning of a couple of teenagers who had been thinking of little else the entire school day.

"Hey, hey, hey. Do I need to call your parents?" Seth said as he slipped back into his spot across the table.

Kate tried to hide her embarrassment by changing the subject. "What's next?"

No one immediately answered. Finally, Seth spoke up. "I just keep thinking, what if this has been going on for years? Who knows how many women have been…" he stammered, then took a deep breath. "You know, tortured or killed."

Kate thought about Hannah's words. *This could change everything.* "We don't know anything yet. I'm hoping we'll find out this was just one terrible event between bad people who aren't even connected to Cedar River."

"Except Clara Riddle. She's Cedar River," Seth said.

They continued to talk but the conversation never found a rhythm.

"Where are we at?" Seth asked.

Jason said, "I'll call Sheriff Burnett again tomorrow and tell him what we know about Robert and Charles Riddle. Maybe Clara Riddle's family is somehow the key to the whole thing."

"Whatever the damn key is, I hope they find it soon," Seth said. "That moving truck is still out there somewhere—these guys aren't done yet."

It was almost midnight when the conversation waned once and for all. Jason reminded the others to keep their discussion private and told them that he would let them know what the sheriff said. Kate finished the meeting by saying, "We don't want to add to any hysteria by circulating hypotheticals. We all know stories *grow* as fast as they *run* through this town." Seth said goodnight after some not-so-gracious ribbing about the incessant tweeting of lovebirds in the area.

Kate and Jason chose to go back to his place rather than hers in case the stresses were adding up for Hannah and causing her Lupus to flare. The fluorescent light over the kitchen sink was on as they came through the back door—the signal that Hannah was in bed for the night. Jason let Kate in, locked the door behind them, then went down the hall to check the front door; the deadbolt was secured. When he came back down the hall, Kate asked, "Do you always check both locks?"

"I used to do it every night when the girls were still here. This might be the first time since."

"Your mom's right; last night changes everything. I looked to make sure you locked the door when we walked in, too. I would have never done that before tonight, but now it's almost involuntary."

They went into the family room, lights still off, and wearily stretched out on the couch in front of the TV. Kate lay in front of Jason, stroking the arm he was using to hold her tight against him. He propped himself up on his other elbow to keep command of the remote. Jason flipped through the on-screen channel guide and stopped when he saw the original *Die Hard* movie was playing on one of the cable movie channels. He hesitated before clicking the OK button.

"It's fine with me. Bruce Willis is a stud in this," Kate said.

"Action movie? Are you trying to turn me on?" Jason asked.

She moved his hand from her stomach up a few inches until it pushed up against her breasts.

"Boy, you don't fool around," he said.

"Actually, that's exactly what I'm planning to do."

She wriggled around until the two were belly to belly. Neither was paying attention when Bruce Willis unloaded his weapon into a bad guy through a conference table.

The couch was a little cramped for Jason's liking, so he suggested, "Why don't we go upstairs?"

Kate pulled back. "No way. Not with your mom here."

"We'll use the guest room. We'll close the door; she won't even know."

"And what is she going to think when she sees me in the morning? 'Well, aren't you a little tramp?'"

"My mom would never call you a tramp," he said. "*Hussy*, sure. But *tramp*? No way." Kate slapped his chest, not impressed with his humor.

"I'm kidding. My mom thinks you're great. I think she's happy we're together."

"Yeah, I'm pretty sure she already likes me better than you—who wouldn't? But I don't care, I'm not going up those stairs tonight—it's too soon. If you want to spend the night with me, I suggest you go get a quilt from the other room that will cover both of us on this couch," she said.

"So I'm not getting lucky tonight?"

"I'm letting you watch *Die Hard*, aren't I? Now go get the quilt."

Jason did as he was told and returned to see Kate lying on the couch watching Bruce Willis jump off the top of a skyscraper with a fire hose wrapped around his waist. She looked up at him and smiled a warm, wonderful smile. He laid the blanket over her and noticed an additional button undone on her blouse. *That's my girl*, he thought. He wanted to savor her—one button at a time.

# CHAPTER 34

## SATURDAY

Jason woke to a stinging sensation at the base of his neck. For a man in his thirties, sleeping on a couch can cause a little stiffness; sharing the space with someone else can be downright painful. On top of the odd neck alignment, he'd slept with his left arm under his body and now it was long past "asleep" and the prolonged decrease in blood flow felt like sharp needles pistoning up and down inside his shoulder. The needles dug in even deeper as he rose onto his elbow.

He looked down at Kate, asleep in front of him. The beauty and contentment in her face were a wonderful contrast to the madness of Jason's last week. He realized that while the search for Liz Pratt had given him purpose through a troubled emotional time, Kate had been the rock on which he'd leaned. And now, after years as just a friend, she was threatening to move right past girlfriend to true companion. He kissed her on the forehead, then got up to work the stiffness from his neck and joints. He did his best to not disturb her, but getting off a single-cushion sofa without being noticed by its other inhabitant was practically impossible.

"What time is it?" she muttered, her eyes still closed.

The sun was barely showing outside and his mom wasn't up yet so he guessed it was between 6:30 and 7:00. He smoothed the hair from her face. "It's still early; go back to sleep."

She rolled over and snuggled tightly inside the blanket.

Jason turned for the hall and rotated his shoulder in small circles then started working on his neck, but the pain lingered. He went quietly up to his room and threw on a sweatshirt and a pair of athletic shorts from the floor, then made his way down to the basement.

The basement staircase opened to a large open space spanning the length of the house. In addition to a large cut-out for considerable storage, three rooms were built in across the opposite wall: a large storage room on the left, and a utility room housing the washer, dryer, and the mechanical components of the house in the center. The smaller room to the right was Jason's office. At the near end of the great room was a weight-training area housing free weights, two benches, one inclined, and a lat pull-down machine. A TV, all-in-one stereo system and dorm-sized refrigerator lined the opposite wall. Jason unrolled a mat in front of the stereo at the far end of the room and started his workout with twenty minutes of yoga. Usually he slipped in a DVD with a specific routine to follow, but this time he chose to move from pose to pose on his own in silence, concentrating the workout on exercises that stretched and toned his back and neck.

He was stiff, not only from the night on the couch but because he'd neglected his three-times-per-week routine for the past couple of weeks. The sweat, which trickled over both temples by the end of the session, was a satisfying victory. His blood was flowing again, rejuvenating his body physically and calming his spirit to a state it hadn't been in a long time. He closed his eyes, pressed his palms together in front of his chest, gathered up the remaining tension in his body, and exhaled.

Getting up from the mat, he walked to the small refrigerator and took a drink from the jug of water kept in the door. The wall behind the refrigerator was littered with pictures of Jason's youth athletic teams; many were displayed along with trophies and medals won by Jason and his teams. When he was a kid, his mom would put the picture of his current team on a shelf in his room. When the next season came around, she put up a new photo and hung the previous one on the wall in the basement. At Jason's request, just before his junior year in high school, the team photos and newspaper clippings went directly to the basement.

In between drinks he studied the picture of his first league championship team—his eleven-year-old peewee hockey team. In the picture, he was on one knee at the end of the front row, next to Seth. He remembered Seth trying to pull at his breezers to make him fall down while the photographer took the shot. Jason returned the favor, jamming his stick under Seth's skate, sending him falling into the next player and toppling the front row like a set of dominoes. Jason shook his head remembering the ten end-line-to-end-line killers that followed as result.

Moving to the free weights, he completed three sets of bicep curls, then completed lifts for his chest, abs, shoulders and back—three sets of each. After a quick full-body stretch, he picked up a pair of dumbbells for a set of tricep lifts but heard footsteps moving around above him, then, a moment later, another set of feet.

He returned the weights to the stand and toweled the sweat from his face. Before going upstairs, he grabbed the water bottle out of the fridge and took another long drink. The peewee hockey photo next to the TV caught his eye again. Standing directly behind him in the picture was Clint Baskett, who towered over the rest of the team. "Even then, you were an oaf," he muttered and rubbed the tender bruise over his kidney. He leaned over and put the plastic jug back in the refrigerator, then shot back up and looked at the face of Clint Baskett again. He turned and ran for the stairs, the refrigerator door still open.

Jason was backing out of his driveway in the time it took to throw on some fresh clothes and give Kate a kiss.

"Where are you going?" she asked.

"To see an old friend."

# CHAPTER 35

Jason pulled into the driveway of a colonial-style house located a few miles east of town. Over the past two decades it had become fashionable in Cedar River to buy small parcels of land outside of town, anywhere from two to ten acres, and build more urban-style houses where family farms had once been. Not long after the trend first hit, developers noticed and bought larger plots, then sold them off in subsets, making money both on the sale of the land and the building of the home. These country developments had become symbols of status and taken on names like Whispering Farms and Prairie Run.

This particular house was not grand in size but sat on an extra-large lot, isolated from its smattering of neighbors. The house portrayed a quiet sophistication, though the large metal outbuilding in the rear sapped a portion of the charm. A classic white barn would have fit better, but, as Jason knew, that didn't come close to fitting into the budget. The owner had told Jason before it was built that he'd one day like to have a couple of horses or even a small hobby farm on the property. As he got out of the truck and jogged toward the pole barn, Jason was no longer sure that the owner had been telling the truth.

The sixteen-foot-high front doors were locked as was the steel service door next to them. He went around to the side of the building and looked in the window. In the far stall stood a box truck with blue tarps draped over it. The tarps did their job for the most part but one had slipped, leaving a small triangle of bright yellow paint peeking out.

Jason's stomach clenched and a cold shiver swept over him. He took a moment to control his breathing, then leaned in again and cupped his hands around his eyes to shield the morning sun. It was definitely a Ryder truck. All the explanations Jason had come up with during the ride over to squelch his suspicion vanished inside two square feet of yellow aluminum.

He turned around and stood with his back up against the cool metal, unsure of the next move. A small-town remodeling contractor wasn't equipped with natural instincts for this type of situation. Then he remembered Liz Pratt's voice, filled with fear and panic as she pleaded from behind the plastic window for help. And he remembered her swollen, bruised face in his truck and the feeling of her atrophied body as they ran through the woods. He knew she would be forever marred by what she had been forced to go through. He pushed away from the wall and strode hard toward the front door.

The door opened after the third round of dogged pounding.

"Tell me you have a good reason."

"I don't know what you're talking about."

"Tell me they're threatening to kill you, holding a relative—something. You've got to have a good reason. Just tell me what it is."

"Jason, what are you talking about?"

"Clint Baskett, Neil." Jason said, stepping eye-to-eye with his mentor. "You said that Clara Riddle was more upset that a man was watching her from the woods than she was about some kids drinking out by her garage."

"Yes. That's what she told me," Neil said. "What's got you so upset?"

"Clint and I have a history so I told the sheriff not to mention me. He told Clint a buddy of his was driving by and saw a woman beaten. He never mentioned a man in the woods."

"I don't know what to tell you."

"Something has gnawed at me from the start—the facts didn't add up. Clara Riddle lived on her own out there for a long time. And remember, I went to see her—she was one tough old lady. She wasn't worried about me or anyone else looking in on her property."

Neil put his hands on Jason's shoulders. "Son, calm down."

Jason slapped his mentor's hands away. "I saw the moving truck in your shed, Neil." Jason's voice was nearing a shout. "I know, all right. I know!"

Neil's eyes furrowed and his head tipped a little to one side. Jason couldn't figure whether it was surprise, delayed comprehension, or admission, as he constructed an excuse. "Come in and we'll talk about this," Neil said, and backed up to let Jason farther into the room.

Jason stepped in, then turned to Neil, closing the door behind them. "We need to call the sheriff, Neil. You need to tell them what you know before anyone else gets hurt… or killed. These are some bad guys—I don't think you understand what you've gotten yourself…"

Cold metal struck Jason at the base of his neck. The pain it triggered made the morning's ache feel like a breezy tickle. A moment later everything went black.

---

Jason's head throbbed fiercely as he muddled back to consciousness. He groaned and tried to shake it away but the pain held fast. His eyes came into focus on two men looking down on him; he recognized both. Neil was on the left, dwarfed by the large Middle Eastern man who had directed the moving crew Thursday night.

Jason tried to rise and put distance between him and the other men, but he realized he was tied to his chair. He tried to look at what was holding him but before he could locate his binds, the large man reached out and clenched the underside of Jason's ribcage, digging his fingers up under the bone. Jason screamed and tried to push the man away but the binds held him still.

"You are going to tell us everything you know or this is the least pain you are going to feel during for the rest of your pathetic life," the man said, tightening his grip for effect. The terror in Jason's screams spiked in response.

Several long seconds later the man released his hold. "Start talking."

Jason inhaled deeply and shook his head. "I don't know anything."

The man was back on him instantly. This time he used both hands, one under each set of ribs. The force of his grip lifted Jason off the chair. Jason screamed and squirmed wildly to escape but the hands did not let go. Ten endless seconds later, the man broke the hold.

The Arab man bent his thick frame until he was eye-to-eye with Jason. "I don't think you understand." His voice slithered from behind his lips. "You are going to tell me what you know and then I am going to kill you. The only question is the amount of pain you will endure before you die."

Jason peered over the man's shoulder to Neil, who gazed back with regret, but didn't move to step in. "Please, Jason. Don't make it any worse. Tell General Attar what he wants to know. If you don't, it's going to get much, much worse."

Jason could tell it was a warning rather than a threat. The other man reached out and Jason retreated back into the chair as far as he could. "Okay. Okay," Jason said.

"The sheriff's theory is that a meth-cooking lab was operating in a secret basement room in Clara Riddle's house. But for some reason it was being moved—they're guessing it's because of a disagreement between Clara and the men distributing the meth." He gave each man an accusing look. "Clara Riddle was killed either because she was threatening the operation in some way or maybe just because it was preferable to sharing the profits." He shrugged. "The kicker is that they think I either killed her or am somehow behind it."

"Why would law enforcement suspect you?" the Middle Eastern man said.

"Because I waited too long reporting what I saw last weekend and then I kept poking around—I don't know."

The large Arab tensed and leaned in for another round of pain, but Neil grabbed him on the arm. "General, wait!"

Attar whipped around and stared over Neil. "Step back, Muhab!"

"Muhab?" Jason's jaw remained open as he worked through the idea. "Neil, please tell me you're not with this guy."

Neil averted his eyes. The general's chest expanded and he smiled broadly. "He has not been your 'Neil' for a very long time. Muhab has been vital to the impending fall of your pitiful country."

Jason stared at the men, the shock of the betrayal burning more than his head and ribs. "How many times were you in my home? How many times were you there alone with my mother? You sonofabitch! Was it all an act? What other secrets have you been hiding?" Jason shouted.

"It is my only secret," Neil said, quietly. "But now I must ask you to share yours. First, I want exact details about what you have shared with law enforcement. Then you will tell me every person who knows what you know."

"I just told you what I know," Jason said to Attar. He was about to address Neil, but a punch rained down.

"Talk!" The general cocked his arm again but Muhab stepped in its path.

"Let me talk to him, General. I don't think he understands what information we are looking for." Attar took a half-step back and Muhab took over the forward position in front of Jason.

"We'll take this step-by-step. Tell me more about the sheriff's investigation."

Jason gave Neil a look that said, "Why are you doing this? Snap out of it."

Neil read Jason's mind. "The general is in charge, Jason. I only have one chance to keep you from suffering. So please tell me what the sheriff knows or I will be forced to let the general use his own persuasions."

Jason could see he wasn't going to get through to his former neighbor and friend, so he told them what he remembered about his interviews with Sheriff Burnett and Detective Mangemelli and their focus on the drug operation. "If they think I'm in on it, there's a pretty good chance there are no other solid suspects. But that's just a guess."

"And he knows you believe the men to be Middle Eastern?"

Jason was about to lie but remembered he'd already told Neil about the men during their lunch conversation a week ago. "Yes, but he didn't mention how it might fit." He leaned forward as far as his binds would allow. "Neil, you can't do this! You're involved in murder—these men have killed people. Do you know that?"

The general's fist came out of nowhere, so hard on Jason's temple that two legs of the chair came off the ground.

Neil gave Jason several seconds to regain the present, then continued. "Your mother said you had your own ideas on what was happening at the Riddle house. We know what the sheriff thinks—what's your theory?"

"I don't know—it's not much different than the sheriff's. Only I'm trying to understand why people would be killed for their involvement in a meth lab—it seems a little heavy. It's no different than what everyone else in town is wondering." The only information he had that others, including the sheriff, might not have was what he'd read the night before about the history of the Riddle family. And he wasn't letting any of that go. If he didn't make it out of this chair alive, Seth or Kate would pass along their speculation to the sheriff.

"But you don't have any working theories?"

"No. I'm as confused as everyone else."

"If that were true you wouldn't have discovered the moving truck in my shed and you wouldn't be tied to a chair right now. You need to be honest with me, Jason," Neil said, then changed the focus of his questions. "What was in the portfolio you had at the restaurant last night?"

Jason tried to act surprised by the question. "Just what I told you; some kitchen renovation plans."

"Jason. I've known you since you were a kid. Remember when you were twelve and you were holed up in your scraggily fort behind the garage? I asked what you were doing and you said you were reading a *Sports Illustrated*. I knew you were lying then, too, Jason. The tone of your voice betrayed you—it was obvious you were looking at something more interesting." He put his hand on Jason's knee. "I'm going to ask you again, what was in the portfolio?"

"I don't know what else to say. It might still be in my truck. Go look for yourself—all you'll find are bad drawings of an armoire."

"You're lying. What does your friend Kate know?"

Jason's eyes widened and his heart jumped into his throat. He tried to regain his composure but it was too late. "She doesn't know anything and neither do I. You already said you are going to kill me no matter what. Why would I lie?"

Neil gestured to the general and the two men walked back toward the living room where they carried on a private conversation. The Arab gave a final nod as if coming to an agreement on something. He walked back into the dining room, Neil trailing, and pulled a chair from the table, faced it toward Jason, and sat down. Neil maneuvered around the leader and squatted down in front of Jason. "We want to know exactly what details led you to my door and everyone with whom you've shared your suspicions. We're going to give you exactly ten minutes to remember everything. If you lie, even once, or provide anything short of the entire truth, I'm going to bring Kate here and let General Attar ask her the questions."

"I've told you everything. I was looking at one of the team pictures in my basement this morning—you know the ones—well, in the picture was the big stupid putz, Clint Baskett, and that sprung the memory of me asking the sheriff to play dumb about my involvement in the search of the Riddle house. That's it. You're the first person I've talked to since."

Neither man appeared to accept the explanation. "It's the truth! If you don't believe me, tell me what you want me to say and I'll say it! Until then, all's I've got is the truth."

Neil shook his head and lifted his wrist in front of his face and made an exaggerated check of the time.

Jason spent the next few minutes imploring his captors to believe him and throwing out indiscriminate facts as he remembered them, but continuing to leave out the information about Clara Riddle and her potential conversion. Neither Neil nor the general reacted to his pleading and soon he was out of things to say. The three men sat a short minute in silence.

"No more time," Attar rose. "Call the girl."

Neil looked at Jason. "Last chance."

*What would keep Kate safe?* Jason needed to get them refocused on him. "What is this all about? Maybe I'd be more help if I knew what you need the information for. What details about the drug-den investigation are you looking for?"

The general smiled at the obvious attempt to stall. He stepped forward and before he spoke, the smile morphed into an evil sneer. "You think we are interested in selling drugs or killing useless women? Do not be so stupid. Addiction and unholy relationships are the afflictions of *your* country. But do not worry, we will change all that very soon. Such Godlessness will be a thing of the past for those willing to follow. For those who do not?" He smiled an arrogant, judging smile.

"Follow who? Follow what?" Jason asked, though he already knew.

Attar looked down on Jason. "Allah," he whispered. "His warriors are poised to destroy your country and send it straight back to hell. Thousands will die across this abysmal country today. And millions more in the coming weeks. America is finally about to pay for its sins against the rest of the world."

"In Cedar River?" Jason asked, incredulous.

General Attar shook his head, disappointed. "Forget Cedar River. You are still thinking small."

"Then enlighten me. Why aren't you in Washington or New York? If you want to send a message, aren't those the places to do it?"

"We are done sending messages! No more embassy bombings or coffee-shop massacres!" The general was climbing toward real anger. "Flying planes into the World Trade Center was an act of arrogance, not war. Osama Bin Laden is a great man, but he is a rebel, not a general. The days of hit-and-run strategies are in the past—single attacks serve no military purpose. They've only increased, rather than decreased, your country's military dominance around the world.

"However, I will say there were benefits that have helped build for this day. The number of Muslims willing to pick up the sword and fight American tyranny has grown exponentially. And the billions of dollars, held back for so many years until an attack against America was thought achievable, have started to flow. Your president brags of how no attacks have taken place since September 2001. He is a fool. We do not plan for more attacks; we plan for war!"

It was clear the man reveled in the opportunity to promulgate his greatness and that of his cause. So Jason sat back and fed his speech. And kept Kate safe. "Do you really think you can build a competent army to fight the U.S. in only the years since 9/11?"

"Our army has been ready for five hundred years. We only required the strategy and tools to execute our victory. I gladly die for Allah, as do millions alongside me. It is that commitment, now harnessed, that will be our advantage. Is there anything Americans are willing to die for?"

*Keep him talking*, Jason thought, *let him show his hand. Think like your opponent, then out-think your opponent.* Jason leaned back in his chair, trying to equal the general's confidence. The antique dining chair squeaked and the joints shifted slightly with his movements.

"Justice. Americans will die to hold on to what is just."

The general's laugh bled condescension. "Come now. There is no justice in America, only greed. The most powerful men in your country are not priests. They are not scholars or healers and they certainly are not judges. No, they are the men with the most money.

"The rest of you, from the president on down, are only their puppets. In your country a person's value is determined by the size of his house and the amount of useless toys he fills it with. But, of course, when you have all you can imagine, you want still more, so the powerful give you credit cards and loans, making the worship of them an obligation, not a choice. Your whole way of life is based on insatiable gluttony and selfishness." Attar spread his arms, offering the well-appointed home around him as an example.

"You are right; we do not have the arms to fight a military giant. But we are very capable—let me correct myself—*fully prepared* to defeat a country based on opulence while it is preoccupied with national economic collapse and the loss of personal, meaningless possessions."

"Are you planning to blow up the Federal Reserve or something? How is that connected to Cedar River?" *Keep him talking! Think!*

"No, no. An attack on the Federal Reserve would be nothing more than a show—explosives versus glass and steel. We plan to attack something much more systemic to the American way of life.

"In a few weeks, millions of people in your country will line up in the middle of the night after your Thanksgiving holiday to buy a trillion dollars worth of goods they don't need, while people across the rest of the world go hungry. How many of those people would line up in the middle of the night to praise their god or to help those in real need? Do you know why that day is referred to as Black Friday? It is the day the retail stores in your country go from losing money to profitability."

General Attar was gaining energy from his speech. "Imagine if that day never came. Imagine the effect on your stock market as retail conglomerates report horrendous losses. Think of the amount of wealth lost by the largest investors in your country. Their money isn't in a vault somewhere; it's in the market the powerful control to drive their endless need for more wealth. They have already lost half their wealth during the last greed-induced recession. How will those men react when they again lose billions and billions of dollars overnight?

"And this time the fall will be much more steep and far-reaching. Hysteria will reign when giant companies and those smaller who supply them begin to lay off millions of workers—workers whose pensions and 401(k)s have suddenly dried up—how will the population view your government who let this happen?"

Jason answered, "They'll do the same thing they did after 9/11. They'll demand the government make you pieces of shit pay, then we'll go on with our lives and you'll go back to clinging to your self-importance inside a cave in Pakistan. It will unite us, not destroy us."

"How will you fund your counteroffensive?" countered Attar. "Your government goes hundreds of billions more into debt every month. The only thing keeping your government running is foreign countries buying up your bonds, confident your economy is strong enough to provide them a reliable return. If that confidence is gone, they will not buy your dollars. In fact, they will sell them. You will have to pay for more military through taxes. The richest one percent in your country already pay fifty percent of all income tax. A ruined economy will sharply reduce their income, thereby dwindling the amount of tax dollars going to the government. Do you think these men, who value wealth more than heaven, will allow the government to take more of it from them?" He sat back down in front of Jason. "It is not a question of whether we *can* defeat your country, the question is: are we prepared to be the first? The Chinese will not be able to afford to prop up your economy by buying up all your debt, because you will no longer be buying all their cheap goods. Perhaps they will invest in their own military instead. Do you see what I mean?"

"I think I do. It looks like we're going to be an Islamic state if the Chinese don't beat you to it." Jason paused. "Except for one thing. You haven't given me one concrete act that will actually cause this great spiral of economic despair. Or how hanging out in some old woman's basement helps your cause."

The general's fist answered Jason's lack of respect. The new cut below his eye was leaking a bead of blood down his cheek.

General Attar spoke to Neil while looking down on Jason with eyes filled with disgust and judgment. "This fool knows nothing. He is far too limited to threaten our activities," Attar said.

Neil glanced nervously at Jason before addressing the general. "What are your wishes?"

"Call the girl. He will pay for getting in our way. He will watch *her die*, before we kill him."

---

Kate filled a bronze watering can and began weaving through the two dozen plants that adorned her duplex. The can was a gift from her Aunt Donna for her college graduation. Kate had worked twenty hours a week at a flower and garden center during college to help keep the size of her school loans manageable. One of the few fringe benefits of working at such a store was the opportunity to take home injured or unsightly plants and flowers at no cost. As a result, Kate probably had more plants per square foot in her apartment when she graduated than anyone else in her class.

As she felt the dampness of the soil under a small ficus tree, she wondered if Jason had a green thumb, or if he even liked plants. She thought for a moment, and didn't remember seeing any plants in his mother's house. There was still so much she didn't know about him. But what she didn't know—those were small things, compromise things. The big things, the core values by which he lived his life, the natural goodness, his quiet strength, his dedication to the people around him, those things she knew—and loved.

Her cell phone rang; the caller ID read *JASON*.

"Hey, where'd you go this morning?" she answered.

"Kate, this is Neil Lockwood. We met last night at Vera's."

"Oh. Hi, Neil." Her embarrassment was obvious. "Why do you have Jason's phone? Is everything all right?"

"Everything is fine. He's doing a little project for me and currently has both hands full. He wanted me to call to see if you could join us out here at my home this morning? I have a little different theory about why Clara Riddle was killed, which he found very interesting. He wanted you to hear it, too."

"Um, sure. What time were you thinking?"

"I need to leave for an appointment fairly soon. Could you come now? Jason thought you would be really interested."

"Um, sure. Give me a few minutes to clean up?"

"That'll be fine. Let me give you the directions," he said.

Kate wrote down the directions, then went into her bedroom to change out of her sweats.

# CHAPTER 36

Attar walked outside and punched a number into his cell.

"We have a small change in plans. Meet me at the QuickMart just off the Interstate west of Cedar River." He looked over at Neil's car. "I will be in a black Volkswagon Passat." He waited for confirmation of the change from the person on the other end, then ended the call and punched in a second number.

"Do you have the twelve contact numbers I gave you?" Attar asked.

General Attar could hear the rustling of papers, then, "Yes, I am looking right at them."

"I want you to call them now. Today is no longer a walk-through. The operation goes live today, on my command. Tell them to prepare for my communication."

"Sir?" The man was more surprised than confused.

"Tell the men to pray for Allah's blessings while they wait. Today they enter heaven as exalted warriors and leave earth as conquering heroes for all history. This will be the day that changes the world; the infidels will soon be destroyed and Allah's people will rise again in their place."

"Praise Allah!" said the man.

"Praise Allah," repeated the general. He ducked back into the house. A car was on the road, speeding in his direction.

Jason heard car tires rolling over the gravel drive outside. He listened for a car door to close, so he could shout a warning to Kate. General Attar anticipated the move and pulled his chair next to Jason's, then aimed his pistol at Jason's groin. "You try to warn her and your genitalia will be sprayed through a hole in that chair before you finish the first word."

Neil opened the door as Kate climbed up the steps to the door. "Thank you for coming, Kate."

The look on her face quickly transformed from confusion to concern as she saw Jason in the chair with cuts and bruises on his face and a gun pointed below his waist. *Don't worry about me,* he thought, *RUN!*

General Attar got out of his chair and slowly walked over to her. In one sudden movement he lifted his .45 and thrust it down at Kate's face. But she was somehow faster; pushing back against Neil and turning away from the oncoming blow. The heavy gun didn't land as intended, but still struck with enough force to open a gash on the back of her head. Jason jerked forward and tried to straighten out of the binds of his chair but the chair's joints, though moaning from the pressure, held together. The general spun and pointed the weapon at Jason, telling him to return to his seated position. The general grabbed a fistful of Kate's hair at the scalp and threw her toward the chair next to Jason. "Sit down!" To Neil he commanded, "Tie her hands."

The general saw the anger growing in Jason's eyes. "The problem with American women is they are as stupid as they are weak. But this is good for you—we will focus on her, making your final minutes less uncomfortable. But for her, on the other hand…"

"But she doesn't know anything! Believe me—she got really pissed off that I wouldn't talk to her about any of this. Why do you think she was so eager to come out and talk to Neil? Because she doesn't know anything about Clara Riddle or meth labs or you." *Follow my lead, Kate.*

"If, after much pain, she still does not know anything, that is okay." General Attar lifted the gun to her head but kept his glare on Jason. "Her suffering will be your punishment for getting in the way."

"Then shoot *me*, you goddamn psycho! But let her go!"

General Attar smiled. "No. She will die. Not just to hurt you, but because she has seen my face." Attar paused as if trying to jog a distant memory. "The last woman to see me in this house ended up with her car at the bottom of the river."

Jason started to say something more to defend Kate then stopped. His face went white and he turned to Neil, who was tying Kate's hands behind her chair. "Neil?"

Neil looked down and did not answer.

Jason lunged forward with the chair still attached to his body, hurling his body through the air head-first at the general's chest. But the general's reflexes were well-conditioned and he easily side-stepped the attack and, like a matador, pushed Jason to the ground.

Attar's throw whirled Jason in mid-air and he fell hard to the ground in the chair, his shoulder taking most of the punishment, his face the rest. He struggled to regain his feet for another rush, but it was done for him as Attar with one hand lifted him off the ground by the back of the chair and set it back on the floor in a seated position. A driving punch momentarily took both the wind and rage from Jason and he was unceremoniously dragged back to his position next to Kate.

General Attar stood over him, waiting for him to regain his breath, then asked, "You knew this woman?"

Jason just stared at the floor, so Attar looked over to Neil for the answer.

"His wife."

General Attar remained silent for a long moment, letting the new revelation carve its way into Jason. Then, finally, as if sensing when a verbal dagger would penetrate most deeply, he broke the tense silence. "What were we to do? She walked in on our group without warning. Muhab was quick with the alibi. I believe he told her we were a group of professors or colleagues of some kind. She likely believed him, but we could not be certain and were forced to bring resolution." The general gestured to Neil, who was now standing to the side of Kate. "Muhab was actually the person who devised the plan for disposing of her."

The general bent down level with Jason, who still couldn't make eye contact, then spoke slowly, pounding him with every word. "He called her later that night, in need of the husband, pretending his car had broken down. Of course, he knew the husband was not there."

"And as Muhab predicted, she offered to pick him up. He gave her a location that would take her across the bridge south of town. But when she came upon the bridge, there was her old friend," he said, motioning to Neil. "When she stopped, I came speeding up from behind and flipped the car into the river." He paused and lifted Jason's still lowered head with the .45. "The first time her car smashed into the rail but wouldn't go over. I had to back up and push her a second time to get the car to jump the barrier." Jason's face was crimson and his body shook from the building pressure. He lifted back to his feet but the general reached out a thick hand and pushed him back into his subordinate postion.

"You killed an innocent little girl in that car!"

Attar raised an eyebrow as if he were just reminded of a missing fact and wanted to confirm it with his own memory. "That is right. I almost forgot. That was the bitch's fault," he said, then looked up at Neil. "Why did she bring the girl?" He paused as if he were skimming a report for the answer, then turned back to Jason. "The grandmother was already asleep? I think that is correct. I recall we were concerned when we heard the woman was able to make a call to her husband as the car was sinking, but fortunately, as is typical with women, she focused on emotions rather than actions. In the end, some unmatched paint and a number of well-placed beer cans were the only clues for the police to go on."

The fuzzy in-and-out call pulsed in Jason's head the way it had so many times over the last two years. *Jason... help us... he was in the middle of the road... Grace struggling... screaming... love you so... sorry...*"

"You piece of shit. You're the best a billion Muslims could come up with?" Jason shook his head defiantly—staring directly into Attar's eyes. "You know why your little plot is going to fail? Because the U.S. isn't made up of just helpless women and children. The first American *man* you run across is gonna make you eat your goddamn spleen, you frickin' coward."

"You mean a man like you?" The general grabbed Jason's hair and yanked his head back, compressing the vertebrae. "Choke on your Yankee disrespect."

Jason forced a response through his collapsed windpipe. "Untie me and we'll see who does the choking."

General Attar checked his watch while continuing to easily hold Jason in his grip. "I would love nothing more but, fortunately for you, I have not the time." He looked at Neil, "Muhab, where is your weapon?"

Neil gestured toward the antique china cabinet. "Get it," Attar commanded him.

Neil retrieved the .38 and the general said, "I need to leave immediately if we are going to keep our schedule. You stay and play the sympathetic friend and get what information you can out of them. Then kill them—the woman first. We will meet in 60 minutes at the original rendezvous point."

"I thought we were driving together?" Neil said.

"Our agility is one of our core advantages, Muhab. We did not plan for this man to show up here this morning, but he did, so we adapt. Crisis creates opportunity, my friend—you are greatly respected for your cultural knowledge and strategic foresight, but we are less certain of your battle skills. The ability to acquire additional information and eliminate a former friend will send a strong message regarding your leadership potential in a new world. Use this opportunity—take advantage of it."

Neil nodded. "I will be thirty minutes behind you."

"This I know. And remember, be nimble—we have the fall-back location if needed," General Attar said and walked out the door.

Neil turned to Jason and Kate, gun in hand, but made no move toward his prisoners. "I am truly sorry about Kelly and Grace. You know we could not have anticipated her walking in on our meeting. If she just would have knocked, rather than bursting through the door like she always did, none of us would be here right now."

"Listen to yourself, Neil," Jason said. "You're blaming Kelly's murder on her exuberance, on her love for her friends. *You* did this, Neil. *You* killed my family."

"I don't mean to blame Kelly for anything. I adored Kelly. I am simply stating how seemingly trivial acts can have such grave repercussions. And I want you to know how Grace's death has affected me. I specifically told Kelly that night to keep Grace with Hannah. What happened to that beautiful girl still haunts me each day."

"What *happened* to her? Something didn't *happen* to her. You killed her!"

Neil lifted the gun in response to Jason's rising anger.

"Was it worth it?" Jason continued. "Do you feel important being involved with a group of lunatics trying to make a statement by blowing up America's Megamall?"

"How did you know it was America's Mcgamall?" Neil walked up to Jason, the gun leveled at his head. "Tell me what else you know."

"It was a guess. It's the only landmark in Minnesota that will make a splash anywhere close to the bombing of the World Trade Center. Plus, your goal is to punch a hole in the U.S. retail market. It doesn't take a college professor to connect the dots."

Neil moved the gun to Kate but kept his eyes on Jason. "Tell me what you know, Jason. Don't make things worse than they already are."

A gun pointed at her face prompted Kate's entrance into the exchange. "You really think shutting down America's Megamall will end holiday shopping? It's not a mall; it's a tourist hub and entertainment center. You'll prevent as much Christmas retailing as you would by blowing up Disneyland."

Neil shook his head. "You are right. That is why Minnesota is just *one* of the targets. Trained units are waiting in cities all across the country for General Attar's signal to annihilate the major shopping malls in each. We don't plan on slowing consumption simply by blowing up individual stores or malls; it's the fear that *your* mall may be next that will bring the economy to its knees. I have to admit, maximizing the fear was my idea." A sense of pride replaced the regret in his words. "Bombers will go out in pairs, one to detonate the bomb, another to transmit his pre-detonation message directly to the Web. The whole world will see the messages and watch the horrible deaths."

"Anti-American propaganda isn't going to scare the citizenry. Weren't you around during 9/11? It only galvanized the country." Jason said.

Neil looked at Jason like he was still seven years old. "The message won't be anti-America or pro-Islam—that is not a part of the equation. The message will be something completely different: first, we will shout our disdain that America has lost its principles and become a materialistic wasteland; secondly, we will warn that the initial attacks are just the beginning of a prolonged series of deadly messages. The country will understand with absolute clarity that stepping into a store is risking certain death.

"The bombers will be masked, so people won't see us as Islamic soldiers; they will see political extremists with a cause, a cause the media will fall all over themselves to justify. When's the last time you saw a story promoting corporations, big business, or greed? I can see the stories now—while they will by no means condone the methods of the activists, they will debate the merit of their claims. You'll have dueling opinion pages; one side will suggest the 'religious right' is creating zealots protesting the secularization of Christmas. The conservatives on the other side will accuse the liberal media and universities of corrupting American youth against capitalism and suggest that their brainwashing is ultimately responsible for the attacks. Everyone needs a villain.

"And through it all, the names Timothy McVeigh and David Koresh will be whispered in conversations around water coolers all across America. Meanwhile, soccer moms will stay home and try to explain why Santa may not be so generous this year."

Kate chimed in. "Times are changing. Your stunt will just push more people to online shopping. Parents are not going to let their kids go without gifts on Christmas."

"Stunt! You think this is a stunt? It's the beginning of the great transformation of America. Twenty years from now America's Megamall will be a grand mosque where millions of people will come to pray to Allah. And as for your cyber-shopping idea, we have operatives working in the distribution departments of a number of large online retailers. Believe me, by this time next week no one is going to want to be the next person to be reported on the news having lost their hand or their life opening a stuffed Holly Horse doll or Fancy Girls' CD."

"So let's say tens of thousands of people are dead and everyone is accusing everyone else of being responsible for the attacks. Let's even assume the economy collapses as Attar wants," Jason said. "What's in it for you?"

Neil smiled an amused teacher-to-student smile. "Nothing. I'm not doing this for me; I'm doing this for the United States of America."

Kate cut in before Jason could follow up. "How does killing thousands of innocent people and leaving their children parentless help America?"

"Think of the wooded acreage Jason owns north of town. A few beautiful trees dot the property but much of it is filled with old, damaged trees fighting one another for nutrients and sunlight. The ground is suffocated with overgrown brush and fallen branches. What was once a beautiful and thriving ecosystem is now just sucking up precious resources to stave off its inevitable death. Imagine what would happen if a bolt of lightning struck there." Neil lifted his arms over his head, then arced them down, as if bringing life to the land.

"The dead branches and decaying grasslands would go up in flames and wipe out everything. Unfortunately, the isolated beautiful strong trees would go, too. But in their place, brilliant green grass would soon cover the land. Fresh pines would sprout from seeds, which need the fire to escape their cones. A variety of other seedlings would blow in and flourish in the new found sunshine and fresh nutrients. It's the same land but it's reinvigorated and stronger than ever before. It's the natural cycle of life. America is that overgrown dying woodland; General Attar and I are just providing the lightning."

Jason watched Neil billowing with pride as he shared his grand story of a planned American rapture. "Your analogies are so goddamned screwed-up that I barely know where to start. But the fatal flaw is that lightning happens naturally. What you're doing is closer to setting a family's house on fire and telling them you did it for their own good. You're nothing more than an arrogant misfit who needs everyone else to be wrong so he can be right. You still didn't answer my question: what do you get out of this?"

Neil shook his head, disappointed. "I understand your resentment, Jason. But if you had enough time to think everything through, you would see the awesome potential this country can realize in its new form. As for me? I get to live in an America where the intelligence of a Benjamin Franklin or the moral fortitude of an Abraham Lincoln will again be held in greater esteem than the market manipulations of Warren Buffett, Bill Gates, or some greedy hedge fund manager. Do I think General Attar is the answer? No. But he can be the change agent America needs. After he falls, and he will, this country can grow again into the great society it once was."

Jason glanced at the clock next to the china cabinet. Time was spinning by and he was still literally looking into the barrel of a gun. So was Kate. Neil followed Jason's gaze and checked his watch. A look of regret washed over the man's face.

"Neil, if America can be reborn into a form greater than anything in its history, let Kate live to witness it. After what you've done to my family, you owe me that much. Keep her here until your work is finished if you have to, but don't kill her. Enough good people have died getting you to this point; she doesn't have to be the next."

"I wish I could, Jason. I wish I could spare you both." His voice held true regret. "But—"

Jason was the only one to see the gun come up outside the dining room window. It was a semi-automatic, larger than the revolver Neil was pointing at him. Aiming it at them was the huge man he fought in Clara Riddle's basement while rescuing Liz Pratt.

"Kate! Get down!" Jason hurled himself at her, crashing them both to the floor as a gunshot shattered the large plate-glass window. Jason looked up just in time to see Neil, who had followed Jason's eyes to the window, knocked to the floor in the other direction by a bullet.

"Omar?" he wheezed.

# CHAPTER 37

Jason landed behind Kate, the corner of the dining room chair taking the initial brunt of the fall. The posts that connected the seat of the chair to its back broke away and the inner spindles exploded from the ensuing concussion. His arms were still bound behind his back but he was free of the chair. He tucked into a ball and pulled his tied hands from his back to his front and silently thanked Kelly for forcing him to try yoga years earlier. He kept his eyes on the open window frame. And from his angle, sprawled on the floor, he saw only cloudless blue sky. A small hill twenty feet from the side of the house gave the shooter a perfect target line to anyone sitting or standing in the dining room. But when they fell to the floor, the shooter no longer had the angle.

He looked over at Kate beside him; she was bent low on her knees with her arms still bound behind her. Neil hadn't bothered to tie her to the chair, figuring she would be dead before she could run anywhere.

"Are you okay?" he asked.

She nodded. It was a strong nod.

He looked back at the window frame. *Think like your opponent, then out-think your opponent.*

The shooter would be coming for them. The house's rear entrance led from the garage into the kitchen opposite the dining room. The front door opened at the far side of the living room to their right, a few feet from the staircase that climbed along the wall to the second floor. The front was closer; he would come through there. But Jason could beat him to the spot. He guessed the gunman would figure his targets were either still tied up, or looking for a place to hide. So Jason did the opposite.

He grabbed one of the long spindles from the demolished chair and leaped forward, yelling instructions to Kate. "Head for the kitchen door but stay low. When you hear the front door open, run out—Go!" He heard her scurrying the opposite direction as he scrambled low under another large window on the front living room wall to the narrow two-foot span that separated the window from the door. He reached up and turned the dead-bolt closed.

He squatted in the space and gambled that the dark curtains at the edge of the window hid him from the attacker. He was on the balls of his feet with one foot slightly in front of the other, holding the two-foot spindle in both hands against his chest. The seconds dragged by like minutes and he started to doubt his initial appraisal. Maybe the gunman outmaneuvered him. He looked at the wall to his right and imagined Kate ten feet on the other side by the door with her hands tied behind her back. If the gunman came through the garage she was a sitting duck. He was about to yell to her to get out of there when… Bang!

The loud crash against the door startled Jason and he fell backward. The door frame gave from the blow, but not all the way. *That's your cue, Kate. Get out of the house. Now!* Jason propped himself back into position as a second crash came, propelling the door open, splinters from the mutilated frame leading the way. The gunman stepped through without hesitation. Jason was right; there was no fear of rebuttal in his movements. Jason rotated at the waist and violently swung the thick chair post into the attacker's knee. The man's scream barely made it past his lips before the wood dowel was racing up to crush the wrist of his already bandaged right hand, dislodging the gun.

The semi-automatic sailed away from them. Jason darted for it but it bounced hard off the hardwood floors toward the staircase landing on the other side of the gunman. The larger man had started falling forward from the blow to the knee and collapsed onto Jason, preventing him from reaching the gun. Jason was immobilized with his hands still bound in front of him. A forearm was quickly across the back of his neck and the other was pressed hard into the small of his back. With his hands bound, Jason wasn't able to create enough leverage to get a full breath, much less overcome his adversary. Two swift punches landed painfully to the kidney Clint had belted the day before, causing him to let out a breathless moan. Then he got some relief when much of the man's body weight, but not his grip, eased off him.

The hulking Middle Eastern man flipped him over onto his back and leaned back on him, digging his right elbow into Jason's chest. Jason could see what caused the man to adjust his weight—his left hand held the gun two inches from Jason's eye. It wasn't the man's natural hand; Jason had just pulverized that one. But at a distance of six inches, the man could have been holding the gun with his toes and still put a large hole in Jason's head.

A cocksure smile curled up the younger man's face, forcing the bulging rage in his eyes to morph into an evil squint. "Enjoy hell, infidel."

A squelching thud made the man's eyes bulge again and he fell on top of Jason. The body was limp, enabling Jason to squirm out from under him. Kate was standing over the body, which was lying face-down on the floor. Blood was oozing out of his neck where the hook of a fireplace poker was still embedded in the muscle and bone.

"He was going to kill you," she said as an explanation.

Jason got to his feet and lifted his bound arms around her. Her tied arms were nuzzled between their wildly pounding hearts as she buried her face into his chest and began to cry. They stood there for a few short moments, unable to absorb what had just taken place when they heard the plea.

"Jason. Help me." Neil's voice in the next room was shallow and weak.

Jason unwrapped himself from Kate and found Neil propped up against the wall opposite the dining room window. His hand covered his ribs where a large blood stain was spreading over the front of his shirt down to his waist.

He was sweating profusely and his breathing was shallow. "You need to call an ambulance. I can't get the bleeding stopped. Hurry." The words were spaced and unsteady.

Jason bent down on one knee in front of him. "Where's Attar?"

"Please, Jason. I don't have a great deal of time."

"Where is he?!"

Neil coughed and the stain grew. "He is going to arm the bomb, then he's supposed to meet me in the parking lot of the Roadhouse restaurant, south of the mall. Now, please, Jason. I need to get to a hospital." His voice was desperate and rapidly losing strength.

"I don't think they have hospitals where you're going, you deluded sonofabitch. But if they do, you better request a double room. I'm gonna be sending your boss there real soon."

"This is bigger than you and me, Jason." Neil paused, trying to catch his breath. "America is going to be reborn. I'm sorry you can't see that."

"To be reborn it first needs to die," Jason said. "I'm not going to let that happen."

Death was coming for Neil. He reached out to clutch Jason for support but Jason backed away. The professor's reach held for a moment as if he were posing, then he slumped forward. Dead.

Jason wondered what he would tell his mom.

# CHAPTER 38

Khalid was waiting for Muhab and General Attar next to the mall directory kiosk inside the south entrance of America's Megamall. Unfortunately, at least for today, Rockwell Outfitters was located on the corner joining the south entrance and the large walkway that circled the building. He kept the eight-foot-tall kiosk between him and the store—the last thing he wanted today was a coworker approaching him and asking what he was doing in the mall when he had asked off his shift the day before.

A stiff jab to his ribs startled him; he spun around to defend himself.

"I talked to corporate again today." It was Jan. "They said you turned down the promotion—what gives?"

"What are you doing here? We agreed that you would take the weekend to yourself." He looked at his watch. "I scheduled the massage for 11:00; you are going to be late."

"That was so sweet of you to surprise me with a massage. I could get used to you surprising me once in a while," she said. "But I got called in, so I had to reschedule. Got to show the bosses I'm flexible, with the regional manager interviews coming up and all." She poked him in the chest. "You didn't answer my question. Why'd you turn down the job? You're leaving a lot of money on the table."

"If I am in line to get the position now, I should be able to receive the same offer *after* I graduate. Also, I did not want to accept a transfer to another store until we know for sure you and I are not going to be together here. Time with you is worth more than a silly promotion," he said.

Jan nervously looked around the kiosk at the store. "You didn't tell them that, did you? You know management is not allowed to have personal relationships with employees outside of work."

"Our secret is still safe; you need not worry," he said.

"Khalid?" General Attar surprised him. The leader tried to act casual, but Khalid could see the disapproval in his eyes.

"Uh, hello," Khalid said.

The general gestured to Jan. "Who is this?"

"This is my boss, Jan," he said, then to Jan, "This is my uncle—" he paused, unable to come up with an immediate alias.

"Muhab." General Attar filled the gap, offering his hand to Jan. "I am very pleased to meet you."

Jan shook it. "Pleased to meet you as well. Khalid, you didn't tell me you had an uncle in town."

"I only visit. Last minute—for job." Attar's English was suddenly poor and his accent much heavier. "I call Khalid and he agree to show me large mall. Find gift for daughter."

"I'm sure you won't have any trouble finding something here," she said. "Just don't get lost. It's easier than you think, especially with the reality-show auditions today. The parking ramps are already packed." General Attar nodded.

Jan turned to Khalid. "I need to get to work. Call me later and we can continue the one-on-one training session." She gave him a wink, then turned and walked toward the Rockwell Outfitters entrance.

"Let us go. It is time," the general spoke like a father to a son, preparing for stronger discipline behind closed doors.

"Where is Muhab? I thought he was coming with you?"

"His role has changed. I will tell you more as we move," General Attar said and started down the corridor that was rapidly becoming more crowded.

---

Jason and Kate cut the twine from each other's wrists and held one another again. But the embrace didn't last long. Too much adrenaline was pumping through each of them.

"My God, Jason. I can't believe this. Who's the man in the other room? He must have been sent to kill us by the guy who left earlier."

"The man in the living room is the guy I fought in Clara Riddle's basement. He's the one who smashed the window in the truck trying to stop us that night," Jason said.

"His boss isn't going to be happy that he shot Neil, instead of us."

"I think his job was to kill all of us, including Neil," Jason said. Kate gave him a confused look so he explained. "He was looking right at Neil when he fired. And remember, Neil was the one holding the gun—he was the only threat. My guess is: Attar didn't think Neil would be able to kill a friend. Either that, or he suspected Neil wasn't completely on board with his idea of The United States of Islam."

"Or both," Kate said.

"Right. And once the attacks are over, what does he need Neil for? He's the new caliph—the leader of all Islam. His vision for America is the only one that matters. He's not going to ask others' opinions; he's going to *dictate* their opinions."

"We need to call the sheriff and let him know what's happening," Kate said, scanning the room for a phone.

Jason dug in his pocket and pulled out his keys. "Yeah, call the sheriff." He looked at the pool of blood seeping from under Neil. "But go outside to wait for him. You've had enough drama for one day."

"Where are you going?"

"They killed Kelly and Grace, Kate. And the last time I waited around for the sheriff, two women ended up dead and another may never recover from her days of torture. I can't just sit around and hope that everything works out this time."

Kate pointed to the living room. "The last time you tried to face one of them, you were literally two seconds away from him putting a bullet through your skull. Next time you might not be so lucky. You need to let the professionals handle it."

"I'm sorry, Kate, but I can't do that. I know what Attar looks like and I know where he's going. Maybe I can prevent a lot of innocent people from being killed by that madman."

Kate looked at Jason; he wasn't going to stop until his family's murderers were caught and she had no right to ask anything else of him. "Fine, let's go."

He shook his head firmly. "No way. You're staying here."

"I saw him, too, Jason; I'm coming with you."

"I don't have time for this, Kate. Just call the sheriff and tell him what happened."

"Do you think you're the only one who gets to do the right thing? They're planning to attack *my* country, too! If there's a chance *you* can save the people in that mall, there's a better chance that *we* can. I go in my car or I come with you—your choice."

# CHAPTER 39

Khalid led the general into the stark-white employee-only concourses along the outer wall of the mall. Fifty yards down the narrow hall they came to a freight elevator; Khalid pressed the down button. They were waiting for the doors to open when a security guard approached. The unusually short man, maybe five-six with boots, stepped into the tight space between the other men and the elevator doors, then turned to face General Attar.

"Where's your ID? You are not allowed in this area without an identification badge." He talked strong and made full eye contact with the general. But having to crane his neck to look up at the man who stood almost a foot taller diminished any dominance he was trying to create.

Khalid answered, tilting his own badge at the man, "New employee. I'm taking him down to get badged right now."

The stocky man gave them the slightest of nods and stood fast for another moment, alternating his gaze between the taller men, then he turned and walked slowly down the hall with his arms out from his sides and bent at the elbows, as if he might whirl around and draw on them with a six-shooter. All he was missing was the cowboy hat and spurs. And a gun.

The elevator doors opened. They entered and Khalid swiped a key card over a reader and pressed the LL button. Attar waited for the doors to close before speaking. He had already briefed Khalid during their trip through the noisy public concourse about dispatching Omar to eliminate Jason Kendall and that Muhab would be delayed because of the morning's complications. Telling Khalid that Muhab was likely already dead would have only distracted the young man from the task at hand, and after the way he froze after killing Clara Riddle, it was important to prop up his confidence and righteousness, not to instill additional doubt.

"Khalid, I hope you understand the significance of your role in our mission. You are changing the world. Not just for today, but for generations. This is the first step to abolishing the infernal and replacing it with the light of Allah. Muhab chose you as his first lieutenant for a reason, Khalid. He knew you were the one who was equipped with the ability to lead and the capacity to take on additional responsibility. You were the person chosen to get inside this place and prepare the way for our historic offensive."

Khalid nodded, feeling unworthy of the compliments from the soon-to-be caliph. The doors opened and Khalid stepped out but the general grabbed his arm. "Think about it—more than a billion Muslims fractured by politics and selfish intentions will be reunited again for the first time since the first years after our great prophet Mohammed rose to greet Allah. You will be remembered forever. On behalf of the entire world and the generations that will live in peace for centuries, please accept our gratitude."

Khalid nodded again. But this time with growing pride. They went to the security office where General Attar received a picture ID badge with the name Ando Kaliq. He pinned it to his jacket, then they walked quickly to the storage area.

Khalid used the padlock key he had copied from Jan's set weeks earlier to open the door to Rockwell Outfitter's small storage space. General Attar guarded the door while Khalid pulled out the stashed backpack with the cable and removed the C4 bricks from the box of old receipts.

The general continued to build up the young martyr's confidence. "This is no small task, Khalid. The man who was to be with you in this endeavor was not strong enough for the task. That is why I am here. I wish, selfishly, you could stay by my side for the rest of this battle. But your place in heaven will be great, better than anything you can imagine on earth."

"It is a wonderful day, General. This may be selfish, but I am very much looking forward to my rewards in heaven," Khalid said.

"They will be well-deserved. You are right to desire such rewards." The persuasion was working.

They were standing in front of the locked mechanical room. Khalid did not have a key or pass card for access to this room. He had something better.

"Hello, Dewayne. I trust the schedule adjustment was not difficult for you," Khalid said to the security guard who joined them.

"Nothin' a little extra green couldn't take care o,'" he said.

General Attar pulled an envelope out of his jacket and handed it to him. "Twelve thousand."

Dewayne didn't bother to count the thick wad of cash before pocketing it. Khalid had always taken care of him. Occasionally, he would even add an extra hundred or two to the agreed-upon amount. It was nice to be appreciated for a change. This installment brought his total payment from Khalid to $22,600 tax-free dollars; $2000 each month (plus bonuses) for the past five months for information about security routines and tactics. Another $10,000 for working the basement on the agreed-upon day. And now, an additional $2,000 for the last-minute bump in the schedule.

Six years on the job and nothing but hassle from his bosses. But finally someone showed him the respect he deserved and paid him accordingly—and it was a government agency, no less.

"So you still think there's a spot for a hard-workin' security analysis guy at the Department of National Infrastructure?" Dewayne asked.

"Definitely. We are preparing for another round of hiring next month and you are at the top of the list," Khalid said.

"Good. I've been gettin' a lot o' offers from other companies, you know. I can't hold them off forever."

"We will not let you get away. Now, if you will make sure no one comes in, we will complete our analysis and be out of here very soon."

Dewayne saluted. "Aye, aye, Chief. The oxygen tanks are inside as you requested." He started for the door. "This worked out real good for me. I was supposed to work the floor for that stupid reality show thing in the rotunda. I'd rather be down here than up there with a thousand people packed into that little circle. No thanks." He saluted again and closed the door.

General Attar took the heavy pack from Khalid and gave the younger man his .45. "Hold onto that while I configure the detonators. We don't want any accidents." Khalid stuffed the weapon in his waistband under his jacket.

With the detonators set, the general moved to the bricks of C4. "Lay out the building schematics, then start lining up the tanks—we are nearly ready to position the explosives." Khalid turned back to the receipt box but was stopped when the general gripped his shoulder. "I could see the way you felt about the woman upstairs. Imagine a world where she and other innocent victims of this godless country learn of Allah's goodness."

"I look forward to such a day for her," Khalid replied.

---

Jason and Kate raced north up the on-ramp to Interstate 35. Jason purposely waited until he was on the state-patrolled federal highway before calling Sheriff Burnett.

"Pat. It's Jason. I just left Neil Lockwood's house in the Whispering Hills development. Neil's dead and so is one of the men who abducted Liz Pratt—the one who smashed my truck window." He glanced past Kate at the thick plastic rattling where the passenger window used to be.

"They're dead? How? When did this happen?" the sheriff asked.

"Neil was shot by the other man who later died trying to kill Kate and me. They're both still in Neil's house. It just happened in the last fifteen minutes. But listen to me. It's part of something much bigger. The men I saw at Clara Riddle's house last week definitely weren't making or selling meth. They're a part of some large terrorist group here to blow up the Megamall. The guy I told you about from the other night is in charge of the nationwide attack. The group's planning to blow up malls all over the country. We're on our way up there now but he's a half-hour ahead of us. You need to get in touch with Homeland Security, the FBI, or whatever agency is in charge of something like this. I'll tell you more later. But right now, call who you need to call."

"But what about—" Jason hit End on his cell.

# CHAPTER 40

"Knock it off, Chris; you're not funny. And you stink."

"What are you being such a bitch about? How about a little thank you for spending all night in the parking lot?" Chris Samuels said, as he ground his pelvis against her again.

"I said stop it. God, you can be such a jerk," she said, pushing him away before storming out of the line.

"Samuels, cool it," his buddy, Matt, said.

"What? We do the dirty work and sleep outside on cold concrete so they can cut in front of two thousand other losers, and then they get to act like bitches? Screw that!" Chris said.

"I slept in that parking lot, too, Samuels, and you don't see me acting like an ass."

"That's 'cause you're pussy-whipped." Chris Samuels took a pull from the plastic bottle of Windsor in his jacket, then offered it to Matt, who declined. "Whatever, dude. Why don't you bitch out too? You're looking at the original 'Punk Master' anyway." Chris and Matt had camped in the parking lot to be near the front of the line of people waiting to be interviewed by the producers of a new reality show where elaborate practical jokes would be played on people at their friends' request. The show was aimed at young adults and they were looking for a fresh face to host the show and emcee the action. Even with sleeping in a crowded parking lot, Chris still couldn't see the producers or the front of the serpentine line, but he'd heard the line behind him was twice the size. He took another sip from the bottle and shook his head.

---

Rhoda Phillips, Special Agent in Charge of the FBI's Minneapolis Field Office, had Jason on speakerphone in a large conference room filled with agents. He gave her a brief overview of the terrorist plot as he understood it.

"And you are sure this attack is happening right now, as we speak?" It was more confirmation than question.

"Yes. I'm absolutely sure about the America's Megamall attack," Jason said. "I can't speak to the attacks on any other malls—I just know there's a plan to blow up large malls all over the country."

"And you are on your way there now?"

"Yes."

"Here's what you're going to do," Phillips said. "Go to the south entrance of the mall." She snapped her fingers at a lead agent near the far end of the oval conference table. "Agent Jackson will meet you there. He'll be waiting for you in a charcoal grey suit, white shirt, and yellow tie just outside the entrance."

"What kind of shoes?" It was out of his mouth before he could do anything about it. Nerves.

"Pardon me?" asked Phillips.

"Never mind. I was just commenting on how we'll be able to identify your agent."

"Mr. Kendall, if that was a joke, I don't appreciate your sense of humor. If what you've said is true, thousands of people are in danger of losing their lives. Do you understand that?"

"Yes ma'am, I do. And ma'am?"

"What?"

"In the last hour I've had two different men point guns at my head. I am quite aware of the gravity of the situation. A situation *I* uncovered, not you," Jason said.

"Understand, Mr. Kendall, we get wild claims into our office all the time. We are working to confirm *your* story as we speak. So you'll…"

Jason cut her off. "Confirming my story? Are you fricking kidding me? There are exactly four people who can confirm my story: two are dead, the third is sitting next to me, and the last person who can give you your confirmation is at the mall right now planning to blow the place to hell, if he hasn't done it already. I'd say it's time to stop clearing the good guys and start chasing the bad guys!"

"Calm down, Mr. Kendall. It's not that we don't believe you. We're just matching it against any intel we have that will provide us additional insight into the plot or its perpetrators." She pointed at her lead agent and motioned to the door and he hustled out of the room with two other agents. "Agent Jackson is on his way and will be waiting for you at the south entrance. Stay off your phone in case we need to contact you before then. Thank you, Mr. Kendall."

Phillips clicked the speakerphone off and scanned the agents seated around the table, most of them with laptops in front of them. "Well, what do we think?"

A female agent sitting to the director's left spoke first, reading from her screen, "Jason Kendall, thirty-six… widower… grew up in Cedar River… graduated from Minnesota-Duluth… lived in St. Paul for a few years… business owner… looks like he moved back to Cedar River a few years ago… no record other than a few traffic violations."

"Did you say he graduated from UMD?" asked a younger male agent.

"Uh," she said, scanning the various information sources. "Yes, that's right."

"He was a big-time hockey player for them—Hobey Baker finalist," said the young agent. The comment was met with furrowed brows, so he clarified. "The Hobey Baker is like the MVP trophy for college hockey."

"Do you think he's looking for another fifteen minutes?" asked another agent.

"I can't say. That was a number of years ago," he said.

Phillips moved on. "Okay, does anyone see anything more concrete that would discredit him or his friend." Phillips referred to her notepad. "Kate Brooks?"

The question was met with silence and noncommittal head shakes.

"Okay. What about his story? Do we have any chatter or other intel that points toward a hit on America's Megamall? Lisa?"

Lisa Martinez oversaw intelligence gathering and discernment. "I haven't seen anything specific to malls or an 'Attar.' There have been regular discussions about the missing students from Lebanon, but intel doesn't indicate they are capable of executing a coordinated attack. Chatter as a whole, throughout known groups, has dropped recently—both locally and in Washington. I've been going through different folders and scanning new info, but haven't seen anything out of the ordinary—again, it's been really quiet."

"Lisa's not the only one looking. Has anyone else come across anything that might support what Mr. Kendall told us? What about this General Attar?"

Again Lisa took the lead. "Attar is a somewhat common name. We have no intel about a *General* Attar, and without a first name, we're grasping at straws."

"Agents Boroski and Timmons, you stay here. Boroski—you keep looking into Kendall and Brooks. Timmons—dig up everything on file regarding General Attar, mall plots, and related chatter. But call Washington first—we'll get our asses kicked if we don't let them in on this one. The rest of you—we're going to the mall." Everyone started moving.

She pointed at individual agents as she handed out additional instructions. "Lisa, you stay on the intel. If you get anything hard, call me. Bert, contact mall security and Bloomington police. Tell them we're on our way but hedge on specifics—I want to meet this Jason Kendall first." She looked down at the table for a moment. The agents waited, silent. "Scratch that," she looked back at Bert. "Tell Bloomington we need their bomb team, but tell them it's just a precaution. And make sure we have a schematic of the mall; that place is like a small city."

After doling out further instructions, Special Agent in Charge Phillips looked around the room. "Any questions?" Getting no response, she scanned the eyes of all the agents around the table. "Okay, folks. This is why we're here. It's what you are trained to do. Let's do this right; each one of us." Then she darted out of the room; the other agents followed with equal urgency.

---

General Attar walked out the south entrance of the huge mall. His pace was brisk but not rushed. He kept his head down, but not obviously so; he knew mall security, and all their cameras, were not an immediate threat to him; they were watching for people *entering* the mall. The day-to-day focus of mall security was not on people who wanted to attack the building, but those looking to cause trouble in it.

Security was in charge of protecting the business's image as much as its assets. They looked for people who wanted to start a fight, or damage mall property; problems encountered on a regular basis. They went out of their way to proclaim both to the public and their own trained employees that they considered each visitor an equal threat. But it was the teenagers whose ball caps sat a little crooked or whose stride was too filled with swagger who caught the attention of the camera watchers. Moreover, it wasn't the entrances that held the majority of the camera operators' attention; it was the food courts, movie theatre lobby, and other areas where the low-hanging-pants gathered.

Attar sat behind the wheel of Muhab's Passat parked in the Rookie's Roadhouse lot across from the mall and waited. He looked down at his watch—slightly ahead of schedule. For General Attar there were two distinct types of waiting: long-term and short-term. He had the ability to calmly sit back and allow critical events to play out over days, weeks, or even years.

But waiting for seconds or minutes to tick by was a completely different matter for the career soldier. In those times, the action never happened fast enough. A simple ten-minute extraction would feel like thirty and waiting just minutes for a call back from a subordinate would send him into a rage and turn a productive call into an angry dictation of personal expectations and character. He knew his impatience could be destructive and he had engaged a number of methodologies, medications, and exercises over the years to curtail it, but to no avail. He peered at his watch again, but this time he couldn't look away. The second hand ticked forward—slower and slower.

# CHAPTER 41

Following Kate's directions, Jason veered south off Interstate 494 onto Cedar Avenue, then followed the ramp onto Killebrew Drive. Two lights later they were pulling into the parking lot of Rookie's Roadhouse. Jason spotted Neil's Passat almost immediately and pulled in behind it, barricading it with his truck. He hopped out of the truck and ran to the driver window. The car was empty.

Jason slammed his hand down on top of the car. "Damn it!"

"So now we know he's still in the mall, right?" Kate said.

Jason looked across the street to the mall, then back at the car. "I guess so. But it doesn't feel right. The original plan was to meet Neil here, which would mean that his business inside the mall would already be completed." He looked back to the mall and the lofted, single-layered parking lot, which looked like a walled concrete terrace protruding from the massive building. "Maybe we should move the truck and wait for him to come out. They definitely aren't going to detonate the bomb until he's clear. No way they'd let any harm come to the great caliph."

"So, how long do we wait?" Kate said.

Jason didn't hear the question. His head was on a swivel, from the car, to the mall, to the restaurant, to the parking lot and around again looking for the terrorist leader.

"The FBI is waiting for us at the mall entrance. Let's follow their lead," Kate said.

"Okay. But we'll leave the truck here so he can't go anywhere."

They crossed the street, then jogged up the ramp to the south entrance to the mall. They waved at the agent with the yellow tie who got to the door a minute ahead of them and offered his hand. "Jason Kendall? Agent Ken Jackson, FBI."

Jason shook his hand and introduced Kate.

The agent nodded, then said. "If you'll both follow me, we are getting set up in the mall security office."

Jason pointed across the street. "We blocked Attar's vehicle with my truck at Rookie's Roadhouse. It's a green Passat."

"We know, Mr. Kendall—my partner is watching it. We'll probably need it moved so we don't spook the unsub. Let's get to the command center; we'll take care of it from there."

They rushed through the wide concourse separating the inner and outer rings of stores. "Keep your eyes moving and stop me if you recognize anyone," said Jackson. Kate kept her eyes scanning to the left and Jason to the right. They came upon a thick line of young people gathered in the middle of the wide corridor.

"What's with all the people?" Jason asked, catching up to the the agent in front of them.

"Auditions for some low-rent reality show. What else would get this many kids out of bed this early on a Saturday?" said Jackson.

Jason veered left as he looked right and bumped into the line of TV-star wannabes. A kid in a jean jacket took great offense. "Sorry, bud—my bad." Jason said.

"Damn right, old man," said Chris Samuels, making a brief motion of physical retaliation.

Jason was moving briskly and didn't even notice the provocation, but the smell of the man's whiskey hung with him.

They got to the small security office in the basement level of the mall just ahead of a flood of FBI agents. An intense woman with jagged features, who looked to be in her middle forties, entered first. She was dressed in a finely-cut black suit that matched her hair. She strode directly to where Jason and Kate were standing with Agent Jackson. She looked past Jason and Kate to Agent Jackson. "These are the wits?" He nodded. "Hang tight. I'll be right back," she said, then turned to the small group of mall security officials and Bloomington police officers.

"Who is in charge here?"

"Captain Willits, mall security," said a balding man from behind a thick mustache that hung well below his top lip. Gesturing to a younger man standing across from him, he said, "This is Officer Vick of the Bloomington Police Department. He's in command of the police station located inside the mall. What can we do for you?"

*What can we do for you?—great. I'm dealing with a customer service rep*, Phillips thought. "Right now I need the blueprints for the mall—all floors including the non-public areas. Then I need you to brief me on your evacuation procedures—there may be an explosive hidden on the premises. What kind of staff do you have?"

Willits spoke first. "We've got eighteen total, four here, two manning the monitors, eight on the floor, and four in the loading bay. That doesn't include the delivery station."

"What delivery station?" she asked.

"After 9/11, we set up a delivery gate in the open lot east of 24th Avenue where vehicles coming into the docking bays for deliveries are inspected inside and out; we use undercarriage mirrors and all. If they pass inspection, we track them all the way to the loading area to make sure no unscheduled stops or detours are taken."

"Has any vehicle ever *not* passed inspection?"

"Not to date, ma'am, no," he said sheepishly, as if she were making some point he didn't understand.

She turned to officer Vick. "How about you?"

Before he could answer, four men in suits burst through the door. Officer Vick introduced Bloomington Police Chief Ray Hogan to Special Agent Phillips. The chief quickly introduced the others.

"Bomb crew is one minute out. We've got another dozen men in the hall and twice that many on the way. Hennepin County is sending men as well," Chief Hogan said.

"I didn't call for additional men—a bomb crew; that was it," Phillips said.

"I understand, ma'am, but we have protocols we follow when it comes to potential attacks on the mall. An action plan, in the event of a natural disaster, local emergency, or terror attack is in place and ready to go," said the chief. "Your office signed off on it," he added.

"The protocols are in place for handling a definite threat. But I think we need to slow down here. We are still checking whether the information we received is credible. If you'll excuse me, Officer Vick and Captain Willits can get you up to speed with what we require at this time."

She took out her cell phone and called the agent in the field office. "Boroski—what do you got on Kendall or the mall?"

"Just more background on Jason Kendall—nothing that points to a lack of credibility or need for attention. As for the mall, it's a complete zero. We're seeing nothing."

"Not good enough, Boroski. Push CIA, NSA, and Interpol. The next time I talk to you, you'll give me something concrete that I can use out here, got it?"

"Yes, ma'am."

Phillips returned her phone to her jacket pocket and walked over to agent Jackson and the two witnesses.

"Jason Kendall, Kate Brooks—I'm Special Agent in Charge, Rhoda Phillips."

Shaking hands with Kate, she could feel the woman's nerves. Jason, though, seemed much more even. If anything, his handshake was a little too dominant. *Interesting,* she thought.

"Mr. Kendall, did you think of anything else that might help us since we last spoke? Or you, Ms. Brooks?" asked Phillips.

Jason told her about Neil's empty car and how he blocked it in with his truck.

"Yes, I know. We moved your truck. If he returns to the vehicle, we don't want to scare him off."

With no new information to exchange, the brief conversation came to a quick and uncomfortable halt. Phillips was about to return to Chief Hogan's group when Kate broke in, "I feel like something could be getting lost in the details of the attack. We're not talking about terrorists. These guys see themselves as a self-proclaimed army who believe they're poised to take over the U.S. I think you need to look at them as such."

"Did they show you evidence of their capabilities?" asked Phillips.

"No, but the guy holding us was adamant that they don't intend to just make a media splash or send some kind of incendiary statement to the world. They were very clear about not being lumped in with traditional terrorist groups."

"She's right," Jason said. "Today's bombings are not just about maximum casualties—it's the first part of a long-term plan to keep Americans from their normal holiday spending as a catalyst to tear apart the nation's economy. Part of their plan involves messages from the bombers to the American public and that's as important to them, maybe more so, than the actual death count. Imagine what will happen on Wall Street if America is too afraid to shop and stops consuming. Companies won't be deciding who to let go, they'll be figuring out who they can keep. I get the feeling this is way more destructive than the sub-prime and lending crises."

Phillips nodded, impressed with the synopsis. She gathered the agents, mall security, and Bloomington police together. "We may be dealing with a group who are here to make a statement to America. And their message is: *go to the mall and you're dead.* According to what the perps told our witnesses, the terrorists are planning to videotape Internet messages before detonating their explosives. So in addition to suspicious behaviors and dress, we need to be on the lookout for video cameras or phones being used for capturing video—anything that will broadcast a message." She looked at Vick and Willits. "They're going to want maximum impact, both visually and in terms of head count. Where would they set up?"

Chief Hogan spoke first. "We're talking about more than five hundred stores and another fifty restaurants. That doesn't even include the amusement park, the Beneath the Sea aquarium, or all the storage and other non-public areas."

"The amusement park is an obvious choice for showing shocking horror," Officer Vick said. "However, we're one of only a handful of malls with such an attraction, so they may think it won't translate. Another dramatic area is the rotunda. A new reality show is hosting auditions there today. The rotunda space is packed and a line of college-age kids trying to become the World's Master Punker, whatever that means, is already halfway around the mall."

Captain Willits added, "He's right. That would be the prime target. Our food courts are huge and always filled with people. If they want maximum casualties and representing all malls across the country, they may strike there. All malls have food courts."

Agent Jackson jumped in. "They will probably vary their approach. They could be in stores, at the entrance, food court, anywhere, but I'm guessing the targets will be dissimilar. Hit one department store and it's like hitting them all—the same way with the food courts, etcetera."

"He's right," Jason said. "The entire reason behind the attacks is to prevent Black Friday from happening. They need to make us afraid to step anywhere near a mall."

He turned to Phillips and saw the questions she'd had about his credibility seemed to have vanished. He directed his input to her but spoke so the entire group could hear. "I just remembered something. Neil told us that they had people in some of the larger dot-coms; maybe Amazon, Best-Buy, or a Wal-Mart—he didn't mention any by name. They're planning to send bombs through the mail to stop people from shopping online, too."

Phillips responded to the assembled group. "That leads us to another issue. We are charged with minimizing any casualties here in the mall but if, in fact, the leader is here, we absolutely cannot, I repeat, CANNOT, let him out of this building. So the question is, how do we evacuate the building without letting him slip out with the innocents?"

Captains Willits detailed the standard evacuation plan. Variations of the plan that would enable the capture of the plot's leader were debated among the ranking officials of each agency, but the unknowns of the attack were great; where, how many involved, types of explosive, and maybe the most important—how soon.

Consensus was building for evacuating all civilians through the main entrances only, which were located on all four sides of the first floor and the east and west sides of floors two and three. Police would shepherd everyone toward the nearest exit where groups of agents would filter out those fitting Attar's description along with anyone with suspicious behaviors or appearance.

The term "Middle Eastern" was not mentioned, nor was the word "profile" used, but the officers and agents knew what they were looking for. In addition to the eyes out on the floor, Jason and Kate would watch four exits each on the security monitors in the central security office to try to spot General Attar. All non-public and secondary exits would be barricaded and heavily guarded.

"Do we need the leader?" Chief Hogan asked. "If the building goes down and people who could have gotten out through other exits are killed, the political fallout is going to be hellacious. Not a person in this room would have a job six months from now."

"Sgt. Vick? How much additional evacuation time are we talking about if we close the secondary exits?" Phillip asked.

"A couple minutes, tops. The anchor store exits are maybe a hundred and fifty yards either side of the main entrances. In the time it's taking to discuss it we would have the people out of those stores and halfway to the parking structures," Vick said.

Both Phillips and Chief Hogan gave him angry glares to let him know they didn't appreciate his editorializing. Phillips gave the order. "Okay, let's move ahead with the main-entry evac plan. Agent Jackson will hand out assignments. Remember, be urgent but do not cause alarm. You set the tone for everyone else. Those of you on the exits, we only get one chance. No one walks through those doors without being visually interrogated."

Assignments were given with the highest concentration of officers sent to the rotunda, amusement park, and food courts.

---

Khalid sat in a leather chair inside a coffee house designed to look like a cozy north woods cabin. A newspaper was open across his lap but no pages had been turned in over fifteen minutes. He wasn't reading; he was praying. He was now just minutes away from greeting Allah in heaven. The fear and uncertainty he felt over the past days were gone. Maybe Attar's words were taking hold or maybe death during the attack had become his destiny rather than his choice.

During the prayers his thoughts regularly returned to Jan. He prayed she would be spared from today's violence and come to know the goodness of the Islamic teachings, which would soon be spread across America. The alternative to converting, he knew, would be dire.

At the next table a young boy said, "Look at all the polices, Mommy." Khalid's eyes flew open and his head darted to the store's entrance in time to see four policemen hurrying through the concourse. He folded the paper and exited the knotty pine surroundings in the opposite direction.

# CHAPTER 42

Twelve black-and-white monitors were mounted in three tight rows on the security office wall. The bottom two rows showed live video of each of the eight main entrances through which customers and mall employees were being evacuated. Jason sat in front of the four on the left; Kate studied the four on the right. The top row of screens flashed live shots from cameras all over the mall. A row of agents kept watch over those monitors, looking for suspicious or out-of-place behavior.

Jason and Kate watched as anyone Indian, African, or Middle Eastern was pulled aside and asked to look into the security camera. An occasional Caucasian man or woman would be asked to follow the same procedure to prevent a charge of profiling or racism by those detained. Agents positioned with Jason and Kate were prepared to relay a positive ID to the agents at the door, but almost midway through the evacuation, neither had even come across a "maybe."

Jason was struck by how orderly the people on the monitors were leaving the building. Even though the visitors were being asked to exit through the nearest doors, rather than those closest to their vehicles, people maintained an orderly and obedient march. He wondered if the people racing down the stairs of the World Trade Center had been so cordial and obedient. He was also surprised by the number of families he saw—women with strollers seemed to be on parade at each of the entrances. *Keep moving—get those kids out of here*, he thought.

A moment later, Jason's eyes widened and he leaned forward. "I think I saw one!" Jason said to the agent on his left.

"Which exit?" asked the agent, his wrist mike already at his mouth.

"It's not an exit. He's in the amusement park. I caught it on one of the top cameras." He pointed at the first camera on the top row, which had already switched to another shot, then to a third. "Can we get this one back to the shot in the amusement park?" he asked to no one and everyone.

---

Khalid stood on a smooth orange path that months ago had the look and feel of cobblestones. He was looking for a place to temporarily disappear inside the Crazy Larry Amusement Park in the center of the mall.

A leading Hollywood studio had recently purchased the theme rights to the amusement park after the previous lease expired, and named it after a popular cartoon character. He had cut through the large park many times to get to other sections of the mall. Khalid was always surprised at how noisy it was. Even with the rides turned off, as most of them were now, rushing waterfalls and piped-in music reverberated loudly off the walls and the bright glass ceiling six stories above. He assumed from the current shut-down the path to his assigned area was also in jeopardy. "Be nimble," he told himself, then looked for a place to hide while he figured out what to do next.

The park was set up like a maze. Real and fake plants grew out of the ground all around, separating clusters of smaller amusement rides and hiding supports for the larger ones. Criss-crossing orange pathways meandered up and down gentle inclines as they wove around the rides and attractions. Around the perimeter of the park were themed gift shops, game areas, and restaurants. Khalid hoped one of those places had a restroom or closet he could tuck into. But one by one they were pulling down their steel doors.

"Khalid, Khalid."

He turned to find Nafi, dressed in a Minnesota Wild bomber jacket, approaching.

"Khalid. What are we going to do? They are shutting down the mall and forcing people out. How are we going to get to our appointed positions?"

"I do not know." Seeing two men in suits appear near the movie theater mezzanine on the second floor, he pulled Nafi into a large group of fake palm trees and ferns. "We are not going to fail. Do you understand?" He was projecting the general's righteousness and strength. "We will assume the others have stayed out of their grasp just as we have. We will complete our mission."

"Perhaps we should go to our positions now. Maybe the others are waiting for us. I must get to the rotunda," Nafi said, and stood to leave.

Khalid yanked him back into the treed cover. "No. If you go and your video partner is not yet there, you will be pushed out of the building before you can complete your task. What if someone wants to look under your coat?" he asked, admonishing Nafi for his impatience. "We will find someplace to wait, then we will go to the rotunda together. If your partner is not there I will use my camera to videotape you. If he is there, I will continue to my post in the department store as planned. But for now, we need to hide."

---

General Attar stared at the massive mall from the window of his hotel room. When his call to Omar went unanswered he abandoned the car and climbed into a hotel shuttle bus leaving the lot. The van took him back to its base at the Radisson Hotel and water park just west of the mall. Built to attract families already planning a vacation at the mall, the lobby was overrun with wet children and harried parents.

The woman at the welcome desk told him all of the large suites, rooms with kitchens, and multiple bedrooms were occupied. But several standard single rooms were still available. He told her he needed to get some work done and asked if any of the available rooms were on the upper floors "out of the way." She explained the hotel required a surcharge for early check-in. He balked at the charge and told the woman he just needed a quiet place to work for a few hours before check in-time. The fee was minimal and of no concern to the general, but he wanted to present himself as a "normal" traveler. After a brief exchange she *happily* withdrew the charge from his occupancy agreement.

In the room, he checked the time on his Blackberry again. He had to assume the worst: Omar failed to kill Muhab and the others in Cedar River and was now in the hands of law enforcement. Perhaps Muhab was, too. Would one of them or both talk before zero hour? Doubtful—asking for an attorney would give them an hour, minimum.

But what about the hostages? They would be a problem; certainly telling the officials everything they knew would potentially diminish the level of success of today's operation. And if law enforcement had Omar or Muhab's phone, they could be tracing his cell right now. But Attar had enough experience to know that politics were a part of law enforcement, and the bigger the bust the slower the pace. For just a moment he considered an early detonation, but kept his confidence in the glacial movements of his enemy and decided to keep the original schedule and enable the full effects of today's operation. Another check of the Blackberry; only twenty-four minutes until the martyrs make their statements live on the Internet, then sacrifice themselves and all the people around them.

How much longer until authorities had his Blackberry's signal triangulated? He went to the room desk, opened the drawer, and pulled out the complimentary note pad and pen. He tore a sheet from the pad and placed it on the hard desk where no impressions would be left. He scrolled to the bottom of his list of two thousand contacts, then counted up. He wrote down every tenth contact, each of which was a moniker rather than a name, until he had thirteen total.

He walked into the bathroom, disconnected the Blackberry's SIM card and flushed it and its tracing mechanism down the toilet. Then he wiped down the useless cell phone, wrapped it in a washcloth and smashed it under his heel. After a quick wipe-down of the room, he was out the door and into a taxi.

He had hoped to make the detonation call from a place where he could watch the aftermath of the destruction with his own eyes. For many months he had imagined hoards of hysterical Americans, fortunate to escape the initial explosions, trampling each other like ants out of a flooded hole. But the success of the mission was more important than his personal reward; he would have to set off the final explosion from the safe house and watch the aftermath on one of the cable news channels.

"Where to?" asked the cabbie.

"Can you get me to 46th and Ewing Avenue in Minneapolis in fifteen minutes?" General Attar asked.

"Of course. No problem."

---

"This is going to be a nightmare. They could be hiding in any one of a thousand places," said Rhoda Phillips. The group of FBI agents, Bloomington police, and Jason were huddled at one of the four main entrances to the amusement park in front of the ride where Jason had seen Khalid on the monitor. Phillips looked around the thirty-foot-high Commotion Karl ride, which spun mild thrill seekers in a sixty-foot diameter circle, pausing at the top for maximum effect. She put her hands on her hips as she considered the best way to search the expansive park filled with small nooks and covers that could be used as hiding places.

"All right, let's fan out and work our way to the other side of the park. Take your time; we don't want this guy to slip past us." She noticed some guests still milling about, herding their young children. "And push any remaining visitors and employees with you. Leave nobody behind—I don't care if it's an old woman with five little grandkids; get them moving. Let's clear this place."

She gestured toward Jason. "Mr. Kendall says we're looking for a Middle Eastern man in his early twenties. Six feet, good-looking, with curly hair. He's not the leader of the group, but he's closely connected to him. Okay, let's go."

To Jason she said, "You stay here. If we find him we'll bring him to you for positive ID. Don't move; if you see something, call one of *us*. Got it? I know these guys messed with you pretty good but don't go trying to be a hero—the country's counting on us catching these assholes."

Jason nodded and Phillips headed up a rising tangerine-colored path surrounded on each side by imitation rock fences with tall tropical plants jutting high into the air behind them. To his right, Jason watched an agent direct a woman and her two small boys out of the park. The woman looked extremely agitated, not with the escort, but with the two giggling boys, who were either twins or close buddies. The boys kept sneaking looks at each other, resulting in louder, involuntary giggling. Their enjoyment only worked to make the mother more angry and soon each boy received a swift rap up the back of his head. *Yep, twins*, Jason thought. A moment later they disappeared over a rise, behind a miniature semi-truck ride.

---

Khalid and Nafi thought they were done when the group of agents first rushed into the park and settled near a ride not far from their perch behind stacks of insulation stored on a second floor overlook above the park. Moments earlier, the two men had left the spot where the agents now gathered. The two had gone through a set of doors marked Stairs A/B. However, they were prevented from moving farther into the mall by a drop-down cage, which was meant to deny access *into* the overlook rather than out. They remained still and watched as law enforcement worked away from them into the maze of park pathways. It wasn't a great hiding spot, but it would need to do for now.

Khalid watched the men slowly creep to the other side of the park, carefully searching rides and looking through and around the small cartoon forms and fake greenery along the way. He knew that once they got to the other end of the park, it wouldn't be long before they expanded the search.

He looked around for a more secluded spot to wait when he noticed one man hanging back from the others. He recognized him immediately—he'd held a door open for him. Handing Nafi the small video camera, Khalid ordered, "Stay here. If something happens to me, set up the camera and make your statement—you know how to transmit the broadcast. Then go to Allah."

"What are you going to do?"

He felt for General Attar's gun under his jacket. "I am going to make right my past sins."

# CHAPTER 43

Chris Samuels was too smart for this. Way too smart. How do you pick the host and chief punkologist of the new reality show, "Master of the Punk?" You play a joke on the group and see who's still standing! He watched the uniform cops and the undercover agents pushing everyone to the exits. But which were the show's producers, the ones in plain clothes or the uniforms? The uniforms looked too cop-like, so he would work the suits. He took the last swig of Windsor, shoved the bottle in his buddy's pocket and said, "Here goes nothin'."

Matt watched as Samuels ran away from the exit and straight for a plainclothes officer, yelling, "Bow before the Punk Master." He knocked down a half-dozen people on the way, then swan-dived atop the agent. Matt wasn't about to be left out. He raced after Samuels, darting to the next agent and launching himself into the woman with a flying cross-body block.

---

The cops and agents were well out of sight when Jason felt the hard steel pressed into his back. Jason instinctively started to raise his arms to communicate to his attacker he was not a threat, but then quickly dropped them. He was absolutely a threat.

"Where is Omar?" asked Khalid, clutching Jason's shirt with one hand and poking the gun harder into Jason's back with the other.

Jason didn't recognize the voice; it definitely wasn't Attar. He recognized the name but didn't admit to it. "I don't know any Omar."

"He was sent to kill you in Cedar River. Where is he?"

Jason glanced side to side but couldn't see any agents. With the loud ambient noise inside the cavernous park, a sacrificial call for help would go unheard. "Are you talking about the hulking Muslim with a brain the size of a golf ball? He's still in Cedar River. He didn't want to come to the mall; probably embarrassed about the iron poker lodged in his skull."

The gun came down hard across the back of Jason's head, causing him to fall forward. Only his attacker's grip kept him upright. If the pistol whip was meant to inflict punishment or intimidate Jason, it missed the mark. He flashed on Thursday night and how he'd backed against Clara Riddle's house in fear outside the basement window when he first heard Omar inside. Now he had a loaded gun in his back, and it was only pissing him off.

"Move. Down there." The assailant shoved him toward an outer corner of the park.

Jason started down a long slope past a fountain featuring a splashing orange cartoon donkey. Ahead he saw a set of restroom doors along the wall; the men's and women's entrances were bumped out with hidden side entries. A family restroom with a standard door was centered between the Men's and Women's.

"Keep going—middle door," the man said.

He stepped inside the family restroom and immediately understood why the mother he saw earlier was so miffed and the two young boys couldn't control their giggling. It looked like a scene from *Preschool Animal House*. Soaked and wadded paper towels were slipping down the large mirror opposite the door and puddles of pink hand soap drizzled off the counter onto the floor near the clogged sink. The rest of the room was equally destroyed—sopping paper towels and toilet paper were scattered about and water had been sprayed over all four walls. Jason wondered where their mother had been—this kind of destruction took some time. He took his first step into the mess and grinned victoriously as his foot slopped onto the flooded floor.

Jason recognized his attacker through the smears and splashes on the mirror. "I know you. You're the dipshit who let Liz and me run out of Clara Riddle's house. Is that what this is about—you like to watch? I can't guarantee anything; not much for peeing in public. Do you third-world guys ever get stage fright?" *C'mon, Jason, Think like your opponent, then…*

The gun moved from his back to the base of his skull as the door lock clicked behind them.

"Some might think making jokes just ahead of death is a sign of courage. Others say it is just an expression of resignation," Khalid said. "But in your case, I am guessing it is stupid American arrogance."

"Let me ask you." Jason bent his legs slightly and shifted his weight to his right foot. "Is it stupid? Or is it arrogant to not surrender when you're surrounded by a couple hundred cops and your brilliant plan is obviously in shambles?" He gave Khalid a moment to think about it, then continued. "And what are you going to gain by killing me? I'm flattered and all, but I don't think putting a hole through my head is going to earn you a Martyr Badge at Camp Allah."

"I would not be so sure. I am guessing you are responsible for all the law enforcement here today. Maybe killing you is exactly what I need to receive Allah's graces. And just so you do not die with any misguided feelings of self-satisfaction, I will let you know the plan is not in ruin. The main explosives, which will shut down this castle of greed, are still armed and secure. They will be detonated any moment with a simple phone call. You may deny one or two brave martyrs' bombs from exploding, but they were only meant to deliver a message before the real destruction takes place."

"And what message is that? We're a group of sick outcasts using religion to justify our pathetic existence? Or don't you know what the message is? General Attar has you losers all so riled up about nailing virgins in heaven, you probably don't care what you're dying for. Virgins or not, your tombstone on earth is going to read, 'Here lies Khalid: Brainwashed Sucker.'" Jason backed up the insult with a patronizing laugh through the mirror.

Khalid's eyes darkened and his gun hand twitched. He started to step back with his right foot to transfer his weight and support the recoil of the gun.

"Die, infid—"

Jason's response was lightning fast. The drenched tile floor was like ice and Jason had plenty of experience fighting on ice. As the gunman rocked back, Jason spun on his already weight-bearing right leg and forcibly swept his left leg around, kicking his attacker's legs out from under him as they shifted. The man flailed in the air for a moment, his arms flying out instinctively to try to regain his lost equilibrium. He got off a shot but his body was working on reflex, not trained conditioning, and the shot lodged harmlessly in the ceiling.

The leg whip rotated Jason so he was now facing Khalid as the Muslim stopped sprawling and started falling. Jason threw himself onto the tumbling man, multiplying the force with which he crashed onto the tile floor. Jason was inhaling confidence. His left hand went immediately to the wrist holding the gun. It wasn't Jason's strong side, but his hand was supported by a locked arm and his full weight leaning on it. Confident the gun was secure, he grabbed a handful of thick curly hair, lifted it, then slammed it back into the tile. Jason lifted the head for a second blow and was surprised at the sudden lack of resistance. Khalid must have still been stunned from the first wallop. He forced the skull into the tile so hard with the second blow that the momentum dislodged his hand from Khalid's head, a fistful of curly hair still in it. The gun slipped from the now limp hand. Jason didn't check for a pulse. The sound of crushed skull told him everything he needed to know. He grabbed the gun and ran out of the room in search of Rhoda Phillips.

# CHAPTER 44

What was a show producer doing with zip ties? And a gun? Chris Samuels thought he was the undisputed winner of the audition until the "producer" he jumped suddenly rolled him over and stuck an elbow on his throat and a gun in his eye.

He sat quietly now, his hands in the ties behind his back, and watched from the sidelines as the mayhem played out in front of him. Fights broke out between cops and civilians, civilians and civilians, men and women, and group vs. group. Those not in the fights were inciting them—all while a mob looking down from the second floor cheered and sent cups, bottles, and anything else they could find raining down on those below.

Chris's girlfriend ran up to him, worry on her face. "Let's get out of here!"

"Do you have fingernail clippers in your purse?" he asked.

"I think so," she said, lifting her purse to her chest. "Why?"

"I need to finish what I started."

---

Jason caught up to Phillips at the east end of the park. He told her and a surrounding circle of law enforcement about his encounter with Khalid and about the bomb set to be detonated after the suicide bombers blew themselves up.

"Did he say where it is?" she asked.

"No. He just said it would shut the mall down," Jason said.

Phillips sent two agents to the restroom, then addressed the rest of the group. "Jackson—alert the agents at the exits to check for existing bombs or booby traps." She pointed at a female agent in a dark blue FBI windbreaker. "See if the structural engineers have arrived—find out where the stress points of the building are." The agent brought her walkie-talkie to her mouth and ran for the command center. Then to the group, "What else would shut down the mall? Think, people—we're running out of time!"

A few ideas were offered, more as questions than strong possibilities. Jason felt the clock ticking—he needed to get Kate out of the building. He turned and saw people at the far exit still slowly filing out of the mall through the security checkpoints.

"Jackets—cold," he said, barely audible. He turned back to the group of agents.

"Jackets—look at all the people leaving the mall—they're all carrying or wearing jackets. Could the bomb be in the heating system?"

A member of mall security spoke up. "He might be right. The mall uses geo-thermal heating and cooling. If they cause enough damage to the system it could shut the mall down for a long time, and possibly for good." Phillips gave him a look that told him she needed more, so he went on. "In the winter, the mall's temperature is controlled with water heated by the earth's constant 56-degree temperature hundreds of feet underground, then lifted, heated a little more, dispersed, and then sent back down for reheating. Not only that, but the main transfer unit is located under the center of the building. If the ground there is disturbed, the structural integrity of the entire building could be compromised. The mall would be shut down for months, or like I said, if it's bad enough, they'd have to bulldoze the place."

The young security officer received more questioning glances. "How do you know all this?" Phillips asked.

"I'm a double major in Civil Engineering and Public Relations at the U of M. One of my professors worked as an advisor to the company that installed the geothermal system in the mall. Maybe we should give him a call; he'll be able to give you all the details about the system."

"We don't have the time," Phillips said. Then into her walkie-talkie, "Get the bomb squad to the heating unit in the lower level. Hurry!"

A communication crackled from the FBI agents' walkie-talkies. "Special Agent Phillips; we have a situation in the rotunda."

"What is it?"

"They're rioting, ma'am. They think the evacuation is a prank. We need backup. We're talking about maybe a thousand kids here, ma'am. How do you want us to proceed?"

"We'll be right there," she said, then brought the walkie-talkie back to her mouth. "Any available agents to the rotunda. Any nonessential exit officers report to the rotunda. And someone bring a bullhorn, goddamn it!" Then to the agent next to her she said, "Jackson, go with the bomb squad to the basement. Time's gotta be running out. The rest of you—let's get those idiots out of the rotunda."

Agent Jackson and another agent ran back through the park while the rest of the group followed Phillips toward the rotunda. Jason was left alone with no direction so he sprinted in the same direction as Jackson—to find Kate.

He caught up to Agent Jackson and his partner a moment later. They were stopped in the park, looking up to the second floor.

At the top of a staircase, between two buildings designed to look like folksy Americana storefronts, two agents were pointing guns at a young Middle Eastern man. The suspect was speaking angrily at the agents, who seemed to be trying to calm him. Jason was too far away to hear the exchange but he could see the man's anxiety rising. The suspect slowly opened his Minnesota Wild jacket to reveal a white t-shirt with the phrase TURN TO GOD printed on it in bold black lettering. Hanging from the jacket's interior were two large PVC cylinders on each side with colored wires running from them. The man started shouting, then looked above him. One agent rushed toward him, but it was too late.

A tremendous, concussive blast reverberated as the man's chest exploded. Steel pellets and human flesh sprayed out like smoke, destroying everything within an eight-foot radius. The agents never had a chance. Their bodies hurtled through the air, one into a wall, the other landing, then rolling unnaturally down the stairs. Blood sprayed from their limp bodies where multiple steel pellets had severed already dead arteries.

"Damn it!" Agent Jackson's words were a mixture of anger, sadness, and regret. "Pike—stay here and make sure nobody goes near that scene," he said to his partner. The man ran for the staircase and Jackson raced for the security office. "Kendall, you stay with me."

---

An accident on Cedar Avenue stopped what the cabbie assured General Attar should have been nothing more than a ten-minute trip, lights permitting. He reminded his fare every few minutes how sorry he was, and that he wished there was a quicker route. Attar told the fellow Muslim he understood but silently wished he would just shut up and stop trying to work the tip. Attar looked again at his watch; the martyrs would be making their statements on the Internet in two minutes. Detonating the C4 immediately following the explosions of their pipe bombs would add the most additional casualties. If he was forced to detonate a few minutes late he would lose some head count but the massive damage to the mall's structure and the martyrs' message alive on the Internet would be unaffected.

"Pull into the nearest convenience store. I need to make a phone call," he said to the cabbie.

"I will need to keep the meter running." *Business is business.*

"Fine."

---

Jason and Agent Jackson didn't break stride when they met the four-man bomb squad in the mall substructure just outside the security office. A man holding large rolled-up printouts waved them in his direction. "I got the plans. The HVAC room is down this corridor."

The six men reached the heavy steel door in seconds and another of the bomb team swiped a card over the reader to allow them entry. Bursting into the room, they scanned the equipment and surrounding structure for explosive devices. Agent Jackson followed a respectful distance behind the man with the floor plans and Jason waited just inside the door and let the experts do their job. Jackson had told Jason that his role was to stay out of the way until called upon so Jackson could focus on being the eyes and ears for the Bureau during the operation.

One team member was moving quadrant by quadrant, scouring the ceiling and reinforcing pillars for explosive devices. He found no wires, detonators, or explosives. "All clear overhead."

Another man used a powered ratchet to open the main heating and cooling boxes and examined the inner workings with his pen light. "All clear in the units."

The third man was charged with looking over secondary equipment and the lower interior of the room. He had the most space to cover but the least amount of likely detonation area. "All clear on the ground."

The team leader who was focused on the most likely targets shook his head. "If there's a bomb, it's not in here, Agent Jackson."

"Holy Cow! You guys is fast," a voice said from the doorway.

The men turned to see Dewayne at the door shaking his head in amazement. "The Department of National Infrastructure will definitely give you a passin' grade on this one."

Agent Jackson rushed him and lifted him by the shirt. "What are you talking about? Who's the Department of National Infrastructure?"

"The guys who were in here before you—about an hour ago, I suppose."

"What guys?" Jackson shouted.

Dewayne tried to calm him. "Don't worry. I'm sure you passed the test," he said. "Did you find they's set-up under the rotunda, too?"

---

General Attar's eyes were leveled on the clock behind the counter of the Holiday convenience store as the woman in front of him labored to select her full complement of twenty scratch-off lottery tickets from the choices displayed through the glass counter. "Let's see. I need six more. How many of the "Let's Play Ball" do I have?" the woman asked the cashier.

"Excuse me, sir, I am looking for the phone," the general interrupted as the second hand passed in front of the twelve. The martyrs were detonating within seconds.

"Outside," the young attendant pointed toward the east side of the building.

---

Wires were duct-taped in a line across a series of steel pillars under the rotunda.

"What are we looking at?" Jackson asked.

"C4 on every other pillar with what's probably propane or acetylene in these tanks for accelerant—to magnify the force of the explosion. It's not terribly sophisticated at the branches, but it's more than enough explosive to send the rotunda up and everything around or above to come crashing down. Maybe the whole building, depending on the architecture."

"So what do we need to do?" asked agent Jackson.

"We need to find the detonator—it's got to be connected somewhere along one of these wires. If we're lucky, one cut and we're clear. If they installed some mitigators, well…"

The men spread out, focusing on the four pillars with the C4 attached. Jason moved in to help; he'd been in hundreds of rooms with exposed wiring. The team fanned out again, each with a specific area or object to inspect. Jason took a quick look at the wiring setup, then followed a single wire running perpendicular to the rest. It ran past the four pillars and ended through a closed door to a small service closet.

"I think I may have something here," he yelled back to the others.

"What is it?" the team leader yelled back.

"A cell phone connected to a small patch of wires. I think we're okay; the light on the phone is green."

The leader's voice changed as he sprinted toward Jason. "That means the phone is ringing. We're being detonated!"

Jason was amazed how fast the man moved under his lead vest. In seconds he was at the cell phone, pushing Jason away. "Find cover!" he shouted.

Jason looked around for something strong under which to shield himself, but as he did, he saw the rest of the group running toward them, not away—no shielding considered. Jason stood with them, ready to face his fate, just like the others who were gathering alongside him.

With no hesitation in his movements, the leader analyzed the explosive's engineering, then started tracing different wires with the point of his snips. He clipped a red wire between the phone and a knot of wires, then moved to the wires between the knot and the C4 and again used his tool as a pointer. He tugged gently at a blue wire, one of several different colors pressed into the clay brick, and glanced over at the men watching at the door. Jason felt the nods from the other men on the team. The leader looked back to the explosive and settled his snips around the wire. "Clear!" he yelled.

A second later, the display on the phone went dark—the call had gone through. The man put his hands on his thighs and hung his head, taking his first full breath in minutes.

"You're sure? Can I call it in?" Agent Jackson asked.

The man didn't move.

"Make the call," said a man next to Jackson.

Agent Jackson gave the all clear into his walkie-talkie and a thunderous cheer from the command center erupted moments later, filling the cavernous tunnels.

---

With the worst of the offending members restrained, the threatening but measured commands of Police Chief Hogan through the bullhorn finally dispersed the crowd from the rotunda. As the mass of people filed through the exits, Agent Phillips and Chief Hogan led the large group of officers back to an already overflowing security ante area. Federal agents and local officers were crammed shoulder-to-shoulder, waiting for detailed orders regarding the large-scale, room-by-room search for the terrorist leader and any remaining associates.

The double doors from the corridor to the mechanical room flew open and the bomb squad strode through, followed by Agent Jackson and Jason. A riotous roar exploded and applause, shouts, hugs, and high-fives were enthusiastically passed around the room. The collection of men and women wore a number of different uniforms representing various agencies, but at the moment, they were a single, bonded unit. The exuberance was greater than anything Jason remembered from his championship celebrations as an athlete. Those days and those celebrations seemed so trivial now. These men and women were heroes of the first order; true champions.

Jason was stuck behind the mass of revelers, twenty yards from the security office and Kate. When the cheering subsided, an assistant Bloomington police chief stood on a chair above the agents and officers and detailed the plan for the intensive mall search, then doled out specific instructions to smaller groups of the various organizations. Jason had a different focus—finding Kate and getting her out of the building to somewhere safe.

He leaned against the back wall, waiting for the orders to be completed when a small crack in the wall of officers opened and through it shimmied Kate, her head rotating side to side like she was looking for a lost puppy. Jason called to her and her search stopped. She sprinted for him, then leaped the final five feet into his arms. Their kiss was full of the angst, confusion, joy, relief, and all the other emotions bubbling inside them. The kiss seemed to last only just a moment and forever.

"Are you okay? We saw that bomber explode on the monitor. It was so terrible! Those poor agents. And their families." She paused and put her hand over her mouth as it began to tremble. "I couldn't find you—the camera shot was so narrow. We couldn't see if anyone else was caught in the explosion." Tears were streaming from her eyes. "Nobody in the security office could say for sure how many were killed in the explosion."

"I'm all right—I was never in any danger," he said. "What about you? How are you holding up?"

"I'm okay—I got pretty freaked out there when that bomber, you know..." She took a deep breath. "But physically I'm fine. I just feel so helpless—like I'm not helping."

Jason put his arms around her and held her close. "Sounds like they still haven't found Attar?"

"No. They're holding some other men that they are pretty sure are involved. Two of them had pipe bombs strapped to them like the one guy. Apparently, one of them was about to detonate himself at a busy exit but the woman behind him in line grabbed his arm and held him still long enough for agents to get to him before he could set off the bomb. One of the agents said the woman basically leaped over some other woman to grab the guy when he opened his jacket, and wouldn't let go until the others could jump in—amazing." Then her voice sank from awe to regret. "But no. They haven't found General Attar yet."

Jason turned away from her and punched the wall as he swore at himself. Kate pulled him back to her and held his face with both hands. "You did it, Jason. You stopped those lunatics. The attack is dead—he lost; you won." Jason looked away and shook his head.

At the other end of the room, the chief finished the assignments by reminding his officers to be thorough and safe. As the group dispersed, Rhoda Phillips made her way to the two civilians.

"It looks like you two get to punch out, at least from this location. I'll find an agent to take you back to our office downtown to get full statements. I want to thank both of you, for everything. I know you've been through a lot today, including getting off to a rough start with the FBI. I apologize for the friction earlier, but you'd be surprised how many threats are called in to us from people just looking for attention, or worse."

Jason responded first. "No problem, just doing your job. Any leads on Attar?"

"No one has shown up at the Passat parked at the restaurant so we feel fairly confident that he is still somewhere in the mall. But it may take some time to find him. It could be tomorrow or later before we can completely comb through this place."

Jason shook his head in disgust. "Frickin' coward. He sends a bunch of kids out to blow themselves up in the name of getting laid in heaven. And now two of your guys are dead while he hides in some closet at the Barbie Store. I know you need him alive, but part of me hopes he leaves here in a goddamned hearse."

"Well, wherever he's hiding, we'll find him." She shook their hands. "Thank you again for all your help. Let me track down an agent to take you downtown."

"Agent Phillips?" Kate said. "Can we just go in Jason's truck? I think we could both use a little break—even if it's just a fifteen-minute ride up to Minneapolis."

The FBI woman looked them over.

"C'mon. Do you really think we're gonna skip out on you *now*?" Jason asked.

"Fine—but straight to the office—we need your statements." She handed Jason her card. "The address is at the bottom."

They had to clear three security checkpoints before being allowed to drive through the final police barricade a half-mile from the mall.

"Still prefer life in the city after all this?" Kate teased.

"I never had a neighbor in St. Paul who wanted to turn the United States into a virgin forest. I can't say that anymore about Cedar River."

"Look at it this way; what's the chance that happens twice?" she smiled.

"That's not exactly a ringing endorsement," he said.

Jason shook his head and changed the subject. "Why do I think they're not going to find Attar?"

"Special Agent Phillips seems like she knows her stuff. I don't think she'll let them *not* find him."

"Think like them, then out-think them," he muttered.

"What?"

"Nothing."

They drove the next few minutes in silence. They were directed by law enforcement through a horde of news vehicles onto Interstate 494. Jason drove west toward Interstate 35 north, which would lead them directly into downtown Minneapolis. He veered right onto the ramp, then suddenly lurched the bulky F250 left, missing the underpass guard rail by inches, and forcing a startled minivan to screech into the far lane.

"Jason! What are you doing?" screamed Kate.

"I know where he is! He's not in the mall. He was gone before we even got there."

"How do you know that?"

"It's something Seth said a couple days ago about thinking like your opponent. I've been trying to do that but what do I know about Muslim radicals?" He looked over at Kate. "Cedar River neighbors, on the other hand…"

He looked back to the road and reached out his hand. "Do you have Phillips' card?"

Kate held it up. "Yeah, right here."

Jason pulled his phone off his hip. "Read me the number."

She did, but it was no use. He tried five times but couldn't get a dial tone.

"Damn it! I can't get a line." He pounded the steering wheel. "Did you see all those news trucks we passed outside the mall? I bet news is out and everyone across the state is trying to contact friends or family who may have been at the mall this morning. The same thing happened when the 35W bridge collapsed in Minneapolis."

Kate turned on the radio. He was right; the mall was receiving full coverage on all the talk stations. Speculation, but no facts, was being reported about what was happening inside the mall.

"Why don't you pull into a gas station? We can call from a land line," Kate offered.

"Won't work. My mom tried my cousin non-stop from our house after the bridge collapsed. She was scared to death because he drove that bridge every day to and from work. She didn't get through to him until after ten o'clock that night."

"What are we going to do?"

He handed her the Blackberry. "*You* are going to keep trying. *I* am going to find Attar."

# CHAPTER 45

Omar's assumed failure in Cedar River changed Attar's plans for the rollout of the national operation. As it stood, he was in the dark about what, if anything, law enforcement knew and who was providing the information. He offset his lack of intel with immediacy and agility. He would set the other cells in motion to strike before the bureaucracy of Homeland Security could coordinate a national plan of action. But at the moment he was again forced to wait—and again not handling it well.

He turned on the television in the living room. Each of the local stations had cut into regular broadcasting to cover the evacuation of the country's largest mall. Soon, CNN, MSNBC, and FOX were also regurgitating the same bits of information. Distinguished looking men and women with heavy make-up were seated in busy-looking studios speaking to the viewing audience from beside a computer-imposed catch phrase graphic. One network called it "Scare in America's Mall," another, "Mall Under Siege." Fox News was the most dramatic: "Heartland Terror?" He wondered if the news networks kept headline writers on staff to maximize the dramatic value and draw viewership. He kept the TV tuned to FOX, guessing they would be the first to broach the terrorism angle and the attack's suspected perpetrators. The live camera shot of the building showed it was still standing, but he was hopeful that the unblemished outer walls only masked severe destruction within.

Finding no hard information, he went back upstairs to the only computer in the house, to check on the download that was holding him up. The screen read, *70% complete*. The grey Packard Bell was several years old, an antique compared to more modern home computers. On top of that, it accessed the Internet through a standard dial-up phone line rather than the dramatically faster DSL or cable modem line. This made working on the Net similar to sprinting through a bog.

He was downloading an instant messaging program that would allow him to communicate critical instructions to the other twelve cells across the nation. Instant messages, unlike regular email, could not be saved and tracked by intervening governments like the United States because they were typed, seen, then gone. Emails went through an electronic mailbox system. Most people didn't know, and conspiracy theorists only suspected, that the U.S. government captured all emails worldwide and filtered them through sophisticated security programs.

The messaging program would have downloaded in less than two minutes on his laptop, but it had already been running on this dinosaur for more than twelve. In addition, before being able to use it, installation of the program required him to restart the computer, tacking another five minutes onto the process. The bright spot was that, all told, it would be only ten more minutes before he was sending messages to his twelve other cell leaders, instructing them to begin their attacks. It would take a National Security bureaucrat longer than that to get permission to wipe his own ass.

He had his modern, faster laptop with him, but chose to trade speed for security at this point. He learned from the talking heads on television that the FBI was on site at the mall and at least one suspect was rumored to be in custody. If they were watching him—either through solid evidence, or by casting a wide net over thousands of "persons of interest," information sent through his wireless data card could be tracked. He considered sending the commands from an Internet café, but didn't want to risk being spotted on the off chance the FBI had his photo on security surveillance and were broadcasting it to the networks.

The seconds continued to pass in slow motion; his subtle ticks were starting to surface. He needed to get back under control. He left the room, went back downstairs, and began a set of two hundred push-ups while listening to the regurgitated information coming in from the networks.

---

Jason pulled the truck over in the middle of a residential block on the western edge of Minneapolis just east of the upscale 50th and France shopping district located in the epicenter of "Old Money" in the Twin Cities, the exclusive suburb of Edina.

The Ford F250 idled in front of a small Tudor-style house. Jason and Kate could see the light from a television flickering in the window. Though modest in size and design, its fashionable location brought the home an unusually high value. So much value, in fact, that the owner had turned it into a duplex, with a garden-view apartment in the basement and a two-level unit upstairs.

"What are we doing here?" Kate asked.

"This is Neil's parents' house, the one I renovated a few years ago." He rolled his eyes in self-disgust. "He said he was having trouble renting it lately—couldn't find the *right* people—down market. In this area, yuppies would be beating down his door with handfuls of money to get into this place." He banged his hand on the steering wheel. "I should have known something wasn't right. I should've figured it out earlier!"

"You couldn't have connected Neil's rental problems with what happened today—not in a million years," Kate said.

"I know, but looking back, so much about him didn't add up. Current things like his connection to Clara Riddle through a church that she stopped attending years ago. And other things like building a house in the country. He was about as handy and focused on nature as I am academic. His move out of town never made sense to me. Until now."

She held up the cell phone. "So what are we going to do? I still can't get an open line."

Jason pulled around the corner. "You stay here and keep working the phone." He opened his door and readied himself to hop out of the truck, then turned back. "Don't give up—keep trying."

"Where are you going?" she asked the question, already knowing the answer.

"I'll be fine. Don't worry about me. Keep dialing," he said.

She grabbed his arm and yanked him back. "You won't be fine! The man's shoulders are wider than I am tall. You can't go in there, Jason. He'll kill you. Do you understand? He—will—kill—you!"

"You're gawking at his shoulders? You didn't hear me commenting on the size of Agent Phillips' breasts, did you? And they were pretty good-sized." He gave her his best forced smile.

She hit him hard on the chest. "This isn't a time for your jokes, Jason. You know what this man has done and what he's capable of. He's in line to become the ruler of a billion Muslims, for God's sake. A small-town contractor isn't going to get in his way. Let's just wait for the FBI to get here."

"His plan is working, Kate. It may not have come off exactly how he drew it up, but you saw all the media trucks—no doubt, it's news all over the world by now. If he's able to unleash the attacks in the other cities, he'll accomplish more than just killing U.S. civilians or scaring the general public. Think of the effect it will have on the fundamentalist Muslims and those on the fringe. What if he *is* able to galvanize them?" Jason exhaled. "We could be talking about World War Three. We all lose if that happens, Kate. I don't care if you live in Mecca, Washington D.C., or Cedar River; you lose. I need to do this."

She wrapped her arms tight around him. "I'll be here when you get back." She kissed him and tried as hard as she could to be strong for him, but couldn't prevent the tears from streaming silently down her cheeks.

Jason got out and lifted the lid of the steel tool chest in the bed of his pick-up, blocking the cab's rear window from view. Safely out of Kate's sight, Jason took the opportunity to rest his stiff upper lip. She was right. He had no chance one-on-one against the larger, heavily trained gladiator. His goal was more realistic: delay the terrorist leader from doing any more damage until help arrived. He closed his eyes and bowed his head.

*Dear Lord: I know I don't do this often enough, but I come to you now asking for your goodness to guide me and keep me strong. Only through your strength, will good conquer evil. Help me to be righteous in my cause and give me the wisdom to use the tools you've bestowed on me.*

*Please keep Kate safe in your arms should I not make it through this test. And watch over my mother—give her the courage to continue to share her gifts with the world.*

He looked up into the moving grey sky in search of the images of Kelly and Grace. They didn't appear, but he knew they were there.

He reached into the chest and pulled out an old insulated jacket with the Kendall Construction logo patch on the front. He felt inside the deep pockets to gauge the amount of space they provided, then looked into the chest for tools with which to fill them.

---

Attar leaped up the stairs to the second floor and into the bedroom to check the progress of the download. It had been more than five minutes and the bars still hadn't made their way across the screen to signal the completion of the download. Below the bars were the words: *94% complete.*

It was another example of Muhab's inability as a strategist—he should have outfitted the back-up location better. "The download should be complete—you fool!" Attar growled. The message box also showed the transfer rate, which was down to 320 MBs per second. The phone modem had slowed to something short of a crawl. Though not an expert on outdated modems, he guessed the modem was being slowed by a spike in local call levels after the attack—another factor unforeseen by his former lieutenant. Another bar appeared on the screen: *95% complete.* Too slow!

General Attar grabbed a ceramic stein holding pens and pencils and hurled it across the room. The stein smashed into bits against the wall, the pens and pencils bouncing wildly off the wall and flying across the room. His attention was suddenly caught by movement through the window where a single man was walking by on the sidewalk.

He appraised the threat, then immediately dismissed it. The man was leaning forward, with his hands shoved hard into his jacket pockets and moving too fast for a trained recon agent. Their job was to take in and memorize as much information as possible. And a strike team would approach in a group of two or more. No, this man was just looking to get to his destination and out of the cold autumn air as soon as possible.

---

When Jason stepped from the sidewalk to the driveway he flipped from walk to sprint. He ran around the far side of the recessed detached garage then quickly curled around behind. He lifted a weathered brick off a stump at the rear corner of the garage nearest the house and reached into the rotting core. Empty. Neil's back-up key was gone. "Damn!" Not only was he without a plan, he didn't even have a way into the house.

*Think, Jason! Why is Attar here? And what are you going to do about it?*

He was at a loss. He studied the house, hoping it would provide a clue. And after a moment, it did. He saw movement in an upstairs bedroom. It was only a shadow, but it had to be Attar. Why is he upstairs? *Think, Jason.*

---

After seeing the man on the sidewalk, General Attar checked the windows on each side of the second floor. He was right, no recon or strike teams were gathered outside the house. When he returned to the bedroom, the download was complete and, even better, no reboot was necessary; the prompt was asking him to log in, which he did. Three minutes later he had sent instant messages to all twelve monikers listed on the hotel note paper. Each of the paragraphs were identical: *We've been breached! Time is extremely limited. Coordinate your team and commence attack immediately! Praise Allah. His kingdom is yours!*

He logged off and leaned back in his chair, but for only seconds. The sound of glass breaking, followed by loud crashes against the side door on the first floor stood him up. He froze, stunned. How could he have missed them? Was it a strike team?

No. Just a familiar voice.

# CHAPTER 46

Jason got lucky… at first. The outside door opened without resistance into a small square entry. The door leading to the basement rental unit stood in front of him, opposite the outside door. The door to the upper apartment sat two steps above on the right. He tried the door to the upper rental—locked. Same for the lower. Surprise was not going to be an option. He needed to find a way to control the situation. *Out-think your opponent.*

He needed both doors open to execute his plan. A pry bar would have been the best tool to accomplish the task but the one he kept in his pickup was at the sheriff's office with the rest of his backpack from Thursday night. He pulled a hammer from his jacket and crashed it through the glass window of the door to the upper unit. Shards of glass fell to the tile kitchen floor. He reached through the open space in the window and unlocked the door, then threw it open.

Getting the basement apartment door open wasn't going to be as easy. It was a solid wood six-panel door that Jason had installed himself. It hinged toward Jason, away from the descending staircase on the other side. It took three powerful kicks to break through the deadbolt. The fourth kick pried the hinge plates out of the wall and sent the door toppling end over end down the narrow staircase. He backed up and stepped up into the kitchen, the broken glass crunching under his feet.

"Hey, Attar, it's me. You weren't man enough to take me on at Neil's house so I came here for another shot. Might not be a fair fight, though;

my hands aren't tied anymore. Maybe I'll keep one hand behind my back—even things out a bit. Come on down; I'll put on some good Muslim ass-kicking tunes."

Jason ran down the basement stairs and turned immediately right, into the tiny walk-through kitchen. He threw open the vented closet door and exposed the furnace and water heater. A fuse box sat on the wall above the heater.

---

A cautious smile spread across the general's face. The man had guts, that was for sure. But what was he up to? Could he be such a cowboy as to come alone? There is no way the police would use the man as bait, and why would they? Even a warrior as tested as him wasn't going to defeat an all-out assault by an armed militia. *Armed!* He reached inside his sport coat—empty. He had given his gun to Khalid in the mall basement and never gotten it back. He had no weapon.

The computer made a 'pop' behind him as its power snapped off. What was this cowboy up to? If the man wanted to fight him, why not come face him? He poked his head down the stairs, which led to the front door straight ahead, the dining room to the right and the living room through an arched doorway to the left. He heard the voice again and, like before, it came from the other side of the house by the side-entry door. "Didn't you hear? Your little stunt at the mall was a complete disaster. For you, not for the mall, I mean. One punk was able to detonate his bomb. It killed a couple of cops—just enough death for you to get the chair and send American missiles raining down all over your homeland."

General Attar checked the windows again—still no sign of back-up. The Cedar River man resumed the smug lecture. "That's right, shithead, we cleared everyone out before your boys could do any real damage. Killed your boy from the other night, too. You know, the one who let me run off with your woman? What was his name? Khalid? Dick? I'm going with Dick."

There was a brief pause before the man spoke again. "Let's go, Attar! Get your ass down here. Or is it like at the mall, you run and hide while some misfit kids do the real work for you?"

General Attar was halfway down the staircase when he spoke. "I didn't need any help drowning your bitch and kid. And I am not going to need any help ripping your heart out, either."

He heard the Cedar River man retreat to the basement, still shouting the mindless taunts as Attar cautiously made his way through the small dining room into the kitchen. He approached the entrance and saw glass scattered beneath it on the tile floor. As he slowly advanced to the sunken entry, the broken glass crumbled under his boots. He stood perfectly still at the entrance for a moment, listening for movement in the lower level. Not hearing any he poked his head in and stole a quick look through the busted door frame down the stairs. He snapped back, waiting for gunfire to follow but none came. *What is he up to?* He took another look, this one a little longer. The staircase was empty except for the fallen door, but the cowboy could jump out at the base of the stairs anytime and start firing. He grabbed a clear plastic sugar container off the kitchen counter and tossed it down the stairs. It hit at the base and smashed to pieces. Sugar sprayed into a three-foot circle. No sound of surprise or movement came from the basement.

Then the front door at the far end of the kitchen and dining room crashed open. He whirled around and saw the thorn from Cedar River blur past, up the stairs to the second story.

---

Jason had waited in the basement until he heard Attar coming down from the second floor, then he ran through the galley kitchen into the back bedroom and out the large egress window he'd installed in the renovation. He ran around to the front door and waited for Attar to track him into the basement. He watched Attar through the front window; the general was reluctant to put himself into the bottleneck. But he also saw something else: Attar was unarmed.

Jason had decided when he first saw Attar's shadow on the second floor, that he needed to get up there to see what he was doing and somehow disrupt it. The only idea he could come up with was to lure the terrorist down to the basement so he could make a break for the room upstairs. But now he could see that Attar had no intention of following him down into the basement. Jason had to act; the terrorist wasn't going to remain at the basement entry much longer. He held the door frame on either side, reared back and kicked harder than he had ever kicked in his life, and used his arms to throw himself at the door at the same time. The door's initial resistance kept Jason's momentum from hurtling into the room out of control. He maintained his balance, righted himself, and ran up the stairs untouched.

He waited for a moment just beyond the top of the stairs and listened. He didn't hear immediate movement downstairs and took advantage of the opportunity to search the bedroom where he'd seen Attar's shadow. Strewn pens, pencils, and bits of mug gave made the room look ragged and angry. The office chair was pulled out and angled, as if inviting Jason to sit down. "What were you doing on the computer, General?"

Attar's voice boomed from the bottom of the staircase. "You are too late, cowboy—the instructions have been sent. You cannot stop it. The abhorrent American way of life is a thing of the past." There was a pause as if he were waiting for a response but Jason just put his hand around the handle of the hammer in his pocket and continued to search for a sign that Attar was bluffing, that he had not been beaten.

Attar spoke again, with almost playful arrogance. "Again, I am conflicted. I would enjoy very much the opportunity to kill you myself, but on this day time does not wait for such selfish pleasures. We both know you are no threat to me. If you were armed, you would have already killed me, but instead you run like a frightened young girl.

"So if you will excuse me, I am going next door to steal a car and kill its owners. What is the American saying: places to go; countries to destroy?"

Jason pulled the claw hammer out of his pocket and raced down the stairs. He may have been too late to prevent the other attacks but he could still capture the mastermind and the murderer of his family. The moment he hit the landing, a steel-toed boot sent him like a torpedo into the wall, the hammer falling impotently to the floor. He didn't have a chance to regain his senses before a stone fist pulverized the cartilage in his nose and blurred his vision. Then two swift punches under his rib cage removed all the air from his body. He was in a weightless fog; the only thing holding him up was Attar's powerful grip.

---

"I may have lied a little," General Attar said with a victorious snarl. "I *am* going to kill a neighbor and take his car. That was true. But the plan is about to be executed throughout this miserable country so I am not in such a hurry that I cannot make time to eliminate the man who has caused me so much difficulty."

He pressed two fingers into Jason's chest between his pectoral muscle and his shoulder socket. It was like pressing a searing iron rod into the cartilage and tendons that held his arm to his body. Jason's head flew back and his eyes bulged. He tried to let out a scream but with no air his mouth shrieked in silent, painful terror.

"People, those who are able to speak, say it feels like a flaming rod through your chest. Is that how it feels for you?" He hurled his knee into Jason's groin and leaned in against him. "I have killed many men. But few have given me such pleasure."

He pulled away from Jason's limp body but before it could slump to the floor, he connected with a reverse roundhouse kick to Jason's head, lifting him clear off the ground. He landed against the front wall just behind the still-open front door. Jason lay crumpled and unconscious; almost certainly dead, but a heel through his skull would leave no doubt. Attar adjusted the limp body with his foot so the head was lying fully against the wood floor.

"What's going on in here? Who are you?"

General Attar looked up to find an old man at the door. He was holding a .22 caliber rifle firmly in his hands but the muzzle was pointed to the floor. The general lifted his arms sheepishly above his head and moved directly in front of him. "It's okay, I'm a friend of Neil's from St. Joseph College in Cedar River."

"Come on now, I just saw someone bust through the door," said the man, his thinning brownish-grey hair wafting in the breeze.

Attar realized the door was perpendicular to the front wall. At that angle, his victim's motionless body was hidden from the man's view.

"I know. I have him tied up in the kitchen. He must not have realized Neil was letting a friend stay here for a few days. I got lucky—caught him off-guard."

"You need any help holding him?" The slouched man showed General Attar what kind of help he could provide by lifting his gun a few inches but keeping it at a downward angle.

"No, but thank you. I called the police. They are already on their way."

"That's funny. I tried 'em a half-dozen times, but my phone's not working. That's why I got this," he said nodding at the rifle. "I don't normally go around the neighborhood this way, but I promised Neil I'd watch his house for him." He lifted his gun again. "So, here I am."

---

Old man Soucheray! His tinny voice dripped with Scandinavian twang. To Jason, it was like the sound of angels. His appearance at Neil's doorstep saved him from certain death, however briefly.

He propped himself up onto an elbow—his words came out so weak as to be almost distorted. "Mr. Soucheray?"

"What the…? Who's that?" the neighbor asked.

"It's me, Jas." The voice was barely audible.

The rawboned man stepped through the threshold, but the general took swift control. He grabbed the rifle by the barrel and yanked it away with his left hand, pulling the unsuspecting man forward. The man's momentum brought him falling toward Attar, who sent him flailing back through the door with a straight right hand. Attar was about to bring the rifle back around to finish the intruder, but the gun had already fired.

---

Jason was still lying helplessly on his elbow, trying to shake the thundering waves of pain that were crashing over him and retarding his equilibrium when suddenly the butt of a rifle appeared right in front of him.

He didn't hesitate. He put his hand around the stock, slipped his finger over the trigger and fired. He saw the blood spurt from Attar's side. But the man gave no reaction—it was as if he didn't even notice. Jason pulled the trigger again. A new hole, an inch above the first, oozed blood. Attar turned to him, pulled the stock from his feeble grip, and brought it down on his skull.

---

Kate stood frozen. After she'd finally gotten through to Rhoda Phillips, she had run to the corner to read the street signs to provide the agent with her exact location. Phillips told her to get back in the truck, lock the doors, and duck down; Minneapolis Police would be there in moments.

But Kate looked down the block to Neil's house. She saw an older man standing at the front door with a rifle. When he took a step inside he was instantly launched back out the door, tumbling down the steps and slamming onto the sidewalk beyond. Then she heard gunshots.

She dropped the phone and ran for the house. "JASON!"

---

When Jason pushed his eyes open, his sight was beyond blurry; it was like looking through waxed paper. His mind was working with the same lack of clarity. Pain seemed to pulse through his entire body. *ATTAR!* He scrambled to find the terrorist, but his body was slow to respond—as far as he could tell. Then a hand settled on his chest. He felt a gentle purpose in its touch. His vision began to clear; Kate was smiling down on him.

"It's okay, Jason. Try to stay still."

His surroundings slowly came into a hazy focus. He was lying on a couch in the living room of Neil's Minneapolis house. The paramedic next to Kate had an irritated look, like his work was interrupted by Jason coming to. Jason struggled to transition mentally from his battle with the next caliph to the current, calmer, scene.

"Attar?"

"Gone. For now," interjected Rhoda Phillips, whom Jason now saw was standing behind Kate.

He looked at her, confused, yearning for more details. She obliged. "Looks like he was bleeding pretty good. A couple of witnesses, including Ms. Brooks, heard two gunshots. I assume from the lack of bullet holes in *your* body, you were the one who got off the rounds."

Jason nodded. Which hurt like a sonofabitch.

"Attar's blood trail led out the back door into the yard. He took a car from the house across the alley. A sixteen-year-old girl was home watching her younger brother at the time. Neither was harmed. The parents were at the Megamall, of all places. He's in a red Audi and losing blood fast. I expect a call from the Minneapolis or Edina cops any minute." She shook her head. "I just hope we're not too late."

"Too late for what?" Jason asked.

"We don't know what's taking place in the other cities," Phillips said. "The director wants to close down the malls in all major cities while the Bureau learns more about General Attar and his group, but the president won't allow it. He says it feeds into the fear the terrorists are attempting to create." She shook her head. "The truth is that he doesn't want the citizenry afraid under his watch."

Jason reached into his front pants pocket and pulled out a small piece of hotel note paper. He handed it to Phillips. "I saw him working in the computer room upstairs. I cut the power but he said I was too late—the orders had been sent. This paper was sitting on the desk next to the keyboard."

Phillips and Agent Jackson looked at the hotel note paper. "Twelve major cities—it fits with what they told you in Cedar River," Agent Jackson said.

His superior pointed to the short number/letter combinations in front of each city. "So what do you make of these?"

"Dollars to donuts those are the contacts' instant message addresses—gotta be. Keeps the communication out of our Internet funnel," Jackson said. She gave him a piercing look—he had just revealed top-secret information to three civilians. She handed the paper to him. "Shut down and evacuate all malls in these cities and the surrounding suburbs immediately. Don't go through Washington. If Attar's attack orders have already been sent, we don't have any time to add layers." Jackson nodded. "And find out who these addresses belong to."

"On it," he said and ran out of the room.

She turned back to Jason and shook her head in amazement. "I'm going to need the paramedic to roll you over—see if there isn't a red cape back there."

"I'm no hero. Hell, I've had more than one person save my life today." Jason's eyes, more focused, flashed to the door. "Mr. Soucheray. Where is he? Is he okay?"

"He's got quite a shiner and nice bump on the back of his head. Other than that, he's all right," Kate said. "He was almost excited about being taken off in an ambulance. He said it'll give him the power at home for a day or two, whatever that means."

"If he hadn't come by, I'd be splattered all over the floor," Jason said.

Kate stepped back to let the paramedic complete his examination. A minute later he gave his initial diagnosis: a fractured collar bone, a possible fracture to the zygomatic bone, a "mangled nose" and possible internal injuries that would require an MRI to assess.

"Zygomatic bone?" Jason and Kate asked simultaneously.

"Broken cheekbone," the paramedic said.

Phillips continued questioning Jason as he was placed on a gurney and prepped for the ambulance but he didn't have any solid answers to her questions. "If you come up with anything else, just yell. I'll have a number of agents assigned to protect you until everything quiets down," Phillips said. "Not that you should expect any trouble. I'd be surprised if eliminating a remodeling contractor is a part of the terrorists' master plan."

"And that's their fatal flaw," Jason said. Phillips tipped her head, questioning his point. "Not eliminating a hayseed contractor, but the intent of their attack. They're trying to collapse Wall Street and, in turn, tear apart Washington. But what they don't understand is that America's soul isn't in either in those places and the people working in those towns don't dictate our survival.

"It's the men and women who own the grocery stores or work in the mill—it's the guy working into the night to come up with the next great invention who's this nation's lifeblood. For two hundred and fifty years men like Mr. Soucheray have been putting down their hammers or shovels or broomsticks to pick up muskets and defend this country.

They know what this country represents—the promise that brought our grandparents and great-grandparents here. It runs deeper than the balance in a 401(k) or the square footage of a house—it's in our soul."

"Is that what you would call what you did today? Picking up your musket?" asked Kate.

"I guess so. No different than a million other guys ready to do the same thing."

# CHAPTER 47

**SUNDAY**

Riyadh, Saudi Arabia.

The lieutenant knocked, then entered the large corporate office. A man was facing a plasma television on the rear wall, watching the coverage of the attempted terrorist attack in the United States. He spun from the large mahogany bookcase to face the visitor.

"You've been watching, sir."

The man nodded.

"Do you think any of the other targets are still a go?"

"Doubtful."

"And what about General Attar?" asked the subordinate.

"Not many men would survive the injuries the news stations are reporting, but I have seen him come through many battles." The man shook his head and turned back to the television. "He shouldn't have been within five thousand miles of that mall. But he needed to be in the action, the general on the front lines. His flaw was that he saw the cause as a means to his ascension to the caliph throne. His center was not on Allah, but on himself. Thankfully, the other commanders do not share such a blemish. A United States in political and economic upheaval would have benefited the cause greatly, there is no doubt about that. But we will make the necessary adjustments and move forward with the operation."

The well-appointed man leaned back confidently in his five-thousand-dollar suit and locked his fingers behind his head, a diamond and gold watch glinting from his wrist. "He had flaws, but vision and strategy were not among them. The United States will fall and the followers of Allah will become the world's next and final superpower."

"Yes, sir. Is there anything you need me to do?"

"Gather the generals!"